SILENCE IN OCTOBER

JENS CHRISTIAN GRØNDAHL is one of the most cele-
brated and widely read writers in Denmark today. Born
in 1959, his literary work includes twelve novels, essays and
several plays. His novel *Lucca* was awarded the prestigious
Golden Laurels Prize in 1999 and will be published by
Canongate in 2002. *Silence in October* is being translated
into thirteen languages.

ANNE BORN has translated many works of Danish, Swedish
and Norwegian literature, including *The Snake in Sydney* by
Michael Larsen, *Vita Brevis* by Jostein Gaarder and Karen
Blixen's *Letters from America*. She is also the author of twelve
books of poetry.

International Praise for
Silence in October

'This novel, which might so easily be another tale about
the debris of a broken couple, is more like the picture of
two existences which, one day, sees their relationship skid
dramatically off course . . . the narrator captures the essence
of life.' *Le Monde*, France

'The surprise hidden within *Silence in October* is the unexpected
power of the style . . . [this is] proof of Flaubert's contention
that a novel should be carried by the style and not the
events . . . The majestic handling of powerful emotions makes
this a great book.' *NRC Handelsblad*. Netherlands

'Ling . . . . psychologically astute. Grøndahl
deals . . . . a theme

first for dramas and then for small talk in the Seventies, and is still as fascinating a subject as ever: the midlife crisis.'
Der Spiegel, Germany

'Aided by long and highly well-wrought thought processes, packed with wisdom, inserted associations [and] eminent observations, the author manages to express the sky-high expectations of love that we have in this day and age, in such a refreshing manner that the thoughts seem new.'
Faedrelandsvennen, Norway

'I wouldn't hesitate to call *Silence in October* one of the best novels of the year. It is a book which dares to wrestle with the great drama which exists within us all. From the tiny perspective: a man, his wife and their children, something great emerges which touches each and every one of us.'
Länstidningen Södertälje, Sweden

Jens Christian Grøndahl's ninth novel presents still further variations on those themes which crop up throughout his work: mankind's journey through time and space, our romantic entanglements, the power and the impotence of words . . . The writing style is masterly and quite superb; seriously virulent and searingly precise. Grøndahl's existential romance will ram squarely in the solar plexus of all those who have just once grown faint at the thought of how little it would take to turn one's life upside-down.' *Eksta Bladet*, Denmark

'A culmination of the literature of the 1990s . . . Grøndahl is brilliantly in command of his novel. In evenly paced, abundantly flowing sentences he recounts one story, then another not unlike the first, moving forward, then back, to Copenhagen, Lisbon, Paris, New York – but still, at all times, the narrative is tightly controlled and the suspense never lets up . . . *Silence in October* is one of those novels destined to characterise the Nineties.' *Politiken*, Denmark

'Grøndahl's meticulous dissection of psychological nuance has won him comparisons with Marcel Proust. Through an accumulation of brilliantly rendered detail, *Silence in October* builds up the contours of a fictional world as flickering and vivid as life itself.' *The Australian*

SILENCE IN OCTOBER

Jens Christian Grøndahl

Translated by Anne Born

CANONGATE
Edinburgh · London

First published in English in Great Britain in 2000

This edition first published in 2001 by
Canongate Books Ltd,
14 High Street, Edinburgh, EH1 1TE

First published in Danish in 1998 by
Munksgaard Rosinante, Copenhagen

Silence in October was translated with the support of the
European Commission and the Ariane Programme 1999

The publishers gratefully acknowledge general
subsidy from the Scottish Arts Council towards
the Canongate International series

British Library Cataloguing-in-Publication Data
A catalogue record for this book is available
on request from the British Library

ISBN 978 1 84195 178 2

Typeset by Palimpsest Book Production Ltd,
Falkirk, Stirlingshire

Printed and bound in Great Britain
by Clays Ltd, St Ives plc

www.canongate.tv

1

Astrid stands at the rail with her back to the town. The breeze lifts her hair in a chestnut-brown, ragged flag. She's wearing sunglasses, she's smiling. There is perfect harmony between her white teeth and the white city. The photo is seven years old, I took it in late afternoon on one of the small ferries that cross the Tagus to Cacilhas. Only from a distance do you understand why Lisbon is called 'the white city', when the colours lose their lustre and the glazed tiles of the façades melt together in the sun's afterglow. The low light falls horizontally on the distant houses rising behind each other over the Praça do Comércio up to the ridges of Bairro Alto and Alfama on the other side of the river. It is a month since she left. I haven't heard from her. The only trace of her is the bank statement showing the activity of our joint account. She hired a car in Paris and used her Mastercard on the route via Bordeaux, San Sebastian, Santiago de Compostela, Porto and Coimbra to Lisbon. The same route we took that autumn. She cashed a large sum in Lisbon on the 17th October. She has not used the card since then. I don't know where she is. I cannot know. I am forty-four and I know less than ever. The older I get the less I know. When I was younger I thought my knowledge would increase with the years, that it was steadily enlarging like the universe. A constantly widening area of certainty that correspondingly displaced and diminished the extent of uncertainty. I was really very optimistic. With the passage of time I must admit that I know roughly the same amount, perhaps even slightly less, and not at all with the same certainty as then. My so-called experiences are not at all the same as knowledge. It is more like, what shall I call it, a kind of echo chamber in which the little I know resounds hollow and inadequate. A growing void around my scant knowledge that rattles foolishly like the dried-up kernel in a walnut. My experiences are experiences of ignorance, its boundlessness, and I will never discover how much I still do not know, and how much is just something I believed in.

One morning at the beginning of October Astrid said she wanted to go away. She was standing in the bathroom at the basin with her face leaning towards her reflection, painting her lips. Already dressed, she was elegant as ever, in dark blue as usual. There is something reticent, discreet in her elegance, dark blue, black and white are her preferred colours, and she never wears high heels. That is not necessary. When she had said it she met my eyes in the mirror as if to see what would happen. She is still beautiful, and she is most beautiful when I realise yet again that I am unable to guess her thoughts. I have always been fascinated by the symmetry in her face. Symmetry in a face is not something one can take for granted. Most faces are slightly irregular, either the nose is, or there is a birthmark, a scar or the divergent curve of a line which makes one side different from the other. In Astrid's face the sides reflect each other alongside her straight nose, which in profile forms a faint, perfectly rounded bow. There is something luxurious, arrogant about her nose. Her eyes are green and narrow, and there is more space between them than in most people. She has broad cheekbones and her jaw is angular and slightly prominent. Her lips are full and almost the same colour as her skin, and when she smiles they curl a bit in a subtle, conspiratorial way, and the incipient wrinkles gather in small fan-shaped rays around the corners of her mouth and eyes. She smiles a lot, even when there is apparently nothing to smile at. When Astrid smiles it is impossible to distinguish between her intelligence and the spontaneity whereby she registers the environment on her skin, the temperature of the air, the warmth of light and coolness of shadows, as if she has never wanted to be anywhere else than precisely where she is. The years have discreetly begun to mark her body, but she is still slim and erect even though it is eighteen years since she had her second child, and she still moves with the same effortless, lithe ease as when we met each other.

I would have put out a search for her long ago if I had not had the statement listing her banking activities, but she didn't want to be found, I understood that much. I am not to look for her. I asked her where she was planning to go. She didn't know yet. She stayed there in front of the mirror for a while, as if waiting for a reaction. When I said nothing, she went. I could hear her voice in the living room as she was phoning, but couldn't hear what she said. There is something lazy, laid-back, about her voice, and now and then it cracks, as if she is always slightly hoarse. Shortly afterwards I heard the door slam. While I was taking my shower I saw a plane catch the early sun in a shining sign, passing overhead between the opposite wall and the roof of the back premises. I had to keep wiping the mirror each time it misted up so as not to disappear in the steam as I covered my face with shaving foam. It is always the same distrustful gaze that meets me in the mirror, as if he wants to tell me he is not the one I think he is, the man in there with white foam all over his face. He looked like a melancholy, weary Santa Claus, framed by the Portuguese tiles that made a frieze of glazed blue plant stems around the mirror. She found them in a foggy village near Sintra, we had driven through the mountain roads' winding tunnels of green, I swore because I got mud on my shoes, while fastidiously and capriciously she inspected the ornamentation on the blue tiles as if they differed radically, and the corners of my mouth trembled when I had a drink of the rough wine that a peasant with his jacket full of straw offered me from a barrel on the back of a donkey cart. At night we made love in a blue hotel, and the shining blue petals and sailing ships and birds on the walls gave her restrained moans an enigmatic tone which made her remote and close at the same time. When I went out of the bathroom she had gone. It was quiet in the flat. Rosa had more or less moved in with her new sweetheart, and Simon was riding around on his motorbike somewhere in Sardinia. It wouldn't be long before we were really on our own, Astrid and I. We hadn't talked so much about it, maybe because neither of us could quite imagine what it would be like. It was a new silence and we moved about in it with a new carefulness. Earlier we had enjoyed the freedom when for some reason the children were not at home. Now the rooms opened out like a distance we either put behind or allowed to grow between us.

A whole world of sounds fell silent. The sounds that the others produced and those I contributed myself and which had surrounded me for years with their continuous themes, subsidiary themes and variations of footsteps and voices, laughter, weeping and shouting. A kind of unending music, that was never wholly unvaried and yet remained the same through the years because it was the music I heard and remembered, not the instruments, the sound of our life together and not the individual words and movements of which it consisted. Our life, which repeated itself, day after day, while it changed, year by year. A life of broken nights and noisome nappies, tricycles, bedtime stories and visits to Casualty, children's birthdays and charter trips, Christmas trees and wet swimsuits, love letters, football matches, rejoicing and boredom, squabbles and reconciliation. During the early years it had gone on growing, this busy, chaotic and polyphonic world, until it filled everything. It spread out among us with all its arrangements and all its planning and all its routines. We stood each on our own side of our new world, and for long periods we could only wave and make signs to each other through the noise and the bustle. In the evening, when all the duties were fulfilled, we sank down together shattered in front of the television news and guessing games and old films, and although neither of us ever dared say it aloud, I was sure that she too sometimes asked herself whether all the details and precautions, all the wearying commonplace everyday business, had not cast a shadow over what was supposed to be the meaning of it all. Only long afterwards did it cross my mind that the meaning was perhaps not to be found in the selected moments I had photographed and pasted into the fat family history book; the meaning of it all was rather linked to the sum of repeated trivialities, the repetition itself, the patterns of repetition. While it was all going on I had only noticed it, the meaning, as a sudden and passing ease that could spread within me when, stumbling with exhaustion, I stopped midway between the kitchen table and the dishwasher with yet another dirty plate in my hand, hearing the children's laughter somewhere in the flat. Chance and isolated seconds, when it crossed my mind that precisely there, in transit through the repeated words and movements of the days and the evenings, did I find myself in the midst of what had become my life, and that I should never get any closer to this centre.

It was in the silence that I realised it, in the void in which Simon and Rosa were by degrees to leave us. The sounds in the flat were no longer a music whose instruments flowed together in a shifting resonance. They made their appearances alone at the edge of the silence like hesitant signals; when I was in the bathroom with the hot water gurgling down the drain, while I shaved and heard her answer me from the kitchen with the barking of the juicer, the whistle of the kettle or the long sighs of the coffee machine. Now that we could at last make ourselves heard, we sometimes didn't really know what to say. I woke up beside her and gazed at her face, turned towards me in sleep, towards the first light of day. When I looked at her as she slept, expressionless, at rest, her features withdrew from the semblance by which I was accustomed to recognise her, the facial expressions of her moods that I knew so well, and it might almost be another face, this face that I have had before me for so many years. I knew her as I had seen her en route through the thousands of days and nights we had spent together, but what of herself as she was, to herself? Earlier we could quarrel over trifles, who should do what, who should have done this and that. Now we had suddenly become considerate, almost discreet. Even in bed we approached each other with a cautiously testing tenderness. It was not quite the same tired or lazy intimate, sleepwalking exchange, no longer the same interchange between spontaneous revival or all too determined passion, when the children had fallen asleep, with half-suppressed groans and exclamations so they should not hear us. It was a little like meeting afresh, as if we were slightly surprised that it was really us, that we were still here. We have been together for over eighteen years, Simon was six when we met. We have never been alone for more than a day or two, at most a week at a time, except for that October seven years ago when we drove through Les Landes, Asturias, Galicia and Trás-os-Montes.

Astrid left the next day. If she had not already gone by the time I had eventually finished in the bathroom, I might have asked her why. But when she finally came home well into the evening and we sat having supper in the kitchen because the children were not at home, it was somehow too late. There are questions that can only be asked at certain moments, and sometimes you get only one chance. If you don't ask in time the chance has been missed. When I served the meal and poured her a glass of wine, her journey was already an accomplished fact, although she had not even packed her suitcase and maybe didn't really know yet where she was going. During the day, the thought that she wanted to go away had made me ask so many new questions that the one querying why she was leaving had grown far too big, far too drastic. I would not be able to ask it without all the other questions thrusting their confused and blushing heads into the silence that followed. For some reason I was sure there would be complete stillness in the kitchen if I put the question. I did not want her to notice that her remark that morning, while she screwed the cap on her lipstick and quickly inspected her face in the mirror, that her casual utterance had prevented me from getting more than half a page written of the article on Cézanne I should have started on a week earlier and which I believed had been planned out in every single sentence. I didn't want to sit there like some heavy-hearted youth fearfully airing his jealous paranoia. After all, we were grown-up people, as they say. And maybe I had exaggerated my unease during the day, sitting in my study trying to concentrate. In any case, surely there was nothing unusual about her wanting to be alone for a while to see something new, now our duties had not only loosened their grip but had actually let go of us and left us to ourselves and each other.

She had phoned from the editing room late in the afternoon to say she would be delayed. I could hear the chittering, cartoon film-like gabble from the loudspeaker as she quickly scrolled through a scene on the editing table. After I had put down the receiver I went over the brief conversation line by line, trying to find a hint of change in her tone, but every single word sounded normal and reassuring, and she had been neither more detached nor more affectionate on the telephone than she normally was. Nor when we were in the kitchen was there anything between us to isolate this evening from all the others. I expected her to talk about her travel plans herself, but it seemed she had forgotten all about them. If she was not merely waiting for me to interrupt her. She chatted about the film they had finished editing that day and, with her usual crinkled smile, described the young director, a very serious, quivering type who had despaired as his favourite shots vanished with the cuts. In a way her work was invisible. It consisted of extracting a story from the unconnected shots the directors brought her, and she made them coherent by excising the greater part. That's how it is with stories, mine as well. I cannot include everything, I have to select from among the pictures I have left, I have to decide on a sequence, and thus my story will be quite different from the one she could tell, even though they are supposed to be about the same subject. While she was speaking I registered each movement in her face. It was the same face as it had always been. At long intervals, through the years I had noticed a grey hair I had not seen before, a line that had grown sharper, but otherwise they were the same eyes that met my gaze through all that had passed between us, the same mouth that spoke to me through everything we had said to one another and later remembered or forgotten.

Later I lay awake and tried to remember the past weeks and months. I tried to find an expression, a gesture, a remark that could explain what was perhaps not a mystery at all. But either no change had taken place, or I had not noticed it. Have I really become so distrait? Apparently. My memory is bad, the days refuse to be separated from each other, they blur so there is only the same well of time in which each day the sky reflects itself anew. Every day was much the same. She went off in the morning and I sat at my table looking out at the row of trees alongside the Lakes which, day by day, was imperceptibly transformed from a wall of rustling green to a gnarled latticework of bare branches in the remains of withered foliage in front of the silent, shining water. She came home and lay down on the sofa while I cooked, we ate, watched television or read, went to bed.

The only change was the silence after Simon went away, and later in the steadily longer intervals between Rosa's visits; the consciousness that we broke a silence when we said something to each other, that we did not as earlier contribute to the same continuing story. More than once I stopped on my way from one room to another and looked at her through an open door as she sat on the sofa reading the paper with her legs pulled up underneath her, absent-mindedly scratching the loose cover with a nail, or as she stood by the window looking over at the row of façades on the other side of the lake as if she had caught sight of something or was expecting something to come in sight over there. When I observed her like this, without her being aware of it, apparently forgetful, immersed in a vision or a thought, she could suddenly look up from the paper or turn away from the view to meet my eye, as if she had felt it on her face, almost like a light touch, and I hastened to make some casual and practical remark to drown out the unspoken question of the moment.

I lay listening to her calm breathing and the distant cars. I thought she had fallen asleep but then heard her voice in the darkness. Perhaps she was surprised that I had not questioned her while we were in the kitchen. Perhaps she had expected me to try to stop her leaving. She lay with her back to me, her voice was calm and matter-of-fact. It might be for quite a while. How long? She didn't know. I put a hand on her hip under the duvet, she did not move. While stroking her hip I thought my question had sounded as if I knew what she was talking about. I asked her if she was going alone, but she didn't reply. Perhaps she was already asleep. When I woke up she was standing in the doorway of the bedroom looking at me. She already had her coat on. I got up and walked over to her. She continued to gaze at me as if reading a message in my face which I myself did not know about. Then she picked up the suitcase beside her on the floor. I accompanied her to the front door and watched her walking down the stairs, but she did not turn round. I could not understand myself. I did not understand I had let her go away without giving the least explanation. Of course I had no claim on her to answer all my timorous questions. The claims we had had on each other had gradually fallen away concurrently with the children no longer needing us. But I could at least have asked, and left it to her to decide how much she would reply. She had announced her decision in such a run-of-the-mill and offhand way in front of the mirror, as if it had been a matter of going to the cinema or visiting a woman friend, and I had allowed myself to be seduced by the naturalness of her tone. And later, in bed, when I thought she was asleep, there had been a distance in her voice as if she had already gone and was calling from a town on the other side of the world. As if by her cool statement she wanted to tell me I must leave her in peace. On the other hand her reply in the darkness might have been an offer which, only now, too late, I realised I had failed to accept. I had often had to drag the words out of her, one by one, with long pauses, when her silence and aloof expression told me something was wrong, that she was feeling hurt or offended. It was an established ritual, a reticence I had accustomed her to allow herself, and I knew my own role in the game, the gentle patience of the humble questioner, I knew its tone and gestures by heart, on the very edge of my chair or bent over her turned-away back, while I mumbled my petition for her mercy. When she stood in the doorway of the bedroom waiting for me to wake up, in the long moment when we stood facing each other, she in her overcoat, I in pyjamas, she had perhaps given me a final opportunity to protest, hold her back, confront her with my unease and incipient jealousy. But I had been unnerved by her unmoving eyes resting on my face. I did not know why, but I knew it would be in vain, as I met her thoughtful gaze, that seemed to look at me from a distant, unknown and inaccessible place.

As I sat by the kitchen window with my coffee, contemplating the pattern of bricks in the opposite wall, as I so often do, I cautiously touched on the thought I had carefully shied away from the previous day. While she was presumably sitting in a plane or a train, and I was yet again scanning the displaced patterns of the joints and the red-brown variations of the bricks, I had to ask myself whether she was travelling by herself in that aircraft cabin, that train compartment. If in reality she was in a strange car beside an unknown driver somewhere on the motorway south of the town. I reassured myself that she would have told me if she had a lover (both of us would have smiled at that word). And that if not, she would have taken pains to hit on a convincing reason for leaving. As far as I knew, she had never been unfaithful to me. As far as I knew. Anyway, I had never been jealous, which of course was no guarantee of anything but my own complacency, but if she really had had affairs during the eighteen years we had spent together, she was a more sophisticated and cold-blooded deceiver than I could imagine. No matter how inscrutably silent she could be when I tried to get her to tell me what the matter was, she was equally bad at hiding her moods. But the thought that she had a secret life in addition to our life with each other did not only seem a threat, it also fascinated me because it threw shadows where I had believed for years that everything was open and unconcealed.

As a rule I was absent several times a year in connection with my work; in reality she had had ample opportunity to launch into an escapade or two. Perhaps her impetuous joy in reunion had more than once been a kind of compensation when I came home and we made love as passionately as in the first years, perhaps her renewed desire had been equally made up of smokescreen and bad conscience. I tried to imagine her in bed with another man. I saw her flushed, inflamed face, turning from side to side, and a strange body crouching over her, locked between her knees, I could even see the strange room. Many years ago, shortly after we had moved in together, she said that if I was ever unfaithful to her she would ask me to see that it was not in our bed, and I was sure that she herself would keep this rule, but as I said, I have never suspected the occasion had arisen. I pictured her before me lying in an unknown room, I invented the furniture, the pictures on the wall and the view through the closed blinds onto a street in another part of town, but I could not imagine the strange man's features, and suddenly I realised that this exercise in jealousy was a blind alley, a trap. In any case our life together had surely lasted too long for a chance affair to be able to shake it, nor had she probably ever imagined in earnest that she would never sleep with anyone but me. The idea seemed absurd, and if she really had an affair it was actually none of my business, as long as it did not change anything between us. But it was precisely that which had disturbed me in the bathroom the previous day, it was that unease which had grown in the dark bedroom and in the doorway only a few hours earlier when she silently regarded me before picking up her suitcase. The increasing feeling that her sudden inexplicable journey, secret lover or not, affected the whole of our life.

I put my dirty cup into the dishwasher and went into my study, telling myself that I must try to live with my unanswered questions, teach myself to live in uncertainty, at least for the time being, without filling the holes in my knowledge with lurid fantasies. It was bound to be quite a while. That was all I knew, all she had said. With the passage of the weeks and no word from her, I do not take her words any longer as a warning, rather an attempt to reassure me. She must have known what she was about to do when she said it, and perhaps she only said it so that I should not lose my head and report her missing to the police. What is she doing? How shall I be able to comprehend the extent of my uncertainty? I leafed desultorily through my notes and watched the ducks' wedge-shaped tracks on the shining surface of the water or the running figures disappearing and reappearing between the dark tree trunks along the shore. I suddenly felt I had nothing to add on Cézanne. After all, others had probably said what there was to say about him without my assistance. I had planned to finish writing the article and deliver it before going to New York, but I was supposed to leave in less than a week, and I had not even got halfway. The trip had been planned for several weeks. During recent years I have written a number of essays on American painters, and among other things there was a retrospective exhibition of Edward Hopper at the Whitney Museum, which I absolutely had to see. Now I was not at all sure whether I should go. Astrid's sudden departure had paralysed me. I could not think of anything but her mysterious decision and the equally mysterious resolve on her face as she stood looking at me in the doorway of the bedroom before leaving. I felt seen through as I stood there, sleepy and speechless in my creased pyjamas, but I had no idea what she had seen with that gaze that penetrated right through me, itself impenetrable and impossible to interpret. I felt her eyes strike a core far inside, how in a few seconds they lit up a place I myself did not know, whether it was because it had been lying in darkness and oblivion far too long, or because at that moment she knew me better than I have ever known myself. I have still not found the words to open that glance for me, it was a look from the other side of the words, and already when she was on her way down the stairs, already while I stood listening to her footsteps, I realised I would keep returning to those moments when we faced each other silently on the threshold of the room where we have slept beside each other for so many years. But I also knew she would not come hurrying back just because I stayed at home and kept watch over her absence. Whether I walked round in circles in the flat or in Manhattan would amount to the same thing, her gaze in the doorway would follow me everywhere.

I tried to pull myself together, and to concentrate on Cézanne. My rough improvised notes suddenly seemed vain and futile. One of them was a reflection I had made several years earlier. I had never really known what to do about it because it introduced a distracting element of psychology into the purely aesthetic meditation on Cézanne's method. The note referred to one of his pictures of bathing women, who in fact are not bathing at all, but have come out of the river and stand or lie on the grass, naked, voluptuous and completely at ease, resting with their sensual weight, as they yield to the movements of the observer's gaze among their bodies and the branches and foliage of the surrounding trees, so that skin, bark, leaves, water and reflections form part of the same circulation of colour, the same round of contrasts and graduations around the clearing among the trees in which there is a clear view, behind the women in the foreground, of the river and the distant opposite bank. And right at the centre of the picture, on the other side of the river, Cézanne has placed two small indistinct figures, almost invisible in the misty remoteness of colour, a man standing on the river bank with his dog beside him. He is too far away to have a face, but it is impossible to miss him there, looking over at the opposite side, face to face with the spectator across the span of the river, and naturally it is the women he has caught sight of, it is their undisturbed nakedness he is spying on in company with his dog. The indistinct little male person reflects the observer's gaze in the perspective plane, so someone standing in the silence of the museum for a moment feels a vague, inexplicable shame, as if his gaze, which without distinguishing between flesh and plants, travels around in the abstract separation of the colours, as if this passive and dispassionate gaze was also a hand furtively brushing the breasts and thighs of the unsuspecting women.

When I heard the telephone I was sure it was Astrid, but it was Rosa calling to ask what time they should come. I had completely forgotten that the previous week we had invited her and her boyfriend to dinner. She sounded so well brought up, just like a real dinner guest and not the demanding, impatient child I had fed with yogurt, then Frankfurters and inventive Indonesian dishes. I tried to write a page or two about Cézanne's discreet voyeur while thinking, between each sentence, of how I was going to explain Astrid's absence. But she had seen to that, I could hear, when during the entrée Rosa narrowed her eyes teasingly and said that now she was probably up in the Swedish Skerries with Gunilla, pulling me to pieces as deftly as the ten kilo of crayfish they were sure to be having for dinner. Rosa's eyes have always been narrow and teasing like her mother's, and the corners of her mouth curl just like Astrid's in a very sensual and sometimes almost spiteful way when she smiles, which she did when she saw my sheepish expression. I apologised for not serving crayfish as starter, which merely made her laugh and stroke my cheek with a tolerant, comforting gesture. Gunilla is a lesbian child psychiatrist from Stockholm with dyed hair, almost copper coloured, and I have never really taken to her and her voluminous screen-printed dresses and her holistic skerries island with outside loo and oil lamps and lumps of amber as big as cobblestones, even though she has known Astrid since she was married to Simon's father, or perhaps just because of that. When Rosa and her boyfriend had left I looked up Gunilla's number in Stockholm, maybe Astrid really had gone up there to stay with her old friend, whom she knew I couldn't stand, maybe that was why she hadn't told me where she was going. I could not really decide whether the thought was a reassuring one, and I was actually relieved when I heard how surprised Gunilla sounded on the phone. I even felt a touch of malicious pleasure. It was obvious she didn't know Astrid had gone away although they rang each other at least twice a week and never talked for less than an hour at a time.

Rosa's new boyfriend must be at least five years older than she is. He was fairly silent during dinner. We had only met once before, but I was still not sure that his silence and the abrupt minimal sentences he framed it with was due to shyness and not to an abysmal contempt. He was one of those shaven-headed young men in black who, like some gang of renovation workers, has undertaken to speed up the Fall of the West so we can get rid of all the outdated civilised shit. In him the dislike of culture had obviously developed into a dislike of everything, maybe with the sole exception of Rosa; now and then he caressed her neck with what most resembled a stranglehold, while fixing me with his small gimlet eyes. But as well as my daughter my gazpacho seemed to meet with approval, as far as I could judge. Before we ate Rosa had shown him round the apartment, she had even dragged him into my study with the breezy nonchalance of a lovingly nurtured daughter who ignores territorial limits, but he chuckled contemptuously at my series of Giacometti etchings and the open monographs on Cézanne on my table. Rosa had told me he was an artist, and I hadn't known whether I should be happy or worried over the enthusiastic glow in her eyes. As far as I could gather he mostly worked on installations and was the man behind an exhibition which had aroused some interest on account of its preserved human embryos embedded in magenta plastic and flanked by a wall of video monitors on which a German porno film with juvenile Thai girls played in slow motion. While Rosa helped me fill the dishwasher she reproached me for not giving him more of a welcome, and she told me in wounded tones that he had read my essay on Jackson Pollock and had been looking forward to discussing it with me. Before I had managed to defend myself the phone rang, and she went in to the installation artist, who in the meantime had installed himself in the living room. I could hear them tongue-kissing in there, and the corridor to the kitchen is not exactly short. Then they were drowned out by my mother's hectic stream of words.

My mother is what is known as an exuberant woman. Everything about her is luxuriant, almost tropical. She asked if she could speak to my charming wife. She says that every time, she doesn't get tired of saying it, she has said it for eighteen years. I said Astrid had gone up to see her friend in Stockholm. She asked if all was not quiet on the Western Front. She uses that kind of expression all the time, and I've often asked myself whether she sounded quite as affected and false when she was young. She can still surprise me, after so many years' acquaintance, not only with her unusually well developed sense of smell where 'smoke in the kitchen' is concerned, as she calls it, but also with her intimidating lack of decency when she oversteps all my boundaries and with an ingratiating 'Cooee' thrusts her head round the door of my innermost sanctum. I'm sure I would have given her inquisitiveness a hard test if I had invited her to camp out at the foot of our bed. Contrary to what might be thought, Astrid thinks she is sweet, and she can still laugh at the swarm of postcards and letters her tireless mother-in-law sends us when she is on tour in the provinces. Her need for communication is insatiable, and she doesn't stop before she has used up the entire stock of note-paper in her hotel room. Naturally, her letters are always about herself and about the present condition of her personality in the midst of a violent avalanche of development which makes her see everything in an entirely new light. This happens at least every other month. She is an actor and although it is a generation since she became too old to play Ophelia or Miss Julie, she has never stopped acting the part of the skittish kitten she must once have been. She called to remind us of the premiere she had already invited us to seven times, of a play a young dramatist had written specially for her. She was hoping to see us both. Her tone was unmistakeable, she had seen through the situation, and I caught myself wishing she would tell me what she saw, but she had already thrown herself into a long-drawn-out account of the 'friend of her heart' as she called him, a somewhat decrepit opera director with prostate trouble and a silk scarf round his neck. It has always amazed me that Astrid can stand her, that she will put up with being my 'charming wife', but she just smiles tolerantly as if it was not her at all who was described in that way. As a whole Astrid is very forbearing, fatuous remarks glance off her friendly smile while she thinks her own thoughts.

As usual my ear was quite hot and swollen when I finally put down the receiver. Rosa and her installation artist left soon after. I would have liked to go on talking to her, it had been too long since we had been together. As a gracious young woman had gradually emerged, wrenching herself free of the gawkiness of an eager child, she too had drawn back from our old intimacy. She used to question me about everything, and I had replied to everything she had asked. I had talked and talked, long before she herself could talk clearly or understand what I said, but as soon as she was ten, she had been the one who talked, she who stubbornly and, permitting no interruption, told me about the world she saw and appropriated, as if the whole time she had to repeat her growing knowledge of it so as not to forget anything. We could still sit in a corner and whisper together, but I noticed more and more often how my questions were left to themselves on the threshold of a new unknown room to which I had no access, and I came to think of my mother, of her heavy-handed lack of restraint, and kept quiet. If I tried to teach Rosa about the pitfalls of adult life, she merely smiled patiently until I had finished. I had to content myself with observing her from a distance, secretly moved, both happy and sad at the sight of her arrogant but vulnerable beauty, which no one had yet had the opportunity to mar. Sometimes I could hardly recognise her, when I saw her chatting and laughing in a circle of contemporaries, unaware that I was watching her, and if she suddenly looked up and smiled at me with those eyes and that mouth, which were both Astrid's and her own, I had to admit I knew less and less about what went on behind her green gaze. It reminded me of what one of my older friends had said when his children left home. That children know their parents better than parents know their children.

I walked aimlessly around the flat when I was alone again. I couldn't make out if it seemed larger or smaller to me than usual. I cleared the table and tidied up, but that was soon done. It was quiet again, but it was not our mutual silence, Astrid's and mine, which one of us could break at any moment. It was a tight-fitting silence which closed around me after each of my sounds, after each car that passed along beside the Lakes. I thought of reading but didn't get beyond the thought. Instead I put on a record, one of my old John Coltrane records that Astrid can't bear, but neither Coltrane's waterfall of notes nor McCoy Tyner's thundering chords would turn into anything except the crackling, slightly hollow, mechanical echo of an afternoon in a sound studio in Manhattan far too many years earlier. I did not know what to do with myself that first evening of Astrid's absence. I walked to and fro in the flat, listening to my own steps and the creak of the floorboards beneath me. At one point I stood in the hall with my coat on, I'd go for a walk, maybe have a glass or two somewhere, escape the silence in the flat and the feeling of being cooped up in myself. Then I discovered I had forgotten my cigarettes, and on the way along the corridor to the kitchen it occurred to me that Astrid might think of calling. I wasn't going anywhere. I sat on the sofa and edited my own meaningless film, channel-hopping between the television offerings of panel discussions, golf tournaments, motor racing and tropical animals. While I walked up and down, I left the television on in order not to be the only person moving and producing sounds among the immovable stillness of objects and furniture. It was the first time in eighteen years that I did not know more or less when she would come home, or if she would come back at all. Naturally we had quarrelled like everyone else, but usually over trivialities and never for long. We had never gone to bed without making peace and smiling at ourselves and each other. The apartment had never, for more than an hour at a time, been allowed to be the scene of those theatrical marital tableaux in which one person stands with her back to the window while the other sits in the foreground pretending to read a newspaper. In all the years that we had been a family and now, when the children had begun to draw back from the ménage, we had moved in a sometimes harassed, sometimes peaceful, but always flexible choreography, in which we met and parted and met again on our way through the days. All the hectic mornings when we sent the children to school, and all the busy evenings when we cooked, had been more or less elegant repeats with imperceptible variations of the same ballet, in which we moved around each other with an intuitive knowledge of the other's movement patterns. Even when we grew more and more alone together we went on anticipating the other's movements and compensating for the other's omissions or fits of inattention, whether it was an electric light bulb to be changed, or a cup grasped in the air before it fell to the floor. Our bodies knew each other in and out and understood how to fall into the same rhythm as we walked along the street or went to bed with each other, even when we turned round in sleep we accommodated ourselves to each other's bent knees and elbows.

I let my gaze roam around the immovable furniture and belongings. She had found most of them. It was she who decided on the décor, with her unpredictable but sure taste. I have often been surprised when she came home with an unexpected lamp, a tea pot or a vase, but even her most eccentric discoveries soon acquired their natural place as logical additions to our universe of intimate objects. The furnishings of the flat did not merely decorate the frame of our life together, they are also traces of her whims and caprices, just as characteristic of her personality as her drawling, crisp voice or her eager, still slightly girlish way of walking on her long legs. Everything in the room was in its accustomed place, but when I looked at the things now it was as if they rejected my intimate gaze. The dark-red carpet we had once bought in Istanbul was suddenly any old carpet, the Japanese woodcut views of Mount Fuji at the end of an ice-blue sea were no longer the well-known landscape of my daydreams but insignificant glimpses of a hostile foreign world, and the honey-coloured mahogany bureau Astrid had inherited from her aunt seemed to me hideous, although its contours and the polished wood's year marks were just as unchangeably engraved in my memory as Astrid's mouth and eyes. Nothing in the room indicated that in a moment she would not come through the door and sit down on the sofa with a newspaper, and I knew precisely how she would sit, in which corner, with her legs pulled up under her, erect and with her head slightly tilted while she read and thoughtfully stroked her neck with the palm of her hand. I remained in the doorway of the bedroom in the same place where she had stood that morning. My duvet lay in a twisted bundle beside hers, smooth and long and airy. My pillow was crushed up against the wall, hers was plumped, full and without a fold, without the hollow her head used to leave. She had taken the time to make her half of the bed, as if she wanted to obliterate her traces before she dressed and positioned herself in the doorway to observe my unsuspecting sleeping face. But she had forgotten to close the door of the wardrobe. She could not have taken very much with her, almost all her clothes hung on their hangers there, and the sight of her lifeless dresses and blouses struck me with a sudden jab, as if she were dead and all that was left of her was her clothes and the other objects that were hers. The brushes on the small table under the mirror, with a few long, tangled chestnut-brown hairs. The Chinese box with its black lacquer lid decorated with gilded herons over gilded rushes, where she kept her jewellery. The rows of shoes, the oldest with dark imprints from her heels. Although her clothes and her belongings bore witness to her personal taste with all its whims, they seemed strangely anonymous now she had left them to themselves in the quiet bedroom. They had so little to say in her absence. The more I had come to know about her, the better, I thought, I knew her, although the opposite might just as well be the case. For all I knew, there might well be still more to know. A bottomless thought. I couldn't remember when I had stopped imagining her secret, hidden sides, when I had grown used to her as she was with the children and me. I could not know whether she kept any secrets at all from me or had ever done so, or whether her hidden sides had been hidden from herself as well. Perhaps she too had become what I thought she was.

For the first time in ages I took out the fat album in which through the years I had stuck the pictures, the pictures of our life. The oldest of them have faded and the colours have become blurred. Astrid breast-feeding Rosa, with young, plump cheeks. Rosa's chubby waddling body on the seashore one summer. Simon as an angler with a cod in his arms almost as big as himself. Astrid in a fur cap, posing with the children beside a lopsided and melancholy snowman. Astrid in front of a golden, tree-covered valley in Trás-os-Montes that autumn seven years ago, and by the rail of the ferry in the middle of the Tagus, in the afternoon sun, with white teeth and the wind in her hair and flashing sunglasses in front of the dazzling façades rearing up behind each other in Alfama and Bairro Alto. I am seldom in the pictures, I took most of them myself, and more than once it has struck me that in a way it was my own absence I was photographing, as when I was in an aeroplane again on my way abroad imagining what they might be doing at home. Rosa on the lawn in front of the sea, naked in the sun with a podgy stomach and wild, wide eyes as she puts a finger over the hose so the water refracts the light around her in a brilliant rainbow fan like the outspread tail feathers of a peacock. Simon with his cheek against the floor boards and a gaze lost in the trafficated microcosm of his toy cars, like a gentle and lonely Gulliver wishing there was room for him on the small empty front seats in his daydream. It had passed quickly, the children were so busy growing as if our lives couldn't progress fast enough, and even the pictures can't stop time. On the contrary, they show how long ago it is since Simon played with cars and Rosa played with water. All the same I am glad I took those pictures, even though I often felt a bit awkward squatting down with the camera. I felt I was intruding on their unselfconscious concentration or spontaneous delight, that I wanted to preserve. I don't know which of the pictures make me most wistful, those where the children don't realise they are being snapped, as if they were alone, or those where they laugh and look into the camera, completely present as they meet my gaze. In one kind of picture I don't seem to be there at all, in the other kind it is certainly not me they smile at but the stupid camera I hid behind. Sometimes I think you take photographs instead of seeing, you forget to look in your eagerness to grasp what is seen, capture it in time's flight. You are absent from your own pictures, not only because you took them yourself, but also because you betray the moments you want to save from oblivion. Before you get the picture in focus it has already become a different image, a different moment. Astrid hardly ever took pictures, she left it to me, she even encouraged me to take them, and when I did, each time I had the feeling of being outside. She is totally present there in the pictures, at one with the moment I plucked out of time's blind growth and stuck into the fat album like the flowers Rosa pressed and stuck into an exercise book. Withered fragments of our life, where she buries Rosa in sand so only her little grinning head sticks up, or paints lines on Simon's face that Shrovetide carnival time, when he was an Indian, while I spy on them through the lens, at a distance, like a doting detective in love.

One of the pictures shows Astrid standing alone on the balcony early one summer morning, when the façade is still in shadow. She leans against the wall, which meets the row of trees beneath her in the vanishing point of the perspective. She looks away, out of the picture, I don't know what at, as if wondering, stopped short between two seconds, between one thought and the next. A restrained musing, perhaps over the years that have succeeded each other so rapidly, over the way her life has taken shape, as if it had happened while she was pondering for a moment as now, occupied in following a bird's disappearance, a changing cloud shape, the wind's creased track on the bright trembling membrane of the lake or how the leaves of the trees alternately turn their shining and their dull side to the wind and the light. If she were disappointed, she would certainly not be able to say over what, yet all the same her happiness seems to her in a vague and indefinable way to be a betrayal. Even though she cannot decide, and anyway has not yet tried to decide, whether it is life that has betrayed her, or the other way round. Life. Can you talk of it like this at all? Can you talk about anything else than the life that is hers? This life, which cannot be thought of without the others', the boy's, the girl's and the man's. Just as she and the others cannot either, as the years pass, be thought about differently, as the years allow her to see them or allow her to see herself in the mirror when she is alone. They are hers, and she is theirs. Is it chance or destiny that has shaped it like this? When was one thing succeeded by another? When did she stop distinguishing? When did it suddenly become too easy and too hard, too all-embracing and actually useless to ask if she really loves the man looking at her through the little aperture of the camera? As when the youngest child asks where space ends.

I sat by the window looking on to the Lakes without lighting the lamp above my desk. The tree-crowns, the mirror of the water and the row of houses on the other side merged together in the darkness, only the lighted windows appeared between the trees like an elongated and uneven, yellow mosaic. Here and there a stone in the mosaic was missing, elsewhere the stones looked as if they had been broken, because a dark ramification of twigs in the foreground splintered the distant square of light. The lighted windows were dimly reflected in the black water, and the folds on the surface made the reflections tremble. As I looked at them from my chair, across the lake, the rows of luminous windows, it seemed for a moment unthinkable that over there behind the dark dolls' house façades strange people were living out their lives, side by side in row after row of unknown homes. Perhaps some of them were watching the same film on television, perhaps some of them lifted their coffee cups at the same time, perhaps more than one of them stood at this moment before a washing up bowl in a kitchen seeing the soapy water shine violet on a plate in the light of the lamp above the sink, all of this in a slightly displaced synchronicity of trivial and everyday movements. But how many of them were thinking that their little world of repetitions and changes, of trivialities and tragedies and sudden felicity, was merely one world among many in the great mosaic? Did someone perhaps also sit behind a window on the other side looking over the lake, thinking the same thing as I did? Were there two of us sitting and thinking of all those windows, all those views and all those doors, all those possibilities opening and closing on each other? Many years before, when I had just moved into town, young and fresh in the world, I had cycled around in the evening, along the Lakes, for instance, and thought there would surely be enough doors to enter. I had cycled beside the water, under the trees, past one door after another, and I had longed to find a door, the absolutely right door that would open onto something I was not yet able to imagine.

She has hired a car in Paris, somewhere on the Avenue Foch. Then driven south. I have the statement of our account, I can see where she has used her card. She has reached Bordeaux late in the afternoon, and booked into a hotel there. She has driven, beside the river, in the stream of late traffic alongside the sooty façades. While I sat at dinner with Rosa and her boyfriend, she was sitting in a restaurant in Bordeaux observing the other guests and vaguely listening to their conversation, a solitary woman travelling through. She has followed our old route south through Les Landes, through the endless pine forests in the drizzle, down to the Spanish frontier. The hours linked with each other in a long tunnel of grey, misty light, as she sat behind the wheel, unmoving and yet in motion, in a car among other cars in the branched delta of the motorway net. Perhaps she was aware of leaving a trail every time she passed her card through another tele-terminal at the filling stations and services en route. A trail of names she must have known

I would recognise, just as I recognised their order. It was the same journey, the same time of year, when Europe fades to a gamut of gold and red-brown and dusty green along the roads, and the suburbs, the factories, the power stations and motorway loops dissolve in the rainy mist among the moving chains of car lights. Perhaps it was even a delayed message she sent me through the computerised statement's list of places, a reminder of something she wanted me to remember. In San Sebastian she went into a bar at La Concha. I can only imagine San Sebastian in the drizzle, the colonnade beneath the row of hotels looking out on the little bay with its corn-yellow sand and the green water and rocking trawlers farther out, paling into transparence in the Biscay fog. I imagine her standing in a noisy bar sipping her *café cortado* while by turns she observed the passing umbrellas beside the sea on the promenade and the shaky, gritty and somehow corroded picture on the television screen above the bar of a remote, incomprehensible war between bearded militia in ragged uniforms, driven by an unimaginable hatred, an unimaginable desire to cut someone's throat or get one's own throat cut in the Caucasian mud. The same pictures I myself watched on those autumn evenings, alone in front of the screen in the apartment beside the Lakes and later in the hotel room on Lexington Avenue, alone with the numbed feeling that time withdraws from us and divides us in the same movement, unaware of its own face, while devouring its children.

We walked between the columns beneath the promenade and over the wet sand. Even at this time of year there were a few late bathers. Their freezing, glistening limbs resembled strayed summer memories when they ran over the sand, stooping and with arms folded. Astrid jumped away when the tongues of foam stretched out after her on the beach, she laughed euphorically after the long hours in the car, her hair curled in the damp air, and her cheeks were cool and sticky with salt. I told her that *concha* means both conch shell and cunt, and she laughed again and pushed at me, so the foam from the waves washed over my shoes. It wasn't as if we felt young again, as they say, it was not a revival of our once unrestrained playfulness. After all, we were the same people we had been the whole time, while everything happened to us at tearing speed. Rosa was eleven and Simon was sixteen, and as I said it was the first time we had been away for more than a week without them. We were apparently the same, and yet we regarded each other with curious, searching and slightly anxious eyes. We were still young, but we knew it wouldn't last much longer. We made love in the afternoon in hotel rooms, we had not done that for several years. We were in motion all the time from one place to another, and with each town we slept in on our way south we grew a little more alone together, left to each other. I lay with my head in her lap, I felt her stomach rise and sink in time to her breathing, I listened to the rain pattering on the shutters onto La Concha, and she squeezed my head softly between her thighs and asked if I could hear the sea. There were other things she might have asked, but she didn't. A couple of weeks before we went away, I had come back from New York, it had been my idea for us to go, I suggested it as soon as we got into the car when she fetched me from the airport. She smiled in surprise, considering the idea. It was the first time the children were not between us, conducting our love, and we swayed slightly in the sudden undisturbed presence of each other. We felt our way forward, I did anyway, while I tried to decipher, in the hotels and in the car en route, whether we were still the people I hoped we were. We went on along the Bay of Biscay between the sea and the mountains, without stopping, almost as if we were in a hurry. We stopped only to eat and sleep, Bilbao and Santander were nothing but names in the rain.

2

While I was finishing my degree I drove a taxi in the evenings. I was twenty-seven that winter. I drove all over the town, now in one direction, now in the opposite, wherever people wanted to go, or where the cool, slightly impatient women's voices over the car radio told me someone was waiting. To the customers their stay in the car was merely a necessary pause as they traversed the distance between what they had left behind and what they were approaching on this particular evening in their life. To me the journeys were a chance web of routes through the city as I took some passenger or other to his destination. Disjointed and insignificant scenes of transport in their continuing stories which I caught just a glimpse of as I listened to the conversations on the back seat or made guesses about whether I had a pusher in the car, a married couple on a silver wedding trip or a business man on the way to his usual appointment with a mistress in leather and rubber. Thus I spent my evenings crossing to and fro among unknown, constantly new stories, endlessly in movement and yet unmoving behind the wheel, in transit from one end of town to the other. One evening in January I was called out to an address in one of the northern suburbs. I waited beside the pavement for a while until a tall slim woman came out of the house with a small boy in one hand and a large travelling bag in the other. She must have been about my age, in her late twenties. Just as they were getting in, a man in shirt-sleeves came running after them. He kept repeating that she mustn't go, that she wasn't going anywhere, although that was obviously what she was doing. His hair was quite long and grizzled, he looked at least twenty-five years older than her and he was clearly what you would call a good-looking guy when his face was not so contorted into a grimace both threatening and miserable. He tried to seize her by the arm but she hit out at him so he had to take a step backwards. She slammed the car door and called to me to start. The boy began to cry and kept on while she talked quietly and calmly to him, I could see him in the rear mirror, huddled into the corner hugging a large teddy bear, hiccuping as he wept. She gave me the name of a street in the city centre and began to hum to him, and on the way in he gradually calmed down. She went on humming the same tune, and sometimes I caught a glimpse of her in the rear mirror, bent over the boy, when the light of a street lamp passed over her pale cheeks and narrow, flashing eyes.

When we arrived and I switched off the meter the greying man was standing on the pavement ready to meet us, still in shirt-sleeves and with the same pathetic yet frightening expression. I was annoyed not to have thought out the short-cut he had taken to get there before us, I who thought I knew the town through and through. He must certainly have driven at speed. He took hold of the door handle but she had locked it and he was obliged to speak to her through the window pane, more calmly now, almost intimately, looking in at her with a sombre, damp gaze. He turned round abruptly when a young woman came out on to the steps. She wore only a t-shirt and clasped her arms in front of her in the cold, looking in alarm at the man who pointed at her and shouted something I couldn't hear. The boy started to cry again. My passenger rolled down her window and shouted to the woman that she would call later, then asked me to drive on. The woman on the pavement took a step towards us, but the man grabbed her arm and I started up the car again. They stood quite still, gazing after us, and he loosened his grip on her arm, as they disappeared out of

the rear mirror. I asked where we were to go now. She made
no reply, she was concentrating on calming the trembling
boy. When we had passed a block or two and I stopped at
a red light, I asked again. Irritably she told me to just drive.
I followed the traffic and improvised my way forward, as
I did when I had no customers in the cab, listening to her
reassuring whispering and humming. It occurred to me that
we might spend the whole evening like this, circling around
the city, unless she thought of something soon, and I glanced
at the pulsing digits on the meter. After we had passed the
Town Hall Square for the fourth time the boy was asleep.
By now she had clocked up almost five hundred kroner.

I took the road alongside the harbour and switched off the
meter shortly before the hovercraft jetty. I pulled in to the
side and turned towards her. What was she planning? She
sat with the sleeping boy's head on her lap, looking out over
the sea. She didn't know. Her voice was faint and cracked.
I turned and studied the crowds of passengers coming out
of the hovercraft terminal, thronging the pavement. When
the last passenger had disappeared and the waiting room
lay empty in the hard neon light, I turned again and asked
if she had no place to go to. She sat bent over so her dark
hair hid her face. When she raised her head her cheeks were
streaked with tears, but no sound came from her. I found a
kitchen roll, I used it for drying the screen wipers with, and
while she blew her nose I suggested a cheap but good hotel I
knew. She crumpled the paper and smiled, almost scornfully.
She hadn't even enough money for the fare. What about her
friend? He must have gone away by now. I was surprised to
hear myself utter the words 'friend' so naturally and 'he' as
if I were quite familiar with the situation. She said he would
be ready to spend the whole night outside her door, if need
be. But was there no one else she could stay with? I offered
her a cigarette and lit one for myself. There wasn't. I studied
her profile in the rear mirror as she sat blowing smoke over

the window pane, letting her gaze lose itself in the reflections on the black water of the harbour, sunk into herself. She seemed to have completely forgotten where she was. I asked if he was her husband. She looked at me coldly in the mirror. What business was it of mine? I shrugged my shoulders and looked away again. I don't know whether I quite simply had the idea because I could not envisage sitting like that beside a quay in the harbour with an unknown girl and her son while evening turned into night. At first she looked at me as if I had suggested something depraved, and I smiled as normally and trustworthily as I could while explaining that I drove all night and didn't get home until well into the morning. She would be sure to find somewhere tomorrow, but she could be in peace until then. Her eyes grew even narrower and fixed me for a long time without blinking, surprised and distrustful. It was as if she only now caught sight of me, as if she was sizing me up to form an impression of who he might be, this strange taxi driver so intent on rescuing her from the mess she had got herself into. Finally she managed a smile, suddenly quite shy, but not exactly grateful. I avoided meeting her eye in the rear mirror as we drove through the town yet once more. I carried the boy up and laid him on my bed, he didn't wake up, just mumbled a little before curling up and sleeping on. There were only two rooms in my flat, she was in the other one looking at the books on my shelf. I gave her an extra set of keys and told her she could just slip them through the letterbox when they left. Suddenly I was in a hurry to get away, perhaps I was slightly alarmed at my own whim. As she stood there I realised she must look rather beautiful when she was not so pale and red-eyed from weeping. She smiled for the second time and asked my name. That was how I met Astrid.

I drove all night until there were long gaps between fares, and even then I went on for another hour, slightly irritated at myself because I'd handed over my bed to a strange girl and her child. When I got home I lay down on the sofa and fell asleep at once. I woke when the sky had appeared behind the rooftops opposite. I didn't really know whether to get up or not. For some minutes I stayed there feeling like a guest in my own home. Then I crept over and opened the door of the bedroom a crack, the bed was empty. I undressed and slept all morning, as I usually did. If anyone had told me that she was the one I would come to live with, this stranger, whom I had rescued from an embarrassing and hazardous situation the evening before, I would have smiled, as you smile at your friends' most grotesque and rambling notions, tolerant and slightly absent-minded, stubbing out your cigarette in the full ashtray among the puddles of beer on the bar counter. But who would have told me that? The future was still remote and vague, something you could at most talk wildly about, like discussing where you might go next summer. When I woke up I could barely recall what she looked like. Of course I was old enough to know how random unexpected meetings are, but I was still too young to realise that the number of meetings is not unlimited. When a beautiful unknown woman returns my gaze in the street I can still play with the idea that life is like a tree branching with possibilities, of ways one might have taken, but it is merely an idea. For I know well enough that trees don't grow in the sky, as they say, and you can't move in one direction without cutting yourself off from all the other ramifications.

When I met Astrid I was not yet old enough to have built up a history. I could still become dizzy at the thought of the profusion of girls' faces in the city and rough sketches of what the future might hold, but the dizziness did not make me blissfully drunk, it sickened me. The alluring twinkle of the casino of coincidences left me with a feeling of homelessness and aversion. I was already tired of standing at night swaying among warm, intoxicated bodies in pulsating noise and flashing lights, where it didn't matter who I was. Tired of standing somewhere in town between one song and the next, bending over yet another strange girl, who hoarsely confided her jolly travel plans and mundane future prospects to me until the music parted us again with its punching beat, as if an angry child was somewhere below us jerking at his jumping jack. If she woke up in my bed the whole thing was suddenly just another passing nocturnal impulse, and I could barely remember the mirages my desire had read into her blank young features. She looked around her sleepily with surprise but I couldn't guess what she saw, not even in my face which, if she could be bothered, she was trying to interpret with the scraps I'd confided to her. She herself was so alien, as I drew her close, a little conventionally, since after all she was there, and she was warm with sleep, and I thought how close one can be and yet know nothing. I looked at her naked body forgetting whether she was beautiful, completely preoccupied by its blind particularities, the shape of her breasts, the scars and birthmarks on her skin. Another body with its handful of genes that a glazier or a clerk and his wife from out in the suburbs had passed on to the precious princess of this night. I stroked the hair away from her unknown face, made a show of examining her features, and she crept close to my side and caressed me vaguely. A touch without content, as if you imagined a language of words that meant nothing, just another sweet and absent-minded little slide through eternity.

I woke up about noon with my back feeling strangely cold and clammy. The boy had peed in my bed, out of his wits because of his parents' marital drama in the night. And now Simon's astride his Kawasaki, no doubt without a crash helmet, as the rocks and the cork oaks and flocks of sheep of Sardinia sweep past him, and it would never cross his mind to call home, that boy I grew used to calling my son many years ago. The dark wet patch on the sheet was the only visible trace he and his mother had left behind, but it seemed she had kept my keys. I tore off the bedclothes and as I carried them into the bathroom I breathed the smell of boy's urine and the scent of her perfume. So she had taken the time to splash some on before she left the grizzled man. If, when I had passed her the keys with a slightly shy gesture the night before, there had been a moment when I thought she was actually the kind of girl I would have looked at in the street, it was merely a fleeting notion. I was still far too taken up with my own private pain. As I lifted up the mattress, between the slats of the bed base I caught sight of the charcoal drawing that used to hang above the bedhead, fastened with a drawing pin. It must have fallen on the floor during the night, that dashed-off sketch of a bird's skull which Inès had once given me, long before I stood at the window for the last time with my gaze following her down the pavement, until I couldn't see her any more through the snowflakes whirled upwards by the wind in confused spirals. I saw her again a year or two ago, one evening when I was coming out of a cinema with Astrid. We nodded and smiled through the crowd, Astrid asked who she was and I replied it was someone I had once known before we met. True, in fact. Of course I'd told Astrid about her, in the time when we had still not finished telling each other our histories. But I didn't tell her that the woman in the cinema foyer was the Inès she had heard me speak of, slightly summarily and distanced, as you talk of the women you knew before the one who is listening to your story. I don't really know why. Was I afraid that she still hid somewhere inside me, that the image of Inès after the chance new sight of her would emerge again and make me suffer or dream in all secrecy? She was still beautiful and dramatic and Middle Eastern to look at, but when I turned to Astrid to answer her curious, but not in the least inquisitorial question, I felt nothing of the pain I once suffered. Inès was just a woman I had once loved, and in the meantime I had dreamed other dreams and nursed other wounds.

I picked up the sketch and searched for the drawing pin. She hadn't even varnished it, my thumb had left an impression on one of the broad lines tentatively outlining the contours of the bird's skull. I rubbed finger and thumb together until the grey charcoal had gone. Eighteen months before, one hot afternoon in late summer, I had gone into the Glyptotek museum, mostly because it was cool. I thought I was the only visitor, but I caught sight of her in one of the small dark halls exhibiting Roman heads. She had her back to me, quite motionless, her black hair gathered into a soft casual knot on her long slim neck. To begin with she was only a silhouette against a distant, sun-flooded door opening into the last of the adjoining halls, a narrow black drawing reflected in the polished stone floor. She was pale although we had enjoyed unbroken sunshine for three months. I stopped, apparently she had not heard me. She was wearing a long black dress, her bare feet were in black shoes with heavy heels and thin straps around the ankles, old-fashioned, slightly sombre shoes which made me fantasise about a slow tango in a brothel in Buenos Aires before the war. Even her pallor had a faint honey-coloured tinge, and I knew immediately that I would touch her, that I would come to feel this pale and yet strangely smouldering completely homogeneous skin on my hands and lips. She stood in front of a Roman emperor, all that was left of him, a tight-lipped face devoid of illusions, disfigured by time, balancing on an iron pole bored up through the stone, as if decapitated. His features were almost completely eroded so that the veins and pores in the stone stood out along the fractured surfaces, from which the nose and lips had disappeared. The face was like a picture which in the course of centuries had slowly faded to the anonymous eternity of

the marble block. I said this to her, or something like it, and
she turned towards me and looked at me with her large dark
eyes, completely calm, her expression seeming to recognise
me from somewhere, although we had never seen each other
before.

Her face still shines through the years that followed,
through the moving reflections and swirls and ripples of
everything that has passed since. It shines down in the green
darkness like the face on a coin that slipped out of my hand,
rare but not irreplaceable. Sometimes I can't see her, at
other times she comes in sight briefly among the changing
reflections of the days, among other faces that I held between
my hands one at a time as if they could tell me something
I did not know. Her eyes have lost their terrible power to
attract, turned greenish like verdigrised bronze and wiped
out in the current of time, but now and then she looks at
me again, at a distance, with an enquiring gaze, with a
constantly more indistinct, incomprehensible question that
year by year grows still more impossible and irrelevant to
answer. We left the museum together. We walked side by
side in the low light, with long shadows between the hot
walls, across the burning surface of the squares, talking
without pause of everything that occurred to us, as if there
were no bounds to what could be said, related and replied
to. We walked alongside the harbour and through the parks,
we went on as if it was impossible to stop, while the last
reflections of the sun vanished in the topmost panes and
the twilight trickled out from between the cobblestones and
grassblades and the calm folds of the water. By sleepwalking
circuitous routes we came to her house in a side-street,
opposite the Jewish cemetery. We postponed what we both
knew was merely a question of time, spoke more calmly
now, with long pauses when we only looked at each other
for as long as we could bear to, staving off the moment when
we would have to touch each other there in her room with its

view of the overgrown graves and crooked headstones with mysterious signs.

There was something old-fashioned about her, about her way of speaking, and it was not due only to her accent. She seemed like someone from another time, as if she had come ashore from one of the great ocean-going steamships with tall funnels, long ago sunk or broken up. Her father was a French diplomat, her mother Persian, and she had stayed on in Copenhagen after her parents had gone on to Teheran, New Delhi and Caracas. She told me she liked drawing, but I never found out whether it was merely something she did while waiting for something else to happen. What else she did never became clear to me, regardless of how much I questioned her, but clearly she had never had to worry about money. Her apartment was furnished in as spartan a manner as a cell in a nunnery, and she apparently ate nothing but frozen ready-made food, but she spent fortunes on taxis, and I have never known a woman who bought so many shoes. Expensive, extravagant, crazy shoes, that she wore a few times before leaving them at the bottom of a cupboard. She showed me her sketches of skulls and fragments of bones. I didn't know what to say about them, about her obsession with death's gnawed leavings registered with wheeling, monomaniacally insistent lines, alternately vehement and fleeting. Her black eyes and black drawings seemed to open onto an alien darkness that I had to refrain from penetrating. From one second to another she could suddenly start and gaze at me in fear, as if I had terrified her with a sudden sound or an unexpectedly hard tone of voice. It happened often, and each time she looked literally shattered. It was at such a moment that we finally gave in to what had been damming up in us on our way through the town. Her body was long and almost lanky, she had small breasts and her feet were long and narrow with bones that protruded beneath the thin skin like the fine bones in a bird's wing. There was nothing in the least voluptuous or indolent in her figure, it radiated an insatiable hunger that conveyed itself to the avid restlessness of her hands and her mouth. To make love with Inès was an unceasing battle that would not stop, an ungovernable, unmerciful rage, as if she wanted to wrench us over an abyss and fall through the empty space with her body locked around mine in an endless dizzy dive. We didn't let go of each other before it had been light for a long time and she suddenly asked me to leave.

It lasted for only just over a year. When it began to snow again, the story had ended, if in fact it had ever become a story, the confused series of cramped embraces, outbreaks of rage, philosophical escapades and rare occasions of slow and silent gentleness. When we were not making love we mostly talked about art, chiefly older artists, Rembrandt, El Greco, Goya and the sketches of Leonardo, his anatomical studies, which naturally appealed to her with their fearless, merciless precision. Among twentieth-century artists only Giacometti and Francis Bacon could elicit her acceptance. She was as uninterested in modern art as she was apparently ignorant of high politics, which surprised me considering her background. She once looked at me in sincere amazement when I mentioned Charles de Gaulle in the past tense, she hadn't realised he was dead. I never saw her read a newspaper, and she had neither television nor radio in her apartment, only an old record player and a small eclectic selection of records including Orlando di Lasso and Gabriel Fauré, Serge Gainsbourg and Astor Piazzolla. But in spite of the huge white patches in her picture of the world I was time and again struck by her analytical perspicacity and detailed knowledge of what interested her, whether it was Indian archaeology, Persian Sufism or Goethe's theory of colour. If I have ever succeeded in writing something about a painter which has not been put better by others, it is due to the conversations in bed with Inès when we lay smoking, still breathless and sweating, while she philosophised her way to an unexpected point with the hair-fine balance between outspokenness and scepticism of the original thinker. She is one of the most cultured people I have known, because her education was of the kind you find only in those who have not studied but sniffed their way forward, out of pure and aimless curiosity, in antiquarian bookshops, libraries and museums, greedily and without regard to scholastic categories.

The only thing she had no wish to turn upside-down and dissect was us, what happened between us, and where we were going. It was just too silly, as she said, and when I once in a tenderly wanton moment whispered something about having children, she laughed hoarsely at my flushing cheeks and timid eyes as she screwed off the lid of the bottle of brandy she always kept on the floor beside her bed. She went on laughing as she drank from the bottle, so in the end I had to thump her on the back between her fragile protruding shoulder blades so she didn't choke. When she straddled me with her back facing me to enjoy the sight of her own excitement in the mirror above the bed, her shoulder blades made me think of the folded wings of a large bird. We would meet at my place or in the street beside the Jewish cemetery, but she insisted that I phoned before I came. I could call at any time, but she did not let me in if I arrived unannounced even if there was light in her windows. On the other hand she could take it into her head to turn up without warning, at any time at all, always vibrating with the same suppressed ferocity that had to be unleashed immediately, often before we reached further than the hall. After our first meeting we seldom went out together and only at night, to bars and inns on the edge of town, never in the centre where we might risk meeting people we knew. It was Inès who wanted it that way. She wanted us to be a secret, that was how she put it, a secret from the world. I soon realised

I was not the only man she was seeing. She didn't tell me about the others but neither did she hide the fact of their existence when I finally summoned the strength to ask. To begin with she was amused at my jealousy and observed it with distanced interest, as an anthropologist observes the odd behaviour of natives. She knew I suffered, and she let me suffer, apparently without sensing she was the only one who could bring my sufferings to an end. Later she grew tired of my questions and my glowering silence.

I was still thinking of her that morning after Astrid and Simon had stayed the night with me. My days were empty and idle, and she invariably turned up when I didn't have anything else to think about or do. Her face and body appeared to me in the gaps during my night driving, and I was always afraid of meeting her. Knowing that we were both in the same town turned it into a danger zone in which both her absence and the risk of suddenly catching sight of her could produce startling attacks of physical pain, as if a hidden hand squeezed my lungs and my stomach. That morning too I found myself several times holding the telephone, about to dial her number. I lay on the sofa for some hours smoking and listening to music until the grey winter light once more began to fade into blue. I went out to get some air, strolled aimlessly around the streets among people on their way home with their briefcases, shopping bags and children, and when I stood outside my door again I could hear Simon's little voice inside. He fell silent and pressed against Astrid on the sofa as if I were a stranger who had pushed his way into what in the course of a day he had grown used to feeling as their territory. She looked up from a comic with an uncertain, searching smile. Was it all right for them to stay another night? I supposed it was, after all I had invited them myself, and really I didn't at all mind being distracted from my gloomy melancholy. She apologised for the wet mattress, and I made nothing of it and said I'd wet the bed myself, you know, until I went to upper school. She laughed politely although it hadn't been particularly funny. I recognised her perfume. She looked different, she had put her hair into a pony tail, and I noticed she had black mascara round her eyes as if she wanted to make a good impression. But it probably wasn't for my sake, it was probably only the sort of war paint women entrench themselves behind when everything else in their life collapses. The black make-up round her eyes gave them a hard, challenging expression that conflicted with the playful, knowing way she suddenly creased her lips into a smile, even when there was apparently nothing to smile at. Maybe she smiled out of embarrassment, maybe to draw me into a confidential, cheerful surprise at finding herself here with her little son in a completely strange man's flat, homeless and left to my unexpected hospitality.

She had been out shopping and started cooking dinner straight away; I sat down and read to the boy, mostly because I didn't know what else to do with myself. He looked at me suspiciously while I read the speeches in bubbles over the little blue men in white pixie caps who lived in a village with roofs made of toadstools, but soon he moved closer, until finally he leaned against me and allowed me to put an arm around his bent little shoulders. Astrid threw a glance at us from the kitchen and smiled, and I looked down at the little blue men, suddenly bashful, as if I couldn't acknowledge to myself what must be the touching sight of the taxi driver sitting and reading aloud to the pathetic child of divorce. The pan was bubbling and simmering, and there was already a scent of garlic and chopped basil, it was almost like playing at father, mother and children with myself as stand-in for the angry, grizzled man we had run away from. It was a long time since I had cooked anything, as a rule I didn't eat until late at night when I drove past a take-away. I took a glance at her standing there behaving as if she were at home, as I had said she should, slightly embarrassed at the empty phrase. If you think about it, empty phrases often slip out of your mouth in the moments that turn out to be most decisive. But I did not know that yet, I merely looked at her between the speech bubbles while I explained a word the boy did not understand. She was as tall as Inès but her hips were rounder, and her calves had a softer curve in the black tights she wore under her short skirt, as if she was going out. But strictly speaking she was already out. Everything about Astrid was different from the woman who had formed my desire so that in the end it would not be known by other forms than hers. I hadn't so much as looked at others since I met Inès, and now here I was taking surreptitious glances at Astrid, simply because she stood there with her back turned, chopping vegetables in my kitchen. Her movements were slower and calmer, even her voice had something lazy about it in contrast to my lost lover's impatient, syncopated intensity. Apparently Astrid had not only masses of time, she even seemed to give herself up to the sequence of movements and their natural tempo without leaving anything out. There was no urgency for her, there was a sleepwalker's certainty in the way she dealt with things that resembled above all enjoyment, as when she let her knife-blade sink through the taut skin of a tomato without using force, so it looked as if it opened up for her quite by itself, with its firm flesh, its moist cavities and green seeds.

While we were eating I didn't give a thought to Inès. We talked as strangers do, of what we did, and avoided touching on the events of the night before as if by unspoken agreement. I asked her about film-making, the same questions that everyone else no doubt put to her, and she talked about the directors she liked, of Truffaut, Rohmer and Cassavetes. I talked about abstract expressionism, about De Kooning and Jackson Pollock, and now and then Simon made us laugh with the penetrating short circuits only children can produce. On the whole everything flowed along easily, and you wouldn't have thought she had just left her husband or that I had just been deserted. When I was in the car on the way out to the airport, where I usually began the evening, I realised almost guiltily that for the first time in weeks I felt lighthearted and at ease. Only when I had crossed the city centre and passed the harbour did I notice that I had not as usual made a detour along the wall of the Jewish cemetery, at a snail's pace, with bated breath. There had been nights when I had hardly any fares because I could not tear myself away from her district and had to go back at regular intervals in the hope of her appearing. As my inquisitorial questions gradually poisoned our hours together, in a rare bout of sympathy Inès had tried to console me by saying she did not see one particular man besides myself, and that she did not prefer any of her lovers to the others. In her opinion their number alone should assuage my torments and prove to me that my jealousy was both useless and out of place. The fact that there were so many of us should make each of us feel that she was unfaithful to all the others with precisely him. I pictured how she gave herself to one after the other in unknown rooms or in the room looking out on the graveyard that I knew all too well. I could not bear being just any man in the series of men she visited or opened her door to, and it did not help when she assured me that it was our differences, our various bodies, faces and histories that fascinated her. I speculated on whether she was the same regardless of whom she was with, or whether to each of us she was someone else, and I could not decide which alternative was the most cruel. When she straddled me on the floor, still with her coat on, her ferocity was unchanged, and when she let me take her, lying passive on her bed, her expression was the same distant gaze. On the nights when she forbade me to come or did not answer the telephone at all, I haunted her street in the taxi or parked on the corner, staring pointlessly at her door. I knew it was comical and humiliating, but I also knew that I would not be able to resist the temptation to humble myself still more.

It had made a difference, a decisive, all-embracing difference, our first meeting in the cool, dim hall among the maltreated Roman heads, when she turned and looked me in the eye without blinking. When I recalled the scene for myself I was no longer sure whether it was she who had responded to my glance, or I who answered hers without knowing the question my eyes replied to. I knew how easy it is to catch sight of someone, and how easily you lose sight of each other again, and perhaps it was a revolt against the whirling chance meetings when I decided to love Inès. Perhaps it really was a decision and not, as I so much liked to believe, her unusual glance that had torn me out of the well-known, stupefied rotation of my days. Perhaps after all she hadn't seen any more, seen further in, when she caught sight of me, and perhaps there was not so much to look for, perhaps I, like everyone else, was merely a changeable, constantly transmuted reflection in the restless, foaming eddies of looks. When I held her face between my hands I tried to find that look again, which had opened to me like a crack in which I appeared to myself, finally released, but her eyes held me at a distance, in check, teasing, scornful or preoccupied. She escaped me when I tried to hold her fast, she slipped away between my hands or pulled me so closely to her that I could no longer see her clearly. Nothing that we did left any lasting trace, all my words dissolved into silence as soon as they were spoken. Each afternoon, each night, it was as if we repeated the same meeting, the same embrace, the same words. We were in continuous motion but we didn't get anywhere. It would not have any future, it was a wrong track, a track outside time, that merely bolted away with us.

But there were also times when she seemed to capitulate,

rare moments when she let me believe I was not merely yet another man in the series of men who passed through her life. Sometimes she stayed with me for several days. I cooked for her while she sat drawing, and when I came home in the morning she was still there. When we tired of making love she snuggled up in my arms and told me sporadic and disconnected stories of her rootless childhood, isolated and jumbled pictures of London, Warsaw and Cairo. One day in early spring, our only spring, it was raining, we lay in my bed leafing through a monograph on Vermeer. We listened to the rain and meditated on the quiet rooms with their soft, clear light, where Vermeer's women sat reading letters or stood pouring milk from a clay pitcher. She said she had never been in Amsterdam, and suddenly she smiled secretly and got out of bed. I could hear her talking on the phone in the next room, and a little later she came in and pulled the duvet off me. A train was leaving for Amsterdam in one hour, she had already booked tickets. She laughed at my languid astonishment and said she was happy to pay. That was when I discovered that Inès always went around with her passport in her pocket. She didn't even want to go home first, just to the bank before we took a taxi to the central station. Her only luggage was a plastic bag with the trifles she managed to buy at the station before we boarded the train, euphoric as children on their way to a holiday camp. I know quite well it is not so, but as I remember it the canals did not run in concentric circles but in a spiral that we followed, Inès and I, as we coiled ourselves into one of our usual philosophical escapades, interrupted by her laughter among the houses with their high white-painted windows. I think we were both happy that rainy weekend in Amsterdam. She seemed younger, which sounds silly, since she was only in her mid-twenties, but from the beginning I had regarded her as someone much older. It was the men who made the difference, of course, all the men she had known, but in Amsterdam I had her to myself, and she really seemed to have forgotten that she knew other men. As if she was taking time off from her life as the dark, debauched, reprobate angel of love who could make grown men howl at the moon. She even let me put an arm around her shoulder as we walked together, something I was never allowed to do at home.

There were no curtains at the windows, in Amsterdam you could look straight in at people, as if they had nothing to hide or did not want there to be anything in their lives others must not see, and for once I felt that's how it was with us too. She pressed close to me as we walked alongside the canals, and could suddenly stop and kiss me in the middle of the pavement where everyone could see. We sat in dark taverns drinking beer and smoking cigarettes, there were twenty-five in the Dutch packs, and we never tired of discussing whether that was the outcome of thrift, or of profligacy. We talked and laughed our way through the spirals of blue smoke and dark green, stagnant water, as if we moved by roundabout ways towards a destination that was constantly being staved off, but in reality we merely went round in a circle. All the hotels were fully booked, and we ended up staying on an old passenger ship. At night we lay in the narrow berth in our cabin, completely still, exhausted by walking around all day long, and I imagined we were far out at sea, between continents. I told her this and she smiled at me, gently indulgent, in almost the same way you smile at a child, stroking my cheek with a slow, almost wistful tenderness that I could not recognise, and which made me happy and sad at the same time.

It was merely a pause on the way to the end, and I moved more and more headlong towards it, the nearer we came. Soon she again replied evasively or irritably when I asked where she had been, or what she was going to do, and the less she replied the more I questioned. Then I was circling around her street at night again when she did not answer the phone, both hoping and fearing to get a glimpse of her secret life. One evening I did really see her come out of her house and walk along the street, and I followed her in the car at a distance without her catching sight of me. It was as if I sat on the passenger seat observing myself as I spied on her, shaking my head with shame, but there was no way back. Clearly I had to completely abase myself before I could get out on the other side. She went into a twenty-four-hour kiosk and came out shortly afterwards with a litre of milk and a bag of coffee. Deep in thought with her eyes down she walked back along her street. I had kept watch on her house since I left her earlier in the evening, for once I knew for certain that she was alone. All the same I stayed on beside the kerb a short distance from her entrance, just far enough from it so that the car would not be visible from her windows. I don't know how long I sat there like some private detective glowering stupidly at her entrance when I suddenly saw a man stop in front of it. I could not see his face but he looked to be a good deal older than me. He wore a camel-hair coat and shiny black shoes. I had not seen him coming, even though I had kept my eyes stiffly directed down the quiet side street. My concentration had sent me into a kind of trance, and he must have sneaked through my field of vision while I was meditating on the entrance telephone board of small shining rectangles or the basement shop's display of wash basins, gas water heaters and mixer taps. Then the camel-hair coat was let into the hall, and I only just managed to get out of the car and over to the street door before it slammed. I imagined he was a rich businessman visiting Inès when his wife was on a skiing holiday in Switzerland, and I visualised him stealthily pushing a handful of new crackling thousand kroner notes under her pillow while she was in the bath. I could hear his steps on the stairs further up, then he stopped and a moment later a door was closed. I ran quickly up the stairs two steps at a time, perhaps in order not to give myself time to regret. I had already rung her bell, it was too late to turn back.

I could hear music coming from the apartment, and I recognised Astor Piazzolla's melancholy rapt *bandonéon*, our favourite music after we had made love and lay stretched out smoking and dreaming waking dreams to the abrupt change of the tango from sweet indulgence to murderous passion. I rang again and yet again before she finally opened the door, rosy with sleep, her hair loose over her kimono, which she held closed with crossed arms. What did I want? I hardly knew myself. I walked past her through the living room and into the bedroom. There was no one to be seen. I turned round, she stood behind me with her arms crossed and her head on one side and an expression full of patronising contempt. Then suddenly it all happened very fast. I grabbed her and threw her down on the bed and she let herself fall, quite limply, with outstretched arms so the kimono slid aside from her naked body. She lay there as she had fallen, regarding me calmly like a spectator waiting to see what would happen. She let me do what I liked, totally passive, abandoned to my desperate fury, and meanwhile I observed myself with an unemotional gaze, out of contact with my blind, furious body. We were both witnesses to my degradation, as I lay there, crouched between her parted legs, nailed by her dark eyes. It must have caused her pain, but her expression did not alter as I penetrated her with a rage that seemed to want to turn her inside out, as if I wanted to punish her for my own helplessness. She lay there looking up at the ceiling, without covering herself, completely lifeless, as I zipped up my trousers and went into the next room. I sat by the window looking over at the churchyard wall in the moving violet gleam from the street-light swinging in the wind above the empty street. I must have been sitting there a quarter of an hour when she came in wearing an elegant evening gown I had never seen her in before. Her face was pale and powdered, and she had put on lipstick and gathered her hair into an elaborate style. She looked beautiful in a dazzling, devastating way. She had her coat over her arm, she was going out, I offered to drive her. She shrugged her shoulders. Neither of us said anything as she sat on the back seat looking out at the streets like any other passenger. I drove her to an address in the embassy district and followed her with my eyes as she went into a spacious building with marble tiles and mahogany panelling. A few days later she came to give me back a book of Dürer's engravings I had lent her. She kept her coat on. I said I was sorry, she did not reply. When she left it had started to snow. I stood at the window watching her vanish among the shining whirling flakes.

Two months later I met Astrid but could not yet know I was nearing a turning-point, that evening we had eaten together for the first time and I was in the taxi again with the customers sending me to and fro through the night. I wasn't going to meet anyone, I wasn't going anywhere. The town was full of sudden meetings and turning-points, but to me they seemed as meaningless in their unpredictable geometry as the movements of the hard balls over the billiard tables in the pubs where I sometimes spent an hour or two when I was tired of sitting behind the wheel. Massive shiny balls that collided with a little click and were sent in new directions away over the empty green desert of felt, now in one direction, now in another until one by one they vanished down into a black hole, out of the game. I could be anyone at all, and I might meet anyone. One meeting could be just as decisive as another, and it would be neither the mystery behind a beautiful unknown face or my own decision to solve it that tipped the scales. But perhaps I anticipate the events and my own interpretation of them. I probably still thought that the story with Inès had been something special, different from all my other stories, otherwise it would not have hurt so much, and afterwards I would have forgotten our confused depressing affair. I still clung to my battered dreams as I sat behind the wheel, sent here and there between the suburbs and the city centre, passive and inexpressive as a billiard ball. She was still my great lost love, it was a sharper, more dramatic world I had found myself in when I was together with Inès. There had been moments when I no longer felt I was hiding anything, where everything in me was translucent and visible, encompassed by her gaze. But if the whole of it had been nothing other than my own delirious visions it was only logical that it had also been I who had destroyed everything by pursuing them so greedily. If the Inès I had loved was merely an image I had held up before her unknown face, it was only a manifestation of cruel irony that I had violated the precious icon of my passion.

I stopped eating and sleeping, I avoided other people as if I were a leper, I sat in the car or lay on my sofa lost in gloomy thoughts, as I saw the smoke from my cigarettes curl in transient spirals before the melancholy view from my window. It suited me well to drive at night through the deserted streets, between the façades of lighted windows. I couldn't have endured the evenings between my own walls, nor did I feel like going out and risk having to meet someone I knew. It was better to be on the move, circling around the unknown worlds of other people, outside everything. In my pathetic desolation I was certain I would never come to love anyone as I had loved Inès, and I was right in a way, in a completely different way than I had imagined. With Astrid it was a different kind of love, not so vehement and blinding. It was gentler, slower, and I took longer to discover it. She liberated me from the hysterical melodrama that had devoured me from inside, until I had ended up as a hollow, ridiculous crock of unhappy love, she lured me into betraying my own inflated, self-consuming heart, and she did not even know it herself. But I do not think I thought like that about it. At the start I did not think about it much at all, I who had pondered until I was near crazy in my self-chosen wounded solitude. With Astrid everything was very easy, very gliding, as if things happened on their own, in their own rhythm. Did I think about her that night, when we had said goodbye at my door as if we already lived together? Did I think of her as a sudden opening, an unexpected promise of pardon? Or was she still only an attractive and surely very sweet woman, who had gone off with her child and found shelter with a broken-hearted taxi driver on night-shift? I thought about Inès among the snowflakes, her dark distant expression in the bed as I raped her, raging with shame and self-hate. On that night too I thought back to a summer afternoon among marble emperors or gods robbed of both arms and legs. I can see myself eighteen years younger, on my way through the night without knowing where, but I cannot repeat the small leaps, the imperceptible slide that leads from one face to another, from one story into the next.

I can't quite distinguish between what I thought then and what I think now, when I am thinking of Inès again because I am thinking of my meeting with Astrid. The stories became entangled with each other and changed in the process, while events wove them together behind me into the pattern I am trying to unravel. I'm searching for a place, a knot from where I can begin my attempt to understand Astrid's disappearance, but I am not sure whether I shall succeed. I follow the threads back to find the logic of the pattern, but the knots loosen themselves between my fingers so in the end I am left with nothing but loose ends. I knit them up again, hesitantly, because I know the story will only be one out of many I could have told with the same threads. How could I know whether one of them is more truthful than another? Perhaps it makes no odds which of them I tell, perhaps they would all turn out to have stitches that are too loose, too slipshod and uneven to be true. I believe this, but still I try, and the more I try the more I realise how little I know and how imperfectly I remember. It is sure to be unsuccessful, sure to be nothing but a fantasy of suppressions and omissions, rough approximations and vague sketches, but that's all I can do. I must discover everything afresh, well knowing that I risk covering up the scraps I might have been able to disclose as I worked. While I weave my way on, it occurs to me how much in a life remains unspoken, in shadow. How does it take shape? When did it take its decisive direction? Where could it have taken a different turning and become another quite divergent story? I stare into the darkness, but it closes around my eyes, I see something gleam briefly, but the gleam dazzles me and immediately switches off again, so only an indistinct fading after-image stays on the retina. For it isn't there any more, it was all so long ago. Nevertheless I go on, even though I know that the truth dwells in the pauses, in the silent spaces between the words. In the end my narrative is merely an attempt to fill the gap where time has gone, hold that gap open, sometimes in the form of questions that cannot be answered, at other times as a tentative answer to questions no one has yet asked.

It was a quiet night in town and I drove home earlier than usual. I took off my shoes in the hall and tiptoed in. She had found an extra sheet and made up a bed on the sofa, my duvet was there too, she obviously thought it was her turn to have the woollen blanket. I was quite moved. As I was cleaning my teeth I heard the floorboards creak in the living room, and shortly afterwards she appeared in the mirror. She stayed in the bathroom doorway smiling apologetically. She couldn't sleep. I was not specially tired either. It struck me I must look like an oaf standing there with toothpaste round my mouth, scrubbing away. I have never liked people to watch me while I am doing my teeth, but of course she wasn't to know that. I rinsed my mouth. She looked sweet

standing there leaning against the door-frame in the sweater
she had pulled over her nightdress, without make-up, with
tousled hair and tired narrow eyes. Most women are more
attractive without make-up, but of course they don't believe
that. Nor do they know they are most lovely when they are
tired. Perhaps because they are too tired to think about their
appearance or be concerned about what one thinks of them.
I have always had a weakness for tired women. Their faces
relax and repose in the features that after all are theirs, they
forget someone is looking at them, forget to take account of
it, and a veiled gentleness comes over their gaze, as if their
eyes rest on something else, something inside themselves or
far away, a different place. That was what it was like with
Astrid as she stood waiting for me to finish, and fell into a
reverie over who knows what. For the first time it struck me
that she was not only attractive. I suggested we should finish
off the half bottle of red wine left over from dinner. We sat in
the living room without switching on the light, we sat smoking in the dimness and the faint glow from the lamp in the
hall, and I can remember thinking how unpleasant red wine
tastes when you have just cleaned your teeth. She spoke
quietly in her brittle drawling voice, almost intimately, as if
we knew each other. She told me no one knew where she
was. It was a long time since she had had this feeling of
being outside everything, hidden in a secret place, and just
at the moment, I must surely realise, just at the moment it
suited her rather well. I said she could stay for some days
if she liked. What would my girlfriend say about that? It
surprised me she assumed I had a girlfriend until I recalled
the half-empty packet of sanitary towels Inès had once left
in the bathroom, and which my guest had of course spotted
at once. I had left it there as a little nostalgic fetish. She must
have read my face through the half darkness and realised her
blunder, for she went on without waiting for a reply. I was
surprised at her frankness. She looked away with her tired

dreamy eyes as she spoke, and sometimes she met my gaze to see the impression her words made on me, but not to appeal to my sympathy. She merely registered me as if watching me listening to her story was a way of getting to know me.

She had met him when she was twenty-one and he was forty-four, the grizzled man who had stood shouting into the evening cold. To begin with she had been his mistress. She was alone in the world. Her parents had died when she was a child, and her only relative was an old aunt. He was married and had a daughter of her age. He was quite a well-known film director, but I had not recognised him when he was outside the taxi in fluttering shirt-sleeves. She had been an assistant in the editing room for one of his films, that was how it had started, as stolen kisses and feverish couplings in the editing room and hotel rooms. She told me how he had overwhelmed her with his insistent gaze, his assurance, his calm deep voice. She had been fascinated by his mature desire and with being the young woman this famous man desired. Everything was different with him, different from the other men and boys she had played at sweethearts with and run away from, but she was still surprised. Talking about it now she couldn't understand why she had had a child with him and why she believed they would live together. But then she had also been surprised, she could remember that, both at him and at herself. He had once taken her with him to Stockholm, where he was to meet a producer. She had lain waiting for him in the afternoon at the Grand Hotel wondering about being there. She could remember the gold-framed birds on the walls, blue tits and robins and suchlike, with their trustworthy little heads askew, looking down at her in bed. She had been almost shocked at their innocence. She was a married man's mistress. It rather amused her to look at herself like that. A precious and awe-inspiring secret, obliged to lie and wait among the little birds. She had looked at her breasts in the mirror, and certainly they were pointed and industrious then like the snouts on a pair of Dutch clogs, and yet what could they be the answer to? She described how she had once caught sight of him with his wife on their way to a film première. Astrid couldn't actually make out what was wrong with her, why she had to be replaced. Desire. The word made her smile, and I imagine she smiled in the same way when she stood at the rail of one of the small steamers in the Skerries, dazzled by the sun's reflection in the water. When he was at meetings she put to sea. When he came back he indulged his desire, grizzled and with a cleft chin, a real man, and she herself gave way, wonderingly. Afterwards she let him talk of the future, until he grew lost in it and lay among the twitterers at the Grand Hotel looking at her, crestfallen, as if waiting for her to find him, drowned as he was in his prospects. She was frankly astonished when he stood at her door with two suitcases one day having 'burned his boats'. He had obviously meant what he said, and she gave way again. She forgot her surprise and hastened to become pregnant, and as she watched the boy grow she began to believe their future was more than words. The bigger he grew the more she believed in it, until the evening I met her, when she had discovered by chance that the film director's desire had found itself a new, sweet young secret with the future before her.

When I woke up she had taken Simon and gone. She had been out to buy bread and left a thermos of coffee on the table. A croissant was waiting on a plate, and a napkin as well, folded under the knife in the style you get in hotels. I wasn't in the habit of eating croissants. In contrast to the previous day the apartment was full of signs of them. Simon's toy soldiers were ranked along the windowsill ready to clash lances between a pile of paperbacks and the stack of telephone directories, their clothes were folded and heaped on a chair in the bedroom, there was even a dress hanging among my shirts, and on the shelf under the mirror in the bathroom stood an entire column of female bottles and tubes. It almost looked as if she had moved in. I continued to spend the days and nights alone and saw them only in the evenings, when they came back before I had to leave. We took turns to cook and in general adapted ourselves to each other in the small flat, adroitly and politely, and when our eyes happened to meet we couldn't help smiling at this unexpected, improvised cohabitation. I was surprised at how easy it was. Even the silence was easy, almost weightless, when we sat opposite each other like the two strangers we were, and couldn't just then find anything to say. She was the first person I had met with whom I could remain silent without feeling uneasy. It surprised me that she could rest in herself so naturally in a strange man's apartment, how easily she became quiet when she had said what she wanted to say, not in the least affected by the silence between us. But we didn't actually have anything to talk about, we were nothing to do with each other, she was merely a stranger camping in my precincts. Nevertheless my sorrowful ruminations were constantly disturbed by Simon's chattering and her crooked smile. Now and again I could feel her watching me while I helped him repair his toys or read aloud from one of the books I had borrowed from the library for him one afternoon when I had nothing better to do. I took no notice when I felt her inquiring gaze, and concentrated on the jolly little plastic men or the stories of animals in clothes. The boy seemed to have grown used to me and behaved as if we had known each other for a long time. When Sunday came we went to the zoo, she had asked if I would like to go with them. I hadn't been there for years and it seemed to me the shiny seals and grubby polar bears were the same ones I had seen when I was Simon's age. He was very disappointed that the bears were not whiter. As we walked on that grey day among the cages and grottoes with apathetic and melancholy animals, for the first time it was hard for me to retain the image of Inès in my inner eye. I heard how Astrid made Simon laugh, and wondered how she had managed to create a feeling of normality around him so quickly. How she pacified his terror over what had happened in simple little ways, by putting his drawings up on the wall or making him laugh in the middle of a bout of weeping by putting on my tea cosy and rushing around the flat blowing the kettle whistle. Afterwards she blushed a little, still with the tea cosy on, when she met my gaze. She must have been in a terrible state inside, but she didn't show it, and perhaps she herself found diversion and comfort by getting Simon to think of something else with her clownish tricks and everyday ease. But when he went on crying, inconsolably, I could see that the perplexity in her eyes was not only concerned with him, but also with herself, and I thought of the decisiveness in her gait as she stormed down the garden path holding Simon's hand with her husband at her heels and got into my taxi, the strength in her voice when she shouted at me to drive on, just drive.

One evening she told me the film director had been outside Simon's nursery school when she went to collect him. He had been beside himself with remorse and self-pity, and I asked if she considered going back to him. She said I should tell her if I was tired of them living with me. I shook my head, that wasn't what I meant. She looked over at Simon sitting on the sofa hypnotised by a cartoon film. No, she had made her decision. She cleared the table as if to end the conversation and started washing up. I sat on gazing absent-mindedly at the screen where the cartoon animals laid spiteful ambushes for each other accompanied by crazy music sounding like the spasms from a roundabout run amok. Simon had flopped down on the sofa, his eyelids were about to fall. I switched off the television and laid a rug over him. I sat watching

him for a while, then went into the kitchen, after all I could
always dry. She stood at the sink, quite still, as if looking out
at something in the darkness. I went over to her, she turned
round. I remember that we stood opposite each other in the
little kitchen for a long time, as she made her eyes even
narrower and looked at me through the cracks, expectantly,
that's how I remember it, but it must have taken a few
seconds at most.

Was she merely waiting for me to make an effort? Was
the movement released by something in me or something
in her, or did it simply occur by itself, independently of
us, in the unexpected pause, the unexpected closeness in
the empty space where our eyes met? I had not thought
it would ever happen, I can't even say I had hoped for
it. I cannot explain the sudden impulse, the vague but
all-important turn that made me lift my hand and let the
back of it slide down her cheek. She slowly moved her head
sideways and leaned her cheek against my hand. I moved
my hand around her neck beneath the soft pony tail, and
she leaned her forehead against my shoulder. Her skin was
dry and warm, and I stroked the light down on her neck
while I tried in vain to imagine how my hand might feel on
her vertebrae, and what she might think feeling it there. I
hadn't touched anyone since that afternoon a few months
earlier, when Inès vanished in the snow. Astrid's neck and
my palm, her forehead and my shoulder, it was a meeting
beyond everything I could imagine, unthinking and strange.
It was something that happened to us without our help, my
hand on her skin, my lips against her head, her hair tickling
my nose, and the unfamiliar scent of her hair. Unknown,
separate worlds, whose boundaries suddenly impinged on
each other. I felt her hands on my hips, she raised her head
and looked at me again, and I had no idea what she saw.
She closed her eyes, maybe it was all too amazing, and we
kissed each other, tentatively, as if we had to learn all over

again what we knew by heart. I could not help thinking of Inès when I kissed Astrid for the first time, I saw her growing smaller and disappearing among the snow flakes, and I thought I had already entered another time, one time had ended and another begun. Astrid's mouth was different, and I myself, I thought, I myself was not quite the same, but on the other hand I wasn't quite sure what the difference was. People kiss each other because they don't know what else to do. You have nothing other than your silly lips, your silly hands that brave the same language while the world changes. Simon was still asleep on the sofa when we went in. That night we let him stay there.

No one knew where she was during the first week we spent together in my apartment, and I myself knew infinitesimally little about her. For that matter, I don't know where she is now, whether she is still in Lisbon or has journeyed on. She vanished in the same way as she turned up, without warning, out of the air one winter evening. I picture to myself that she is alone, alone again, as she was when she got into my taxi with her little son to leave everything she knew. I imagine her sitting at a window looking onto a strange street, where children shout in a language she doesn't understand and the trams rattle past the glazed tiles of the façades, thinking of the time she hid herself in the home of a man she had never seen before, and wondering why he should have been the one she came to live with for so many years. I try to call her up before me, just as the grizzled film director must have done, alone in his house, when he realised she had slipped through his hands, and thinking she must be somewhere in town, in an unknown, inaccessible place. Perhaps she walks over the Rossio at the end of the day between the battered trams and the smoking charcoal braziers of the hot chestnut vendors, through the crowd of leisurely strolling people, and perhaps she thinks how easy it is to change direction, how little it takes. Perhaps she walks along the river watching the small ferries blacken on the gleaming water in the low sun over the river mouth, behind the hair-thin cables of the bridge that look as if they are about to burn up, themselves only a silhouette among the silhouettes of people walking along the quay.

3

I went to New York five days after Astrid had left. I couldn't know then that she was in Oporto. She had quite simply disappeared. I had almost decided not to go, and when the plane took off I regretted it. It was no help to reassure myself that she knew my travel plans and when I would be back. Sitting in the plane I realised that it was not only my anxiety and unanswered questions that had paralysed me in the days after I had seen her vanish from the stairway landing carrying her suitcase and heard her steps growing fainter as she descended. It was simply that I missed her, and the loss grew stronger, more crushing, as the days passed without any word from her. Previously, when, for one reason or another, she was away for a few days, we had joked and said it was good to have a little holiday from each other. I positively enjoyed having the flat to myself in the evening, when Simon and Rosa had gone to bed, and besides I had plenty to do keeping up the domestic routine without her. I liked being alone with the children, I was closer to them when they were left with me, whether I helped them do their homework or took them out to eat because I couldn't be bothered to shop and cook. I didn't have any time to imagine what Astrid was doing. Now I had all too much time. I could not explain why, I had no tangible reason, but during the days after her departure I grew more and more convinced that I was about to lose her. Previously it had only crossed my mind as a theoretical possibility that a misfortune might occur, that she could be ill or simply fall in love with someone else, but it had been easy to brush my worries aside. Her presence had erased them, and I had smiled as one smiles at the fussy warnings that insurance companies give of how dangerous it is to be alive. Just as one never really believes anything will happen to oneself, I could not imagine anything happening to her or to the obvious, almost banal, fact that we were together. So much was she a part of my notion of myself. I felt as if I had been woken out of a dream and was now looking around me at a world that only superficially resembled the one I had been familiar with. When I woke in the morning and caught sight of her duvet lying smooth and immaculate beside me, it seemed to me that my world had become a strange place, or rather that there was no longer any clear boundary to separate our home from the rest of the world. And when I let myself into the silent, empty apartment where we had lived together so long, it was like visiting a place where you had once lived: the realisation that only for a time do you grow used to feeling that it is precisely this place and nowhere else that is home. It was seven years since I had last been in New York, but the town looked familiar, rising grey and vertical on the other side of the East River as the taxi crossed Queensboro Bridge. Once again I stood in the strangely cross-illuminated shadow at the bottom of the streets' deep shafts, confused and weightless with fatigue in the restless, unceasing stream of cars and faces, the same stream as always. When I arrived in my hotel room I went to bed at once, but could not fall asleep. I lay looking out of the window and watched the sky grow darker above the top of the glass façade opposite. I dozed a little, and when I looked again the dark blue, monotonous reflection of the sky was broken by brightly lit squares in which men in white shirts sat bent over their bluish screens or walked around the floors like ghosts wearing ties in the dreamlike, shadowless light. It was already night in Europe.

I recalled the empty, aimless days after Astrid left. Each

time the phone rang, it might be her, and I tensed as I lifted the receiver and heard myself utter my name. One of our friends rang to invite us to dinner, and I strained to sound casual and credible as I said that Astrid was in Stockholm visiting a friend. I had not the least desire to socialise, but I sensed it would seem more unusual if I refused than if I went on my own. If I were to produce a plausible reason for saying no thanks I should have given it right away instead of explaining why Astrid was unable to come. I said I would look forward to it, and felt irritated with myself for the rest of the day. Incidentally, it surprised me that there were so few calls for her. Normally the phone rang constantly, more often for her than for me. She must have safeguarded herself with the Stockholm manoeuvre from people who might call her, as she had done from Rosa. If that was the case she had obviously planned to travel for quite a time. But she must have realised that the Stockholm pretext would have run out of steam after a week had passed. Friends seldom visit each other for an indefinite period, and the plausibility of the story would soon be replaced by curious or worried enquiries. So I guessed the motive for her white lies was for her to slip away as adroitly and unnoticeably as possible. Once she was gone, it wouldn't matter. That she had not told me the same tale was understandable, considering I would be likely to ring her at Gunilla's, as in fact I did. Presumably she did not want me to be worried, but on the other hand she must have foreseen the state I would be in over her mysterious departure. Perhaps she had been surprised that I did not insist on an explanation or try to hold her back. Perhaps she had been relieved I didn't. Perhaps she respected me for it, perhaps it had merely confirmed her secret reasons for going away. This was the confusion my speculations reduced me to, sitting in my study poring over my notes on Cézanne. Having spent the rest of the day writing different versions of the same section over and over again it was a great relief to take a taxi out into the northern suburbs and look forward to an evening with nicely tempered Italian wines and nicely tempered conversation about all and sundry.

It was a dinner party like so many of those we went to over the years, with the same people. Now and again a couple divorce, one vanishes from sight, and after a period of time the other introduces a new face, but otherwise it is the same more or less regular group that has stayed together, at a distance or as close friends. Some of them I have known since I was young, among them the host, a well-known architect, and his wife who was my sweetheart for a short while, long before she met him, long before Inès and Astrid. She runs a shop selling humanistic artefacts from India and Bali, and when we talk she always puts an intimate hand on my knee as a little painless memory of that distant summer when we were young together. We should have been eight with Astrid, but luckily no one was surprised at her absence, and after I had repeated the Stockholm story to the couple who arrived last she was mentioned only in passing. There I sat with my dry martini like any other grass widower, with my back to the dusk in my friends' garden, concentrating on appearing relaxed. I looked around the stylish interior with its modern, fairly expensive furnishings, which carefully avoided any flamboyant sheen, and were placed so harmoniously piece to piece that the room created an airy, almost puritanical impression. I would have created much the same atmosphere in my own home if Astrid hadn't possessed a weakness for mixing sedate antiques with eccentric kitsch. For the first time ever I felt like an outsider, a newly arrived member of the company. I took part in the conversation only when I was asked about something, and didn't really listen to what the others said. They chatted about the usual things. It struck me that even though there was something new to talk about each time, it was still the usual kind of topic, not only because as a rule I could guess in advance what one or another of them would say of this or that, but also because the way they expressed themselves neutralised the differences between the subjects. They were all treated with the same approved irony, the same casual, fastidious distancing as if, sitting around the fire in the heavily atmospheric twilight of the villa, we belonged to a chosen, exclusive élite, who subtly, heads aslant, observed and commented on the folly of the world.

I cast my gaze around the cluster of familiar faces. Each one of us is a constant bearing on the others' horizons, witnesses to their lives, and because we have known each other so long, we aren't at all aware of the passage of time. We belong to the same age group, our lives have more or less taken their definite shape, and yet we are still not so old for the future to seem long, indeed almost remote, just as when you are out sailing the horizon doesn't seem to move from the spot. Most of us have had children, some early, some late, and most of us have done what we are doing for so long that we have nothing to prove to anyone, but each time we reach a goal we have already started to make new plans. We can't imagine anything could be different, we still don't give any weight to the fact that our story is getting longer than our future. And yet it is a long time since we took over our places from others. Here and there an old white elephant still trumpets away, but otherwise we are the ones in charge now. It's just that we haven't discovered that only for a while can we allow ourselves to smile benevolently or tolerantly at the youngsters fidgeting behind us. We can't really picture their hunger and self-consciously pompous stridency being replaced by smug, tolerant causeries, when they sit where we are sitting now. Of course we do not have an answer for everything, we can still ask questions. We refuse to believe we shall ever be as pompous and bloodshot with red wine and achievements as the old fools we have replaced. We still laugh at them when we see them clutching onto their reputations like anxious dotards raking through their drawers with trembling, liver-spotted hands in terror that their home-help has stolen some of the silver. We are not without scruples, we do have our ideals, and we can still manage to say something outrageous and amusing. We recall the amazing sensation of feeling the warmth of the seats when we finally sat down. We have not forgotten what it was like to be cold, and sometimes we find it hard to believe that we really are sitting here. Nevertheless we can't quite understand why it should be so hard for the new ones to stand outside in the cold waiting. It won't hurt them to wait a bit longer, just as we ourselves had to wait. We can't fully understand what it is like to be them. There is far too much hate in their eyes. We can't imagine what it will be like for our successors to feel our warmth in the empty seats, even though the warmth is always much the same.

One of the men in the party, a museum curator, had launched into a long exposition. Something about an exhibition he had recently seen. He was as prolix as ever and his expression as intense. He bears a slight resemblance to Stravinsky, and he knows that himself. He has been bald ever since he and I studied the history of art together, and he speaks in the same insistent, almost inquisitorial tone as he did when we spent whole nights discussing how subtle it was of Marcel Duchamp to drop art and devote himself to playing chess for the rest of his life. He hasn't changed, he has just grown older, but he interrupts himself still more often with sudden noisy laughter, as if he is crumpling up his whole edifice of ideas before the eyes of his deferential listeners, merely to leave them with an embarrassed and offended feeling of having subjected themselves purely for the sake of his enjoyment and not, as they believed, with respect for a deeper insight. Preoccupied as I was, it only gradually dawned on me that it was Rosa's boyfriend, the installation artist, who was the subject of the monologue.

In the opinion of the curator his casts of embryos and child pornography in slow motion were a parodic example of the avant-garde being stone-dead, for if tradition no longer had any authority for rebellion to attack, if the provocation itself was part of the endless disguises of tradition, then the word 'avant-garde' was merely an unkempt excuse for not knowing the job, not having any ideas, only a scanty fig-leaf for what was at bottom the bourgeois ambition to call yourself an artist. In the end Rosa's boyfriend was still only one of those young opportunists who disguised their grubby Oedipal tricks as art historical patricide and proceeded to jump straight out of the gutter into Who's Who. Everything my bald friend said was what I myself could have found to say, and actually it should have delighted me to hear how he made the company snigger at the scornful, black-clad young man who, possibly, to my secret chagrin, might become my son-in-law. Nevertheless, and I didn't quite know why, I felt like coming to the rescue of Rosa's hard-boiled and mulish beloved, and I had already involved myself in a long exegesis, the first of the evening, without exactly knowing where it was leading, when the curator looked at me tauntingly over his steel-rimmed spectacles as I came to a halt to take a pull at my cigarette. Incidentally, he had seen our indomitable iconoclast at a private view with his tongue down my daughter's throat. His narrow steel-rimmed eyes scanned my face searching for an involuntary twitch he could make capital of in his revelation, but I remained unmoved as complete silence fell for a second. He wouldn't have said that, I thought, anyway not in those words, if Astrid had been there. I might just as well give up, the others had already given way to the uproarious avid laughter that deafens the embarrassment when someone's bounds have been overstepped. But it was not dangerous, I could safely laugh at myself in their presence, it was merely the small obligatory repetition of the original initiation ritual of friendship in which you have had to humble yourself once and for all as a kind of mutual pledge, as if you must mortgage your self-respect before the others respect you, so no one should think one member gets more credit than the others.

Before we went in to dinner I took myself up to the bathroom to be alone for a few moments. I sat on the edge of the bath, staring stupidly at our hostess's opulent bottles of perfume and dried cornflowers hanging in coy little bouquets tied with lavender blue bows like a charming feminine touch in all the barren white sanitation. The five-year-old 'after-thought' of the house had left a yellow plastic duck with big blue eyes in the bath, and it rocked and smiled encouragingly at me, as if trying to infect me with its good humour. I caught myself wanting to throttle it, as if its naïvety were a genuine, live innocent's blue-eyed frankness towards the world and not a designed, moulded plastic ingenuousness, and at the same time I felt guilty over my impulse as if it would have been a real wrongdoing to punish the plastic duck for its happy ignorance. Suddenly everything seemed so impalpable and distorted, as if seen through water, in this home where I had so often been with Astrid, among these people who were supposed to be my closest friends. Why had I come? What was I doing here? How had they become my 'closest friends', this flock of easy-going, vain, self-congratulatory and intellectually constipated examples of the academic middle class, sitting there washing down their blasé remarks with Brunello, as if their acquired cosmopolitan gestures could mask their rapacious ambition? As if their culinary humanism and their car trips to Tuscany could make anyone forget that every one of them came from a suburban yellow-brick housing block smelling of blood sausage every afternoon at five o'clock. A futile god-forsaken suburb where the weather was always grey, and where their mothers 'who stayed at home' had vacuum-cleaned their way through frugality wearing only nylon stockings on the hair-cord, and longing for something better. As if their mundane distancing and their muted, sure taste and all the slim volumes of verse on their bedside tables could hide the fact that they had been pushed out between the thighs of these worn grey pensioner mothers with bad backs whom they visited only seldom and reluctantly because they were slightly ashamed of their permed poodle curls and polyester trouser suits, sitting there in the housing block beside the oil-cloth with glossy magazines, rolling their own cigarettes and reading about 'the celebrities' and perhaps now and then getting a glimpse of their own children in the glossy, glittering and awe-inspiring world into which they had vanished.

How had I come to be one of them? How had I grown old enough to sit and laugh at an angry young artist merely because he was just as fanatical in his adolescent anger as we were lukewarm in our studied, well-shod maturity? Did we laugh at his warped, megalomaniac dreams of changing the world because we ourselves had made our warped ambitions resemble something more adult by decreasing them, lowering the range of our sights and aiming for the available possibilities? Did we smile at his existential funk because we ourselves had long ago gone down on all fours and reduced ourselves to social animals? When the curator had speared the young avant-garder so uninhibitedly with almost passionate cynicism, was this other than a hidden defence of his own disillusioned shamelessness, an indirectly backward-looking approval of all the times he had kissed the arse of a minister of culture, chairman of directors or prominent artist in order to get where he was now? I was surprised at my own anger, strictly speaking neither the museum curator nor the others had done me any harm. Was I sitting here on the edge of the bath silently reviling them because I needed to unload my growing disgust for myself? Or had I merely come to see them as they really were, now nothing was as it used to be? I visualised the curator, his expression during the brief silence before the others' laughter broke out around me. He had looked at me as if he knew what with all my strength I was trying to hide. Besides, I was sure that Astrid would have come to the defence of Rosa's installation artist. She was no more delighted with him than I was, but she accepted him because Rosa loved him and at least she tried to hide her scepticism when our daughter was around. Even before the children started to grow up she taught me that I might as well stop influencing them with my own preferences. The children's upbringing was one of the few things we could quarrel about. Again and again I criticised her blind trust that all would be well if the children were only left in peace, and time after time she pointed out that I only tried to control them and form them to accord with my own perfectionist criteria. She had been right, I had to admit that now, when in any case they were out of my reach. Simon and Rosa behaved with the same supreme skill and self-assurance as their mother, and if I didn't care for Rosa's installation artist, that was my problem. It would only be hers if I was tactless enough to reveal my scepticism. As I sat scowling on the edge of my so-called friends' bath I wished Astrid had been there to defend her daughter's lover, now that I had failed. As a whole the evening would have gone differently if Astrid had been with me. They would not have laughed at her as they had laughed at me. When Astrid entered a room the tone of the conversation altered. She exercised a remarkable influence on those around her by her mere presence, probably without knowing it herself. In their eyes she represented something unattainable, because she had been born and brought up to take everything for granted which they themselves had dreamed of and struggled and degraded themselves to gain. They were afraid of her because of the negligence she could allow herself, when they constantly had to be on the watch to take care they held their glass properly or used the right cutlery. She came from what was once called 'an old family' and even though her parents drove their Jaguar over a cliff-top on the Amalfi drive when she was only fifteen, they had managed to teach her the naturalness you only find in people who have had centuries in which to become civilised. She was never embarrassed and knew nothing of the anxiety and scorn of snobbery, she could talk to anyone and everyone and behave normally wherever she went. When she left boarding school she put her privileges behind her, and when I met her there was nothing in the least worldly in her lifestyle, but she comported herself with the same invulnerable naturalness, and even if she had happened to pick her nose at table, she would have done so in style.

Astrid was inviolable. Even the most intimidating comment, even the most offensive idiocy glanced off her crooked smile and indolently narrowed eyes, and I couldn't count how many times I had seen a puffed-up, self-aggrandising stud or scheming little jade creep off with their tails between their legs having failed in their intention after trying to muscle in on her. She herself decided when she would reduce the distance that surrounded her like an invisible defence, and when she did so she could be both surprisingly generous and unexpectedly direct, but no one could ever guess what she was thinking, not even I. If she had been there that evening, on the way home she would have entertained me with her observations and interpreted them, without malice, but with an almost merciless curiosity, because she simply never tired of marvelling over the little games people play with each other, the invisible commerce of emotions and social status in which the prices swing from hour to hour. On one of the last occasions we had been out to dinner together, on the way home she had analysed every single couple there and made me aware of every small movement, each unguarded remark, each of the flickering side glances I had not noticed myself. It might have been her experience of the editing room that stood her in good stead here, her professional knowledge of how the studied mien and involuntary twitches in a face comment on each other and change meaning, all according to the story they are appearing in, and the place they have in the story's sequence of scenes and dialogues. Once again she amazed me with her acuity, although I couldn't resist reminding her that our friends must certainly talk about us in the same dissecting manner. Like her, all the others thought that only their view was privileged because every one of them felt themselves at the mid-point of their own universe, in which we others were merely planets and moons, and in which precisely their good sense, fear and desire determined the direction and course of all movements. She shrugged her shoulders, but I persisted, saying you could never know whether someone looked at you with an uninterpretable expression which you were unable to see through because it covered some arcane knowledge. She smiled elusively, almost as if the idea amused her, keeping her eyes on the white lines streaming towards us in the headlights.

She was driving, I wasn't quite sober. She drove fast, she is actually quite a speed merchant, but she drives with the same assurance with which she handles the sharpest kitchen knife. I contemplated her listening and smiling secretive profile and her eyes fixed on the motorway, while persisting with my train of thought in a somewhat muddled and uncertain way. I asked if she had noticed that people always seem diminished when you talk about them. As if you had to make them smaller to make room for them in your perspective. Shouldn't that in itself be enough to sow doubt in your own judgement? And if everyone looked at everyone else from their limited but totally different viewpoint, who then could assign themselves the right to be the one who saw accurately? If all the many opposed and crossed and overlapping views were equally right, then each of us was no more than the unlimited, but also incoherent and contradictory sum of distorted, abbreviated and incomplete reflections in each other's eyes? I named the curator as an example. We knew he slept with his students, but his wife didn't know. On the other hand she may have known that he snored or suffered from haemorrhoids, which his trim little girlfriends at the academy of art didn't realise. We knew he had slandered a colleague in order to gain his present post, which he held as the uncompromising and altruistic protector of the absolute élite of art, whereas we could not know whether at this moment he was ridiculing my catalogue texts, although he had told me how excellent they were. Conversely we may well have been the only ones who knew that once, when we were on holiday with him in Greece long before he was married, he had leapt into the sea from a sailing boat far from land to rescue an abandoned puppy, which Rosa had insisted on taking on board. Astrid's lips creased into an inscrutable smile as she changed gear to move into the overtaking lane. I went on, encouraged by her expectant smile. But one thing, I said, was how little we knew about each other. And something else, how much we actually knew about ourselves. For if you were never really able to assess yourself, if you always had a blind angle, a white spot in which you could not see yourself, then you would never obtain self-knowledge, regardless of how hard you were on yourself, perhaps precisely because you are always either too hard or too tolerant where your own self is concerned, and if furthermore there really was someone who saw you as it were full-length with an unknown, inscrutable gaze, with secret, inscrutable knowledge, perhaps even without your noticing it, would you then have to resign yourself to the fact that your real, full and true identity remained a secret behind this unknown stranger's eyes? I stopped, my mouth dry after the stream of words, and suddenly she laughed. I didn't know whether she was laughing at what I had said or at something else that had struck her. She went on laughing, not maliciously, almost heartily, with her eyes on the road, as if it was there, among the red rear-lights of the cars, that she had caught sight of whatever was so amusing, while I sank back in my seat exhausted as the lights of town came to meet us.

Perhaps she was only laughing at my words. It was Astrid who taught me to laugh at myself. To her, words were no use for getting close to reality, in her opinion they were rather an impediment. She admired my rhetorical skills, but not so much for what I said, more as you admire someone who is good at water skiing or tossing pancakes up in the air. To her words were merely a kind of pendant, like speech bubbles. When she listened to people she always took account of who they were, including when it was I myself who had spoken. For instance, if we were going out in the evening, and she had changed her clothes for the fifth time before the mirror in the bedroom, it didn't help if I said she looked lovely. That's what *you* think, she said with a crooked smile, but still looking sceptically in the mirror as she inspected herself. We were equally sceptical, she and I, of the unpredictable cracks between reality as it is and the descriptions of it in which people reflect themselves. But where my own doubts have made me twist and turn the words endlessly, it seemed as if Astrid had drawn the opposite conclusion once and for all. She preferred to keep quiet and let the words die away as if it was only through silence that truth became visible. If I said I loved her, and she was the first woman I had been happy with for more than a few hours at a time, she merely smiled and stroked my hair from my forehead with a shy gesture, as if my words were an over-extravagant bouquet of flowers. She was modest about words, particularly big ones, therefore it seemed all the more powerful when she herself suddenly embraced me from behind and whispered that she loved me. Once I asked her why, but she just smiled and said *because*. Because what? She looked at me as if she was surprised I could bring myself to ask. Because you're so stupid, she replied and kissed me on the brow. To her there was no why or wherefore, and there was almost a touch of disappointment in her smile, as if I had come to reveal that I was not as sure as she was. But as reticent as she was towards words, towards the belief that everything can be explained, and as cool and reserved as she could seem to those around us when we were out, she found it equally easy to let herself go when we were alone together. She gave herself to me without hesitation, in her own playful, careless manner. She was generous with her tenderness, almost careless, because her caresses were not little letters greedily or fearfully waiting for an answer, but extensions of herself, without reservation. Sometimes it was almost as if she dazzled me with her love, as when she made herself invisible by kissing my eyelids with her warm soft lips. But when she laughed at me that night in the car on the way home from yet another dinner with our circle of friends, it may not only have been because as usual I lost myself in my own words. Perhaps she also thought I was making unnecessary worries for myself. Although it amused her to see through the cock-fights and mating dances of the social game, when people reflected their self-esteem in each other's lust or envy, deep down she seemed unaffected by what others thought of her. And although she might spend a long time before the mirror before she was reasonably satisfied with her appearance, I do believe it was as much for her own sake, as a game, when she tried on one dress or blouse after the other, just as once long ago she had passed the time dressing and undressing her dolls. That was the secret behind the sleep-walker's assurance with which she carried herself when she associated with other people, and I was the only one who could see it, because only I knew she was as much at peace with herself when she was out as when she came out of the shower and walked through the apartment naked and dripping under her fluttering kimono.

I ran the cold water in the basin and lowered my face towards the jet. There came a cautious knock at the door. I felt the skin of my face contract and observed the small drops glinting like sweat in the bright glare from the light above the mirror. I was in the wrong place, everything was wrong, I shouldn't have come. It had been a mistake, I should have thought up an excuse, no matter what, or not have excused myself at all, simply said I could not come. I should have sat at my desk and thought about Cézanne or just looked out of the window, into the darkness over the Lakes, over at the lighted windows at the row of houses on the other side, all the windows looking into others' unknown lives. At that moment all I wanted was to be at home in front of the window in my study, alone in front of the view. Astrid might even have tried to phone, I was not to know, perhaps everything was different from what I believed. But what did I believe? That everything was over? That she had gone off with someone else? That I would never see her any more? That there had been an accident? That she had taken her own life? I was like a blind person stretching out his hands into the empty air without finding anything to grasp. But why did I imagine the worst? The knock came again, and I recognised my hostess's worried voice through the door, the old girlfriend I had fooled around with one long-gone summer when neither of us knew what else to do. If fate had dealt the cards differently, I might have been the one she shared this bathroom with, but wouldn't I then have long since turned into someone else? Someone who couldn't stand her dried wild flowers and Balinese textiles? Someone who grew sick and tired of mauve silk ribbons and oriental designs? Someone who one day might chance to pass a strange, unknown Inès or Astrid in the street, as she walked by herself smiling at something she had come to think of, after which he would go on in the opposite direction, homewards, absorbed in vague, diffuse daydreams. I looked at my face in the mirror, spotted with little drops as if I had a fever, and I visualised Astrid as she had stood in the doorway the morning she left, I saw her strangely distant and yet insistent, all-penetrating gaze, itself impenetrable. I dried my face and opened the door and smiled as naturally as I could. No, there was nothing wrong, just a bit of an upset stomach, no doubt it was all the black coffee I drank when I was working. The others had gone in to dinner. We went downstairs, and on the way she turned and asked how long Astrid would be away, still with a little of the worried look on her face like a remnant she had forgotten to wipe off, and I speculated on how much my own face gave me away, and if she might have guessed everything was not as usual, as I replied that she was coming home in a week's time.

I pretended not to notice the others' curious glances as I sat down at the table. They were discussing a big Mondrian exhibition that had just opened, and I pointed out that Mondrian did not, as you might think at first, plan out his compositions before executing them, but on the contrary felt his way forward by intuition, as can be seen from his unfinished pictures, where you can make out how the charcoal guidelines had been wiped out and drawn on top of each other until he had found their correct complementary order. In other words an art form slightly reminiscent of that to be found in the abstract expressionists, who used to paint over the same picture many times before it was completed, which merely served as a reminder of how it was superficial to differentiate between constructivism and expressionism. I could hear it was going well, my voice was calm and self-assured without sounding didactic, even the curator regarded me benevolently from behind his spectacles, as if wanting to show he had always known he could rely on me, and our hostess, my old summer sweetheart, looked at me with something almost resembling tenderness, as if I had returned after a long convalescence. While I sat there expanding on Mondrian and thus made my comeback into the circle, I met the eyes of now one, now another, and asked myself, who I might seem to be in their eyes. To some I was an established, sometimes even feared, art critic, to others I was the man who had been able to conquer a woman like Astrid, to one or two of them I was an arrogant, aloof and self-absorbed intellectual who smoked too much and most probably didn't even know how to replace a bulb without getting a shock, and to the curator and our hostess with the dried flowers I was someone who had transformed myself into all this from having been a passionate, awkward and precocious young man, who had once wasted eighteen months of his youth letting himself be torn to pieces by unhappy love for an exotic-looking bitch everyone would have told me I hadn't a chance in the world of keeping hold of.

There was a great deal they didn't know, a great deal they couldn't know. There was everything I hadn't known myself while it was going on, and there was all I knew while it was happening, but didn't know any longer, either because I had forgotten it, or because I was no longer quite the same. For I'm not quite the same as when I met Astrid. I can see it from the few photographs where I am present. There aren't many, because I have always hated being photographed, I've always felt caught out, whether it is because I make too much effort to look natural, or because I stiffen at the thought of being reduced to a single grimace out of all the grimaces, one single moment out of all the hours and days. In any case, I always get tense and far too self-conscious when someone points a camera at me, because I suddenly feel it isn't me being photographed but someone trying to look like me. I can see my features become sharper in the pictures, but I can't decide whether it is my real face that gradually becomes recognisable through the soft indefiniteness of the young skin, or if it is my original face that is gradually distorted by the folds and furrows of the years. When I meet my own eyes in the pictures of our life, my normal slightly sceptical expression, it is as if the man in the picture looks at me and wonderingly asks himself: Is that really you? Perhaps Astrid feels the same way, although of course it isn't something we think about every day. She too is someone different from the person she was when she sat on the back seat of my taxi one winter evening humming to her little son, as she left everything she had believed in. She must have wondered too when she saw the old pictures of herself whether those really were the same eyes that met her gaze across time. The same eyes that had once answered the insistent gaze of the grizzled film director, as if she could read from it the person she would become. We have changed alongside each other, keeping in time, and so we didn't notice at all that we were changing, just occasionally, as when the children, tall and leggy, came rushing up to us across the sand in summer or when we saw them from the window going to school, did we feel surprise at how big they had suddenly grown. Each stage wiped out the previous one, in the children and in ourselves, so there are only the pictures and our own imprecise recollections left, and although we have continued to change we have only in rare moments thought about the change and only as something that happened to us, not as something that tore us along with it and took us away.

I can hardly remember what it was like to be me, before I became the man who was with Astrid. When I think of myself as young it is as you think of a pair of shoes you once had, a pair of worn-out shoes you threw away long ago. You think of them as your old shoes just as you talk of your old self, although the shoes were new once, and strictly speaking it is you who have grown older. I have hardly any pictures from that period. I have only a single picture of Inès, taken in Amsterdam. I have never shown it to Astrid, there has never been an occasion to do so, and if she has in fact seen it, she hasn't said anything about it, perhaps because if she did she would reveal that she had searched my study. The picture is between two pages of the monograph on Vermeer, beside a colour print of the famous painting of a girl with pearl ear-rings and a blue turban, standing in a dark room, surprised out of her solitude, with slightly parted lips and a timid expectant look in her eyes, as she turns towards the light to meet the strange, penetrating gaze. I am in the picture myself. I am sitting beside Inès, my arm around her shoulder among the Japanese and American tourists on board one of the boats that sail around the canals of Amsterdam. We are all looking up, and some of us wave to the photographer. It is the same picture he has taken thousands of times before, the unknown photographer. I can hardly make us out among the other tourists on this spring day in Amsterdam long ago. A flock fortuitously brought together, who half an hour later will be scattered to all the winds, and of whom several must have died long since. We all look happy, perhaps because we are in Amsterdam, perhaps because the sun has come out at last and gleams on the green water and on the still-wet raincoats and folded umbrellas. Our faces are so small that the features are almost invisible. I have to pore over them through a magnifying glass to bring us into view, Inès with damp hair and her head leaning towards mine, looking so sweet, not at all like a bitch who makes men howl at the moon. Our eyes are small and indistinct like black motes in the picture's fog of diminutive particles that reproduce the colours of hair, skin, coats, boat and water. Our eyes are no more than minute black holes in the halted moment's area of colours, reflections and shadows, insignificant perforations into all that went before, out to all that was to come, memory and uncertainty, limbo and flickering hope.

I can't remember what I saw, I can't remember anything about our boat trip through the canals of Amsterdam, and I ask myself if I would be able to remember something out of all I have forgotten if I didn't have the picture of myself sitting beside Inès, looking up and smiling. I wonder whether it is the picture of us that shadows everything I may have seen. Inès leans towards me, tender and girlish, whether it is for the sake of the photographer or because after all she wants to have a picture in which you can see how sweet she could be. I can remember her spicy scent, the Maja soap which always makes me think of Spain even though we never went to Spain together and it is only her name that sounds Spanish. She has a flat paper bag in her hand and I know there's a postcard in the bag, she had just bought it in a museum and I can remember the picture although I can't see it, a dead pheasant with blind extinguished eyes, hanging from a hook head-down, painted with meticulous strokes without traces. I can't remember what I was thinking as Inès leaned her head against me, I only remember what it meant, or what I hoped it was to mean even though it has long ceased to matter. My eyes look at me like small black pinpricks in a remote faded second, but I cannot look inside, they are too small, it is too dark in there behind my young face in the pale unexpected spring sunlight above the canal. I know I loved her, but I can't remember what it was like to know that, how it felt. I know my love tore and dragged at me, but I can neither recall the pain nor the unexpected outbreaks of seeping happiness. I can tell myself that in reality it was not Inès who made me suffer, that I merely flayed myself on her until I bled, that it was not her that I loved but my own intoxication, my own poisonous chocolate-box picture of who she perhaps might be, and what I so much wanted to make her into. I can tell myself that my young, hungry and tempestuous love for Inès was a blind alley, a mirage, but I cannot know it. The memory of her quickly lost feeling, soon I could no longer sense anything, where before there had been pain. The wound healed and became a shiny scar without nerve fibres.

I looked round at the others as I continued to talk about Mondrian and explain to them that it was wrong to regard his primary colours and vertical and horizontal lines as emblems of the rationalism of an anti-metaphysical century, and that his apparently extreme concrete abstractions should rather be understood in the light of his theosophical mysticism, an ancient oriental dream of cosmic harmony. I drew their attention to the richly painted landscapes of his youth with their dim forest fringes and mirror-calm lakes at twilight and argued that in reality Mondrian was an incurable romantic, and they listened intently, almost devoutly, even the museum curator nodded his bald head encouragingly. Suddenly I thought he looked like a caricature of himself with his shiny pate and his flashing spectacles and almost satanically conspiratorial smile meant to signal that really nothing in this world could surprise him in the least, and that of course he was just as familiar with Mondrian's spiritual leanings as if we were talking of his own uncle incarnate. I looked at our hostess and she gave a kittenish smile so the thick layer of powder on her cheeks threatened to crack. Apparently she couldn't get enough Mondrian and widened her eyes as if it were those she listened with, and not her ears, which she had decorated with something reminiscent of gilded fir cones. She too resembled a caricature of the crazy kid I had tumbled in the sea grass with, she didn't even refrain from bending forward slightly on her elbows as an invitation to get a peek inside her scoop-neck blouse. She had crammed her breasts into a black bra that must have been at least one size too small, presumably to recall their once so legendary abundance. But what about me? Was it really me sitting here showing off my knowledge of Mondrian? Wasn't I myself a caricature of the polished art expert who could say something well-chosen and witty about any and every painter providing he was dead and famous? I smiled, no doubt absolutely charmingly, at my old girlfriend and thought of the time she had seduced me in a bathing hut. I could almost recall the feeling of wet coconut matting on my buttocks and her cool, domed breasts when they slipped out of her bathing suit. While I smiled at her as a kind of acknowledgement of her symbolic little flirtation over the table, I thought of how the earliest experiences we have with each other determine the keynote of the music we later come to play together. She was a year or two older than I was, and that had been enough for her to be well embarked on her erotic career, whereas I was still a bit of a jaywalker. When I was young I felt I was different inside from outside, someone other than the slightly clumsy, shy youth she had taken under her experienced wing. I had imagined that one day I would leave uncertainty behind me and at last be myself, fearless and imperturbable. I longed to come into view and show who I really was. I was open to everything then, I concealed nothing and everything was free to go right through me. I was far too easily shaken, susceptible to the smallest vibration, and I anxiously felt myself reflected in every glance that fell upon me. Now I sat here and sent her my very best roguish smile, but was that really me, was that what I had become? A discursive charlatan going a touch grey with chiselled features, who could sit and serve up Mondrian in paper-thin slices? Had I paid for my adult self-assurance, my firm views, my unswerving powers of judgement, by stiffening into this talking mask? Was there still someone behind the mask, did it still hide a secret difference?

I made them laugh at the story of how Mondrian had left the Stijl group, offended because Van Doesburg had betrayed the principle of strictly vertical and horizontal painting by placing his squares aslant because he found diagonals more 'dynamic', and while they laughed at this example of almost fanatically puritan and formalistic enforcement of principle, I thought it was precisely this genial, mature and well-tempered laughter that divided an artist like Mondrian from such a band of complacent, conformist and intellectually indolent culture snobs. But actually I could not care less about Mondrian, just as I had not been able to enthuse over Cézanne in the days that had passed since Astrid left. For the first time ever I had lost any desire to write, any expectation of excitement at seeing the sentences follow one another, see the words pull themselves out of the chink at the end of my fountain pen in long, vibrating wavy blue ribbons of damp signs that dried into the paper. I began to write after meeting Astrid, and I began to live from writing when Rosa was small. If I had been prevented from writing I should certainly have felt suffocated by the accumulated triviality of the everyday, but on the other hand I had only been able to breathe in the flat, silent and unmoving world of pictures, because there was a real, noisy, moving world that drew me into its turmoil all the time, spoke to me and demanded answers. One world had called me when I was in the other one, and my adult life had consisted in travelling to and fro between them every day. When one closed itself behind me and the other opened itself up to me with the hullabaloo of the everyday, in the midst of the confusion, while hunting for a tin of anchovies, I could fall into a reverie over the way the empty bottles in the larder could remind me of one of Morandi's humble and crookedly melancholy still lifes. Similarly, in the middle of my meditations on Brancusi's porous marble eggs I could not help thinking of the pale down on Astrid's buttocks when the morning sun touched them as it slanted in beneath the blind. It had been a vulnerable, changing and unpredictable balance I had maintained, and I had never imagined being relegated to one of these worlds alone, cut off from the other, but when Astrid left, the apartment became as still and silent as one of Hammershøi's deserted, grey rooms with white doors gaping onto emptiness, and I had nothing to add, nowhere to go.

I became the person I am through living with Astrid. Everything people connect with my face and my name came into existence while we were together, not only what I have written but also many of my quirks, reaction patterns and habits, all the things people find attractive or repellent in me. If it is true, as some say, that the first impression you get of others is also the one that lasts, and determines how light and shade are distributed in the more detailed picture that gradually forms, then with the years I have become the unknown taxi driver who one winter's evening long ago drove Astrid and Simon into town, and whose eyes a few days later she, wonderingly, but actually not with surprise, looked into as he lifted his hand and stroked her cheek. Anyway, that's how I picture the change which has taken me away from the gloomy young man sitting beside Inès in the boat on a canal in Amsterdam. He and the taxi driver are actually almost the same age, but the taxi driver Astrid caught sight of is someone else, someone unknown whom she and I have learned to know simultaneously. It was she who caught sight of him first, it was her glance that released me from the young man in Amsterdam and his scourged longing. She knew nothing about me, she did not know who I was, in her eyes I might have been someone different, not an unrequited young man who kept hitting his head against the same wall, raving with jealousy, shame and wounded vanity. Astrid liberated me, and she didn't even know it. The world grew amenable again, I no longer felt like an expelled monster sneaking along beside the wall, love was no longer a losing concern, and I promised myself I would never again love in vain, that I would not once more stand with all my emotions on my sleeve like a war

veteran promenading his bravery medals from a war no
one remembers. It all passed very quickly, but it was a
slower, more casual, almost aristocratic way of loving, not
a feverish, enervated hunger, not a drumming with white
knuckles on a closed door. To begin with I was dizzy with
lightness, with Astrid everything seemed possible, I did
not need to weigh my words, but nor was it necessary to
invoke every caress with pathetic declarations or anxious
questionings. We still knew infinitesimally little about each
other, and yet it felt very natural that Astrid and Simon quite
simply stayed on in my small flat. I began to drive in the
daytime when I didn't attend lectures, and when I arrived
home in the evening they were already there. It was a new
and remarkable feeling, that someone was there, that I found
light and voices when I got home. In the evening we put
Simon to bed on the sofa before retiring to the bedroom,
and soon we took it in turns to take him to nursery school
in the morning.

One morning when I was walking along the street with
him, an elderly woman came running after us with something in her hand. Smiling, she gave it to me and said my son
had dropped his glove. I hadn't seen him lose it, I hadn't even
noticed Astrid put gloves on him, and I smiled back slightly
flustered, for a moment quite ashamed, as if I had lured the
child away from his mother and was also irresponsible and
inattentive. If the woman had children herself they would
have left home long ago. There was something motherly in
her smile which seemed not only directed at Simon but also
at me. To her I seemed a sweet, slightly distrait young father
who couldn't cope with everything I had become responsible
for, and when I went on with Simon's little hand in mine and
replied to his unpredictable questions, I secretly relished my
false status. He asked about everything under the sun, and
as I replied it struck me that to him I represented a limitless
universe of knowledge, about as large as the Alexandria

library, so that I was not only a double-dealer to passing elderly ladies, but in a way was also shamming to him when I gave such cocksure answers to his questions about how far it is to the sun, and what happens to you when you die. Like the library in Alexandria, my own ideas about the order and meaning of things had long ago gone up in smoke, but nevertheless this youngster took me at my word, unshakeable in his faith in my powers of judgement. When he grew tired of walking I lifted him up on my shoulders and let him hold on tight to my hair. I wondered at how light he was and thought that as we walked along in the dense thundering morning traffic he was left completely to me, a stranger who had kissed his mother without quite knowing what he was doing, simply because it had occurred to him. I also thought about the grizzled film director, who had stood in his shirt-sleeves one cold night and shouted at Astrid in the taxi. Once she must have believed it was with him that her life was to take shape and become a story. I carried the proof of this on my shoulders, the proof that she must once have thought like that about the shouting man. Simon pulled at my hair and my ears, to draw my attention to something, and while I answered at random I thought that the small proof of love in the flying suit I was carrying with a firm grip of his winter boots, was the only thing which remained when her dream fell apart. He had come toddling out of the story when it was a thing of the past, just as once he had struggled his way out of her body. He had gone with her out of one story into another none of us had foreseen or so much as dreamed of. I would never be Simon's father, I would always be another man in another story, and as I walked hand in hand with him in the wintry blue morning alongside the roaring stream of cars, among the busy pedestrians with little white clouds of cold air around their mouths, I thought that the time of great blue-eyed frankness was past, gone was the empty-handed innocence in which nothing is written in advance, and you can be anyone at all, and anything can happen.

Astrid must have thought something similar those first times we woke up together in my bed and stretched out for each other with sleepy, slightly cautious caresses. She too must have asked herself how much of her had stayed behind in the blind alley she had left, and if she was quite the same now she exchanged the same caresses with another. Our meeting was pure coincidence, and we both enjoyed the feeling of tricking the rest of the world in the first weeks we were together in my cramped flat, where no one could know she was, and where no one yet knew that I no longer lay alone pining away in my forsaken state. I felt a lightness, at last I was free again, and I laughed for the first time in ages. The months passed, we started to go out together and meet each other's friends. Astrid divorced the film director, and when spring came we found a larger apartment. Our story had begun, had already found its tone and style, and the more often one of us talked about our meeting one winter night in a taxi, the more it sounded like the creation myth of our love. Gradually, as the anecdote was circulated, it made our chance meeting resemble an hour of destiny, and as time passed, the years before our meeting were reduced to a prehistoric wilderness of overgrown paths, failed experiments and uncompleted sketches. But sometimes when I heard myself telling the story yet again, it only intensified my memory of the accidental nature of our meeting. I recalled the weightless, dreamlike feeling of suddenly having stepped aside from my course into another world, where I too was someone different from the man who had gone astray in his immature obsession with Inès. In brief fleeting moments before I fell asleep, on the threshold between thought and dream I asked myself if it was so easy to love Astrid because I had finally learned to love, or because I had learned to love less. It was only a

passing notion and I forgot it just as quickly when I was in
her company again. For example, when we went into town
together on one of the evenings Simon was with his father.
She liked dancing, and when she stood in the throbbing
music and the whirling lights with closed eyes, twisting
around on herself, turned in on herself, she was like an
island in the midst of the din and morass of flickering
variable silhouettes, an island I let myself be washed up on
as I embraced her. She had not done much dancing when
she was married to the film director, it hadn't been his style,
and so it had stopped being hers. He had made her feel much
older than she was, and when she met me it felt like regaining
her youth. That's how she described it, as if she had taken
the wrong turning in time and had found her way back to
the starting point, a little nonplussed that she had become a
mother in the interval. And she really was very young when
she rolled around in bed playing tickling games with Simon,
she was more like a big sister being childish again. It was
strange to stand embracing her in the swarm of dancers, as I
so often had stood with an unknown girl on one of the many
nights I had spent in town. It was strange how we stood like
such a pair, who have just bumped into each other, young
and unruffled, and at the same time were already two who
belonged together.

I shared a taxi into town with the curator and his wife.
When I decided to take my leave they had already rung for
one, so I could hardly decline. I kissed our hostess goodbye,
and she looked intimately into my eyes and laid her palm
on my chest, lightly touching my skin with her fingertips
between two buttons, saying I must take care of myself.
I smiled, a little fatuously this time, and said of course I
would. What did she actually have in mind? A little flirt of
remembrance in Astrid's absence, while her husband stood
looking out for the taxi? Should I with a passing flutter of
lust assure her she was as attractive as she used to be? Did she

just want to remind me that in her way of thinking she had a kind of first priority on my cock because she had had her fingers on it before Astrid? And what was I actually to take care about? That she didn't come at me with her long red nails? What had she seen? Was my face really an open book? Was she the one out of the whole party who had observed me with a secret, inaccessible knowledge and seen what was hidden from myself? The thought was quite as irritating as it was disquieting. It had started to rain and we ran out to the waiting taxi, a little ridiculously, as if we could avoid the drops if we ran fast enough. The curator sat in the front seat, I was in the back with his wife, a well-upholstered but quite attractive woman with short, sensible hair. He, who had ravaged the parties and bars of our youth like a wild and Dionysiac centaur and invaded the knickers of every single beauty he felt like seducing, in the end had married this mild, retiring and unremarkable woman, and I was not the only one to have been surprised at his choice. To begin with I thought it was a case of some kind of moral reform, and he did talk about having children with an unctuous piety that I would never have ascribed to him, but they didn't have any, and soon he went on the rampage again like any fox in the hen-house. An old fox eventually, but one who hadn't lost his taste for young flesh. I wondered why the new generation of beauties just like their now mature and eternally pregnant predecessors went on falling for his bald, lean and not especially virile appearance. I learned the explanation from a mutual acquaintance, a poet, who himself continued to look not a day over twenty-five. I had to remember, he said, that young women always fuck upwards. The curator may have become flabby, but his eyes in the steel-rimmed spectacles radiated the irresistible charm of power.

He did nothing to hide his raging unfaithfulness from others, apart from his mild and totally unsuspecting wife, apparently he relied on his friends to shield her from the bitter, lecherous truth. I was pretty piqued and didn't refrain from telling him so, whereas Astrid was remarkably unaffected by his grotesque treachery. When I asked her what she would say if I romped around as freely as our friend, she merely kissed me on the forehead and said I would never have the nerve for that. She observed his digressions without condemning or excusing him, from a distance, as if they were a matter of neutral, arbitrary events which were not worth having an opinion on. That was probably true, and in fact I admired her for her ability to distinguish between the sides of him she found unpleasant and those she admired. She had a weakness for cynics, for their ruthless, blasphemous humour, and the curator could make her laugh till the tears came into her eyes. I'd been seated some way from his wife at dinner and we had not had much chance to talk. Now she obviously wanted to be friendly, because she asked quite innocently how Astrid was, and what kind of film she was editing. I answered her questions and we carried on quite a lively little conversation as we drove into town. I have always had a calming effect on shy people, they feel safe in my company and quickly loosen up, which can be a bit of a burden, but also a saving grace when you're shut up together, as in the back of a taxi. In the end she grew quite sloppy and begged my pardon for her husband's disparaging remarks about my daughter over the drinks. I brushed it off and said strictly speaking it was her boyfriend and not Rosa who had been mentioned disparagingly, and the curator immediately took advantage of my defensive evasion tactics. 'Quite right, it wasn't at all about Rosa, and why was she getting mixed up in it? Surely you can say what you like when you're among old friends?' His wife said there must be some limits, they were only young, and what if I should happen to think Rosa's boyfriend was a nice bloke? The curator snarled at her 'nice bloke' and repeated his scathing description of the artist's completely ludicrous and pathetic avant-garde attitudes. I tried to mediate between them and soon found myself in a situation where I was standing up for his wife. Their wrangling continued until she asked the driver to stop at a kiosk and went in to buy cigarettes. While we waited, silent and rather ill-at-ease in the presence of the expressionless driver, he suddenly turned in his seat and looked at me in a way I would almost call desperate. He said I was lucky. What did he mean? Yes, I was lucky because I had Astrid. I didn't know what to say and concentrated on keeping my face calm as I met his distraught glance in the half-light. His vinous breath wafted right into the corner where I sat. There was something he wanted to talk to me about. Had Astrid ever told me that he had tried to sleep with her once when I was out of the country? Apparently he was not at all worried about the driver, sitting there with his blank face swallowing every word we uttered, while staring listlessly at the long glittering tracks of the raindrops on the windscreen. I mustn't worry, it was a long time ago, at least five years. Anyway she had rejected him, how could I imagine otherwise? His eyes blinked behind the neon reflections of his spectacles with a flash of demonic joviality that distorted his solemn, almost humble face into a theatrical two-faced grimace, as he went on with his confession. It was after a dinner like tonight's, his wife had been ill so he had gone on his own. He had driven Astrid home, the two of them were alone in his car. He felt they'd enjoyed themselves so much together, there seemed to be a special contact that evening, and you never know, he wasn't to know, was he, how she and I got on. They talked about everything, in the way you can with Astrid, I wondered if anyone knew what he was talking about, and when, as they drove, as if by chance he laid a hand on her knee, she left it there. I looked out through the transitory fans of transparency the wipers made on the windscreen. I could see his wife standing in the kiosk, resting on one leg in the queue and apparently absorbed in the pictures of hamburgers and hot dogs above the counter. Her face was quite white in the neon light and her gaze distant. He didn't know if Astrid even noticed the hand, she wasn't totally sober, but she did not push it away, and there really had been, what should he call it, this contact, so he left his hand there where it lay on her knee. When he stopped at our entrance he tried to kiss her, but she merely turned her face away smiling, and before he could say anything she had said goodnight and slammed the car door shut after her. Neither of them had said anything about the episode. Had she really never told me about it? I followed his wife with my eyes as she stepped out of the illuminated sphere of the kiosk, suddenly just a dark silhouette approaching. The curator slapped me on the thigh and smiled in a conciliating way. Now at least I knew what kind of a shit my friend was.

I couldn't pull myself together and go to bed, although it was past two in the morning. Again I sat in the dark in my study looking out over the deeper, more limitless darkness of the Lakes. As far as I could see it had stopped raining. The glow from my cigarette was reflected in the windowpane, its slightly stronger, slightly redder smouldering when I sucked in smoke was the only sign of life. The lights had been switched off in the windows on the other side, only the street-lights shone and the faint orange gleam in the sky, the glow from the city's lights, that has always reminded me of the firelight over the creepy fantasies of judgement day in Hieronymus Bosch. The lamplight only reached part-way up the row of façades over there in insufficient fans on the brickwork between the dark windows, the rest of the walls faded into the darkness, the same darkness as over the lake, so that the shining wet asphalt of the street on the opposite bank seemed severed from its surroundings, an outstretched ribbon of light beneath the blurred and incomplete ghosts of the houses, stretching out into black nothingness. The view made me think of the famous picture by Magritte, *L'empire des lumières,* depicting a gloomy house beside a nocturnal lake surrounded by dark trees, illuminated only by a single mysterious and ominous lamp, paradoxically and subtly placed beneath a pale blue sky with white clouds. At every other time I would have embarked on a study of the context to discover precisely what it was about the view that made me think of the picture, as so often a picture had me hunting for an early sensual perception, the particular light in a half forgotten doorway or side-street which for a moment brushed the edge of my mind, only to fade and grow dim the next moment. With time my recollections had transformed themselves into pictures and merged with the recollection of all the pictures I had seen, until I was no longer sure of the difference and had difficulty in distinguishing one kind of memory from the other, because anyway both were equally diffuse, equally distorted, abandoned to the impulses, preoccupations and anxieties of the moment. Now I no longer cared about Magritte, about the mastery of the lights, I merely sat staring stupidly out into the darkness because I knew I would not be able to fall asleep. Besides, I had always thought Magritte was an unusually facile and inferior painter.

I asked myself what I would have said to the curator if his wife had not sat down beside me on the back seat just as he had finished his confession. I was afraid it would not have made any difference if she had come precisely then or two minutes later. He had paralysed me, forced me into my corner in the back seat of the taxi, and he must have known himself that I was defenceless, disarmed. But why had he told me that story, and why on this evening? Why had Astrid never told me about it? Was it because he had lied? But why should he lie and show himself in such a bad light, even risk losing my friendship? And why had Astrid kept silent about an episode that with a little goodwill and a light edit would only have demonstrated her faithfulness and constancy? Perhaps because otherwise, if, with an ironic and calming smile she had told me about the little occurrence, I might have gone and confronted the curator with it and thereby in fact heard his version, the one in which she had let his hand stay on her knee, whether it was from forgetfulness or misunderstood tact. Perhaps because in reality, whether it was only for a short distance or for an hour during dinner, she had contemplated or at least played with the idea of what it would be like to sleep with the museum curator, and because the mere thought, although it had never been put into action, to her seemed shameful and half-criminal. I came to think of Astrid's surprising tolerance towards his affairs with his female students. Was she so tolerant only because she wanted to excuse herself for her own small tête-à-tête with him? I thought of how she had laughed in the car on the way home from a dinner party like tonight's, when I had philosophised over what people really know about each other, and used the curator as a grotesque example. Was it him she was laughing at? Was it me? Was it herself? Was it quite a different story I would never come to hear?

Perhaps it didn't matter whether the story was true or not. In any case if it was true, nothing had happened. A few minutes too long for a hand to rest on my wife's knee could easily be relegated to the scrap-heap of fortuitous mishaps and misapprehensions. After all, so much happens en passant. If on the other hand this fully innocent story was pure invention, it merely strengthened my sneaking feeling that the curator had not told it to me to exult and pride himself on the fact that even Astrid, the unconquerable, impregnable Astrid, had wavered for a moment under the influence of his renowned talents as a seducer. That rather he had told it to me in order to ascertain that he had seen aright when he glimpsed a crack in my apparently so relaxed façade of grass widower, earlier in the evening as

he described how the installation artist had made free with
my daughter for all to see. Perhaps he had merely invented
his piquant little story to let me know he had understood or
anyway sensed, ferreted out, sniffed his way to discovering
there was 'something in the wind' or that 'the knives were
out' or there was 'a rift in the lute' or whatever it was my
mother had hinted at on the phone. But why should he be
at all interested in what went on between Astrid and me?
Perhaps he was speaking from the heart when his dull wife
had gone to buy cigarettes and he impressed on me how
lucky I was. Perhaps because all his little student doves, no
matter how smooth and supple they might be, were only
a form of extremely sensual but nevertheless despairing
sublimation. Perhaps because like so many others he had
surreptitiously lusted after Astrid and so was relishing the
knowledge that I was about to lose what he himself had
never been anywhere near gaining. I tried to remember
what had actually happened on that trip to Greece many
years ago when he had so heroically rescued Rosa's puppy
from death by drowning, perhaps to make an impression on
Astrid with his resolute, tanned and still muscular life-saver's
body. But I couldn't find even a syllable of a single scrap of
one alarming picture to illustrate my suspicions. That holiday dissolved into a cracked film of quivering heat haze
and fleeting shadows, gleams of light in a bottle of retsina
beneath an awning of plaited bamboo, crimson lobsters, the
children's burned shoulders and bleached hair full of sand,
the turquoise blue finger of sea behind the shutters and
Astrid's shadowy body waiting for me in the afternoons in
the semi-darkness of our room.

When I woke up I did not know where I was. It was dark
around me, and the darkness was parted by a vertical, frayed
strand of yellowish light, falling from the ceiling and almost
down to the floor, as if a crack had opened in the wall and
the light was coming through it, the strange, unrecognisable

light from another place, another day. I turned on my other side and caught sight of the narrow strip of lighted windows through the curtains I had not completely drawn before I fell asleep. I sat for a long time on the edge of the bed, dazed and confused, before getting up and going over to the window. The white shirts had stopped circling around each other in the buildings opposite, the offices were empty but still fully lit, without a shadow. I stood at the window watching the night traffic down on Lexington Avenue, the regular chain-drive of the cars' red and white lights along the formless, changing but undifferentiated mass of bodies passing each other in opposite shoals on the side-walks. In a short while, when I had taken a bath and changed my shirt, I would go down in the elevator and mix with the crowd at the bottom of the shaft among the columns of shining glass, reduce myself to a particle among the particles fluctuating amongst each other beneath me, each in its own direction and yet swallowed up by the same stream of continual, unstoppable, directionless movement.

4

The sun had reached the other side of the block when I awoke, it was already throwing its afternoon light on to the façades on the opposite side of the Lakes. It occurred to me that for the first time since Astrid had gone I did not feel any surprise at her absence. For the first time I did not expect, in a moment's forgetfulness, to hear her sounds in the bathroom or the kitchen, the trickle of water on the tiles, the clink of a teaspoon on a saucer. I had begun to accustom myself to solitude and spread myself out in it, now that I did not need to show consideration for her. I had fallen asleep in the middle of the double-bed instead of keeping to the half which usually made up my nightly territory. I threw my cigarette stubs into the lavatory pan, a habit Astrid had cured me of many years ago. I played all the jazz I hadn't listened to for years because she couldn't stand it, and I made do with a sandwich in the evening, when for eighteen years we had kept on cooking a hot dinner every day regardless of how tired we were. In less than a week a part of me had grown used to being alone, completely unaffected by my thoughts constantly circling around her disappearance. I could see the details of a life without her even though I still did not have the remotest idea of their perspective. As I walked aimlessly around the apartment on bare feet or sat passively at my desk watching the shadows growing under the trees along the lake shore, it occurred to me how quickly even an exceptional state acquires a dull tinge of triviality. When I had decided to go to New York as planned it had been almost in spite of this state and probably also in spite of Astrid, who had given herself this mysterious advantage in a process about which I had only vague and anxious ideas. The only thing I knew was that a change had taken place, in her, in us. I did not know to what. There were times when I felt violently wronged, but soon after I collapsed again into vegetation and self-reproach because I had just allowed her to leave and because I could not imagine why she had gone. I was convinced it was my own fault but at the same time I had to ask myself if I really believed that I alone was responsible. If this too was not yet another manifestation of my usual self-obsession, my all-too-many fruitless speculations that went on circling irremediably around my own freezing ego like the moons around a barren planet. Perhaps it was meaningless to ask why. Perhaps even she herself wouldn't have been able to give an answer.

When I was again hunched over my notes on Cézanne that afternoon I realised that I might as well give up. As far as I was concerned Cézanne's apples could rot in peace. If my former life was about to fall apart I would at least concentrate on seeing it happen without being distracted by ambitions or promises that had lost their power over me. I rang the editor who had commissioned the article, and to my surprise he was full of understanding even though I didn't even make any attempt to explain. Afterwards I felt how stupid I had been in my fruitless efforts during the last few days, obviously Cézanne did not matter, unless it had been my blunt tone on the telephone which had made the editor so amenable. I was usually very polite and was surprised to hear how brusque, indeed, almost unfriendly, I was being to him. I felt quite cheerful when I put down the receiver, but that could have been because the sun was shining and filling the apartment with a warm, living glow. I decided to go for a walk, now I had extricated myself from my duties. It was a long time since I had strolled along the streets without having to go anywhere, without anyone waiting for me. Through the years with Astrid and the children, the town had gradually become a mere backdrop to my purposeful and planned activities in one sphere or another. There were streets I used every day, but also districts where I hadn't been for years because I had no reason to visit them. The town had long since ceased to be the alluring, strange and promising world of opportunities and potential, of crossing paths and glances, which I had once explored, curious and full of youthful expectations. It had become ours, Astrid's, the children's and mine, almost as familiar as the rooms of our apartment and their furnishings, and I moved around it like a sleepwalker although I knew our town was only one of the millions of parallel towns that the other inhabitants had each formed according to their memories, routines and disappointed or fulfilled hopes. That afternoon, while I walked around aimlessly now in one direction, now in the opposite, the town was again an unknown labyrinth, and although I knew every crossing in the net of streets, I had the feeling of getting lost. It was Friday, people crowded the city centre and there was the usual hectic, expectant mood when the weekend is approaching with its measured hours of leisure and dissipation, adventures and attempts to escape. Now and then I caught a glimpse of myself in bus windows or the dark glass of display windows when I walked through a ray of sunlight between buildings, and I asked myself as I had done at dinner the night before, if it was really me, the man fleetingly passing through his own transparent reflection among the pedestrians and bus passengers and the immoveable wax mannequins in the windows. At other times I peered in vain for myself in the broken-up, momentary reflections of window panes, but saw only the other pedestrians' chance, insignificant bodies and faces, as if I was merely a lost pair of eyes that were not in the film playing between the light and my retinas.

I went into a café to read a newspaper, but could not even concentrate on the headlines, the great events in the world outside were too small and indistinct in my field of vision, dominated as it was by Astrid's absence, a sudden, enormous vacancy which the human crowd of the afternoon penetrated and frequented. I could only sit in my corner and watch the passers-by with the same apathetic and homeless feeling you can have when you sit in a café in a strange town watching people whose language you can't understand. Although the air was cool they had put tables and chairs out in the sun, and there were as many people outside as in. A girl sat alone at one of the tables furthest out, she must have been about Rosa's age and was dressed like Rosa, in the same casually inventive way, in a big coarsely knitted roll-neck sweater and a pair of shabby, Prince of Wales tartan men's trousers she must have found at the Salvation Army shop. Like the sweater the trousers were several sizes too big and there would have been something comical and clownish about her figure if she were not sitting so elegantly with her legs crossed and her cigarette raised in an absent-minded, world-weary gesture as she slowly kept watch over the square through her narrow sunglasses, backwards and forwards past the fountain's tassels of pulsing foam and the flock of pigeons scattering in fluttering explosions at regular intervals. Her copper-coloured hair was gathered at her neck and kept in place with a pencil coquettishly pushed through the loose knot, her thin face was covered with freckles, and I suddenly became intensely interested to see who she was waiting for, what kind of young man she might have fallen for, arrogant and unapproachable as she looked. I ordered another cup of coffee, sharing her wait with her as she gracefully sipped her tea. Then she raised her head and directed her gaze on a point at the end of the square, expectantly, until the person she had caught sight of had seen her too, whereupon she lifted her slim hand and smiled. I looked in the same direction and tried to get a glimpse of the young man she was waving to, until I saw a girl detach herself from the crowd and a moment later recognised Rosa, as she took the last steps over to the table and embraced the red-haired girl.

I quickly unfolded the newspaper as if in the course of a second I had become absorbed in an article about economic growth in southern China, and straight away felt irritated with myself for the abrupt manner in which I had concealed my presence, as if I had a bad conscience. Abashed, I asked myself if I had really been sitting keeping a secret watch on the red-haired girl like any other old lecher who doesn't want to acknowledge his own covert and futile lasciviousness. I who was still far from old, and who had been no older than Rosa's youthfully rebellious installation artist when I became her father. Why hadn't I just waited until she happened to catch sight of me, waved cheerfully and let it be up to her whether she felt like coming over to say hello? Why hadn't I just drunk my coffee and on the way out feigned surprise, kissed her on the cheek and exchanged a word or two before leaving them to their own company? The longer I stayed sitting in my hiding place behind the business pages, the more inept it would seem if Rosa discovered me. But I couldn't bear the thought of looking her in the eyes, I couldn't endure Gunilla in Stockholm hearing yet again the feeble lie that made Astrid's absence into something normal and credible, and I was far from sure of being able to keep up the mask and hide my inner turmoil of disquiet and unanswered questions. All the same I couldn't help peeking over the newspaper now and then. There was absolutely nothing in the least arrogant or world-weary about the red-haired girl now. She had pushed her sunglasses up on her forehead, no longer masked as an exclusive and unapproachable Bohemian, and she nodded approvingly and laughed aloud at what Rosa was telling her. I could hear their laughter and remembered how many times I had heard that sound from Rosa's room through the closed door when she had girlfriends visiting. The muffled giggles from a secretive and inaccessible world of blushing dreams and poisonous intrigues. When she began to grow up Rosa had gradually withdrawn from our old intimacy and confided solely in Astrid, and I was completely unqualified to guess what it could be that made the two girls outside alternately move their heads together and throw them back with hilarity. We were still affectionate with each other, but when she had visited us I could feel from her light, somehow elusive way of kissing me goodbye, that apart from the increasingly rare conversations with Astrid it was only our washing machine and a few practical pieces of fatherly advice or fatherly thousand-kroner notes that she still had any use for. The rest she found elsewhere, some of it with the red-haired girl with the pencil in her hair, some with the cropped installation artist and some with others I had yet to meet.

When at some point the red-haired girl came into the café and went downstairs to the toilets, Rosa sat gazing thoughtfully across the sunny square where the human throng gathered and scattered in randomly changing formations. I could have got up and gone out to her, I could still make out I had just caught sight of her, but I sat on there. It occurred to me that I shouldn't have known what to say to her. Here, sitting each on our own side of the big glass pane looking onto the square, I suddenly saw that we had come to the other side of the years when we could enter one another's innermost selves by hidden channels, some of which had been concealed even from ourselves. It would not have taken much, I could merely have asked how she was, well knowing that she would smile and say she was fine, but it was precisely that balance between distance and intimacy, between tenderness and politeness that I was not sure I could maintain. I was actually quite happy that she

had no use for me any more even though now and again I
allowed myself a little bout of wistfulness, but I would not
let her see that for once I was the one who might need her
because I was at a loss and felt the ground slide beneath
me. I wanted to shield her from the sight and shield myself
from her seeing me like this. I had a strong feeling that
she only moved with such great self-assurance in her new
world because she knew where she had me, and because she
reckoned I was always as unshakeable, at ease with myself,
whether she had need of me or not. But I could also feel that
I myself would not be able to bear her surprised, perhaps
even frightened glance when she saw I knew even less and
was even more vulnerable and confused than she was. She
enjoyed teasing me but she did so only because she was
unable to imagine it could really hurt me, and that was in
fact why she teased me, to make a show of shaking my
equilibrium, secure in the knowledge that she would never
succeed. If she had just turned her head halfway round to
see what had become of her friend, she would have seen
me, but she went on looking in front of her, smoking her
cigarette, given over to unknown thoughts. She looked very
lovely and mature, sitting there in profile with half-closed
eyes and the cigarette between her soft lips. She resembles
Astrid more and more, Astrid when young, she has the
same thick brown hair, the same narrow green eyes and
broad cheekbones, but as I sat observing her that afternoon
I could also glimpse the last, blurred traces of the features of
the child she had been not so long ago. I walked again beside
the Lakes with her plump little hand in mine answering her
impossible questions, again I walked up and down the floor
with her at night as she screamed like one possessed and
vomited down my back. Again I stood in the hospital one
night and saw her come into sight between Astrid's thighs,
violet-blue, covered in blood, with her blind prune face that
made me think of the dark, constricted faces uncovered at

the bottom of a peat bog, but alive, indomitable and terrified, roaring, head hanging downwards, boxing with clenched fists in empty space. It was not so very long ago, and now she sat in the sun smoking with her eyes screwed up.

Astrid, Simon and I spent our first summer by the sea in a house she had loaned from some acquaintances. She had just divorced the film director and had refrained from all financial demands, not only out of pride, I think, but also to get it over with as quickly as possible. Her decision had floored him, since she was the wronged party, but it only made bad worse that she didn't try to fleece him. He had been unfaithful and yet he was allowed to keep his house and his money, so all in all it was a pretty shabby part he came to play. In the long run Astrid could not keep him in the dark about where she had moved, but she always asked me to leave her alone when he came to fetch Simon. Naturally he did not fail to comment on the humble surroundings she obviously preferred to the fashionable villa in the northern district, but the next moment he could burst into tears in front of his son and ex-wife, completely broken down with remorse and making humble pleas for one more chance, despite everything and referring to 'all they had had together'. Simon was quite impossible when his father was expected, he didn't want to go to Tivoli or the cinema, more than once Astrid had to tear herself free of his arms to get him out of the door, and when he had finally gone with his contrite, grizzled father, she would furiously batter the apartment with the vacuum cleaner or clean the windows. When she mentioned the film director it was as if she talked of a mistake, an aberration, a blunder, which she could only come to terms with by distancing herself wonderingly and ironically from the girl who six years before had succumbed to a mature man's formidable passion. In her account of their years together, her love for him became a young infatuation, a crazed illusion that had been allowed to go on much too long and take everything too far, and I never told her what I thought when she spoke of her first marriage like that. That perhaps she only diminished her own and the film director's feelings into lightweight erotic grimaces in order to be able to convince herself that our own emotions were as reliable and inevitable as gravity itself. Because she anxiously had to assure us both that I was the man in her life and not just a chance taxi driver, the first one who happened to come along. We were still young, and perhaps we were both afraid of our own youth, of the haste with which love had changed face. It may also have occurred to her in unguarded moments that the new face of her love might turn out to have been only another mask. We still had so little life behind us, we were not yet to know that history is just as uncertain and ambivalent as the future. We still believed that the past could be exorcised with occult gestures, we still believed that our warm breath alone was enough to blow life into our hopes.

It was unplanned, but we did not view it as a misfortune when Astrid found herself pregnant in the spring. It was just another accidental occurrence that came to change our life. She did not say anything to me about her suspicions until she had been to the doctor and had them confirmed. When she did tell me it was in the same off-hand manner as when she said she was fond of me, with the same modesty towards the words as if she had to weigh them in her hands, surprised at their weight and remarkable appearance. When she had managed to say it, one night when we lay side by side, while she absent-mindedly played with my hair, I had the same feeling about her as I had had when some months ago I'd seen her standing at the sink in my kitchen and had gone over and touched her for the first time. It was with the same recklessness, the same dizzy feeling of life opening out to me and yet again I sensed the reply at the same moment as the question voiced itself. Why not? She looked away when she had spoken, waiting, and I took her face between my hands and smiled, as I met her questioning gaze. Why should I not have a child with her? If my life was not to take form now, when would it? What had I to wait for? What had I to fear? It was my calm smile that convinced Astrid that it could be the two of us, that it was no longer a mere idea, a hope in the sequence of hopes that sets one in movement while one is young, and makes one wander here and there. I had no idea what I was doing, but I did it none the less, and the breathless feeling of leaping without hesitation into the unknown, the liberating weightlessness of the leap itself, filled me with a remarkable certainty, one I had never known before. She was in the third month when summer came and we settled into the house by the sea. We didn't tell anyone where we were. It had been impossible to keep the divorce secret, the papers had printed front-page pictures of the well-known film director who had been deserted by his beautiful young wife, and I had to disconnect the phone for days when Astrid's whereabouts were revealed. The house by the sea was our hiding place while we waited for new divorces and deaths to attract the interest of the vulgar world of noisy headlines and greedy toothy grins in the limelight Astrid had taken her leave of. It was early summer, the beach was still empty, only Astrid, Simon and I were in the house, and the weeks flowed together as the colours of the sea do in the course of the day. In the end we couldn't distinguish the days from each other, just as you don't notice the sea changing colour, pale grey in the morning, dark green in the afternoon, violet blue in the evening, flecked with the dazzling reflections of the low sun.

The sun had just disappeared behind the horizon. Simon and I were kneeling in the cool damp sand engaged in digging a trench at the edge of the sea so the waves could fill the moat around the sandcastle we had spent the afternoon building, a sombre grey medieval fortress, with conical towers made from his little bucket. We quite forgot to talk to each other, completely absorbed in our laborious engineering work, and we hadn't noticed the sea growing dark beneath the orange and green sky. The wind blew off the land and the little waves collapsed exhausted on to the wet sand. We slowly succeeded in conducting the water into the moat, but only for a moment at a time, then it sank down through the grains of sand leaving only a feeble scrap of foam. I heard Astrid calling me, obviously it was time to eat already, but Simon seemed not to hear her and I went on with the digging although I had begun to doubt whether it was any use. Astrid called again and I looked up. She stood at the top of the steps that led up to the house behind the slope at the edge of the beach where rose bushes grew. She called my name again, and then once more, louder than before, only my name, her voice was shrill, almost hysterical. Only when she called again did it strike me something might be wrong. I threw down the little plastic shovel and ran as fast as I could. She was pale and she began to cry when I reached her and caught sight of the trickles of blood running down her bare legs beneath the thin summer dress. I carried her inside and laid her on a sofa, then rang for an ambulance. Simon started to cry too when he saw the blood on her legs, and she tried to comfort him, glancing over at me by the telephone. I don't know how long I sat holding her hand and stroking her hair without finding anything to say except the same few inadequate and banal sentences before at last the ambulance came. She wanted me to stay in the house with Simon, who had crept into an armchair, mute with terror, and soon afterwards I stood beside him watching the ambulance vanish along the quiet road in the twilight. I went on talking to him while cooking, as much to soothe my own anxiety, I talked about everything that occurred to me, about the moat we had dug around our baronial castle of sand, about the deserted medieval castles where the knights had once sat feeling bored while they waited for a dragon to come along. Later on I settled him under his duvet on the sofa in the living room and stayed with him until he fell asleep. I went outside and sat down at the top of the steps from where she had called me. I sat and looked at the glass-like, transparent reflection of the water beneath the pale evening sky. There was nothing to see and yet I stared into the empty, unmoving surface of the sea as you can stare into a wall because you don't know where else to look. I could see the little edged outline of the sandcastle against the sea, which had risen in the meantime so the waves beat with regular intervals at the foot of the walls that rose like a dark, fragile island in the shining foam of the surf. Just as we had begun to believe it could be reality, what had begun as a chance meeting, a chance impulse, a show of hope, now threatened to leave us again. Just as it was beginning to take shape, its own as yet incomplete and half-formed body, no longer only dependent on our ideas, our feelings, embraces and words. For the first time in my life I spoke to someone who was not there. I spoke to Astrid, alone on the steps in the twilight I begged her to hold on, not to give way, as if my saying it would make any difference. I went on sitting there as it grew darker, I sat smoking in the evening chill among the rose bushes on the slope and peered at the first stars emerging in the cold gaping vault of the sky, and I realised in a different manner, more exposed and naked than before, that I was not the only one who was alone as I sat there getting a stiff neck from gazing up at the stars' dead light, that we too were alone together, Astrid and I, abandoned to ourselves and each other.

In the morning we went to visit her. They had told us she would have to stay in hospital for a few days. They wouldn't promise anything. She was exhausted with worry, and Simon was terrified at the sight of his pale mother in the white bed. She spoke to him calmly, explained what had happened and asked him about our sandcastle. It was still standing, he told her, the waves had not covered it. He smiled as if that was quite a miracle and totally forgot his anxiety. I came to think of how she had hummed to him in the taxi that evening in winter when their world had fallen apart. It was the same calmness she had spread around her then, even though inside herself she had been in turmoil. She had made him stop crying by humming the same silly tune again and again as I drove them through town. She had no idea where she was going and still she had been able to hum to him, calmly and gently, as if he did not need to worry about where they were and what was happening around them as long as he could nestle in her arms. We went to see her in hospital every day. It was apparently just a question of lying quite still, the crisis was over, she had held on. Up to then I had not been alone with Simon for more than a few hours at a time, but he had already grown accustomed to regarding me as the man in his life. All the same, I wondered at myself when I kissed him goodnight and later in the evening crept up and opened his door a crack to see whether he was asleep. It was the first time anyone had need of me, needed me just to be there. He corrected me kindly when I forgot to put a pat of butter in his porridge or brush his back teeth, and he helped me write shopping lists to make sure I included everything. We spent most of our time on the beach, I taught him to swim, and after a few days he let go of my hands and took his first strokes quite fearlessly. A fortnight after Astrid came home from hospital he swam with us right out to the sand bar. He laughed when he saw her admiring face and said that now we were actually four as we were swimming, three in the water and one in her stomach.

I did not forget my wakeful night on the slope by the sea. In my memory it is on the steps of black-stained wood that our story begins, that it becomes a story which began one winter night as an inadvertent coincidence of circumstances.

As far back as I could remember my thoughts and feelings had been like a distance between the person I was inside and the world flowing around me, its days, places and faces. It was as if I was always somewhere else, and I longed to wipe out that distance, I so much wanted to open myself up and allow the light of places and other people's eyes to fall upon the unknown one who hid in the darkness there, but the light and the eyes never penetrated far enough, there was always a last shadowy corner where he hid himself, the person I ought to be. When Inès turned towards me one summer day in the semi-darkness among the indistinct Roman heads I thought that at last here was someone who had caught sight of him, and I tried to hold her fast, as if I could see in her eyes what I hoped she saw. When I met Astrid I had in the meantime given up the idea of being different from any of the figures moving between days and places, a face among the faces in the city's interchange of hurrying changing reflections. But on that night when I sat staring out at the disappearing, almost invisible transition between the darkness of sky and sea, everything that I was concentrated into the two little words I went on repeating in a hushed voice among the rose bushes, until the words no longer meant anything in particular because they contained everything: *hold on, hold on*. And that evening the following winter when I stood watching Rosa come into the light, covered in Astrid's blood, it seemed as if at long last I too came in sight. While Astrid screamed with pain and emptied herself of the child that had taken shape inside her, I felt that the distance had finally been covered, how my love was no longer merely a feeling, a question, a gesture into thin air, how it had become something that definitively existed between us, someone who filled her lungs for the first time and emptied them again with a roar.

Our first years are a bright mist of fatigue and happiness, of days and months that lost their firm outlines in the

momentum, dissolved in the dizzy whirl of speed at which
everything took place. I recall them not as stationary, fixed
moments, I recall them as a movement on the spot, the same
spot. Our first years are a glade in time, and I remember the
feeling of having arrived, as if I had been lost among the
tree trunks in a dense forest, on blind, overgrown paths,
until I finally came out into the light and caught sight of
the sky again. I really came to believe that it was Astrid
I had been waiting for without knowing it. I believed I
had arrived at the place where I ought to be. The days
flowed together as if they were one same day, one same
night that turned gently around each other, and I was no
longer impatient for the time to pass, I no longer dreamed
it would take me somewhere else. The days resembled each
other and I had masses of time, and when another year had
passed I marvelled yet again that the changes were fruits
of repetition, of the repeated cycle of everyday events.
We did the same things every day, and meanwhile Rosa
and Simon grew between us with faces whose permanent
features were emerging from their soft skin. We exchanged
the same words and caresses, and meanwhile their register of
tones and nuances grew, until a quick glance, a fleeting touch
or a half-expressed sentence, depending on the context, took
on a special meaning which we alone understood how to
interpret. Each time we had a meal with the children,
each time we made love again, our words and smiles and
movements held all the previous evenings and nights in
their repetition, in the repetition's annulment of the flight of
time. The days did not obliterate each other, they no longer
devoured each other but were united in the same peaceful
rhythm of parting and reunion, of business and sleep, as if
we had pitched camp in the midst of time. Sometimes I was
bored, but the boredom was not as before a pain caused
by the repeated undermining of my gaze and my thoughts.
When I was bored it was rather a kind of meditation on the

unheeded physiognomy of trivial details, the pale reflection of the winter sun on the party wall in front of the kitchen window, the dry, crisp, ribbed peel that crackled when I picked up an onion, the drop of water that slowly swelled below the tap and gathered the light before giving up and falling like a silvery comet into the grey steel of the sink. When I was bored it was actually not boredom, rather a long moment of unthinking rest in the centre of gravity I passed again and again in the course of the day, and in which all fluctuations, all movements, took their strength. I could completely forget myself for hours at a time, whether I was changing Rosa's nappy or reading aloud to Simon, whether I sat at my desk watching the words come into view on the paper, or was in bed with Astrid feeling her desire awaken beneath my hands. The whole time there was something around me that grasped me and pulled me with it out of solitude, out of myself and into the profusion of events. Even when I was alone in my study I was only a pair of eyes and a pen, one with what I saw and what I was trying to say. Those were the years in which I couldn't distinguish between duties and freedom, to me it had come as a liberation that every day, every hour of the day there was something I had to do, and I was all the more engrossed in my work because of the knowledge that I did not have the whole day to myself.

I often had to travel for my work, and once again when I found myself early one evening in an ugly hotel room looking out of the window at a strange town, I could see them clearly before me. Simon in his room painting tin soldiers, absorbed in the dark blue colour of the Northern States' uniform jackets. Rosa in her little plastic bath tub singing to herself as she washed the hair of a doll with a film-star smile. Astrid in the kitchen washing spinach with red fingers under the cold tap and for a moment contemplating the wrinkled folds of the spinach leaves that looked like the folded skin on her swollen fingertips. When I phoned home I sometimes didn't really know what to say. I asked them to tell me what had happened during the day but I didn't feel I had anything much to talk about, and the little everyday words that used to overflow with meaning when I had their faces before me, grew thin and inadequate and incapable of reaching across the sudden distance. As a rule I had looked forward to an interruption of the repetitive pattern of daily life, but as soon as I had left I would almost always start to miss them, and I could feel quite desolate when I roamed around the streets of a strange town, left to my own devices. Whole days could pass when I did not speak to anyone but waiters and hotel receptionists and exchanged only the most vapid, strictly necessary comments, and if now and then I met an art dealer, a curator or a critic I warmed myself on the conversation in a humiliating manner, as if I were a homeless person who had been invited in out of sheer compassion. I felt more exposed when I was travelling than I had formerly, and it often struck me that in the streets of a foreign town, where no one knew me, I was merely a Mr Anybody who spoke with a strange comic accent and behaved rather hesitantly, without the reserved naturalness of movement of one on his way to a place where he is expected. Astrid often laughed at me when I phoned home for the second time in a day and asked how things were going, as if something special was going on in my absence.

During the winter of Rosa's seventh birthday I went to Paris for a few days to see a big Giacometti exhibition at the Musée de l'Art Moderne. I spent an entire afternoon walking up and down among the tall bronze people on their gigantic feet, thin and bony, their arms at their sides and their expressionless, narrow, loosely modelled faces slightly raised, as if they were listening for something. I had written about them before without managing to pinpoint what it was that made the air vibrate unnoticeably around them each time I saw them again. It was not only because they themselves were almost nothing but lines in the air, with hardly any dimensions, as if the air were a piece of thin paper on which Giacometti with quick strokes had produced their contours like rents in the light into an unknown darkness. There was also a quality in the space around them, the invisible, transparent space between their reduced physique and my gaze, which reached out to them and fumbled in the void into which they threatened to vanish. While I circled around the fragile, expressionless and introverted men and women in the white gallery, it dawned on me that it was the air itself they made me see, tottering on the edge of invisibility and absence. Not only did they withdraw while I looked at them, in towards the innermost limit of spatiality. It was as if my eyes chafed at their bronze bodies and stumbled forwards in a free fall as they squeezed themselves in. As if the thin lonely figures, if I looked at them too long, would vanish completely. Perhaps the reason for their making such an unconquerable impression on me was because of the resistance my eyes met when they gazed at the figures so greedily. This last, impassable limit that separated us and prevented them from becoming one with the air before my eyes. This was the limit which Giacometti had apparently continued to search for. After the experiments of the earlier years his work was no longer a matter of renewal, of the continuing extension of the field of experiences. From then on he had stayed in the same place, concerned only with the very final hesitation before the point at which presence and disappearance open to each other. And perhaps I am thinking of Giacometti again because it is the same boundary I myself go on approaching, and which I cannot cross when I visualise Astrid again, standing in her overcoat in the bedroom doorway, unmoving, as she waits for me to wake up. I rise, go over to her, I stand face to face with her and meet her eyes, and she has already vanished. She stands before me, but she isn't there any more, she looks at me and it is as if she looks through me, as if she were alone and I was merely a thought.

But there is another reason too for me to be thinking of that winter day in the Palais de Tokyo. As I walked up and down in the quiet gallery among Giacometti's bronze silhouettes, I suddenly felt a hand on my shoulder. When I turned round I saw Inès, standing there smiling at me. I hadn't seen her since I followed her with my eyes among the snowflakes, after we had said goodbye to each other. There were one or two grey threads in her inky black hair, and she was wearing glasses, but they only served to emphasise the Persian beauty of her eyes, and the slightly sharper, slightly deeper lines around her arrogant nose only strengthened the features I remembered so well, and which had once been the watermark of my sleepless nights. It was almost eight years ago. We made polite enquiries about each other's life, and I told her about Astrid and the children, rather cursorily, I felt, as we walked side by side under the plane trees beside the river. She walked as quickly as ever, with the same mercurial nervous gestures while she talked. When I turned towards her I could see the steel girders of the Eiffel Tower plaiting themselves in and out of the bare tree crowns behind her swift, registering glances. She said I looked older, and it suited me, and I smiled, unsure what to reply. We went into a café on the Place de l'Alma. We sat beside each other on a long upholstered bench from where you could look at the square. She had lived in Paris for a year or two, she might stay on. She told me she lived alone although I had not asked. She did not make clear what it was she did, a bit of everything, it seemed, just as before, money was obviously still not something she needed to worry about. It sounded a little lonely, a little aimless, although she took pains to sound like the anarchic, dissolute woman I had once known. I told her I wrote about art and she listened as if really interested. I grew a little bolder and talked of the difference it had made to have children, and she smiled at what I said, with a smile that could seem both sincere and sympathetic in a slightly condescending way, according to how I chose to interpret it, as if it was still demonstrably the fêted fluttering demi-mondaine who was now amusing herself with my new, bourgeois status as happy paterfamilias. Gradually we ran out of news, and in the increasingly long pauses I sat watching the waiters' mechanical, almost hysterically punctilious and effective movements, feeling her gaze resting on my face. She already knew I was a father. I looked at her. She was calmer than I remember, no longer afraid to hold a gaze, but her nostrils still widened a little when she smiled, and her teeth were as dazzling as before in her honey-coloured face. I couldn't really decide what it did to me to see her again, how deep the sight of her penetrated. She had once seen me in the street with Rosa in her buggy. She asked what my wife did, and I told her, a little abruptly. Now she was the one to watch the waiters officiously rushing around. She would like to have a child too. I looked at her in astonishment, and she read my expression and smiled at herself. Was that so strange? I didn't reply. I lit a cigarette and watched the passing silhouettes below the grey sky above the Place de l'Alma and felt her hand rest on mine, at first quite lightly and as if by chance, the dry warmth of her palm.

She had been about to call me several times during the winter we parted, and later, the next year, when she guessed I must have given her up. Of course she was not to know I had found someone else. Over the years she had realised what she had thrown away. Even though time had passed, she couldn't help thinking that it might have come to something with the two of us. She probably hadn't been very nice to me. I shrugged my shoulders, I expected I was as much to blame. She asked if I was happy. Yes, I said and replied to her glance, yes, I was happy, but I said it after a pause, as

if I had had to think about it. The word sounded wrong in
my mouth, 'happy'. That word was both too big and too
small, at the same time quiveringly ecstatic and too flat and
pastel-coloured to describe my life. She slowly stroked the
back of my hand, took it in hers and turned it palm upwards,
as if she were a gypsy who could tell my fortune. I let her
keep it and regarded it as it lay in hers on the seat beside
her knee, that shone faintly through the black tights under
the seam of her skirt. She too had met someone else, a year
or two after we parted, they had been together a long time,
and there had not been anyone else in that time. She smiled
again, now slightly tentatively. She had really tried. They
were still together on the afternoon she saw me in the street
with Rosa, but it didn't work out after all, and since then
she had sometimes thought of me, and not only because
she had seen me with my little daughter. She had thought
of that time. I had been very young, I had loved her so,
what should she say, so excessively. We both laughed at
the word. She had almost been obliged to guard herself,
defend herself against my young, ravenous love. I pressed
her hand kindly, and it made me feel old for a moment.
But no one else had loved her like that before and certainly
not since. So fearlessly. I took back my hand and lit a fresh
cigarette. She asked if I was busy. We might have dinner
together, she would be glad to cook. I looked at her again
and hesitated, until I came out with an excuse that was not
too feeble for us both to live with. We talked for a while of
Giacometti, of the ambiguous balance of the bronze figures
on the edge of absence. It sounded far-fetched. She wrote
down her phone number on a serviette before we left, and
when we were out in the noise and grey weather on the Place
de l'Alma she kissed me quickly and told me to ring if I had
time. I watched her as she ran down the steps to the metro
with her long black coat flapping, thinking that she had
not kissed me on the cheek, as you might have expected,

and of the feeling of her lips on mine, which I had almost forgotten.

On the way back to my hotel I congratulated myself for having refused Inès's invitation so resolutely, but I did not throw away the serviette with her number, as I had thought of doing. I left it on the bedside table among the day's receipts and loose change. Not until after we had parted had I realised in earnest that she had been fishing in a fairly uninhibited, even shameless way, all the more amazing considering we had not seen each other for eight years and only by an absurd coincidence had visited the Palais de Tokyo on the same afternoon. I had not even known she had moved to Paris. If I was indignant afterwards over her approaches, it was just as much because I had allowed myself to be influenced by them. But was there actually anything wrong in talking of the past or admitting that she looked back on it with regret or at least a touch of nostalgia? Wasn't it I who had immediately misinterpreted her hand, which she had laid on mine in mere friendship, her eyes, which with wondering familiarity had examined the changes in my face? Could she be blamed for my suddenly recurring memories of her knee and her lips? Perhaps not, but still, she must have known what she was doing. She could not but know that her words illuminated my version of the story from an unexpected, unforeseen angle. And she had not merely asked whether we should eat together, she had suggested dinner at her place. I could visualise it all too easily. Had she really thought about me? Had I not been the only loser in the game? Was it in reality I who had 'picked the longest straw'? It was a faded triumph, it had come too late. When she left me I felt only sorrow and disgust for myself, and since then Astrid had made me forget her, surprisingly quickly, it seemed to me now. But what if I had not met Astrid? What if the grizzled film director had not followed the taxi that evening I drove her and Simon to her friend in town? Then

she would have been merely another passenger who paid
and disappeared into a doorway out of sight. And what if
Inès had come to me in my sentimental solitude? Ought
I to have been more stubborn, more persevering, then,
since I loved her so immoderately? Could it have been
our child I was pushing in a buggy a few years later, as
I passed an unknown Astrid in the street, without giving
each other a glance? The idea was too perverse for me
to maintain for more than a second or two. Once again
I felt confused, thinking how little it would have taken
for my life to have turned out another way. The actual,
arbitrarily coincidental and mutually trivial circumstances
would merely have fallen into place in a slightly different way. The unnoticeable little displacements between my
thoughts, feelings and impulses need only have undergone
slightly other displacements and influences at a slightly
different time. What if one winter evening I had not left
the table without knowing precisely what I was doing, to
walk into my kitchen where Astrid stood with her back
to me, still only an unknown young woman whom I had
helped out of a jam? What if I had never put my hand on
her cheek? What if she had flinched away from my touch?

The cherished life that had been mine, in which I had
finally become myself, finally at home in the world, settled
in my love for Astrid and the children, was nothing more
than a blind, tentative shoot in time's desultory ramification
of possibilities. Neither more nor less in tune with my
innermost self than all the failed shoots that had withered
and fallen along the way. One single branch had grown
strong and put out new shoots, because we wanted it, and
because circumstances made it possible. Quite small devia-
tions in the blind growth of chance could have prevented
it ever coming to fruition. Yet perhaps there had been a
hidden, frightening connection between the withered and
the surviving shoots. When I stood in my kitchen one

winter evening and raised my hand to Astrid's cheek, it was also a rebellion against Inès, against the grievous state in which she had left me, and it was treachery against myself, against the passion I had been one with and which threatened to devour me from within. I saved myself, but only by betraying myself. I could only step over the imperceptible threshold of my new life by turning my back on the old one. I could only transform this in itself coincidental and random step towards the crossing of a threshold by convincing myself that there was a world of difference. Thus nor could I really know who it was that caressed Astrid's cheek and took her face between his hands. If it was the person who loved Inès so hopelessly and uncontrollably, his caress in the kitchen could not be totally sincere. And if it was a new and still unknown edition of myself who a few months later smiled calmly when Astrid told him he could be a father, shouldn't he perhaps have hesitated with his reckless *why not*? He should rather have considered why, but he still knew neither her nor himself well enough to know the answer too. He surprised me. Before I could look round they had become a family, he and the girl I had picked up in my taxi. It had come to me like an unexpected gift, and he accepted it before I had time to feel whether it was what I wanted. He had obviously settled into me for good, and I grew used to him speaking and acting in my place, until it was impossible to distinguish us from each other. Eight years later as I sat in my hotel room in Paris thinking of when I loved Inès, it was like thinking of someone else's love, and yet I had to ask, uneasily, with bated breath, if it was only myself I had betrayed, if I had not also betrayed Astrid.

I see her standing before me in the doorway of our bedroom with an expression that seems to see something I do not know, from within a place I do not recognise. I see Rosa sitting on the other side of the café window, out in the sunshine, looking away across the square, I have no idea at what. Her hair and her skin and her laughter were the living material proof of my love. It was her child's eyes that had made me into a father when I walked up and down with her in my arms, her little, weightless body, left entirely in my care. Her trusting look later, when I walked holding her hand beside the Lakes, and she suddenly stopped and asked me anxiously when time would come to an end, completely reliant on my reply. Now she was sitting at a café table smoking, remote and alone. When I saw her sitting there with her cup of coffee and her filter cigarette on the other side of her childhood, I had long since stopped comparing my brief young love for Inès with my love for Astrid. Time itself made the difference. As I sat behind my newspaper observing Rosa's profile in the sun outside, I recalled the story the museum curator had told me in the taxi the night before. Now as I thought about it in daylight it seemed to me grotesque and hard to believe. I could simply not imagine Astrid having a fling with my bald old student friend, not with him anyway. There was something distasteful, tacky, about his confiding in me, which made me want to clean my teeth. I should never be able to accept his offer of a little chewed-over sickening dollop of knowledge, dripping with saliva and vindictive vanity. I had to keep inside the boundary of what I knew, on the threshold of the bedroom, face to face with Astrid and everything I could not know. She looks at me, in her coat, with her packed suitcase, and I cannot imagine what she sees, through what she sees me. Perhaps she too has faltered between one step and the next, perhaps she too, in the imperceptible transitions on the way from one thing to another, has asked herself whether she was moving in the right direction or had lost her way without realising. And yet she did in fact go on, with only a faint shadow of doubt behind her eyes, as one day gave way to the next. Until she lay awake again in the darkness between the days, pushed a thought ajar and let the cold air waft in from the unknown, not quite certain if it really was herself lying beside me, or someone who just resembled her. Perhaps she also thought of the whirling fortuitousness of it all, and perhaps with the years she thought that it is not the roads and the faces that make a difference, the roads that open out to you all the time in all directions, the faces that approach you all the time and pass by. Perhaps with time she also came to think that it is only she herself who, step by step through days and years, goes to meet a difference. A difference that has never been written in her heart because it can only be written in footprints. Because her love doesn't care who she loves and why.

Some years ago when we were leaving a cinema together and I greeted Inès through the crowd, she had long since been merely an old, quenched flame which I burned myself on in my erring youth. But perhaps I had taken too long to realise it, perhaps I had realised it too late. Astrid noticed the beautiful, exotic looking woman who nodded and smiled briefly at me on the other side of the foyer before disappearing into the street, and she asked me who it was with casual curiosity, as if she was not really interested. I told her it was an old acquaintance, but I didn't say it was Inès. It may be that she guessed it, but it may also be that she didn't bother to wonder who the unknown woman might be. It was already a long time since I had told her about the lost love of my youth, it was a long time since we had stopped telling each other stories of our past, perhaps because it gradually took up so little space in comparison to our own story, perhaps because we really believed everything had been recounted. Why didn't I just say it was Inès? My concealment made me think much more about this fleeting encounter than I might have done if I had told her the woman in the cinema foyer with the hawk's nose and grey lines in her black hair was identical with the young woman who had once been the object of my stormy longings. I had told Astrid about her the summer after we met, when she was pregnant with Rosa, while we were still interrogating each other about everything that had preceded that winter evening when our lives took their decisive turn. We were in bed in our room in the house by the sea, Simon was asleep in the next room. Her face glimmered indistinctly in the blue half-light of the summer night, and I caressed her forehead and cheeks as if I could brush away the fine dust grains of twilight from them, just as I brushed the sand from her calves and feet. I described, hesitantly to begin with, how I had abased myself, devoured from within by jealousy, how I had spied on Inès and besieged her until she could no longer breathe in my presence, and I did it in such an ironic and distanced manner that my very tone of voice told her that it was not just a past chapter but also a delusion, an infatuated dream, out of which she, Astrid, had woken me. She listened to me with a thoughtful, crooked smile as if wondering that I could really have been so crazed and beside myself with frenzied passion. She seemed almost fascinated by my account and questioned me on apparently irrelevant details, and I allowed myself to be swept along, I depicted and exaggerated the portrait of the passionate madman I had been until I noticed a flicker in her eyes as if she was forcing herself far too much to look at me. I kissed her and said I loved her, it was not until I started living with her that I had learned to love, because she had released me from my self-absorbed phantoms. She crept close to me and whispered in my ear not to say any more, it wasn't necessary. She took my face between her hands and looked at me with tender, veiled eyes in the twilight. 'We are here, you know,' she whispered. 'Isn't that enough?' I caressed her warm body until I could see she was ready, and entered her, cautiously at first, because I recalled the evening when she had stood at the top of the steps calling me, with the blood trickling down her legs, but she merely smiled and told me not to be afraid. It wasn't a disease, after all. Afterwards we lay there quietly, still twined into each other, listening to the waves breaking under the window, their abrupt fall and the sucking, purling sound when they withdrew.

On that winter evening in Paris when I sat watching the light fall behind the shutters until it was only a dark blue remnant at the bottom of the darkness of the room, I regretted having let Inès kiss me goodbye and disappear into the metro below the Place de l'Alma. I had been alarmed at the thought that I might succumb to her nostalgic luring tones as a kind of delayed revenge, as if in spite of everything I could pick apples from a branch I myself had sawn off. As I sat there in the growing darkness, again looking into Inès's eyes behind her strange new glasses, seconds before we parted in the grey winter light, I felt a desire to take a step aside from my course, to draw her to me and breathe in the scent of what had never come to anything. I felt like spending one night in the world that was no longer there, sinking away into her for one night, locked between her arms and legs in an old fury, until she would finally let go and I would finally feel my old anger had left me. Perhaps I really believed that I would be able to lay to rest the old ghost by embracing it. Perhaps it was only my dormant anonymous desire persisting in my imagination because she had so unexpectedly offered herself to me. My short-sighted, insatiable and unscrupulous lust, that was perhaps the banal truth behind all the masks of sensitivity. Her answering machine was switched on. I listened to her melodious, sensual voice speaking French to all and sundry, and only when the bleep was followed by silence, my own silence, did I discover I had walked into a trap. No matter what I said, and regardless of how casually I said it, she would realise why I called. A single sentence, even the most banal and offhand, would be enough to betray me, betray Astrid, betray my new life, my new, cherished self-assurance, that had given me the courage to pick up the receiver and dial the number on the serviette, which I should have crumpled up and thrown away while there was still time. Even if I let her understand, in the most neutral and reserved manner, that I wasn't averse to the idea of seeing her again, I would risk my desire shining through. With a few apparently innocent sentences on her answering machine I would have given her proof that I too had lost my way in the ramified wilderness of chance, that my life with Astrid and the children was after all merely a resigned capitulation to whatever had been possible, whatever had panned out, after she left me. It would have been Inès who had remained faithful to our sincere, young love, and I who had forsaken it because I had not had the courage to suffer and wait, and who now, when she stretched out a hand, seized it immediately, wet with tears of gratitude and foaming with pent-up passion.

I had just put down the receiver when the telephone rang. I let it ring once or twice before picking it up. It was Astrid. She wanted to know what time I would be landing the following day, and if I wanted to be met at the airport. She asked if anything was wrong. I myself thought my voice sounded completely normal. I said I had been asleep when she called. I told her about the exhibition I had seen and she repeated an amusing comment Rosa had made that morning. Suddenly I missed all three of them terribly, and she laughed at how fond I could be on the phone, just because we hadn't seen each other for a couple of days. I soon forgot about my meeting with Inès, and when I occasionally remembered it at intervals of a few weeks I felt surprised to have forgotten it as quickly as at the sight of her I had allowed myself to be overwhelmed by doubts and nagging questions. If I occasionally lay sleepless at night listening to Astrid's peaceful breathing beside me in the dark, it was not because I was haunted by Inès and her eyes and lips one afternoon in the Place de l'Alma. Nor was it because I imagined it to be Inès lying beside me in the dark, in a different apartment somewhere else in town, in another life. It was not the reunion that had shaken me, it was its after-effects, not the passing fit of desire in my Paris hotel room when I dialled her telephone number, but the unexpectedly chill light that had been thrown onto my present life, my sudden irresolution in the dull grey light over the Place de l'Alma. It was these sudden dizzy attacks of weightlessness that kept me awake and made me turn towards Astrid's invisible face and put an arm around her sleeping body, as if I was afraid of levitating from the bed and drifting away into the bottomless night.

I haven't been alone since she turned up one winter evening holding a little boy by the hand and got into the back seat of my taxi, and it is even longer since she herself was last alone. She was young when she had Simon, and she had been still younger when she met a grizzled man with confident hands and an insistent gaze that seemed to mould her when he looked at her and embraced her. She had smiled, the young woman, at his adult melodramatic desire, but in the end she had given way, maybe tired of playing hide and seek, maybe because she longed to be seen. She had been almost invisible when he caught sight of her. She had still been a child when she spent the summer holidays with an aunt who one morning told her that her parents had driven over the edge of a cliff in Italy. The rest of her childhood had been spent at a boarding school, until at last she was free to do what she wanted, but she was at a loss what to do with all that freedom. She was alone in the world, all confused by the thought of everything that was possible, bewildered at the sight of the countless ways opening up to her, the crowd of faces coming towards her, and she had not yet decided on anything at all when the grizzled film director cast his eyes upon her. No one could tell her who she was, no one was going to come and tell her that. At the beginning it had amused her that she could drive a grown

man crazy to such an extent, and later it had fascinated her to
be the secret in his life, invisible to all others and sometimes
also to him when she closed her eyes while he clasped her,
beside himself with passion. Until, that is, she decided she
wanted to come into view, perhaps because she was afraid
of disappearing completely if she kept on giving him the slip,
she, the precious secret he was so clever at keeping hidden
from his wife and his daughter. She could have been his
daughter herself, and yet she gave in when he grew tired
of his mystery mongering and one day appeared at her door
with his suitcases and his dramatic gaze. She thought that
after all it might be love, what had begun as a secret chase
where the young prey roused the old hunter with her wondering or absent-minded smile. She convinced herself it must
be love, and she stood by her decision once she had taken it.
She adapted herself to it, as she adapted herself to being with
the little boy and his father in the white house in the northern
part of town, and she let time pass. To begin with she did
not think anything of it when her grizzled husband came
home later and later, and when one evening she discovered
why, there was a long moment when she just fell and fell, in
a bottomless and endless descent. When she felt the floorboards
under her feet again she was not in the same world as before.
They had not lived in the same world, she and the grizzled
film director. It was not her, it couldn't be her, this young
woman who had borne their child and cared for it, while
he was in another part of town with another, still younger
woman, and the only thing she knew was that she could not
stay an hour longer in a house grown suddenly so alien.

   She didn't belong anywhere when she sat on the back
seat of a taxi with her little son, but she had tried that
before. Perhaps that was why she hesitated only for a
moment when the taxi driver offered her refuge in his flat for
a few days. For he seemed nice enough, they were even about
the same age. So she stayed on there. She must have asked

herself later how it had happened, how she caught sight of him, why he was suddenly not merely a helpful taxi driver whose flat happened to be empty at night. Did such things happen, just like that? To begin with it did not mean anything, and that may have been why she gave herself to him, because it did not need to mean anything. He was only a chance taxi driver, to him she could be anyone at all. He was in no hurry to tell her who she was, he let her think what she pleased while he embraced her. He wasn't out to abduct her, he was not going anywhere in particular, the man who drove all over town every night. She may have asked herself if it might not be dangerous when she discovered she was pregnant, but she couldn't help smiling when she had told him and he merely looked at her calmly and said *why not?* Yes, she may have thought, why not, actually? It was his calmness, she told him later, it was that which had convinced her, when instead of being seized with panic he merely looked at her like someone who knew what he was doing. She had to love a man who could look her in the eyes so calmly, a completely strange woman who confided to him that she could make him a father if he felt like it. His astonishing *why not* made her forget to ask herself why it should be precisely him. She had to love a man who dared take the chance when it occurred because he knew that in any case it was coincidental who you ran into and when, and because he dared believe it might be now his life should take shape, and not next year or the following one. It was not until it had happened, after the decisive step had been taken, blindly, that her love discovered its reasons. To begin with she just liked his eyes, his eyes and his calm voice, such a chance thing. She told him once, and he smiled. 'Yes,' he said, 'it doesn't matter why one loves.' One morning she woke when he spoke her name in his soft, calm voice, and she had opened her eyes and discovered that it was here she belonged, in his calm gaze that seemed to completely encircle her on all sides. His affectionate, slightly melancholy eyes seemed to open a great space around her in which she could be herself, in which she could run as hard, as far, as she wanted without disappearing. But she no longer had any wish to run, as she had run when she was young, when yet another smitten puppy or yet another desperate grown man thought they ought to tell her who she was and mould her features with their lustful hands. When she was young she had believed she was someone else inside, a strange person that only a strange, unknown man would be able to recognise. She had deserted one man after another, young or mature, out of disappointment because clearly he was not the one who could lure this beautiful unknown into the light. Whoever should it have been? She laughed at herself as she described her young restlessness. As time went on she could not think about who she was without thinking of the life that had become hers that winter evening when she left the grizzled film director because she had discovered she no longer lived in the world she had believed she lived in. Everything before that evening gradually seemed to her like loose, obliterated, rejected sketches for what was to come. But it is many years ago since she talked to me in that way about herself. It became unnecessary to talk so much. After all, we were there and that was enough.

I cannot unravel our first years, I cannot distinguish between them. Even when I unwind the years into the long thread of the narrative, and no matter how much my story winds backwards and forwards between then and now, there is a difference in the thread and the ball of yarn. Even if the ball is made up of the same thread it is not in itself a story. It is merely a huge globe of compressed days and places that supplant each other, so the innermost ones have long since disappeared into the soft darkness of the ball. As I gradually unwind the thread into the light the ball grows smaller and smaller, and it loses its weight, until only the weightless line of the narrative is left, the line's long series of continuous points that twist and turn in my attempt to interpret the years' convolutions and entanglements, round and round, the years turning around themselves in time with the earth's perpetual spinning rotation of repetition and change. It's funny how you always talk about time as if it is a place where you move back and forth. Perhaps it really is a place, the place where all days and hours exist beside each other, perhaps you tell your story in order to find a way through memory's labyrinth of moments separated by oblivion. But there are several ways through its crooked paths, and if you go one way you cut yourself off from all the others. You make your way into the labyrinth while unrolling your ball of wool, and when it runs out you have only a loose end to hold on to. Slowly you return, tracking down yourself. Now and then you hear voices behind the thin walls of the dark, now and then you see a gleam of light where you thought there was only a wall, but you keep to the track, afraid of dropping the thread and getting lost. In my memory I am everywhere at the same time, at each single moment, remembered or forgotten, not quite the same from place to place. In my story I can only be in one place at a time if I am to find the way between the places and discover how I went from one place to another.

Rosa leaned her head back and closed her eyes in the sunshine, so her long hair fell softly over the back of her chair. I imagined her sensing the light like an orange fog through her eyelids, listening to the clicking footsteps of the passers-by and the voices around her at the other tables. When you close your eyes you are in the midst of everything. The sounds of the world and your own thoughts blend with each other in the same invisible space. There was the hint of a smile in the corners of her mouth, it was either the warmth on her face that made her smile or something she was thinking of. She raised a hand and stroked her neck, as slowly as a caress, and I recognised the movement, Astrid did that too when she was thinking, at the same time self-forgetful and yet sunk into herself. I too closed my eyes for a moment and it seemed to bring us closer together. Why couldn't I just get up and go out to her, why were we sitting here each on our own side of the wide café windows, my daughter and her father? I was ashamed of hiding from her, but I knew it would also be somehow shaming to go outside and meet her gaze. I was ashamed of Astrid leaving me. If sometimes, when the darkness was too dense or too bottomless, I had had to embrace the sleeping Astrid, afraid of slipping away from her, a single look from Rosa had always been enough to confirm where I belonged, that it was here my home was, not merely some random point on the globe. Her gaze had held me fast like the invisible cord of a kite, and she didn't even know it herself, in her eyes I was the one who held the cord, so she could safely shoot up into the air and explore the heavens. When I was in the labour room with her light, new-born body wrapped in a blanket, I was overcome by a crazily nervous fear of dropping her, and I mumbled the same words in my head as I had spoken out into the summer night when I sat between the rose bushes on the steps to the beach, *hold on*. When I opened my eyes again she was looking over at the glittering jets of the fountain as the wind whipped them, so the water blew sideways in a scattered snowstorm of shining drops and foam, ceaselessly renewed, constantly vanishing in the same pulsing movement. I had held on. Now it was time to let go.

I saw her red-haired friend come up the stairs from the toilets and approach among the tables. She had put on lipstick and her red mouth resembled a sharp, freely hovering sign in her pale freckled face. She caught sight of me and smiled faintly. I smiled back and held her gaze as she came nearer and passed, and I managed to register a faint blush under her freckles before she glided out of my field of vision. If I had looked away at once when she saw me, my embarrassment would have betrayed that my gaze was not by chance. Now it was her turn to be embarrassed, because I had reciprocated her fleeting, cheerful smile with eyes that read her face with interest. Perhaps she had smiled because it had occurred to her in passing that the man reading the paper in the corner actually looked rather good. Perhaps she had sunned herself for a second in my attentive gaze and at the edge of her consciousness touched on the thought that I was a man and not just a man who could be her father, at which she had immediately pulled in her antennae, afraid I might have interpreted her smile as encouragement. Perhaps, and now it was my turn to blush, perhaps she knew I was Rosa's father, perhaps she had blushed because my glance was a disconcerting transgression of role-play. I made use of the newspaper again and stole a glance like an observant cat's past the headlines at the two girls in the sun. If the red-haired one knew who I was she gave no sign of it to Rosa. Again they took it in turns to speak and nod or smile at what the other said, and at one point, when I once more felt reasonably comfortable with the situation, she suddenly looked past Rosa and in through the window, and briefly caught my eye. She did this once or twice more, as if she wanted to assure herself I was still there, keeping an eye on her. My eyes roamed restlessly around the headlines and I was conscious of every single twitch in my face. A little later when I looked up from the paper again they had gone, and I sat on looking out at the cups they had left, Rosa's friend's with a faint red impression of her underlip on the edge like a greeting to my forty-four-year-old confusion.

I walked along Strøget, the pedestrianised street, into the evening sunshine, which made the human crowd melt together and branch out again in a black, strolling forest of silhouettes with long shadows plaited into each other on the dazzling flagstones. The low sunshine in the gap between the façades ate its way into the silhouettes in the backlight, frail and tenuous as Giacometti's bronze figures. The light dazzled me so I could not see the faces in the black stream of figures before they took the last step towards me and stepped out of their dark outline with a look that brushed mine, the second before we passed each other. I felt that at each step I passed through another's gaze, to be succeeded a moment later by the one walking behind me, just as the strange faces were transformed in front of my eyes when they came to meet me in turn, out of the shadows. It was as if they not only passed me, but also passed through me, just as I in turn passed through their eyes in the same movement into the light, the same rhythm of footsteps and rocking faces, where I constantly caught sight of another, myself ceaselessly seen by another and again another, as if I too could not remain the same for more than a glance, a second at a time.

5

I left the hotel and rambled around the streets between Fifth Avenue and Times Square, in the crowd of pedestrians between the buildings with their vertical slabs of lit windows and the horizontal stream of car lights. I observed the faces passing through the islands of light in the darkness, new faces all the time, strangers as I was in this city where everyone comes from somewhere else. It is the only strange city where at each step I take I am not reminded that I am a foreigner, where my accent and my appearance are only yet another difference between all the differences that counterbalance each other. If the taxi drivers and bartenders and waitresses get impatient with me it is not because they regard me as a foreigner but because they consider me to be a New Yorker who is merely intolerably slow or indecisive or awkward. In New York I can be whoever I wish, as long as I don't forget to give a tip. That evening I calmed myself down by drifting along with now one, now another stream of pedestrians in the grid plan of streets. Fatigue acted as a local anaesthetic, only my sight and my hearing were exempt from the pleasant feeling of lethargy, and everything I saw and heard were repetitions of something I had seen and heard before, the car horns, the disconnected words, the shining buildings and the river of faces. It was like stepping into a film I had seen hundreds of times, the same street scene that appears in all the films set in New York, but without leading me from one scene to the next, rather as if the film ran in loops and I myself moved on the spot. As I went on without stopping I saw the city twist and turn around me, it was the city that moved and I observed it, passive and unmoving, from a far distant place in myself.

I thought of all the people who had come here, driven by flight from something or driven by a vague hope of something else, who had walked the same streets I walked now, in the same deep chasms that opened up to each other at right angles between the square, unapproachable buildings. Once again it struck me that this city, which has attracted so many people from every corner of the world, does not itself have a visible, noticeable centre like those of European cities in which the streets, if you walk through them long enough, always meet at the same point. Old, sooty, mysterious cities where you arrive one evening by train and soon after leaving the station come face to face with the illuminated apostles and saints on the façade of the cathedral. Here all the railways are underground. When you have first arrived you can merely float around the streets crossing each other at regular intervals. In itself the city does not give you a feeling of having arrived at the enchanted, perspectival vanishing point of dreams and hopes. In reality it is an invisible city, its streets no more than the invisible netted screen in the travellers' inner image of the places they have left and may have lost for ever. New York is only visible to those who observe the city through the faded transparent memory of the wheat plains of Ukraine or Armenia's mountains, a slum district of corrugated iron in Puerto Rico or the inundated rice fields of Guangdong. It is so easy to find your way here, yet in a subtle way you can get lost because the square monotony of the city plan does not help you to trace what it really was you were looking for. But that evening it suited me perfectly, I was not doing anything that evening. I ate at a diner on 52nd Street, one of those merciful, functional places where you can eat on a bar stool at a long counter without feeling embarrassed because you are on your own without a companion. I sat looking out at the traffic behind the mirror-imaged beer ads of red neon rods in the window, behind the pane's blurred reproduction of my silhouette in the garishly lit window, bent over on the bar stool, transparent, so the passers-by on the pavement seemed to walk right through me, homeless beggars with outstretched cardboard beakers, beautiful busy women of all races. I looked at my watch, added on six hours and tried to recall precisely what I had been doing at the same time the previous evening.

I had been standing in a corner of the stage with my back to the empty seats in the auditorium, watching my mother's rubbery, red-painted lips that revealed her sparkling white crowns in the smile of a beast of prey every time someone came up to kiss her cheek during the little *nachspiel* after her première, which she had called to remind me about on the evening I had Rosa and her installation artist to dinner. She had been just as self-conscious and theatrical on stage as usual, and as usual the cackling, maniacally affected gays and exalted prima donnas with roving eyes flocked around her to avow how absolutely wonderfully and superbly she had once again surpassed herself in sophisticated, expressive insight. If she had ever had even mediocre talent it had long ago been lost through her insatiable hunger to be loved by her audience, who had laughed and wept gratefully and emotionally down there in the dark for years, thankful that with her raffish and frivolous grimaces she sanctioned their coarse, low comedy sense of humour, and moved that with her crocodile tears and her heaving, ample bosom she raised their trivial and sentimental passions to fateful and universal stories of Great Love. Formerly her wasp waist and deep, shadowy cleavage had ensured her one role after another as a weak and enchanting woman at the mercy of her emotions, and on the whole she was an ideal example of the belief that what you lack in your head you must have between your legs, which one theatre director after another had in fact had the opportunity to confirm. In the end age had forced her to take 'mature parts', but this had merely made the critics discover new and subtle sides of her talent, purified by the humble wisdom of experience. The thought of growing old filled her with terror, and she was still too stupid to comprehend a word of the dialogue she bawled and wailed her way through, but when her nearest rival on the boards was disabled by a thrombosis, the role of *grande dame* of the theatre became vacant, and it fell to her because there were no other suitable candidates.

As I sat in the dark watching her sloppy gestures in the bright footlights, my reasons for never going to the theatre were once more confirmed, and I regretted not having stayed at home. But after I had seen Rosa and her red-haired friend vanish into the crowd and at long last had gone home from my walk, the evening had opened up before me in the silent apartment, empty and dull, and I had seized on my mother's première as a feeble excuse for pretending everything was normal for an hour or two. Now I wished I was back at my desk staring blindly at the lighted windows in the façades on the other side of the lake. My father sat a little further along the row, he had already fallen asleep five minutes into the first act. He had been in the foyer, alone in the high-spirited first-night crowd of sweating men who clearly felt uncomfortable in their newly pressed funeral garb, and their wives, who looked all the while as if they were about to collapse even though their long Thai silk dresses were consistently ten centimetres too short. My father was as elegant as ever, scanning the foyer with his customary nervous gaze, more suited to an insecure teenager than a distinguished septuagenarian. I felt sorry for him when I saw how relieved he was to catch sight of me, and at the same time ashamed of my own sympathy. Not until we had stood chatting for some minutes did I notice he had forgotten to ask why Astrid was not with me. Perhaps he had spoken to my mother, perhaps he was glad that for once there were only the two of us, or else he was merely distrait. No one would be surprised that he was on his own. My mother despised his new wife, she had made no secret of that on the few occasions she had met her, and her contempt for her ex-husband was all the greater because he was satisfied with such an inferior substitute when she herself had ditched him. She couldn't care less whether he came to her premières or not, but even though it was almost thirty years since she had left him he kept on turning up, furtive and conscientious, 'to make her happy', as he said.

I seldom saw him. He had moved to the other end of Denmark a few years before I met Astrid and the distance had made it easier to refuse his invitations. I visited him several summers in a row with Astrid and the children, and each spring he rang again and asked if we would be coming in the summer, but after each visit I had found it hard to be friendly towards his new wife, a potter who was twenty years younger than him and interested in astrology and bio-dynamic vegetables. When we went to visit them in their little thatched pancake house she fell upon me as if she hadn't spoken to a civilised person for months, and excitedly insisted that I must justify why, many years ago in an article, I had written that craft could not be on the same footing as art. Out of consideration for my father I refrained from telling her what I thought of her clumsy and very ethnic pots and bowls, a reticence that only made her persist further and in a victorious voice explain my cold and distant arrogance by saying I was a typical Scorpio. But I might have lived with her aggressive inferiority complexes and her musk-plant scented, esoteric provincialism if I had not had to put up with being a passive witness to my distinguished father subjecting himself like a whipped dog to her wayward and neurotic mood swings, whether she

explained them by the moon's phases or his masculine
lack of feeling for her bio-rhythms. My father had been
an engineer before retiring, he had built bridges and dams
in Africa and the Middle East, and now he spent his time
lighting incense candles and serving herbal tea for his holistic
partner and giving her Tibetan foot massages and fondling
her astral body while allowing her to instruct him in her
twaddle about the emotional life of plants. I was not resigned
to his choice until Astrid with a crooked smile once made me
aware that in my rage I had quite overlooked the fact that
he was apparently happy. I think she was right, and perhaps
the leap was not after all so great from his old blind faith in
mathematics to his new ecological piety, both were carried
by the same resolutely radical consistency, the same fear
of life's irony and unanswered questions. In my view his
new marriage was a parody of his marriage to my mother,
only with the difference that the degradation was no longer
painful, merely ludicrous. Behind the concrete engineer's
masculine exterior a kind but nervous heart always beat, in
its loneliness pleading to be loved, naïvely believing that it
was something he could deserve. When I was a child he sent
me postcards from towns with strange names, and I kept the
cards with African or Arabic themes in a box under my bed.
He was always engaged in building a bridge or a dam or a
power station somewhere or other in a tropical country,
often he was away for months at a time, and every morning
I sat feeling the porridge oats swelling in my mouth while
waiting to hear the clatter of the letter box and the soft slap
on the hall floor. I have kept one of his cards, which I find
particularly moving today. It is not the aerial photograph in
itself that moves me, the sunny view over a tongue of land
densely built up with white high-rise blocks surrounded by
the improbably blue sea. Nor is it his laconic note on the
back about the temperature and his own well-being, dated
9th October 1965. It is the printed text, in small type above

his faded handwriting: *Beirouth Moderne, Vue générale et les grands Hôtels de la Riviera Libanaise.*

I learned from early on to look after myself, my mother always slept late, and when I came home from school, she had usually gone to a rehearsal or was 'on the radio', if she was not resting behind the closed door of their bedroom with the curtains closed. My school friends' mothers were always ready in their suburban homes wearing their aprons with hot cocoa in the pan, but she lolled on the unmade bed reading the paper with a cigarette in the corner of her mouth, unapproachable and blowsy in a dissolute way that offended my puritan boyish mind. We did not meet until the evening when at long last she emerged from her boudoir, heavy with sleep and provocatively voluptuous in her open kimono, to heat up a tin of soup or a thawed ready-to-eat dish for us before vanishing again to 'get ready' before she left me to my own company and took a taxi to the theatre. Only when she gave interviews to 'the magazines' did she tidy the house in a rush so it looked like a home for once, when we were to be photographed together, she bending over slightly, with her chin pressed into my hair so the photographer had the benefit of both my plump childish cheeks and her equally bulging bosom. Even I have to admit she was beautiful then, unnervingly beautiful when she leant over me, powdered and with her hair piled up, to kiss me goodbye before she walked down the garden path to the waiting taxi, her high heels clicking, her hips rocking in her narrow skirt. Her beauty had the effect of a vague and incalculable threat, it alienated her from me because it was so clearly meant for others, and when she bent to kiss me on the cheek with her soft, full lips, her perfume and her white, domed breasts in the low-necked dress made me feel like an ugly little manikin who, undeservedly and as a specially divine grace, was brushed for a moment by the murderously gentle light of a world in which I would never get on. We seldom talked for very long, and if we did, it was usually in the form of a continued monologue, as if she was thinking aloud just because I happened to be there, when she sighed and said how hard it was, how everyone harassed her so much, and how sometimes she felt like 'running away screaming'. I visualised and heard it, how she ran along the suburban road, screaming, in her petticoat and with hair flying. I am not exaggerating when I say that my mother's communicativeness towards me in extent and content more or less corresponded to what my father found room for on the backs of his postcards with camels, Bedouin tents, minarets, elephants and African villages. Terse, brief messages which apart from observations about the weather merely stated that he was well and hoped I was well too, and that he was looking forward to seeing me again. Only seldom did he go any deeper and then merely with the vague assurance that he 'was thinking of me'. I never got to know what he thought when he was thinking of me. But it never occurred to me to reproach him for his shy brevity. I took it as a proof of his indisputable and sovereign masculinity, engaged as he was with his bridges and dams and power stations, which in my eyes he constructed almost with his own bare fists, with a stubbled chin and tropical helmet and exerting inhuman feats of strength, as, dogged and unswerving, he defied the baking sun and wild animals and the incorrigible laziness of the natives. In the evening I lay in bed imagining that one day he would take me with him, how we would leave my slut of a mother to her afternoon sleep and her theatre, how I would stand on the desert sand and pass him the monkey wrench, and how, dripping with sweat and paying no heed to me he would take it and with muscles playing would tighten the last nut in a steel bridge across a godforsaken wadi in the white-hot heart of the Sahara.

The day before he was to return from his engineering exploits there was a dramatic change. Instead of spending the afternoon in bed my mother was seized by sudden energy, she stormed around the house putting things to rights and vacuum-cleaning, she beat sofa cushions and aired the rooms, and what during the past weeks had come to resemble a brothel after closing time, was transformed in the course of a couple of hours into a solid, bourgeois home of the kind I envied my schoolmates. For the first time in weeks she went shopping and exhibited a hitherto unsuspected gastronomic potential, and when my father finally stood in the doorway, sun-tanned and fabulous, she flew to him and flung her arms around him, clasping him so hard that in the end he had to laughingly release himself from her amorous embrace. For one single evening I was in heaven, the calm cloudless heaven of bourgeois life, and my mother and I sat at the table listening with smiles and wonderment to his stories of exotic lands. For once my mother's dazzling beauty was not a threat, and I did not find it at all painful when I saw her kissing my father, putting her arm round his waist and stroking his bottom seductively. She played that role too, so not an eye was dry, but as early as the next day she began to be irritable, and I saw how my father, the bridge-builder, the turbine constructor, the imperturbable concrete expert, had to exert himself to please her and receive even a single casual caress. Again she retreated to her bedroom in the afternoons, and when he came home she produced dinner sullenly and grudgingly from what was in the fridge, and his gentle voice and entreating eyes only made her still more distant and short-tempered. When she had gone off to the theatre we took refuge on the sofa, in Kipling's, Cooper's and Stevenson's world of palpable dangers and simple virtues, but more than once I saw him, through the half-open door of my room, after he had said goodnight, sitting with his whisky in the living room gazing into the air, alone in his own home, and I listened to the ice cubes chinking in his glass and how they hit his teeth as he downed his drink. Sometimes I woke in the night to hear them quarrelling on the other side of the wall. I must have been about thirteen when I slowly discovered what went on. To begin with there were only forebodings I could barely put into words, when he had gone away again and I heard her behind the door of their bedroom, whispering on the telephone with a strange, ingratiating voice, or when it was not a taxi but a private car waiting for her in front of the terraced house. Several times she rang home in the evening, suddenly very affectionate, and asked if it mattered if she stayed in town with a friend, after all I was 'so big now', and anyway I was used to getting up alone in the morning. One evening I had told her that I was staying the night with a friend I often visited not only to play, but also to be surrounded for at least an hour or two by a little homely everyday life. But during dinner my chum suddenly got stomach ache, and I was sent home. In the night I was woken by the sound of my mother's low laughter on the other side of the wall. At first I thought she was laughing in her sleep, or I had dreamed it, but when I heard her sighing continuously and rhythmically, I was about to go in to her, convinced that she must have fallen ill like my friend, an epidemic might have broken out, but I stayed in my bed when I heard a deeper groan blending with her half-stifled, intermittent sighing. In the morning I cautiously opened the door of her room slightly, she was asleep alone in the wide bed, and on my way to school I was almost sure that it had been only a dream.

As time went on she did less and less to hide her unfaithfulness, or else I learned to interpret her manoeuvres, because inadvertently she had lifted a corner of the veil that covered her secret, profligate life. Just as she had left me to my own company, now I started to leave her to hers, and when I was not with a friend I went into town and roamed around. It was thus, by chance and almost from boredom, in the winter, when it was too cold in the streets and the parks, that I began to visit the museums and gradually became aware of the motionless and mute universe of pictures, where my gaze could release itself from my nagging thoughts and give itself up to the forms of light and shade, the presence of faces and places. In the museums I could be in peace, no one spoke to me, no one turned their back on me, and there were days when I played truant to sit in the quiet galleries and allow my gaze to lose itself in the hermetic landscapes and halted events, the unchanging moments outside time of portraits and still-lifes. I sat for hours at a time until there was no longer any distance between my eyes and the mythological gestures of naked figures surrounded by clouds and flowing cloaks, no marked transition between my thoughts and the azure blue sea behind the closed shutters in a dark room where someone had left a violin. Although the pictures had been painted at greatly varying dates, and although they opened their frames on to widely different sceneries, they always left me with the same both evident and surprising idea, that the world did not consist of different, mutually separated places, that the world was one single connected place, which was merely very large. It was at that time I began to see things as they are, literally, as it were, precisely as if the world was syllabic, as if it consisted of syllables, of the light's vowels and the shadows' consonants. I observed dead things and forgot the time. I stopped listening to what people said. It worried them, I could see, encouraged by my own indifference to their disoriented expressions. I didn't care whether they understood me or not, and I stopped making an effort to make myself understandable. I stopped doing my homework, but could still give random answers to this and that without completely failing. They wanted answers to everything, and I made a half-hearted attempt out of politeness, until I began to answer by coming out with the same sentence: 'I don't want to answer.' Giggles sounded around me. 'Did I

not want to answer?' The teachers' injured feelings and anger
took me by surprise, for the simpler I made things for myself,
the more complicated everything became. One morning one
of them stopped me in the corridor and, leaning against the
row of hooks holding damp coats, looked at me doubtfully.
Did I intend to go to seed at the age of thirteen? I couldn't
help liking him for the expression and smiled pleasantly
as I informed him that I was only twelve. He turned up
his eyes and said he was going to weep, but he didn't.

I sat at my table in the classroom reading the names of
those who had sat there before me and carved their runes
in the varnish. I gazed at the world map of waxed canvas
unrolled in front of the chalk clouds and sloping rows of
meaningless numbers and signs. Africa resembled a buggy
that was tipped forwards, and my own country looked
like a pixie with a cold, speaking admonishingly to his
children while the wind blows down his neck. I did not
think of my father any more, he was far away beneath
the cruel sun among concrete mixers and building cranes,
while his wife opened her legs for her unknown lovers.
I imagined sandstorms, the monsoon that whipped the
palm leaves, the deltas, the lake villages, the deep clefts
in the mountain chains, the long drawn-out wailing from
the minarets in towns where you slept on the roof. I no
longer took part in the community, I had quite simply
forgotten the necessary words, the ordinary exchange of
information about family conditions and holiday plans that
make people trust each other. Even love slowly released
its hold on me. There was a girl in my class who had
breasts, pointed and very obvious behind the tight cotton
blouses she wore. She sat in the row in front of mine,
sway-backed, with her elbows on the desk. Her fair pony
tail brushed the skin of her neck, and her shoulder blades
were outlined under the white cotton like folded wings
around the dotted line of her vertebrae, which disappeared

into her trousers lining, the waist pulled tight with a belt over the reversed heart shape of her pelvis and bottom, a swelling, pale blue, washed-out heart. Her eyes were blue and her earnest beauty made me think she would be able to understand me better than anyone else, if I could only find the right words. I imagined her blue eyes would be able to see things just as I saw them, things as they were. I had been to her home with some of the others, we had sat on the floor drinking tea and listening to music. There was always a bright lad who could say something funny, and I watched her as she laughed her pretty laughter at the brainless cracks. I was the last to leave, we sat opposite each other while the empty turntable rotated and the candles burned down. Words were a barrier between us, a gigantic building with empty rooms where we would never be able to find each other. I had danced with her once, at a party. We 'danced on the spot' in the half darkness, as you dance to slow numbers, close, and I could feel her through her clothes and breathe in the perfume of her newly washed hair, but I did not know how my hands should advance from their prescribed places on her hips, she was so near and yet so far. One afternoon, after I had begun to be eccentric, she caught me up on the way home from school. We stood by the wire fencing of the school sports ground. She asked what the matter was, why I avoided them. Behind her the grass spread out like a steppe between the empty goalposts. She was an envoy, she had not come of her own accord, 'they' had sent her because they had noticed what her blue eyes did to me. Her breasts pointed scornfully at me in their clean, soft cotton whiteness. The conversation was a gift of charity, her blue eyes gazing at me, a conspiracy. I looked at the grass. I was always surprised by the enormous distances on the field when we went out there in our shorts and the others spread out and grew small around me on the green space. I avoided the ball as far as possible, and when on rare occasions it landed where I was, I left it willingly to my nearest opponent. I stood there watching her vanish on her bicycle between the horse chestnut trees of the suburban avenue, I watched the moving light flashing at regular intervals on her white back, treacherously.

I don't know if I had really expected my father to intervene in my mother's flagrant unfaithfulness, or what I had imagined he might do. Throw the china about? Beat her? Cut her throat with the Arabian dagger he had brought home for me, and then stab himself in the stomach with it? She grew ever more careless with her subterfuges and digressions, even when he was at home, but he took no notice of anything except at night, when he thought I was asleep, and he waited up for her. I heard him through my door when she had at last come home and he voiced his pathetic, humiliating questions. If she answered him at all it was with anger or jibes. Once I heard her say that if he went on with his ludicrous jealousy she would have to take a lover to satisfy him. As a rule the nightly scenes ended with her going into their bedroom and slamming the door behind her, and shortly afterwards I heard him in there, presumably sitting on the edge of the bed, if he wasn't actually kneeling, despondently begging her to forgive him and assuring her of his deep love. At other times she left the house and he again sat in the living room with his whisky and cigarettes, as it grew light outside and the blackbirds began to sing along the deserted road. More and more often she did not come home from the theatre at all, and it might be several days before we saw her. My father revealed new sides of himself when we were alone, he cooked and washed and asked me how things had gone at school, and I lied because I thought he deserved some good news in the midst of all the misery. But I couldn't return his affectionate care in the afternoons, when I got home and he was already going around the house in an apron. I entrenched myself in my room and only replied reluctantly when he knocked cautiously and came in and sat on my bed. I knew I wounded him by my distance, as if he wasn't suffering enough as it was, but his unhappy eyes and gentle, dispirited smile made me even more taciturn and reserved, and in the end he went away, stroking my hair tenderly so I turned quite black inside. When I went home one afternoon in early summer she had come back after several days. She stood at the window in the living room looking out at the road, he lay on the floor with his face to the wall, crumpled up and shaking as if with cold. He didn't see me and she only turned round after a long moment in which I stood listening to the incredible, shocking sound of my father weeping. Her face was completely expressionless, slack and white with exhaustion, and she looked at me as if I were a stranger who had gone the wrong way. I made my decision on the spot and went into my room to load my backpack. They didn't notice me leaving the house, totally engrossed as they were in their own drama.

The ruin was barely discernible behind the trees and overgrown shrubs in the front garden. In one place the roof and ground floor had collapsed together into a clearing in which pieces of beams, broken bricks and crushed tiles were piled up beneath a frayed hole open to the sky. I had often explored the wrecked house on my way home from school, or when I cycled around on Sundays along the quiet roads. I could spend hours at a time sitting on an old damp-stained sofa, sunning myself or watching the rain passing unhindered through the hole in the roof and hitting the dust in dark patches among broken glass, remnants of wallpaper and shattered window frames. The place was at the end of a cul de sac, ending at the edge of a wood. The wood had started to spread into the wild garden and the wind had blown seeds in through the windows and roof, so the cracks in the cement of the basement floor had opened wider beneath the slow steady pressure from the plants' growing net of roots. The green stems pushed their way right up through the fallen floorboards, and the fresh shoots brushed against the torn wallpaper in what had once been the drawing room. In a few summers they would reach the crumbling stucco in the remains of the ceiling.

When I placed my bicycle against the tumbledown wooden fence and approached the house through the tall grass for the first time, I had the feeling of being watched. It was completely quiet on the road and in the wilderness inside the fence, where the ruin came in sight behind the thick foliage, gaping with its black window openings staring like a skull. I crawled in through one of the empty eye sockets, ducked under the fallen rafters and balanced along the edge of the wide crater in the floor, alternately dazzled by the sun and fumbling in the half darkness. The staircase to the upper floor was almost intact, and I went on along a passage with doors, which on one side led into the open air, where a section of the house had finally disappeared. At the end of the passage there was a room which apart from the hole in the roof was more or less preserved. It was here the sofa stood, among walls covered with book shelves in which a few books had been left behind, bound in mouldy leather, with yellowing worm-eaten and damp-stained pages. On the floor I found a rotting gold frame without glass around an old photograph of a white, now yellowed steamship with a tall funnel sloping backwards. The ship lay at anchor on the greyish sea off a coast with grey palms that framed the view with their curved trunks and ragged leaves. I also found water. A mouldering cracked rubber hose, rolled up under the house wall, turned out to be fastened to a tap hidden behind the thick growth of ivy. Remarkably enough it was not completely rusted up, and I was quite euphoric when I saw the spluttering, red-brown stream change colour and become transparent, glinting in the sunlight like newly polished silver.

To begin with I had merely played with the idea of having a place I could retreat to, a place no one else knew about. In the preceding weeks I had secretly smuggled various useful things from my parents' house, books, preserves, some packets of biscuits, diverse kitchen utensils, blankets, a sleeping bag, a primus stove, a transistor radio and a hurricane lamp. I had discovered I could just fit on the mouldy sofa if I lay on my side with bent legs. It was to be my bed. I made use of the hours of daylight to organise things, and when dusk fell the former library almost resembled a home. I talked to myself encouragingly as I listened to Brahms's violin concerto on the transistor and heated a tin of tomato soup over the primus. I had done it, I had moved from home, it was no longer merely an idea. All the same, I had trouble falling asleep on the first night, and I lay awake for a long time listening to the distant cars on the motorway and the mice rustling below, while trying to distinguish the constellations of stars. In spite of my careful preparations there were things I had forgotten to think of, for instance, toilet paper. That did not become topical until the morning when I was woken up by a bright ray of sunshine, which made the dew shine on my sleeping bag. I trained myself to use the grass, which reached up to my knees, and on the following days I chose a new place each time. After almost a week had passed I had gone all the way round the house, and when I returned to my starting point my leavings were already so hardened that they no longer smelled, and the earth looked after the rest. My trousers were soaked with dew when I made a path through the wilderness of stalks and stems the first time, with my arms above my head to avoid nettles and thorns. As I squatted at the bottom of the garden and looked up at the house, I imagined the window of my new room was a square pupil looking at me without blinking. I hadn't brought my school satchel with me, and this omission made me take the final decision to stop going to school. In the morning I roamed around the roads and stole food from the back entrances of supermarkets where the lorries unloaded. In the afternoon I lay on my sofa and read or watched the birds that flew through my room.

I soon got used to the inconvenient details and laborious routines of my new life, I even grew used to the mice, and went so far as to take them into my care. The ruin was the natural meeting place for the wild cats of the district, and on my depredations at the supermarkets I secured some tins of cat food, but at night I could hear that the cats still preferred the genuine article. I even maintained my personal hygiene to a certain extent, every morning I washed at the cold tap behind the house, and afterwards I washed my underpants by beating them on a stone as I had seen African women do on television. I felt like a Robinson Crusoe, who had of his own accord gone on a journey of discovery around this desert island in the suburb's almost cosmic tedium of interminable well-groomed gardens. When I listened to the radio it seemed like receiving signals from a distant planet, and one afternoon, when I heard the news reader giving a description of a missing boy with my name and my appearance, my first reaction was that it must be a funny coincidence, an unknown boy who was my double. Naturally I had realised my parents would probably be worried, although they clearly had enough to deal with, but I didn't dream of telling them where I was. It fascinated me to be one of the missing persons you hear about now and then, for whom marl-pits and lakes are dragged, and I thought of Leslie Howard's cheeky jingle in *The Scarlet Pimpernel: They seek him here, they seek him there, those Frenchies seek him everywhere. Is he in heaven, is he in hell, that damned elusive Pimpernel?* Sometimes when my mother isolated herself in her bedroom she had half-apologetically, half-deprecatingly said she needed 'to be herself'. Now I understood what she meant, now I could finally 'be myself', far from the others' words and eyes, all their irrelevant stories and futile plans. But I was only 'myself' because I forgot myself in my ruin, lost in books or in my room's endless variations of sunbeams, linked shadows and jagged leaves. When I was seemingly lost in daydreams and deep inside 'myself' I was all the more present and aware of the visible world's unheeded and wonderful details. I forgot about time and everything I knew. In the evening when I went for a walk in the garden my eyes were in contact again with all they saw as if they awoke from the stupor induced by thoughts and words, and I watched the light extinguished in the grass, blade by blade, as my shattered house was slowly submerged in blue. When I sat among the grass blades and closed my eyes and felt the last rays of sunlight leave my face, I repeated, as a private liturgy, a pagan evening prayer, some lines from a poem we had read in English. I couldn't recall the poet's name but the first lines were engraved in my memory like a mantra which, even better than Leslie Howard's rhyme, interpreted what I was feeling: *I'm nobody, who are you? Are you nobody, too? Then there's a pair of us – don't tell! They'd advertise, you know. How dreary to be somebody, how public, like a frog* . . . I don't remember the rest, only the image of public frogs came back each time I listened to the voices on the radio croaking their news and views, their details of missing persons and lottery results and shipping forecasts into my dripping, rustling, rattling, soughing silence.

I remember it as a whole summer, but in reality it only lasted a week or two. I forget how my father found me, but one day he was standing inside the fence calling me, gently and cautiously as always, as if I were a runaway cat. I showed him the way through the ruin and pointed out the places where he should put his feet, and when I had sat him on the sofa I asked in a well-brought-up way if he would like a glass of water. He held up the glass to the light before drinking as if he didn't really quite rely on me. So this was where I had hidden myself. I said I hadn't hidden, I had just moved, and he looked at me mildly. He had moved too. I expressed surprise that it wasn't my mother who had left. It was best like that, he said. After all, he travelled so much. He had found a place in town. He said my mother missed me, and he looked as if he believed that himself. I asked if it was painful. 'Yes', he said, smiling almost apologetically. He praised me for the way I had made myself comfortable, and laughed when I told him how I obtained food. When he rose to go he handed me a handful of hundred-kroner notes, so I could 'provision myself in a more organised manner'. He didn't try to persuade me to give up my hermit existence, he knew well enough that would be superfluous now I had been discovered. He stood there for a little while after saying goodbye, and I hugged him. He looked quite surprised. When I think of my father I like to visualise him turning for a last time to wave to me among the broken beams and crushed roof tiles. The next day I went home. My mother told me he had gone to Yemen, he would be there for several months supervising the construction of a turbine plant. For a while she did her best to live up to the role of single, caring mother, not least in the week when my parents' divorce filled the garish front pages of the tabloids. She even baked biscuits one Sunday, but soon she resumed her afternoons behind the closed door of her bedroom, and frequently she did not come home until morning. One evening, standing in front of the mirror in the hall painting her eyelashes while waiting for the taxi, she suddenly looked at me and said, as if it was something that had just occurred to her, that my father was a poor fish. I felt like answering, coming to his defence, but I didn't, angry with myself for leaving the little words hanging in the air when she went out to her taxi with a quick kiss of the fingers. We left each other in peace. Sometimes she slept at her successive lovers' places, at others they spent the night at our house. They always treated me with express politeness, as if I were an adult, and I grew used to the varying faces appearing in the doorway of the bedroom in the morning when I was getting ready for school. Although I resumed my old existence, the stay in the ruin had marked a turning-point. The tale of my escapade travelled all around the school, in the others' eyes it invested me with something fabulous, and from being the reserved eccentric of the class I became almost sought-after. Besides, in the long run the house was more comfortable to live in than the wrecked villa, and when some years later I started to go to bed with girls I even came to appreciate my mother's egocentric way of life. She couldn't care less who spent the night in my room, and it merely amused her that it was seldom the same one. At least her son wasn't a poor fish.

I learned to get along, I taught myself the rules of the game, the sweet innocent game that means nothing because it can mean anything at all. But when on yet another light Nordic night I lay in my room or among the sand dunes on the beach with my hand buried in yet another bold or timid girl's knickers, there was always the same gap between the hand and my head, between the person I was inside and the probably quite sweet but undoubtedly chance guy into whose eyes she gazed deeply while he feverishly tried to roll the condom the right way. I contemplated the tender scene from some far-off place, deep inside, and thought again of the happy weeks in the ruin where I lay looking at the stars beneath the hole in the roof, in harmony with myself on my mouldy sofa, watched over by only the feral cats and trembling mice. The hermit looked at me coldly from his dilapidated, dry-rotten kingdom, and I felt the coldness of his eyes, but I couldn't see him, I saw only the dull snowflakes of the stars framed by broken rafters. Each time yet another girl whispered sweet nothings in my ear, and each time I answered her in the way you do answer, I thought it was

merely words, merely a barter in the dark, one word for
another, a caress for a kiss, a romantic glance for a dizzy
little fall between her charming thighs. The difference was
still too great, the difference between inside and outside,
which I had been allowed to forget for a while in the
house where the birds flew around inside the walls and
trees grew up out of the basement floor. When I saw my
mother painting her lips and puttying her face before going
off to her lovers, I asked myself why she had ever lived with
my father. But they had been so young, only slightly older
than I was, they had been mere children who lost themselves
in the light nights. Perhaps it was merely a chance night in the
sand dunes or in a rented room that had tipped the scales,
an accidental encounter, a sweet little dizziness to which
they had attributed far too much significance. Perhaps they
had only surrendered themselves to each other because they
were tired of all the rushing around. As it had turned out, I
was forced to ask myself whether my very birth hadn't been
a slight misunderstanding. If in her eyes I should have been
someone else, another time. But as I began to turn into
an attractive young man, she started to take more interest
in me. She pumped me teasingly and inquisitively about
my adventures and took me into her confidence, as if I
was really interested in hearing who she slept with and
where. We were 'chums' now, I was the only one who
'understood her'. When my father was in Denmark I went
to see him in his apartment in town. As before he talked
about his bridges and dams, but I just listened absently to
his accounts and replied evasively to his cautious questions
about how things were at home. Suddenly it seemed a long
time since I had dreamed of standing at his side on the
building sites in the tropics, and when I received his always
laconic and insignificant postcards they seemed to me to
be just as childish as I had been when I kept them in a
box under my bed to take out when I couldn't sleep.

He didn't wake up before the curtain calls but was the first to rise, and he clapped with great enthusiasm as if he wanted to compensate for the snooze he had taken during the performance, when my mother stepped out on the stage alone, received the bouquet presented to her by a blushing ticket-seller, and curtsied with studied humility to the enthusiastic audience. 'Enthusiastic' was hardly the word, people were just about foaming with ecstasy, their eyes shone like born-again Christians', they stamped and clapped so hard you would think their palms were quite raw. My mother had done it again, yet once more her limited but routine, indeed, even overdone, repertory of high-flown and vulgar grimaces had coerced the audience into feeling that here they witnessed life itself, genuine, deep and amazing life, and not the cheap, grey, and insidiously shabby imitation they took a break from for one night, and shortly, when the lights came on, would go home to again, blissful and crestfallen at the same time. After the last curtain call I accompanied my father and the other special initiates up behind the stage for 'the little festivity' she had so zealously phoned to remind me of. I kept in the background as I saw her screw on her smile and offer her cheek for his humble kiss. I could see, thirty years later, how he still tried to combine a certain intimate, old familiar closeness in his expression with the survivor's light, social and untouched tone. This was the moment he had come for, which he had searched for through the years, as if he could never finish proving to her and to himself that the old wounds were healed. But before he had managed to get his receipt in the form of just one single warm and acknowledging glance she had offered her cheek to the next admirer. To her he was only one well-known face among the many now flocking around her like the seven little dwarves around Snow White, just as innocent and touchingly naïve in their devotion. To him she represented an old injury, a slight but disfiguring limp you try to deflect attention from by always being well-groomed and always smiling obligingly at the world. He looked around him at a loss, alone again now that his mission had so suddenly been brought to an end, and I hid myself behind a group of managing directors' wives who were standing in a cloud of perfume listening raptly to the art director, with dangling wrists and voiced s's depicting the artistic crises he had been through during his work on the performance. When I glanced in my father's direction again, he had gone.

I was about to seize my chance to sneak out into the wings when my mother caught sight of me and steered her way through the obstructions of champagne glasses and bristling cigarettes, purposeful as a heat-seeking missile, loudly giving voice to her maternal joy of reunion so everyone turned to look at me. Had she been terrible? I had to smile at her anxious little-girl face. She knew what I thought of her dramatic efforts, although I had always restricted myself to indirect comment in the form of equivocal ironic comments, but before I could answer she had put on a quite different, falsely aggrieved and sorrowful mask. Where was my delightful wife? She had been looking forward *so* much to seeing her. I mumbled something about Stockholm but she saw through me. She is not just stupid, I thought, she's also cunning, which in her case has never been any contradiction, and her intuition is the sharper because it is the only thing about her that can't be bribed. What was the matter with us? From the way she said it you would think Astrid and I were two children who had quarrelled over some toy. I pretended not to understand what she was talking about, hoping that would make her reveal how much she knew, and where she had got it from, but again I had miscalculated, for she contented herself with patting me on the cheek and twittering that it would all be all right, and with a sparkling smile she turned to the photographer, who had been standing about fidgeting to get a picture of the diva arm-in-arm with her faithful son. The green and red after-images of the flash had barely faded before I was again left to myself in my corner of the stage. It was I who had had to give up getting her to reveal herself, not she, she had merely resigned when she realised I was not of a mind to satisfy her inquisitiveness and pour out my heart to her on the spot, in the middle of the jungle of carnivorous eyes.

I followed her with my eyes as she embraced a pretty woman in her mid-thirties I seemed to have seen before somewhere or other. She looked almost alarmed by my mother's overwhelming cordiality and leaned against the man at her side, who was now allotted the obligatory kiss on the cheek, an elderly sun-tanned man, lean and furrowed, but still upright, with wavy white hair and a hard, insistent gaze. A few seconds passed before I recognised him. Of course he had been invited, my mother had acted in several of his films, and if I wasn't far wrong she had also had an affair with him once, long before he met Astrid, when she and I were still toddlers. As I saw him put a brown, wrinkled and liver-spotted hand on my mother's back, I asked myself if I had never actually considered that he was the same age as my father, the film director who had stood out in the winter cold long ago, in shirt-sleeves, still grizzled, and called to Astrid in the taxi, less than a minute after I saw her for the first time. Now he was here, with the young girl from that time, the next discovery for his restless desire, whom he had been unable to keep his hands off, even though he could be his own son's grandfather, and even though at that point Astrid was still really young and trim. When he had realised Astrid was not coming back, he had stayed with her successor after all, he had even had a child with her to stop her from running away, now he had to face it, his time for conquest would soon be past. She too could almost be his grandchild, but no one thought of that when they saw them together, he had worn very well, and although her stomach wasn't quite as flat as it had been before she had a child, all in all he still looked what you'd call a man who'd hit the jackpot, as he stood there discreetly supporting himself by leaning on his young wife. If he was really nice to her, she might stay with him until he died. It was almost ten years since I had last seen him. When Simon was thirteen he had asked us if he could be excused from visiting his father. It had become more and more painful for him to go out to the villa where he had once lived, and where the film director was so busily occupied with his new family. I don't think it was just because he felt like the rejected child, I also think he was old enough to see the real reason for the visits. His father only wanted him because his son's courtesy visits confirmed that his betrayal had been forgiven, and that therefore it had been forgivable.

Astrid accepted, reluctantly and out of regard for Simon, that she had to deal with him. He only phoned every few months and if she happened to answer the telephone she always looked upset and thunderous when she went to call Simon. She never spoke of him other than as 'your father', never just 'father'. She never forgave him, but neither apparently could she forgive herself for once having played the role that her successor did later on. The role of his cock's sweet little secret. But in spite of everything she wasn't staunch enough to excuse herself from his sixtieth birthday. I have often been amazed at how strong a grip these conventional family occasions have on us, regardless of how we get on with our family. No Christmas Eve passed without my mother joining us for dinner, despite the fact that I happily passed several weeks at a time without contacting her. How can it be we are so sentimental about dates not set by our feelings but by the calendar's completely inane highlights? In Astrid's case it was all the more remarkable because her parents had died when she was still a child. She had no siblings, Simon, Rosa and I were her only family, and she had chosen us herself, whereas she had long ago rejected any familial relationship with the film director. It can't even have been for Simon's sake that she turned up at the séance, for he merely shrugged his shoulders at the invitation that came flopping through the letterbox one day, illustrated with a pretty tactless picture of the film director in bathing trunks with his arm around his new wife and his new child on his shoulders, taken, naturally, in front of the absolutely politically correct peasant's house in Provence, where else? There he stood, the charmer, with his intense eyes and a hand on his new wife's firm buttocks, bluff and virile like another Picasso look-alike. He would be pleased to see us. Yes, naturally he would be pleased to gather his harem for a day and act the kindly pasha, stroking his chin as he admires the fruits in his perfumed garden. When we arrived at the residential road where I had once waited in my taxi as Astrid came storming down the garden path holding Simon by the hand, the birthday child stood ready with his new family in an exact replica of the invitation, receiving his guests, although not in bathing trunks, but in a pink shirt and summer sailor-suit, as if it was not Picasso, after all, but rather Visconti he was trying to imitate. I could see his smart new wife was ready to swoon with terror at the sight of her predecessor, but Astrid reassured her with a conciliatory sparkle in her eye, while the film director shook my hand in a long, imploring pincer manoeuvre. Everything was ready for the great peace pact on this summer Sunday in his imposing white villa with its palatial window panes and black glazed tiles.

So now he was sixty, Astrid and I were in our mid-thirties, Simon was thirteen and his new wife was twenty-something. His first wife was in her late fifties, and his daughter from the first marriage was our age, while his little 'afterthought' was three. I don't mention it out of pedantry, I am merely trying to maintain perspective in this convoluted account in which time and place shift around in irregular spirals. But I couldn't help thinking of it when I discovered I was seated next to his first daughter in the big marquee erected in the garden to create space for the numerous guests, 'in case the weather did not smile on us'. This precaution had been unnecessary, the sun was baking on the canvas, the air was heavy and smelled of rubber, and before we had finished our starters it was like sitting in a sauna. It's easy to imagine what it is like to sit in a sauna in tie and jacket. The sweat dripped from my eyebrows as I tried to converse with the daughter, a grey bony woman with thin lips and a practical hair-do, who looked ten years older even though, as I mentioned, we are the same age. She was a nurse in a cancer ward, and when I had managed to warm her up she entertained me throughout the whole dinner with the ethical problems concerning the use of pain-killing morphine medication in the terminal stage. Should the pain be eased when there was no hope left even though morphine in itself would kill the patient in a short time? Wasn't it a *slide* in the direction of euthanasia? I visualised the emaciated patients in their over-large hospital nightwear, clutching the stands to which their death-inducing drops were attached, staggering in the middle of a frozen lake. While considering what I myself would prefer I secretly observed the nurse's mother, the film director's first wife, a stout woman in a gaudy loose-fitting smock dress, who laughed loud and long at her own jokes. She had obviously determined to be Junoesque instead of just fat, and instead of harbouring a grudge she had decided on a life-affirming, almost jovial attitude at this great reconciliation feast, in spite of the fact that she had lived alone ever since the film director deserted her in favour of Astrid. The corners of the cobalt-blue silk scarf that hid her double chins arranged themselves among the lettuce leaves on her plate, as she bent forward across the table to advise her ex's new wife on child upbringing, and the bashful girl nodded piously to the motherly exhortations out of sheer happiness in the heavy, rejected woman's demonstrative manner. But all the same, now and then, when the fat lady raised her glass, I saw her casting quick nervous glances at Astrid, who had naturally been given the place of honour on the host's right. As usual Astrid was equal to the situation and smiled politely as one smiles at strangers, at the harmless little anecdotes from their mutual past that the film director attempted, glistening with sweat in his damp tent. Sometimes he put out a hand and rumpled Simon's hair, and I saw Astrid's eyes grow distant and the boy shrink away each time, although he smiled dutifully. We got talking about children, the bony nurse and I. She had never had any herself, she lived alone like her mother, but she travelled a lot, she told me bravely, on her own in Mexico and India, and almost succeeded in making her exotic journeys sound like dreams come true. The film director himself was the first to speak, unconventional through and through as he was, after all, and in the speech he made for himself he thanked one by one, with shining eyes, the women who had meant so much to him and 'enriched his life', if he might so humbly express it, 'although it had not always been too easy'. His new wife sat like a girl on the edge of her chair playing faint-heartedly with the bread crumbs on the tablecloth as he spoke. His plump ex-wife put her head sideways with a heartfelt smile as a tear coursed its way down her powdered cheek. His youngest daughter sat under the table pulling blades of grass from the lawn. The eldest stared down at her empty plate, given over perhaps to thoughts of euthanasia or her last walking tour in Nepal. Simon had left the table, I couldn't see him anywhere. Astrid turned her back on the speaker and fixed my eyes with slightly raised eyebrows and curling lips.

I left the theatre without saying goodbye to my mother. It was a long time since I had last strolled alone through the

town late in the evening. I enjoyed the cold air on my
face and the dry sound of withered leaves crunching beneath
my feet as I walked under the trees of Kongens Nytorv, and
I was quite cheered at the sight of the white illuminated
façade of Hotel d'Angleterre, flickering promisingly behind
the crooked trelliswork of the tree crowns. As always on a
Friday, the town was full of people flocking in front of the
cafés, the same cafés where I myself had once stood swaying
in the throng, happily intoxicated and light of heart with
vague expectations. As I passed the queues of young people
pushing at each other, impatient as moths to get into the
light inside, I suddenly felt old and tired. It was their town,
at least in the evening, not mine. I remembered what one of
my friends had said a few years ago. 'When we're standing at
a bar counter like that,' he said, glancing at a crowd of noisy
kids, 'and one of them suddenly turns round and shouts "Hi,
Dad," then it's time to go home.' Was I going to catch sight
of Rosa for the second time that day, I wondered? I looked at
the girls, painted and powdered, dressed up as hardened, lost
women, much older to look at than the red-cheeked boys in
baseball caps, whose loutish, sheepish jokes only made them
smile like tired fashion models. Behind their unmoving and
faultless masks another film was running, in which the light
was sharper and the shadows deeper, in which adult men
with calm, grey eyes and rusty voices and a dark, painful past
carried them away in black sports cars out to the big white
hotels by the sea. A slow film pervaded by slow, sad strings,
in which the wind lifted the light curtains between the half
open shutters of deep, shadowy rooms, so they could feel the
coolness of the wind on their skin like a strange, unknown
glance as they lay waiting with closed eyes. I had a hot dog
at a sausage-stall in front of Nørreport Station, it was many
years since I had last tasted one, but I had not eaten all day,
I'd quite simply forgotten to eat although I had masses of
time. I went slowly homewards. The neon signs opposite

the Lakes were reflected on the surface of the water in a vibrating coloured haze, and I stood a while watching the neon hen laying her neon eggs, as I had done so often with Simon and Rosa. The last neon sign of the row on the roofs was a leaf from a calendar. The date shone red against the black sky, the 17th of October, it would soon be a week since Astrid left. I was tired. During the past few days I had had to mobilise all my energy to maintain an illusion of normality, to Rosa, to the curator and the other dinner guests, to my parents, and at the same time constantly revolving in my mind the same questions I feared the others would ask. Where had Astrid gone? Why had she left? Tomorrow I would be in a plane, out of their reach, alone at last with my unanswered questions. Somewhere behind me a man sat on a bench in a shiny worn parka with a cord round his waist, spewing a torrent of abuse at all and sundry, surrounded by his bulging, mouldy plastic bags. I had often wondered what was in those bags. As usual the light on the staircase went out before I was at the top. When I reached the last landing I saw the glow of a cigarette faintly smouldering in front of our door. The glow rose into the air with a sudden movement, and a moment later the light came on again.

Rosa's boyfriend had been tonsured since I last saw him. Only a dark shadow of hair growth remained on his bony crown but it didn't make him look in the least formidable, he rather resembled one of those Moroccan street boys whose heads are shaved when they have lice, looking neglected with their filthy little hands outstretched. The installation artist stretched out his hand too, not to beg for alms but to shake mine, a manifestation of civil urbanity I had not expected him to descend to. Did I know where Rosa was? He went straight to the point without beating about the bush, but in a voice that was so low and subdued that I couldn't understand how I could ever have felt intimidated by this polite and serious young man. I replied I had no idea, as I decided to keep silent about Rosa's presence in the café in the afternoon. Anyway, that was some hours ago. Had I any idea where he could find her? It occurred to me she might possibly be with her red-haired friend, but I shook my head and suddenly had a comfortable feeling of solidarity with my daughter. He stood there looking down at his cigarette stub in a lost way, it had burned down almost to his nail, but he obviously didn't like to throw the stub on the staircase floor while I was watching. I asked if he would like to come in to put out his cigarette. He threw it into the guest toilet, it seemed we had the same habit. It was a good thing Astrid didn't see. He walked around the living room, I was obviously not going to get rid of him easily. I said I was going to New York next day and had some shirts to iron, but he just looked at me without getting the hint, amazed at what that could have to do with Rosa. He had not seen her for twenty-four hours. Good Lord, he should only know. Had they quarrelled? He looked at me again, this time with a searching glance, then shrugged his shoulders. He didn't understand it, she had just gone, suddenly. At first he thought she had gone down for some cigarettes. He had been looking for her all over town. Classic, I thought, she went out for cigarettes and never came back. At least Astrid hadn't made use of such a hoary old pretence. I didn't know what to say and asked instead if he would like a beer. Now I was stuck with him in earnest, and on the way through the apartment I thought abashed that we were developing quite a mutual fate, two abandoned men.

He sat at the kitchen table looking at me while I got out the ironing board. He said he had read my essay on Jackson Pollock. I smiled at him and began to iron the collar of one of the damp shirts rolled up beside him on the table. What did he think of it? In reality I was not interested in what he thought of my essay, I could almost guess. He lingered, as if he was reflecting in order to discover what he did think. It had an interesting point. That way he had not said too much. I always start with the collar, I said, and then I do the sleeves, the sleeves are the hardest. He gaped at me as if not sure he had heard aright. I looked down at the flat shirt sleeve and pressed the iron along the edge to make a sharp fold. It was not that he was usually jealous, he said, lighting a fresh cigarette. It's really pointless, I said, they get creased anyway on the flight, no matter how carefully I pack them. Did I have any suspicion that she was seeing anyone else? I met his eyes. Someone else? He looked away, his eyes were shining brightly and I was afraid he might start to cry, this tonsured young man in a worn leather jacket. If she did, she probably wouldn't tell me. He smiled bitterly and took a gulp from the bottle. A few weeks ago he had seen her on the way into Kongens Have with an older man, well, not really old, about my age. He caught sight of them by chance, from the bus. Had he asked who it was? He blew air from his nose, but it sounded more like a giggle than a snort. Would *I* have asked? I shrugged my shoulders. He had asked if there 'was someone', he had asked several times, but it always ended in a quarrel. She felt she was being watched. She said she had never promised him anything. I looked at him again, he was looking down at the floor. I wanted to say something friendly but I couldn't think of anything although I knew every single thought rummaging under his tonsured crown. Then he rose quickly and thanked me for the beer, I didn't need to see him out.

Now he was going out into the dark again to shamble around, alone and rejected. I understood his position but I had forgotten what it felt like. I could only smile at myself, at my young, bleeding heart when I once stood at a window and watched Inès leaving me amidst the whirling snowflakes. My wounded self-esteem barked despairingly in my head as I drove around town with

the night's passengers, like a mangy starving cur running
in circles and snapping at its own tail. I smiled at the
installation artist too after he had gone, but it was not a
malicious smile. I thought of everything he was going to
suffer and how really the worst thing was being so sorry
for himself. Ironically enough my own daughter had been
the cause of my having the opportunity to confront myself
when young. I remembered her sitting in the afternoon sun
in front of the café, a thoughtful, introspective Rosa who
sat contemplating the fountain and the pigeons, unaware
that I was observing her. I could not have reached her
even if I had knocked on the window and waved. She
resembled Astrid more than ever with her mass of brown
hair and wide cheek bones and her narrow eyes that saw
everything without revealing any of it. A young Astrid, so
young that she had not yet met me. A young woman who
had just grown up, alone in the world. Perhaps she really
had been on her way to meet an older man, not old, just
older than herself, someone like me, just as the young Astrid
too had once walked through town with quick, stolen strides
as if she were a secret agent in the adult world, on her
way to meet a married man with grizzled hair and strong
hands. Perhaps that was how Rosa had walked through
the town when she had said goodbye to her red-haired
friend with a conspiratorial smile, on her way to an adult
man with furrowed cheeks and a calm, self-confident gaze
which seemed to enclose her completely on all sides as
if she could sink into that gaze and disappear into it,
let it take her, unresisting, to an unknown destination.

Perhaps Rosa walked through town with the same determination I picture in Astrid when she walked beside the
grizzled film director along a corridor of the Grand Hotel
in Stockholm and let him open the door of the anonymous room where no one knew that in a little while
she would be lying with this married man between her

girlish knees. The same determined sleepwalker's stride that in its time had carried Inès through the streets from one man to another. Secretive, treacherous strides into something unknown and menacing. Perhaps Rosa smiled too at the helplessness of this mature man's desire. Perhaps she already suspected she was merely his little gesture of defiance against boredom and the weight of days, perhaps she laughed at him when he clutched at her young body with his adult, breathless lust as she closed her eyes and vanished between his hands into the free fall of a blind moment. Rosa, Astrid, Inès, perhaps it was the same urge to disappear from the eyes of these helpless, grown men, to surrender themselves and slip away in the same movement, just as they bent over their young bodies to possess them. The same secretive smile when they vanished through an invisible door in the wallpaper between the comic pictures of little coloured birds at the Grand Hotel. Each time they rose from yet another strange bed, it may have been with the same weightless feeling of being strange and unknown themselves, as if their faces were painted shells which those poor married wretches had broken so they crumbled between their lustful hands. Each time they left yet another man and walked alone through the evening town they felt again the cool air on their skin, as if there was nothing but a thin porous membrane where their faces had been. No one had better tell them who they were, as they walked there in the streets, Inès, Astrid and Rosa. It is the same young woman who walks like this through the night with quick strides and wide open eyes, so the strange faces pass freely through her gaze, one after another, like fleeting reflections on the whirling stream of darkness. Unknown faces with unknown eyes that open to her and close behind her again, as if she constantly crosses yet another threshold without ever going forward. She always wants to be somewhere else, but she does not know where, she only knows that every single room and every

single town will be a trap. Thus she goes on, as if she were
a letter without a sender and without an address, a letter to
everyone and no one, all the time being torn open and all
the time being sealed up anew before anyone can read what
it says.

6

It was cold and windy the day after my arrival. The air was clear between the square grey buildings that cut their way into the uniform blue surface of the sky, themselves cut through by the sharply outlined shadows of other buildings and the water tanks on the flat roofs. In the afternoon I went for a walk in the side-streets of old warehouses between Greenwich Street and the Hudson. There was nobody to be seen, only the endless stream of cars on West Side Highway, beside the river. The neglected industrial façades reminded me of Edward Hopper's towns. A few hours earlier I had been in the Whitney Museum in front of one of his solitary women. She sits in a room with pale green walls, she has sat down on the edge of the bed. She looks out of the window at the water tanks of sooty wood similar to those on the roofs above my head, between the grey and dark red walls' faded, peeling names painted in capital letters. She is blonde, she is still young, and she sits looking out of the open window in the pale sunlight falling in on her equally pale face, torso and thighs. Her face is expressionless and her body is presented without the slightest suspicion of desire, almost a little clumsy, as Hopper painted them, a little stiff in the joints, which only serves to strengthen the immobility of the picture, the impression of a long moment's completely unmoving stance in the flight of minutes and hours. I might say her gaze is absent, but at the same time it is fully and completely there, resting on the edged outline of the buildings and the conical zinc roofs of the round water tanks or perhaps on a distant point between them, outside the picture, at the end of the view from the window where an invisible barrier prevents her calm gaze from reaching further. There it stops while she sits on, perfectly still, halted in a pause on her way through the day, where nothing is to happen, where she is alone, where there is nothing to say nor anyone to say anything to. Perhaps she is listening to the deep note of the distant traffic, perhaps she hears neither the muffled noise of the cars nor the horns and occasional shouts that probably reach her through the open window. She looks neither particularly unhappy nor the opposite, she just sits on the bed in the silent, pale green room, in the transilluminated silence of the picture which is also her silence, the silence of her body and her thoughts. She may have fallen into a reverie, as if she has fallen out of time, alone with herself, but no longer than is quite ordinary and unremarkable. In a little while she will get up from the bed and dress and go out into the day, out into town and on through life, but not yet, not just now. She will sit on for a little while and allow her thoughts to open out and widen and extend, until they can no longer be thought. It is not that the world is empty. The world is full of houses and things, and emptiness is just the arbitrary yet necessary distance between houses and things. The special thing in such a pause in the day's course is not emptiness. What makes her sit on, what makes me stay in front of her, is not that the pause is empty, neither are the pale green walls empty, or the sky in the window above the roofs. They are there, we know, the walls and the sky, they just happen to be there. What for a moment makes us hold our breath, she on her bed, I in a gallery at the Whitney Museum, is rather the totally banal, but still only in the pauses, and only slowly dawning, observation, that the houses and the things and the bodies and the light and shadows look as they do. That the world is what is present, at any time, at any place. That there is nothing more to it.

I walked along the wide pavement beside the Hudson in the direction of the World Trade Center. Runners in jogging gear overtook me at regular intervals or came towards me, breathing hard and red in the face. On the left cars streamed towards me on their way up to Holland Tunnel, a ceaseless river of lacquered sheet metal, like a noisy, moving reflection of the river on my right side, peaceful, grey-blue and very wide at this point. On the other side of the river I could see the Colgate clock, an enormous white face that seemed to float on the water, quite small at a distance, rather the size of a watch face. It was about four o' clock, so it was ten at night in Copenhagen and nine in Portugal. I did not know then that at that point Astrid had arrived in Oporto, she might have been in her room at the Infante de Sagres or walking beside the dark river and under the steel bridge towards the Cais da Ribeira, as I went on down Chambers Street and turned up by West Broadway back to Soho. The bank statement showed she paid her hotel bill with her Mastercard the next day and continued on south. It was not like her to choose the most expensive hotel in town, but we had stayed there together seven years before. Perhaps that was why, perhaps it was because she had driven from Santiago de Compostela to Oporto in one stretch and needed a comfortable night. The statement helps me not only to reconstruct her movements, I also use it to remember what I was doing myself at the same time, constantly subtracting five hours or adding them. We were displaced in our relative movements, each in our own time zone, our own continent, both of us far from the town where we had lived together. Later that afternoon I was in the cinema on the corner of West Houston and Mercer Street, for some reason I still have the ticket. I did not attend to the film, but it suited me well to sit in the dark and watch faces and places succeed each other. As long as the film lasted I did not need to walk restlessly through street after street without knowing what to do with myself. As I sat in the darkness of the cinema she may have been sitting on her five-star bed looking out of the open window, out into the tree tops of Filipa de Lencastre. I can't remember if they were planes or fig trees. I expect she had a bath before going out to eat. She came out of the bathroom in the hotel bath-robe, with a towel tied like a turban around her wet hair. She opened the window and lit a cigarette and sat on the edge of the bed in front of the view of the square, motionless with fatigue. She listened to the invisible cars and the voices of the invisible people down in the square, while her gaze sank into the darkness among the dark green, dry leaves of the trees, faintly illuminated from below by the street lamps. She sat on there for a while, with her arms stretched out behind her and her palms resting on the bedspread, as the glow ate its way through the cigarette between her lips. Perhaps. It is just something I imagine, but perhaps she knew I would try to visualise her in the places we once visited together. Perhaps it was on purpose and not only for convenience that she used her Mastercard all the way to Lisbon instead of cashing money on the way. Perhaps she did not merely want to show me she was taking the same route we had followed seven years before. Perhaps she also wanted me to see those places again and visualise her alone in those places, where we had been together. As if something particular had happened on that journey, something decisive. As if en route, without noticing, we had passed a decisive point.

It had rained the whole way to Santiago de Compostela. I have a picture of Astrid standing on the square in front of the cathedral lifting her face to the drizzle. The lacy Gothic of the granite façade seemed to dissolve in the fine rain, flickering like a distorted vision in the white light, and in my memory it is as if the denticulation and her features touch each other through the rain. I put her wet shoes on the radiator in the hotel room and held her chilly feet in my hands until she fell asleep. The next day we crossed the Rio Minho on a small ferry rather like a barge, and continued southwards through the desolate mountains. We could drive for a long time without saying anything. Sometimes she would point through the side window because she had glimpsed an eagle high above or a distant house washed pale blue so it had the same colour as the sky. Now and then one of us switched on the radio and hopped forwards and backwards between channels, but the signal was poor because of the mountains and the music constantly faded into scratching sounds. There was hardly any traffic on the mountain roads. We were far away. At home we were not used to spending so many hours at a time together. We parted in the morning and met again in the evening, and when we were together the children were generally around. It was an unaccustomed feeling to sit motionless beside each other for hours as the mountainsides opened and closed before us in time with the bends of the road. At home we always had something or other to do, either trivial or interesting, in the car there was nothing to be done except to go on, all the time on the way to the next town. As we drove through Trás-os-Montes, I thought yet again how fast the years had gone since the winter she moved into my flat and broke my solitude. The years were like a train in the night that goes so fast that the lighted windows flow together with the speed and you see nothing. I thought about how much of our time had been taken up with doing the same things every day, as the months passed and the children grew and we talked about all that happened. In the evening, when everything had been done and the apartment was quiet and we lay down beside each other, it was sometimes like meeting again after a long separation. Slightly hesitant, slightly fumbling now and then, like seeing each other again after a while and having to search a little before you can take up the thread. Had she been happy? Like myself, she must have been too busy to even ask, happily occupied with everything but herself. Like myself, she was immersed in her work, like myself she let herself be whirled around by the roundabout of family life, so the surroundings faded into a swarm of lights and colours.

Distances grew longer between the villages in Trás-os-Montes, and pauses when neither of us said anything grew longer, until she looked at me again and smiled with her narrow eyes, as if everything was as it had always been. I can remember pulling in to the side because she needed a pee, at a place where the road made a curve through the round, grass-covered mountains. I stayed in the car while she walked in among the mossy projecting rocks and withered grass and the prickly evergreen bushes. She vanished from sight when she squatted down, as if she had been swallowed by the naked knobbly landscape with its meagre growth of brown, grey, grey-green and rust-red under the pale sky. It was perfectly still. There was only the sound of my seat creaking slightly under me, the wind in the grasses and the distant trickling sound from the place where she had disappeared. Perhaps it didn't matter, my being unable to think of anything to say to her. Words had never been what bound us together. They had merely been the sound of our story when we talked of everything under the sun on our way through the years. We hadn't needed so many words, we seemed to understand each other without them. A look, a gesture, a sigh or a smile was enough. The story told itself. But at some point I must have lost sight of her, even though she was there the whole time. Because she was always there, and because she was so close. As when she kissed me and her face widened out so I could not make out its outline or proportions and saw only her blurred skin and huge eyes. I had not seen her for a long time. That's how I was thinking when half a minute later she appeared in the landscape again, as if out of nowhere, and came towards the car through the dry grass. She screwed up her eyes against the sun as she looked down into the shadowed valley behind the thin transparent mist. Her shadow went winding, long and without joints, across the shining grass blades as she walked, as if it lived its own life beside hers. It was an interval in the story, this journey, not a continuation, and we moved through that interval, among the bare, monotonous mountains, without having the story to tell us where we were going. That's what I was thinking as she came towards the car, while she looked around her one last time, still alone for a moment in the unmoving landscape. That was why I did not know what to say.

When I came home from New York the second time and was waiting for my suitcase among the other passengers at baggage reclaim, I caught sight of her behind the glass fronting the arrival hall. She had not seen me yet. She stood among the others waiting there, neck stretched, with her arms crossed, fidgeting with the car keys as if they were pearls in a rosary, a little impatiently, a little anxiously, as if doubting for a moment whether I had been on the plane. For another few seconds I was only a passenger among others who stood waiting for their particular suitcase to come in sight on the conveyor belt. Then she smiled and waved, and I waved back, from one moment to the next her husband again, hers among all the men in the world. In the seconds as she stood peering through the glass wall, not knowing I was observing her, she was still the woman I had left. The next moment, when her expressionless face broke into a smile, she became the woman I had returned to in order to continue where we had left off, where I had let go of her. A week or two earlier, in the middle of September, I had been in a plane again on the way to New York. I sat looking out at the empty sky above the clouds, wondering as usual what Astrid and the children were doing. No doubt they had already eaten, Rosa would be putting plates in the dishwasher, Simon would be in the living room, completely lost in an opium den in Shanghai with red dragons on the walls where at this moment Tintin stuck his head out of a Chinese vase as tall as a man. Later on Astrid would read another chapter aloud from *Huckleberry Finn,* maybe one of the chapters about the nights on the great river, about the flickering lights on the shore and the voices rolling across the water to Huck and Jim where they sit on the timber raft smoking a pipe as they drift with the current. She would kiss them goodnight, put out the lights in their rooms and sit down in front of the television's brief, leaping flakes of everything that was happening at the same time in another place, and if she had not drawn the curtains, she would be able to see herself, in one of the window panes, far away in the darkness, a diffuse, blurred and transparent figure on the sofa, her face merely a yellow patch in the lamplight, with dark shadows where her eyes were. She might light a cigarette and look through the blue-grey swirls of smoke past the screen's changing, synthetic colour combinations into the darkness behind her reflection, knowing nothing of the cat which rose at the same moment and stretched in the ray of sunlight on the floor beneath a window in the East Village, before running out into the corridor where a tall young woman in her late twenties was coming in through the front door with a brown paper bag full of foodstuffs in her arms and, with the cat at her heels, walked through the apartment, switched on the telephone answering machine and listened to my voice announcing that I would land the same evening soon after eleven.

In the spring I had spent a month and a half in New York to work on my collection of essays on post-war American painters. I stayed in Brooklyn Heights with an acquaintance of my father, a Lebanese cardiac surgeon whose wife had died the previous year. He was at the hospital or with a woman friend on Long Island most of the time, and I had the house pretty well to myself. When I was not in my room watching the grey squirrels in the trees in front of the gloomy and very aristocratic terrace house, I took a train from the station in Clark Street to Manhattan to spend the morning in the archives of the museums and university libraries. They were peaceable, uniform days, and I was happy in my solitude, completely absorbed in my book, which slowly but surely began to take shape. Of course I missed Astrid and the children when I sat eating my lonely pizza in the evenings surrounded by the high oak panels of the cardiac surgeon's opulent dining room, but not as much as I had expected. The artists of the New York School filled my horizon and ousted Astrid, Simon and Rosa from my field of vision. There was an ocean between us, and in their absence ideas came to me and arranged themselves continuously in one undisturbed, unbroken movement, as ideas do when you begin to write at the proper moment. My friend the museum curator had given me various telephone numbers of people he thought I might like to meet, among them an art dealer who had known both Rothko and Pollock, a distinguished critic and a young Danish artist who had moved to New York after leaving the academy. Very talented, he had said with a little smile and a sly glance behind his steel-rimmed spectacles. But I felt like contacting neither the art dealer nor the critic, either because of my usual shyness and fear of seeming pushy, or because I was getting on so well with pursuing my own ideas that the interpretations and views of others would only have been a disturbance. And as for his talented young painter, his sly recommendation left me only with a vaguely insulted feeling that he was trying to lure me out onto thin ice with one of his discarded conquests from the academy, one of those ambitious and well-equipped fallow deer in overalls adorned with decorative paint spots he romped around with behind his wife's back. As if he wanted to put me to the test in the hope of proving I was not a mite better than he was.

Besides, it was of course American and not Danish art I had flown the Atlantic to write about, and moreover I had come precisely to write, so all in all I could see no reason to seek diversion from my comfortable hermit existence in Brooklyn Heights.

One afternoon I was sitting smoking in the sculpture garden behind the Museum of Modern Art, contemplating the moving reflections of clouds and skyscrapers in the low ornamental pools. I had spent several hours on the collections, guided through the store rooms by an assistant who stood at a respectful distance and looked on as I made notes about some of the pictures I wanted to refer to in my book. As I sat glancing at people and listening to snatches of their conversation, I asked myself what exactly it was in the New York School of painters that was so important to discuss, so many years after their lucent painting had in turn been succeeded by pop art, minimalism and conceptual art in every possible aspect. Wasn't there something naïve and unfashionably romantic in their pathos, their existential notion of the intensity of brush strokes, the strictly personal expression? Hadn't the world become too self-conscious and ironic in the meantime? Was there any sense any longer in tending the individual and authentic that could not be exchanged or reduced, in a world where everyone drove the same Japanese cars as they played merrily and without commitment with the cultural masks of identity, as if it were fancy-dress time all the year round? I could easily find reasons for smiling wryly at the puritanical conceit of the American painters of the Forties and Fifties, when you listened to Charlie Parker with the same gravity as when you heard Stockhausen, and strutted around Greenwich Village in black polo-neck sweaters with a dog-eared paperback edition of Camus or Sartre in your back pocket. But I had kept going back to their pictures when I grew tired of the ironic airs or dry theorising of more current art. Where

Andy Warhol's sham anonymous cans of soup already seemed outmoded, long past their sell-by date, Jackson Pollock's and Mark Rothko's, Franz Kline's and Clyfford Still's canvases were still the same. They were the same kind of hermetic fields of paint unfolding themselves in a mediation between the hand and the eye, without the intervention of language or interpretation, a pure and autonomous presence of colours and contours. These canvases were what they were with an integrity that could still move me. You need not know anything to look at them, they could hang anywhere because they did not require an art institution or tradition as a background for ironic or theoretical games of meaning and meaninglessness. I loved looking at them. When I stood before them again I felt that their absolute presence, devoid of references, demanded my own presence, a concentration without thought, resting in the centre of the eye's gravity, precisely here, exactly now.

I enjoyed sitting lazily and apathetically in the garden's niche of purling water and lowered voices between the enormous buildings and the restless, crosswise humming of the right-angled streets. I felt a desire to stay as long as possible before getting swallowed up in the traffic outside again, but perhaps too, for the first time in days, I felt like being surrounded by people without having to keep moving the whole time. It suited me well to sit there, a stranger among strangers, at rest among the skyscrapers for a quarter or half an hour in scaled-down alertness. It seemed almost like relaxing one's guard to sit like that, slackening the rope of one's watchfulness, dropping off with closed eyes in the middle of Manhattan. At one point, when I opened my eyes after a short nap I caught sight of a woman who had sat down opposite me on the other side of the pool. She could have been in her mid-twenties, perhaps thirty, she had fair, short hair with a side parting, and she was wearing a black tailored suit, and dark sunglasses making her face and the triangle of bare skin in the neck of the jacket seem even paler. Sunglasses were in fact not strictly necessary, since the sun did not reach down into this crevice between the tall buildings, and the dark glass could only make it harder for her to read the book she held up in front of her, unmoving, with crossed legs. Pale and interesting, I thought, but I couldn't help looking at her, especially not after I had managed to make out the letters on the book jacket. It was *The Fall of the King* by Johannes V. Jensen, in Danish. I hadn't read it since school, and the only thing I remembered clearly was the scene where a horse is slaughtered on a snow-covered field, in which the author, with graphic precision, describes the red, violet and brownish innards twisted about in the snow. As I looked at her, my mind's eye pictured a strange, both beautiful and cruel connection between the sobriety of the brutal image and her discreet, androgynous elegance. I smiled at myself, but all the same I went on playing with the idea that this might be one of those absurd coincidences you are always hearing about and that the elegant young woman might be identical to the talented artist whose name and telephone number the curator had jotted down as he sent me a sly glance. In which case his slyness had been justified, considering how uninhibitedly I was devouring her with my eyes. Ashamed, I buried myself in my notes on Jackson Pollock and Barnett Newman and wrote down a couple of supplementary comments with steely earnestness, and when I looked up again, a Hassidic Jew sat smoking a cigar on the chair where the reading beauty had been.

I forgot her in the train back to Brooklyn, engaged in observing the groups of motionless exhausted faces carefully avoiding each other's eyes in the overfilled compartment, each on their separate way somewhere, and when I happened to look anyone in the eye by mistake I immediately directed my gaze at a fictive point outside the window, where the grey walls of the tunnel rushed past. I did not think of her again until I had written out the notes of the day and sat looking at the grey squirrels in the trees in front of the Lebanese heart surgeon's house. They moved at the same speed and with the same jumping wave-like movements as the green curves on a screen registering heartbeats. The image of the beautiful stranger was very clear to me, her regular features made even more expressionless and motionless by the sunglasses, her bare skin in the otherwise modest V-neck of her jacket. However naïve it might be I could not relinquish the idea of the totally improbable fluke, that I might perhaps have been sitting opposite the curator's talented lady friend in the afternoon in the sculpture garden. As if in this city of all cities it would be particularly unusual to come across a young woman who understood Danish, for instance, because she was a Dane. It annoyed me to be wasting time on such a futile whim, and I told myself it was just another example of the kind of rubbish that builds up in your head as you go through the day. Of course I had noticed her only because I was alone in a strange city. Could it really be anything else? I looked at my watch, it was six o' clock. It was midnight at home, Astrid must have gone to bed by now. Perhaps she was lying there thinking of what I might be doing, perhaps she had already fallen asleep. Our lack of synchronism suddenly made me sad, as if it was not only the ocean and the time zones that separated us. I had never been unfaithful to her, and though the idea had now and then tempted me, when a beautiful unknown woman looked at me with an appreciative glance, it had only been in the form of diffuse and fleeting fantasies. The idea of making a pass at a strange woman seemed humiliating. Should I stand with my hat or my cock in my hand soliciting a little adventure? Besides, I would never be able to manage the smoke screen of feints, white lies and strategic suppression of facts that I would be obliged to spread around me in order to meet my fairy-tale princess in secret. But the practical problems of infidelity were not the only things that terrified me. If I deceived Astrid and lied to her, if there was something in my life that she must not know, I would not only reduce her to less than she was, I would also diminish myself until I was nothing but a miserable calculating gnome. That was my reasoning when on rare occasions I was distracted by some woman's luxurious legs or dreaming eyes, but months could pass where the idea of a digression did not so much as cross my mind. When Astrid teasingly told me that some woman or other had glanced at me with interest, as a rule I had not myself noticed. I didn't really believe her and took it as a good sign that she actually had to tell me about my inadvertent success with the ladies. If she said something like this at all, it must be because she couldn't dream of being jealous, and that, of course, was because she had no reason to be.

Was I not happy, perhaps? As I watched the nervy grey squirrels cavorting around in the tree tops out on Orange Street, I recalled the afternoon in Paris some years earlier, when Inès had put the same question to me. The word had seemed so inadequate and at the same time so inquisitorial, 'happy', as if by being expressed in the form of a question it already held a silent accusation, because I was not sitting there in the café on the Place de l'Alma overflowing with happiness like an ecstatic porker. It was the kind of question you asked when you were young, because you still had only the words to brace yourself with, all those words you adjured yourself and the world with because you hadn't yet formed the world and it hadn't marked your shining, hopeful mug. The fact that Inès had had to ask that question at all must have been because she had neglected to part from her youth and let go of herself. The years had gone by for her just as they had gone by for me, but she obviously still clung to the idea that every possibility was open, even those she had rejected. If she had really believed, even for a moment, that she could make me forget my wife and children and throw myself into her arms just because she happened to turn up one afternoon in the Palais de Tokyo, out of the blue, it could only mean that she had learned nothing. I had sensed the futility beneath her off-hand account of her improvised and uncommitted Parisian life, free as a bird and insidiously lonely. She was still only responsible for her own pretty arse, and even the most passing fluctuations of her mood shadowed, as they always had done, events in the world outside her closed blinds. She was just as intense and quivering as in the past, but the intensity had acquired a slightly mannered touch. She still subscribed to the overwrought idea of 'living in the present' and so she had come to a halt. She clung to her precious freedom like a small saver who studies his savings book, shiny with age, every evening. As she gradually grew older she would change into one of the grey subscribers to great and passionate love, sitting on a bench in the shade in a straw hat with her summer coat buttoned up to her chin, gazing after the young couples in love and envying them their enamoured ignorance.

I knew very well I was being unfair. Hadn't Inès said she would like to have a child? Hadn't she merely been unlucky? Why couldn't I just accept that I had escaped unharmed from the most painful defeat of my youth, whereas she regretted, when it was too late, what she had thrown away? Was I nursing an old grievance? Would it have been too ironic if it should suddenly turn out to have been she who had suffered most? Had I been afraid that my old feelings for Inès had merely been in hibernation when I directed my hopes at Astrid's new, unknown face? Probably it was all of no consequence now. The only thing my reunion with Inès had left me with was her simple and at the same time all-encompassing question in the café on the Place de l'Alma. It was not the recollection of Inès that brought me to think of her question, it was much worse. It was the recollection of a totally strange blonde in a black suit, with whom I had not exchanged a single word and had gazed at for less than a minute all told. She looked like one of the indolent beauties in Astrid's French fashion magazines, and then she might well be a formidable girl from Ikast with both feet on the ground, and *The Fall of the King* was merely one of her accessories on a par with the very filmic and mysterious sunglasses. I felt a complete fool as I sat glowering at the innocent, frolicsome squirrels, a fool in my own eyes. *Was it possible I had not been happy?* Possible, yes. It was so long ago since I had last considered the question, and anyway now I was on my own. I couldn't reach out to Astrid and test my feelings. But if I wasn't happy, what then was I? Not the opposite, at least. Perhaps neither. Was that the secret behind my immoderate irritation at the naïvety of the question? That I was neither cold nor hot, but lukewarm, and so spat the question out of my mouth instead of answering? Had Inès reminded me of something that afternoon in Paris, something I preferred to forget, or something I had actually forgotten?

It was not so much my old unhappy love she had reminded me of, it was rather the way I had loved her, wildly and ravenously, without restraint, totally exposed and defenceless. Afterwards I had explained to myself it was bound to have gone wrong with Inès and I could not reproach her for having protected herself against my reckless passion. No one could stand being loved like that, and if she had allowed me to I would certainly have loved her to bits and pieces. It had been an immature, self-absorbed love, I told myself. It had not been Inès at all I had loved but my own besotted image of her, a gilded icon that shone mysteriously in my waking dreams. No one was so mysteriously and utterly wonderful. My fanatical adoration was almost insulting because she would never have had a chance of living up to

my exaggerated notions about her. And of course she herself
had sensed that, which was why she had decided to hasten
the time when she had to disappoint me. But why then had
she taken my hand in the café on the Place de l'Alma? Why
had she reached out to me in such a transparent manner,
when I had suddenly turned up again as if dropped from
heaven, seven years after she had made off through the
snow? Because it was not at all so marvellous to be free
and without obligations in a one-room flat in Belleville?
Perhaps not only that. Perhaps she had reached out to
me without any ulterior motive, merely to touch for a
moment the memory of a dream that was too beautiful
to be forgotten. It was obvious that my young passion
had been an infatuation, that she had never been what
I wanted to make her. But all the same she had kept
the naïve, faded image of this unknown illusory woman
I had invented, she had not been able to relinquish that.
Perhaps my illusions about Inès were like those on early
Renaissance altar pieces, by Giotto and Cimabue, their
chaste visions of the blessed virgin with the pure, defenceless
eyes and ivory white cheeks in the Uffizi, the Louvre and
the Metropolitan Museum, like pieces of wreckage from
cancelled time. The cruel princes of the Italian city states
were dead, their victims and the victims' bereaved were
dead, their sufferings forgotten and the machinations of
power accounted for and relegated to the archives. Only
the dreams remained, weightless hallucinations of that foul
and bloody life, painted with fine brushes and preserved as
a greeting from the dead to an unknown future. Perhaps not
even a prayer to be remembered but rather a recollection
of interior movements which had disengaged themselves
from the flesh of the dead long since turned to dust. The
recollection of an imploring glance that had painted the
world more beautiful than it was simply to be able to endure
it. My besotted fantasies about Inès were very far from the

truth of who she was. But they might have been very close
to the truth about the person she would have liked to be.

I myself had become the person I was while I had been
living with Astrid. The mature, responsible father and
husband she occasionally teased about other women who
desired him behind his back. As the years passed and he
gradually took shape I had no wish to be anyone else. I no
longer felt the distance between inside and outside that had
made me so melancholy after I had left my self-imposed exile
in the ruin and returned to my suburban youth, in which my
mother came and went en route between her changing roles
and changing lovers. That gap between my interior world
and the world outside which I had believed I could cross
with my love for Inès, and which had merely opened wider
when I reached out for her with my impatient hands. One
day I suddenly found myself on the other side of the gap,
and I hardly knew how I had crossed it. I had become the
man who was married to Astrid, father to both our daughter
and her half-brother. Our life together filled me to the brim
with all the everyday repetitions and the repeated moments
of sudden lightness when I discovered I had forgotten myself,
one with the continuous movement that whirled us through
the easily flowing, foaming current of days. And the part of
me that was not engrossed and pervaded with everything
I did with Astrid and the children, was correspondingly
absorbed in my scribbling, so there wasn't a single crack
between the two, only the swift unnoticeable transitions
which gave me the feeling that my life was unfurling like
one continuing gesture. Yes, I was happy, and not least
because I just didn't have the time to ask myself such an
odd question. I was happy, but I didn't dream that Astrid
and I would merge into one single four-legged creature
of joy. We were two and we went on being two who
parted in the morning and met again in the evening in a
continuous rhythm of departure and reunion. I was happy,

but my happiness was not to be fulfilled in selected scenes, weighty with all the significance I attributed to them. It was not the recollection or expectation of a rapt present, in which Astrid and I were united in the absolutely right light, and in which we ourselves and everything that involved us melted together in one glowing moment of mutual passion. My happiness was not so theatrical, it was more patient, more discreet. It was a joy that could stand daylight, and it didn't matter if it was a little stained, or slightly creased. It was the movement and direction of the current, not the fleeting ripples and reflections on the surface, it was that which carried us on, we only had to keep afloat, and so we never asked each other where we were actually going. It would have been meaningless to ask. We didn't have to go anywhere, only further on together, from day to day through the years that came, like nomads who make their home in a different place each night and yet, as soon as they have pitched their tent, can say they are at home again. Only occasionally at night, at intervals of months, I lay in the dark beside the sleeping Astrid and asked myself how it had actually happened that I came to accompany her and whether I really had not left anything at all of myself behind en route. Whether he was all I was in the whole world, and whether he might just as well have been another, this man lying here, who early in the morning Astrid would regard tenderly and sleepily while she waited for him to wake up and emerge once again in her eyes, as he stretched out his hand to her cheek, warm and slightly swollen with sleep. Alone in the dark room beside her invisible sleeping body, in the minutes before my consciousness wrapped itself up in itself and rolled over the edge, I sometimes imagined myself hovering above a delta of tributaries branching out into meandering streams which constantly divided anew the higher up I went. One stream resembled the other so they were hard to distinguish, and yet each flowed in their own winding course, but seen from so high up it seemed to make no difference which one you followed on the way to the endless, monotonous sea. Yet was there something I had forgotten, after all? From my dizzy bird's-eye perspective I couldn't catch sight of myself down there, I could not tell if I had lost my way in the ramifications of the delta, whether it made any difference at all, whether in the end it wasn't just a question of floating with the stream.

As I sat there trying to see if it was the same squirrel or another popping up among the leaves where the first one had vanished, I saw the Lebanese heart surgeon parking his car in front of the house. He was in his early sixties and had a pleasant olive complexion. His curly black hair was smoothed back from his high forehead, and his grey and black moustache completely covered his upper lip, which merely contributed to the unchanging sadness in his Levantine eyes. He jumped out of the car, surprisingly agile, almost eager, and opened the door for a slender little woman with big sunglasses and a yellow scarf tied firmly under her chin. She must have been roughly his own age. When I had had dinner with him after I arrived he told me very frankly how he had met her on a golf course in New Hampshire, precisely a week short of a year since he had buried his wife. The slight lady in the check trouser suit had made him want to live on, that was how he expressed it, the man people queued up for to do their bypass operations. He had insisted on hearing everything about Simon and Rosa, looking attentively at me with his dark, oriental eyes as if everything I told him was of the greatest importance to him. His eldest son lived in Cairo and the youngest had settled in Düsseldorf. He carried his lady friend's travelling bag for her and gallantly offered her his arm before they went up the steps to the house. Half an hour later a cautious knock sounded on my door. He smiled apologetically as if to excuse himself for intruding in his own house rather than leaving it to me from cellar to attic. They were giving a little cocktail party the next evening, he wanted to introduce his fiancée to his friends, I would be more than welcome. There was something touching about the studied American manner in which he pronounced the word *fiancée,* his accent was usually unmistakable. But it was even more touching that he used that word at all. Today I could wish I had spent that evening with him and his grey, frail lady friend and not only to show him that I valued his hospitality, but as he stood announcing his invitation, I had not the least desire to appear as the European lodger who had been invited to join in out of politeness, an exotic item of the house's inventory. I could hear in advance the questions people would ask and visualise how I would answer them yet another time while the person who asked had already turned away to another guest. Off the cuff I fabricated an excuse and said I unfortunately had a dinner date with a Danish artist who lived in Manhattan. He only smiled and withdrew, and as he went downstairs it struck me that I hadn't needed to explain who I was going to see. Obviously she still haunted me, the black-clad beauty from the sculpture garden behind the Museum of Modern Art. On the spur of the moment I felt caged in my room. I had become accustomed to walking around freely in the large silent house, now I could hear my host and his friend talking and playing music down below. The aggressive sound of a fruit liquidiser drowned out *Das wohltemperierte klavier,* and just as I had adjusted myself to Bach he was replaced by Ella Fitzgerald. I couldn't get to grips with my notes but went on sitting by the window because I didn't know what else to do. The afternoon light was as golden as the street name, Orange Street, it spread in beams and fans along the walls and sidewalk, just as lavish and luxurious as the sedate terraces of brown brick behind the wrought-iron fences, and the air was perfectly clear, with a touch of coolness, sharply outlining the shadows of the lobed leaves against the sun's hard afterglow on the trees' bark.

Now that I had made myself homeless for an evening I might as well try to turn my pretence into reality and call the unknown Danish painter. If nothing else I could then confirm or disprove my naïve theory that it was she who had been reading *The Fall of the King* earlier in the day. But at the mere thought of calling I got butterflies in my stomach, and it was not only my inborn reluctance to contact people I don't know that awoke them. I also had a vague feeling of guilt because, stupid or not, I had established this link in my consciousness between the telephone number the curator had written down and the elegant young woman I had secretly spied on in the sculpture garden. What was happening to me? Had I not after all set my mind at rest with all the good reasons for my never having deceived Astrid with so much as a single affair? And anyhow what was wrong with sitting and looking for a short while at a girl who was obviously aware of her attributes and clearly dressed to be looked at, and who furthermore had planted herself right in my field of vision? The fact that she was probably Danish and that for a single-minded moment I was reminded of the telephone number on the scrap of paper the curator had given me with a raffish glint in his eye, was surely not an association that necessarily came within the sphere of criminal intent. On the contrary I convinced myself that the only right thing to do was to call the girl, make a dinner date and thus prove I had nothing to fear either from her or from my ten-year-old, entirely monogamous desire. When I saw the heart surgeon and his lady friend get into the car, dressed for dinner, I went downstairs to telephone. She answered at once. She sounded neither particularly surprised nor particularly enthusiastic when I introduced myself and made my suggestion. As we were talking I continued to picture the pale woman in black with the boyish hair-cut. She was not from Ikast anyway, I could hear. Her voice was surprisingly deep and she spoke slowly, as if she had to consider even the simplest words and phrases, maybe because her thoughts were elsewhere. It turned out that she had no plans for tomorrow evening. She suggested a Thai restaurant in Spring Street and even offered to reserve a table, perhaps to compensate for her preoccupation. My mood improved as soon as I had put down the phone. I would have dinner with her, I could tell her about my book, she would talk about her painting, we might even exchange gossip about Copenhagen artists, and afterwards I would take a taxi back to Brooklyn. It would have been strange to spend a whole month in the town without meeting anyone except my host. I dialled my own number in Copenhagen. It took a while for Astrid to answer. She had gone to bed, it was after one o' clock at home, her voice was hoarse with sleep. I apologised and asked how things were, and if anything had happened. Why do we always think something will happen when we are away? She told me Rosa had had her hair cut, and Simon's football team had won a match on Sunday. I said the book was going well, and we exchanged the usual tender nothings before saying goodbye. I would like to have continued talking to her. That night there was something despondent and bachelor-like about going to bed in my room on Orange Street, where the street lights shone through the leaves of the trees with a synthetic glare.

I worked with concentration all morning and managed to finish writing a section in which I discussed the technical and expressive differences and likenesses between Jackson Pollock's layered explosions of oil paint and Morris Louis's vertical, thinly flowing veils of colour. In the afternoon I went over to Manhattan. My dinner date was not for several hours. I spent part of the time at the Metropolitan Museum, although I had already been there once or twice, and afterwards sat in the sun in front of the Loeb Boathouse

allowing my thoughts to wander as I observed the angular
silhouettes of the tall buildings above the trees in the park,
the folded reflections of the sky in the lake and the vibrating
image of the water along the grooved cliff of black granite
towering on the opposite shore. There was still plenty of time
as I strolled southwards along the Avenue of the Americas.
The transverse streets between the rows of vertical building
blocks opened out against the empty, blue and pink sky
above the Hudson. Dusk fell as I walked. Suddenly it
seemed somewhat hazardous to be on the way to have
dinner with a completely strange woman, and I almost
blushed at the thought that she might get the impression
I was 'after something'. But on the other hand she could
just have said she was engaged. Unknown as she was, I still
visualised, lacking a more precise description, the reading
beauty in suit and sunglasses when I finally reached Soho.
There were ten minutes left before our appointment when I
found the restaurant in Spring Street. I went into a bookshop
and took a look round. On the way back I caught myself
smoothing my hair, as if it made any difference how I
looked. There was a queue out on the sidewalk, and I
took my place among the people waiting, gazing round
as if I really knew the face I was keeping a lookout for.
I observed every single woman who passed along. A hefty
girl with red cheeks and a snub nose crossed the street and
aimed straight for the queue. She wore a pair of lobster-red
tricot trousers which looked as if they were about to split
around her broad thighs, which quivered at each stride she
took. Was she the one I was waiting for? Was that why the
curator had smiled so slyly as he wrote down her phone
number? A broad smile lit up her face when she caught
sight of a black woman waiting some way in front of me.
Why had I actually been so terrified at the thought of it
being the cheery girl in lobster-red tricot I was to discuss
art with as we ate deep-fried vegetables with chopsticks?

What was I actually up to? The next female pedestrian was a tall, leggy girl, walking with long strides at the side of a black man in leather jacket and cap. She herself wore a black leather jacket and shabby jeans, and I concluded they must be a couple. I went on with my spying, still somewhat ashamed at the evaluating glance I had directed at the girl in the red trousers, when the black leather man turned into the bookshop I had just left while the leggy girl walked on hurriedly towards the queue, her searching gaze moving along the line. But she stopped some way off, and when I looked in her direction again she was talking to a stooping young man with unframed spectacles. I looked at my watch. Was the chic beauty from the sculpture garden letting me wait after all? As the queue slowly advanced I listened to the conversations around me and glanced covertly at the speakers, the hefty girl in tricot who was laughing loudly at herself, and the leggy girl in leather, who gesticulated with her long slim hands, telling the stooping man about a film she had seen in her nasal New Yorker accent. You could see she'd just had a shower, her long hair was still wet. Her hair was unusually long, about the same length and colour as Botticelli's Venus, and her luxuriant golden-brown locks were a strange contrast to the worn leather jacket and her narrow, slightly hard and angular face, pale, almost transparent, it seemed to me, and completely without make-up. The stooping man held up a lighter for her, and as she bent her head a little forwards to light her cigarette she glanced at me briefly with an indifferent expression in her grey eyes. The man lifted his hand in farewell and crossed the street, and the leggy Botticelli girl looked at me again, with her head slightly aslant, smiled a question and came towards me. I wondered why I had not recognised her deep voice.

If the Lebanese heart surgeon had stayed out at his lady friend's house on Long Island, if he had never held his cocktail party, or if I had accepted his invitation, or gone to the cinema instead, if I had never watched a strange, Danish blonde in the sculpture garden behind the Museum of Modern Art and by a ridiculous association confused her with the unknown woman hiding behind the telephone number given me by the curator with a diabolic expression, if he hadn't given me the number, if, in brief, everything had gone differently, I would never have met Elisabeth. That would probably have been better, or it might still have gone wrong, only in a different way. It's useless to speculate on the ramifications of chance, the crazily budding alternatives of eventualities that wither one by one, as events gradually succeed each other, jostle and push each other on until nothing can be changed again. All the same I can't let go of the idea of how easily, how smoothly, everything could have developed in another direction when I think of the importance I later ascribed to an evening in Soho seven years ago. The events in themselves do not mean anything, they are as weightless as anything that never happens, never unfolds. The story does not take place in New York, in Copenhagen or in Lisbon, it is not about Elisabeth, Astrid or Inès. It is played out in my confused head as I travel in my mind between the cities, to and fro in memory, and the figures moving through it are only shadows of the women I am describing, flickering, indistinct and intangible when they glide across the inner cave walls of my skull. The cities and the women are merely names echoing under the vault of the cave, and it is the echo of my own lonely voice I hear as I attempt to interpret the bewildering shadow play on the wall at the very back of my head. Perhaps I have never known these women, perhaps they, like the cities, are nothing more than the handful of moments I remember, the disconnected and fleeting angles of vision in which the faces and the streets came towards me. I have forgotten so much, and there is so much I have never known, never seen. My story is an interpretation of interpretations, it is nothing but my hesitant, irremediably distorted recollection of the significances I have ascribed to certain places, certain faces, and of how the faces and the places changed their significance on the way.

In the years that have passed since that evening I have asked myself whether Elisabeth was especially beautiful at all. Not in the same way as Inès or Astrid, not in the obvious, I had almost said universal, way in which they had always been regarded as beautiful women. Elisabeth's flowing, unruly Botticelli hair was beautiful, but she herself was no beauty, and when we finally got to our table and studied the menu, slightly formal and smiling carefully, I was almost relieved that with her appearance she had definitively freed me of the sexy, black-clad daydream from the sculpture garden, which had irritatingly clung to my thoughts during the past few days. There was nothing in her way of speaking or looking at me that so much as hinted that she viewed me as a man other than in the strictly social and clothed sense. She didn't speak nearly as slowly as she had on the telephone, on the contrary she was rather lively, but she made the same sudden pauses, as if she was searching for words or lost in thoughts of something completely different. She was easy to talk to, and before the first course arrived I had already told her I was married and had children, as if I must quickly transform what had threatened to become an obsession into a totally harmless evening. I even told her about the woman reading in the sculpture garden and about how I had wondered if it might be her. That amused her, and when she had finished laughing she asked why I hadn't cleared up the mystery on the spot. I said I was far too shy for that, and she looked at me in amusement and said I didn't seem particularly shy, but still without the least touch of coquettishness. There was something almost boyish about her as she sat there in her shabby T-shirt with the name of a baseball team on it, I don't remember which one. There were moments when she could look like a slim boy with her narrow pale face, although a boy with hair right down to the hips. She was almost clumsy and several times nearly knocked my glass over. When I looked at her I felt very adult in my tweed jacket and freshly ironed shirt, even if she must be about thirty, and there could only be six or seven years between us. It turned out that we liked the same painters and shared the same aversion to much of the art produced later. She was particularly fond of Mark Rothko and Morris Louis, that was why she had left Copenhagen after the Academy to settle here. Among other reasons, she added, tossing her head and looking distant for a moment. She wanted to be close to the pictures she stole an arm and a leg from, she said and smiled again. It made me think of the curator's expression when he wrote down her name and phone number, smiling his foxy smile. I found it just as hard to imagine what he saw in her as I would have to understand what she might have seen in him. I asked her how she came to know him. She explained that he had been in charge of a group exhibition of young artists' work, in which she'd had a picture. She said it casually, without so much as a hint that there was anything I must not know. Later, shortly before I returned to Copenhagen, I asked her straight out if they had been together. No, she replied, brushing the tip of my nose with her index finger in a funny, cheeky gesture, as if she was playing for a moment that I was the one who had been disappointed. But he had tried it on all right, she must say.

That evening I had no idea, no expectation that I would ever have the chance to ask her. Just as I had been comical in my own eyes when I hung back from the heart surgeon's invitation before finally dialling her number, now I was composed, sitting talking to her while the Thai food made the sweat trickle down our foreheads. She was surprisingly good at eating with chopsticks, considering her boyish awkwardness. I kept on waiting for something to crop up that we disagreed on, an area where we had not developed kindred ideas, and at one point I debated with myself whether she might just be playing up to me, but the seriousness in her subdued deep voice made me reject the idea, her searching gaze absent-mindedly noting the talking and smiling faces in the restaurant when she hesitated in order to find the right word. Not until I had paid the bill and we were walking among the old cast-iron façades of the district, did it emerge that she had read several of my articles and essays. That was why she had agreed to meet me. Did I think she went out to dinner with whoever came along merely to have the opportunity to speak Danish? My text on Giacometti had particularly interested her, the observations on withdrawal, the point of balance between spatiality and absence. The only thing she disagreed with me about was my enthusiasm for Edward Hopper. How could I be so wrong? He was incapable of painting people, his women's breasts were never of equal size, and he could never get them to stand on their feet so you believed in it. The most she would admit to was that his colour combinations were original, for example when he juxtaposed grass green and mint green, or strawberry red and aubergine. Moreover, his bloody boring fire escapes and fire hoses in slant sunlight adorned just about every other girl's room in the provincial backwaters, mind you. I enjoyed her pert arrogance and protested just to get her to go on. We sat on the sidewalk in front of a café at the far end of West Broadway. Behind her the World Trade Center towered with all its empty, brightly lit offices glittering in the darkness above the old warehouses. I tried to make her tell me about her own pictures, but she made light of them, and even her modesty seemed sincere. I asked if I could see them, she was evasive, she didn't know if she dared. What did she mean by that? She smiled and looked away, she was afraid I would like them as little as she did herself. But she found a pen and wrote the heart surgeon's phone number on the back of her left hand as I was taking her home in a taxi. If she should change her mind and I still felt like seeing them. When we had said goodbye and the taxi was on the way across Brooklyn Bridge, it occurred to me that the evening had gone precisely as I had foreseen. If I'd ever imagined anything else it was probably only because I had become a bit strange, sitting by myself in front of my window in Orange Street, with only the scurrying squirrels for company, and I still think there was no ulterior motive in my hoping she would not wash the back of that hand too thoroughly.

I worked steadily during the days that followed, and only thought briefly of Astrid and even less of my meeting with Elisabeth. It could still have ended like that, before it had ever begun, just an evening among so many others, without any consequences, quickly forgotten. Seven years have passed since I put that story behind me, and it has long been fruitless to ponder on whether the story began because I was ready for it, without knowing that myself, or whether it seized the chance to begin because circumstances offered. Nevertheless I did speculate over it after Astrid had left and I strolled around Soho once again as the autumn wind pulled at my coat and trouser legs. When I looked through the list of exhibitions in *The Village Voice* I discovered that Elisabeth was showing in a small gallery on the top floor of a former storehouse in Wooster Street. I had not actually thought of going to see it, but as I happened to pass it on the way back from my walk beside the Hudson, I went up, quite tense at the thought that she might be there. As I stood among Elisabeth's wide, almost monochrome canvases, reaching up from floor to ceiling in the bare, shabby space, Astrid might have been standing on the Cais da Ribeira in Oporto, with her back to the crumbling, old façades tottering on each other's shoulders across the river. I can't recall which of us said that the district beside the river resembled an Asiatic lake village with its broken, soot-blackened tiles and lines of heavy dripping washing and blinds rolled down over balcony bars in front of the windows roaring out football transmissions and family feuds, separated only by narrow alleyways with shops as small as broom cupboards lit by a single grease-spotted bulb. The black alleys daylight never reached and where we walked together hand in hand past groups of emaciated drug addicts with lacklustre eyes and the toothless little old women carrying their burdens on their heads. While my eyes slowly separated the faint graduations of colour and by degrees called forth the vague, barely visible contours in Elisabeth's flat but only apparently empty fogs of colour, Astrid may have been standing on the quay beside the dark river looking up at the traffic passing high above her head on the steel bridge linking the city centre with the southern bank. At that time I did not even know she was in Portugal. Perhaps she thought I must be in New York by now, perhaps she hadn't given a thought to where I was that evening a week after she had left me. Until she went away I had been absolutely sure she knew nothing about Elisabeth or about what had happened then. She never asked me, but perhaps she did guess after all that something must have taken place. If so she made no sign she knew. Perhaps I had revealed it without realising, not by anything I said but by something in my silence as we drove through Tràs-os-Montes among the solitary villages with grey, decaying stone houses and black, kneaded mud in the alleyways where chickens and cattle were free to roam. Perhaps she had merely considered it as a possibility when late one evening we arrived in Oporto and strolled around the illuminated cathedral. Perhaps the suspicion had grown in her like a little invisible hole in her thoughts that let the cold air in as we stood beside the parapet along the slope above the river and laughed at the boys playing football against the cathedral wall. As we smiled at the names of the port wine houses spelled in high neon letters over on the southern bank, well-known English names which suddenly meant nothing, shining in the night sky.

7

Elisabeth called three days after we had had dinner together in Soho. It was a Sunday. I was surprised to hear her voice, I had thought it was Astrid phoning when the Lebanese heart surgeon knocked at my door in the morning, still in his dressing gown, and said there was a phone call for me. Did I still want to see her pictures? Yes, I did. Our conversation had inspired me, her enthusiastic, self-forgetful way of speaking of the artists we both liked, and if in weak moments I had doubted whether there was anything new to be said of such a thoroughly interpreted and canonised movement as the New York School, every doubt had evaporated the morning after our meeting. Was I doing anything that afternoon? The suggestion took me by surprise, I had only just had breakfast and had actually planned to spend Sunday in Brooklyn, write for a few hours and afterwards perhaps go for a walk in Prospect Park, which I had not yet visited. She lived near Tompkins Square, between First Avenue and Avenue A. It was a quiet sunny Sunday in the East Village, there was hardly any traffic and I enjoyed strolling with the warmth of the sun on my back among the low brick houses with black-painted fire escapes on their façades. The jagged outlines of the fire escapes and their twisted, zigzag shaped shadows on the walls made me think of Franz Kline's dramatic abstract architecture of broad black brush-strokes, which I had been writing about that very morning when the heart surgeon knocked at my door. There was a lazy, laid-back atmosphere, almost idyllic, although in some places it was still a rough area. The homeless basked in the sunshine among their shopping trolleys filled with junk, muffled up in their filthy coats, even the vigilant pushers stood closing their eyes against the sun when there were no customers. The Puerto Rican mothers took walks with their buggies beneath the trees in Tompkins Square and shouted jovially to each other in Spanish, that soft, childish variety of Spanish the Latin Americans speak, and the down-at-heel punks with their green Mohican hair and rings in their noses and eyebrows had taken off their leather jackets to sun their thin white arms. Some black guys with dreadlocks sat among the flickering patches of sunshine, beating their drums in a shining, drifting cloud of marihuana. It was a district sought after by young people, especially if they were artists or dreamed of the artist's life. Everywhere there were small theatres and galleries in basements and vacated shops, and if you sat long enough in one of the chic alternative cafés you could listen to their grandiose plans for the next exhibition, the next play, concert or performance. Most of them were hopelessly untalented, but the East Village crowd formed a closed circle whose members confirmed to each other that they were cool, and rather than aspiring to a breakthrough on Broadway they seemed to prefer the studiously ragged and Bohemian cosiness in which they could feel young and subversive, long after they had passed thirty.

I found her house and rang the bell. A long time passed and I was just about to go and find a telephone box when she stuck her head out of a window on the third floor. She hadn't expected me so early. Her long hair hung down vertically like a halted, golden-brown waterfall around her face, as she smiled and told me to let myself in and threw the key down on the sidewalk. The staircase was narrow and scruffy and there were several doors on each floor. Hers was open, I knocked lightly before stepping inside. The apartment consisted of a kitchen diner and one large room where she worked and slept. She was in the kitchen, opening a tin of cat food while a white cat rubbed itself around her calves. She had bare legs and feet, very long and chalk-white legs beneath a pair of synthetic indigo blue football shorts, and her hair hung like a musketeer's cape around a checked washed-out man's shirt with so many missing buttons that her stomach showed when she moved. Was she dressed so lightly because she had not expected me until later? She smiled and made a humorously apologetic gesture with the can before kneeling down and serving the impatient cat. Then she rose again and flung out her arms, suddenly a bit shy. Well, this was where she lived. Would I like a glass of wine? She had already set out the bottle on a tray with two glasses and a bowl of salted peanuts, an excellent Orvieto, I noticed, and she carried the tray into the room and put it down on the worn floorboards, almost ceremonially, between a battered sofa and an old deck chair with striped canvas. Her easel stood at the opposite end of the room, on the other side of a rolled-up futon, between the canvases leaning against one wall in stacks, with the stretchers outwards. I chose the sofa and she crouched in the deck chair with her long legs pulled up underneath her, watching me as if to see what I thought. Again I felt old in a vague way, although I was only thirty-seven that afternoon, as I sat breathing in the smell of turpentine and oil paint in her apartment, and fixed her grey eyes for slightly longer than I would otherwise have done, so as not to let myself be distracted by her folded and, something I could no longer ignore, particularly well-shaped legs. She rested her glass against her pink knee and gazed into the corn-yellow liquid for a moment, turned the glass around and said she had almost not called me. I cleared my throat and asked why. She blushed a little as she looked up at me. She knew quite well she was not really good, not yet, she still had a long way to go. We had had such a good talk and she was afraid she wouldn't be able to live up to everything we had spoken about, so I would think she was just full of big words without knowing how to put them together. Her face didn't seem nearly as sharp as it had done a few evenings before, in artificial light, but I was struck again by the contrast between her unruly, romantic hair and her angular features, the prominent chin, the narrow mouth, the pale grey eyes and long nose which was a trifle crooked. Her nose had a bend in the middle, which gave her a slightly degenerate profile and led you to recall certain dukes, astronomers and encyclopaedists of the eighteenth century. Her face, devoid of make-up, radiated an almost ascetic spirituality in contrast to the unpractical luxuriance of the hair. The golden-brown locks were constantly in her way so she had to stroke them away from her forehead while she spoke. They constantly interrupted the conversation like something irrelevant and lacking in seriousness which she brushed aside, impatiently or mechanically as she tried to pursue an idea, find the words that could take her on in the direction of what she was attempting to approach in her thoughts.

She was relying on me to express my honest opinion. There were so many people who just patted her on the shoulder for one reason or another, but what I had to say would mean something to her. She had read what I wrote, she was sure that at least I would be able to see what she was striving for. I said I was glad she had plucked up the courage to call me, and told her how our conversation had helped me to overcome the doubt I had sometimes felt about my plan to write on the New York School. Her genuine enthusiasm had convinced me, I said. She smiled, embarrassed, and took a sip of wine. It had been quite unexpected, I went on, to meet someone who thought the same way about Morris Louis and Mark Rothko, no one seemed to take any interest in them any more, they had been canonised and then forgotten. I felt I might have exaggerated my doubt as well as the constructive effect of our meeting on my work, but she looked at me attentively as I spoke, and after all it wasn't totally wrong, merely laid on rather thick, for the sake of clarity. Again she supported the foot of her glass against her kneecap and gazed into the wine, as if looking into a crystal ball. It was not only because she was shy about her pictures, that she had hesitated to call. I lit a cigarette, and she looked at me briefly as I blew out smoke. She had also been afraid I would misunderstand her. People talked so much. She was not to know what the curator had said about her, perhaps I thought – no, she interrupted herself, that sounded utterly daft. What did? I asked. She smiled ironically, perhaps I believed she was the sort who ran after married men. We laughed over that, and I said she didn't give that impression at all, and besides, the curator had said only nice things about her. I didn't say anything about his conspiratorial smile, instead I said that actually, I had thought the same when I called her, that I too had been afraid she would misunderstand me. As a whole it was astonishing how much we had already talked about us. When you meet a woman, at first you talk about anything else, anything out in the world that may interest you. Later on you talk mostly about each other, about your own story and the other's and about the sensational fact that you are together until you again start to talk about the world outside, if you don't stop saying anything at all. Perhaps Elisabeth too thought we had talked enough about us, for she suddenly rose with a cheerful remark that she might as well get it over with, and began to pull out canvases from the stacks along the wall.

Her pictures were certainly not as impossible as she made out, but her own evaluation of them was actually quite precise. Her sources of inspiration were still visible, but it would be wrong to call her an imitator. There was a huge gap between the confidently balanced abstractions I saw at the gallery in Wooster Street seven years later, but the rudiments were there already, the awareness of colour and attitude to the material, and above all I could see that she was not satisfied with easy solutions. But there was still something subdued and 'felt' about her canvases, a slightly too busy use of sponge and thinner, as if she was afraid of being too obvious, of adding flesh and bone to her compositions, an anxiety which made her weakest pictures too decorative and eager to please. She had gone into the kitchen, I could hear her washing up, she dropped cutlery and pans on the floor, clumsy as she was and clearly terrified at the idea of what I was thinking about her work. When I was alone with her pictures and passed from one to another, concentrating on finding out what to think about them, I felt both serene and crestfallen. What I had repressed during our dinner in Spring Street because I was so relieved to be freed from my futile daydreams of the mysterious beauty in the sculpture garden behind the Museum of Modern Art, had announced itself the more painfully when we met again and sat opposite each other, I on the ravaged sofa, she in the deck chair, with her beautiful long legs folded up under her chin so the comical football shorts, probably without her noticing, crept up in tight folds along her perfectly arched thighs around the little curve of her sex. I had done my best to censor away that part of my field of vision as she was telling me how her fear of being misunderstood had almost stopped her from calling me, but I couldn't hide my attraction from myself, and it would be hard enough to keep it from her. How depressingly trivial it was. Could I really not meet a woman who thought and talked on the same frequency as myself without immediately getting ideas from the sight of her thighs just because they were lovely, and because she unwittingly exposed them to my ferocious gaze? Even when she clearly suggested that the mutual wavelength we had been lucky enough to find should be kept free of irrelevant erotic noise. I went into the kitchen to join her. She sat at the kitchen table with the cat on her lap, apparently immersed in a newspaper article. I sat down facing her and said what I thought about her pictures. I spared neither my acknowledgement nor my critical objections, where they were concerned I was even a little brutal in my honesty, and I speculated on whether I might perhaps not have been quite so honest if she had not given me to understand that our new acquaintance was absolutely platonic. Was I even punishing her a bit? Or was I merely completing the clarification of the kind of relationship we were to have which she herself had introduced, to cut myself off definitively from the risk of committing follies? She looked at me and took pains trying not to blink, absent-mindedly scratching the cat behind the ear. Silence fell when I finished speaking, and in the silence the cat jumped down from her lap with a soft thump and stretched before slinking into the next room. Now she didn't even have that to occupy her hands with. She cleared her throat, pushed the hair away from her cheek and said I was right. She was glad, she said, that I had been so direct, it was almost like getting a present, and in reality she did know where her weak points were, but it was sometimes easier to realise when it came from someone else, that only happened rarely, she could really put my criticism to good use. I almost felt too sorry for her and tried to retract a little, but she persisted in her self-criticism, until I was forced to praise the best pictures fervently to put an end to all this honesty.

She said she was looking forward to reading my book on our mutual painter favourites and asked why I had doubted whether it was worth writing. I wondered whether she questioned me on my self-doubt in order to redress the balance between us, now she herself had revealed her uncertainty, but I couldn't make out whether she asked because it gave her pleasure to shake the pedestal on which she had apparently placed me, or because my confession of doubt had increased her sympathy. I replied that my problem was the same for anyone wanting to write about artists who were neither academic nor literary. The paradox involved in writing about the New York School was that the strength of their painting actually derived from its consistently non-linguistic character. Their non-conceptual pictures evaded every description, every verbal characterisation, and you would never be able to contain them or the effect they had on you even if you used the most sensitive vocabulary. Something would always remain which could not be expressed in words, and it was this remnant, this experience beyond words that made you keep returning to them. An experience that could only be expressed in painting itself and only unfold in the meeting between the eye and the purely physical, non-referential presence of the picture. A combination of consciousness, matter and form that could not be interpreted because it was unique in the deepest and most unfathomable meaning of that word, whereas language always had to make use of similarities and contrasts, in other words, of comparisons, in order to set the consciousness in motion. The only linguistic statements that came anywhere near what I was talking about were perhaps the paradoxes of the Zen Buddhist sages, because to them the exercise of disciplines such as archery and calligraphy elicited the same spontaneous insight as that which on rare occasions occurred in the meeting with a perfectly accomplished picture. She listened with an intense gaze that seemed to register every movement in my face, while at the same time in her thoughts she was in a totally different place, and I must admit I was quite moved by my little toast to pure painting. As I was speaking I actually decided that something like this should be the preface to my book. With such a self-critical prelude I wouldn't have promised too much. Suddenly she rose, as if she could not take in any more, and suggested a walk. There is a limit to the number of ways in which you can be together with someone in an apartment, you can sit opposite each other in different seats, or you can go to bed, and when the latter possibility is excluded, there comes a time when you are tired of the first one, especially when you don't yet know each other so well and the pauses in conversation should preferably herald a deeper stage of mutual contact. We had already become quite close through our love for the New York School, and now that was enough, now something different must happen if we didn't want to risk ending up in a blind alley. I scratched the cat politely under the chin while she pushed her bare feet into a pair of worn-out basketball boots. She put on a scruffy old raincoat and a pair of scratched sunglasses and lifted her hair up over the coat collar with a shy smile, as if she wanted to excuse its immoderate growth, and soon afterwards we were down on the street.

She walked fast, with long energetic strides, and as I walked beside her I noticed for the first time that we were of equal height, if she wasn't a bit taller. All the same, we must have looked an odd couple, she in her bombed coat, with bare legs and dusty canvas boots, I in my tweed jacket and polished shoes. I felt hopelessly conventional, almost like a cop in plain clothes, as we walked through the East Village, which seemed to be inhabited by cosmopolitan village originals, so that eccentricity had become the norm while the normal was a quiet sensation. What could she have seen in me, an intellectual bourgeois creature in tweed jacket and newly ironed, pale blue shirt? I felt a stranger, not quite myself, and wondered what kind of relationship we were establishing. There was nothing in the least flirtatious or tacitly significant in the way we spoke to each other, and I felt reassured by the idea that anyway it could not be the start of an affair, now I had visited her at home and we had gone out again, into public, neutral space. Was it the start of a friendship? I pictured Astrid and the children. They had finished dinner now, Simon was most likely lost in some star war or other on his computer, Astrid was probably reading a bedtime story to Rosa, and I saw her on the sofa with the small figure who had almost disappeared inside the duvet she had dragged with her into the living room. At the same time I was walking here in the afternoon sun on the other side of the Atlantic ocean beside a girl I knew hardly anything about, far away from my life, my town, my daily round, where every step I took was a step along familiar, well-trodden paths. We followed the Bowery for a while past the dusty shops with equipment for restaurant kitchens and traversed Little Italy and Soho towards the Hudson. From time to time I pointed out some anonymous detail that had caught my attention, like a naïve tourist, as I described to her how my experience of pure painting corresponded to my experience of the mysterious presence of things when you concentrated on their physiognomy alone, detached from their purpose or significance. I told her about my childhood when I had moved away from my parents into a ruin to vegetate over the passage of light and shadows across the collapsed remnants of walls and fallen beams. She understood me, she had been like that as a child too, and like me she could fall into a reverie over the pattern in a manhole cover or the torn posters on a wall. We talked about the special, though uneventful moments when the sudden lightness of an unconscious, inadvertent movement and the light that falls upon it, and the shadow that it briefly outlines, when all this is united in an inscrutable way with one's gaze, as if the movement arose and issued from the eyes that follow it. At one point I happened to kick a big rusty nut on the sidewalk so that it ran over the sunlit paving, balancing on the edge of its own shadow like a runaway figure eight, and hovering in a diminishing spiral until it toppled over and turned into a nut again. She bent down to pick it up, then passed it to me with a smile saying it was from her to me so I wouldn't forget our meeting. I still have it in a drawer somewhere. Then she suddenly asked me to tell her something about my wife, as if for safety's sake she wanted to remind me of our tacit agreement, in case I might have misunderstood something.

It was quite strange to hear her speak the words 'your wife', and equally strange to talk about Astrid, summarily describing her, rather like the way people give a description of themselves in a lonely hearts advertisement. Thirty-eight, film editor, narrow eyes, wide cheek bones, slim, chestnut brown hair that gets curly in wet weather, previously married to a well-known film director, mother of two, the eldest from the first marriage, likes Truffaut, crayfish parties, tramps beside the sea, antiques, Catholic kitsch and trips to southern Europe, cool and reserved in the opinion of others, but in fact intuitive, considerate and sensual behind the façade. Was that Astrid? She suddenly seemed so remote and small to my inner eye. Had I said too much already, or should I have said nothing at all, because that would be too little anyhow, regardless of how much I said? Both. But yet another threatening question hit me when we reached the West Side Highway and walked in the direction of the World Trade Center with a cool breeze in our faces on the wide sidewalk beside the sparkling river, among the puffing joggers, along the same stretch I would take a week after Astrid had left. It is the same thought that has pursued me ever since the morning she stood in front of the mirror and casually announced that she wanted to go away, so casually I forgot to ask her why. The same question that poses itself each time I see her again before me, standing in the bedroom doorway regarding me, a few minutes before she vanishes. Do I know Astrid at all? Do I know anything about her except what I know about the years we lived together, the things we did together, and the fragments she told me about the time before we met, just as summarily as the description I had given Elisabeth? And does she know anything more about me? Elisabeth asked how long we had been married. Ten years?! She shook her big hair incredulously but respectfully. So it could be done then! I laughed and kept my voice light as I spoke of being liberated from the impatient and egocentric expectations of youth, of the happiness that could tolerate daylight, tolerate getting creased, and while she listened and looked at me attentively, I suddenly felt it all sounded so thin and pale, and it seemed to me that she too could see and hear the faint shadow beneath my adult smile and confident words.

But it was true, wasn't it, that was what it was like. Wasn't it? I asked her about her own situation. Now I was the one who had a balance to redress, I who had exposed myself and expected a disclosure from her, give and take, just as I had repaid her artistic self-criticism with the account of my occasional writing crises. We had stopped to look out over the deserted quays and the empty river, the wind had freshened and pulled at her hair and her coat, and she pushed aside the locks that blew across her face as she smiled faintly and looked out at the pale blue and blue-grey and petrol-blue water ruffled up by the wind in restless fleeing flurries. It was a long time since she had been together with anyone. Two years earlier she had found herself pregnant, he was an artist too, back in Copenhagen, it had ended badly. That was when she came to America. She had grown used to being alone most of the time, she didn't mind, although sometimes she had to ask herself whether she wasn't getting too good at it, at being alone. Now and again she felt like going home. It was a tough city, you didn't get anything handed to you on a plate, but on the other hand she liked having to fight. She didn't really know what she'd expected. Sometimes she missed being in a place where people knew her. A speck of dust flew into my eye, it felt like a pine cone and the tears ran down one cheek. She turned towards me like someone suddenly waking and opened my eyelid with one finger, but she couldn't see anything, and suddenly the speck had gone. A couple of seconds passed before I said it had gone, in which her fingers still rested against my cheek and you can say I made use of the moment, that I withheld relevant information, so to speak, as I lightly took hold of her wrist, as if I wanted to remove her hand. We stood like that for a little while, not long but long enough, I with her wrist in my hand as we looked into each other's eyes, I with my red, tear-filled eye, then she made a movement with her hand and I let it go, and she turned to the river. I mustn't get fond of you, she said. No, I said, and looked in the same direction as she did, over at Colgate's clock that caught the sun so you couldn't make out the time. Then we stood there for a while, quite close together. A crazy, aimless place to stand, with our backs to the calm, monotonous Sunday traffic, and the deserted, sooty warehouses. She turned her face towards me, serious and with a new gentleness. You are strong, she said. Why would she think so? I said nothing. She said she was cold and wanted to go home, I could get a train from Church Street, she said. I said I would walk part of the way with her. She said I didn't need to. I said I knew that. We started to walk. I tried to find something to say, something light, anything, but managed nothing except scattered and rambling remarks separated by endless pauses, on the way back to the East Village. I couldn't make out if she was the one who had been good at hiding her feelings or I who had been blind. As a whole we had been clever at misunderstanding each other. We hesitated in front of her street door, she took a long time to find her keys. When she had opened the door she turned to me and said goodbye. I kissed her, she made no resistance. I hope you know what you're doing, she said. I said I knew. I hadn't the least idea.

They are the same things you do, the same movements,

and yet you feel it must be different, mean something else, because it is another person meeting your eyes or closing her eyes as you bend over her. Why did I take it so much to heart? Was it because for ten years I hadn't slept with anyone except Astrid? Was it merely what is said to be 'a digression'? Well, I'd apparently been digressing for a long time, although unaware of it myself, long before the afternoon I sat gawping at a modern young woman in the sculpture garden behind the Museum of Modern Art, completely led astray by the utterly improbable hypothesis that she might be identical with this Elisabeth I had originally no intention of calling, supposedly in defiance of the curator's raffish expression, as if he had given me the telephone number of the most luxurious tart of all time, but certainly just as much in fear of what I myself might think of doing. But if it was not a question of just another weary married man who wanted a bit on the side now he had a break from the daily round, and right over in America at that, far from any curious or judgmental eyes, then Elisabeth was merely an extra in my private little drama, the absolutely chance object of my pent-up desperation. That was how I put it to myself later, chafing with shame, but I was more tender as I stood in her apartment once more that afternoon and embraced her among her canvases, while the cat rubbed itself jealously around my trouser legs and her bare calves. We remained standing for a long time without moving, she with her hands clasping the revers of my jacket and her head resting on my shoulder so her hair tickled my nose, locked in that long embrace, unable to move, perhaps because neither of us knew where we were going. I came to think of another embrace in another apartment, another twilight hour, when I had walked the town off its feet with Inès after she had turned towards me, standing alone in a quiet shadowy gallery among the weathered marble portraits of forgotten emperors. And I came to think of the chasm that had opened up in me when I left my childhood ruin, where I had lived for a couple of weeks with the mice and the wild cats, lost and happy, and moved home again to my parents' empty, silent house. That intangible distance I believed I had put behind me many years later when Inès drew me to her in front of the window looking out onto the Jewish cemetery with its crumbling unreadable headstones. As I stood holding Elisabeth tight it seemed as if I had stepped across the same distance a few minutes earlier when I took the last stride over to her and opened my arms. As if the old distance had opened up again while Rosa and Simon grew between Astrid and me as time went on with us, without my seeing it, perhaps because I had so much more than myself to look after. Was I about to deceive Astrid, or had I, through the years with her, deceived both her and myself? Had I after all left the most primordial part of my self when I took the decisive step and seized the chance, that evening in my kitchen when I caressed Astrid's cheek for the first time, since she happened to be the one who had turned up in my loneliness? Nor had I known then exactly what I was doing. Slowly Elisabeth loosened her grasp of my jacket, I let my arms sink down, and she took a step backwards, looking at me, shy and slightly confused. I had no idea what she read in my face, but she must be able to see something, exposed as I was to her eyes. She let her coat fall to the floor and undressed before me, until she stood completely naked, face to face with the strange, fully dressed man who had invaded her life, as if she wanted him to know what he was taking on, see her as she had been created with her small breasts and prominent ribs. Then she went over to the rolled up futon and spread it out, kneeling to straighten the sheet, and I noticed the greyish dirty colour of her heels and missed her already, although she had only gone a few steps away. I could hear the police car sirens up on First Avenue. A noisy salsa tape from a car radio echoed among the façades, grew louder and died away, and through the window I saw the shadow of a pigeon's flapping wings approach the fire escape's folded, hatched shadow on the wall of the house opposite, at the top where the bricks still shone with the low sun's deep glow. The sunlit flapping pigeon and the pigeon's flapping shadow approached each other until the distance between them was wholly harmonised as it landed on the top step of the fire escape and folded up its wings.

To tell the truth it was not at all unforgettable, the first time Elisabeth and I lay together on her hard futon, watched over by the white cat, who sat in the doorway with impeccably folded paws like a household sphinx, to whom nothing human was strange. I was inclined to believe her when she said it was a long time since she had been with a man. The angularity of her body seemed to be transmitted to her movements, and our venture developed into a hectic and hoarsely breathing rough and tumble, until we had to give up. She lay with her cheek resting on my thigh as she regarded my still aroused cock with a disoriented wondering gaze. I came to think of a famous photograph by Man Ray in which a silent film beauty from the Twenties with a dark pout and long eyelashes bends her head in the same manner as she regards a primitive African statuette. We both laughed, not only at my comparison but also because I should have come to think of it at all, and we went on giggling now and then as we crept close together in the dusk beneath the heavy woollen poncho that served as her duvet. She asked if I was disappointed. I wasn't, not a bit. I was almost relieved at not having to perform brilliantly the first time, after so many years of having Astrid as the steadily more biased witness of my sexual prowess. I had never quite believed that any other woman would be as satisfied in her place, whether I suspected her of being modest or of overrating what had now become hers, merely because it was hers. But I didn't say anything about that to Elisabeth as we lay close together beneath her poncho, and to my surprise nor did I have a trace of bad conscience, perhaps because there was nothing demonic or overly exotic to be felt in her long narrow body against mine. It was just another body, different from the one I was used to. I tried to explain to her how I was feeling, how it seemed like having traversed a distance in myself, a distance that had grown through the years I had lived with Astrid, without my having noticed it, because it had opened so slowly and gradually, but she laid a finger on my mouth and told me to stop.

Later on we never talked about Astrid. Nor did we talk about us, about what had happened between us, or what was going to happen. The future was taboo. We discussed art, our work, what we saw and heard and what we had once seen or heard, and we avoided touching on the inevitable day when I would return to what was my life. We pretended it was not approaching, and settled ourselves in our soft shining soap bubble, delighted that it stayed aloft. We did not count the days but the hours, and so the three weeks that followed became a small eternity. We spent most of the time in her apartment, and took long walks without a destination or went shopping in the middle of the night at the Korean greengrocer's on Avenue A. I cooked for her, hearty Spanish casseroles, and she managed to put on a kilo while we were together. We also learned how to make love to each other, but there were nights when we just lay chatting and quite forgot that forbidden lovers are supposed to fuck like mad. Every other day I went over to Brooklyn Heights and slept at the Lebanese heart surgeon's house to work for a few hours next morning, but just as often I sat writing in Elisabeth's kitchen, while she worked next door and the cat went to and fro between us like an affectionate messenger. My book progressed more quickly than I had expected, neither Elisabeth nor her cat distracted me, on the contrary

I found it easier than before to focus on the themes I was pursuing, and when I read aloud to her the pages I had written during the day I could hear they were better than most of what I had written so far. The heart surgeon was rarely at home, he apparently preferred his lady friend's house on Long Island, and only once was there a message that Astrid had called. I myself rang home a few times and was amazed at how unaffected I was when I asked what had been happening, or talked of my book. As far as I could hear she didn't suspect anything. I would not have believed that treachery would feel so easy and effortless, and I listened to her voice with the usual tenderness, slightly delayed by the satellite link, as if Elisabeth and she really existed in worlds apart and the boundary between them went straight down through myself.

We spoke to hardly anyone apart from the times when we were in one of the cafés in the East Village and her friends came over to say hello, nonchalant artist types who shook my hand politely, stealing curious glances at me as they exchanged local news with Elisabeth, mildly wondering what kind of bourgeois specimen she had raked up. She made no special effort to introduce me to her world, and I was only too glad to have her to myself. Only once did she take me with her to a fashionable private view in Soho. The gallery was in an old converted garage with frosted glass windows facing onto the street, so the cool white space formed a hermetic abstract sphere around the exhibit and the specially invited guests standing in groups with their backs to the pictures, conversing animatedly with each other while keeping an eye on whoever came and went. Nobody noticed me at my observation post in the furthest corner, I was momentarily invisible. I was surprised to see how many people knew Elisabeth, and from my corner I watched my graceful ragamuffin of a lover being kissed on the cheek by middle-aged men with pony tails and black

T-shirts under their pin-striped suits from Saks. So they too were part of her world, the world I had disturbed and to which she would return when I had gone home. Even the artist was clearly one of her oldest and dearest friends, a little Italian with thinning hair in a white suit and sandals, who had to put his head back to look up at her as they stood giggling together. He was the only one who allowed himself to smoke, and he puffed away at a full-grown Havana cigar as he told her a story that was so funny she doubled up with laughter. I couldn't help noticing how he jovially put his little hairy hand with the smoking Havana on her buttock in the washed-out jeans full of holes, as he stood on tiptoe in his sandals to whisper something in her ear, totally indifferent to the obviously well-to-do women in pink and lemon-yellow Chanel creations fidgeting for an audience. Again I was reminded of the curator and his foxy smile. Was I a laughing-stock as I stood here, completely thin-skinned because of love in this clinical, hectically humming place?

The day before I left we went out to Coney Island. We had a beer at a bar on the promenade, where elderly men in dented baseball caps sat bent over in silhouettes beside the sea. The ugly cries of seagulls resounded inside the bar, which naturally was called the 'Atlantic', and behind it the ferris wheel was spinning in the empty pleasure park. The television was on above the bar, the football pitch was almost the same green colour as the walls in that scruffy place. The players jammed together on the pitch in a confused bunch of numbers on their bowed backs and the next moment spread out again like a flock of heavy, clumsy gulls. One glittering aeroplane after another approached in the sky over the sea and prepared to land at John F. Kennedy airport, and the anglers out on the jetty dropped their lines into the water again and again. They had tied little shiny fish onto their lines as bait. Behind them, on the other side of the park, were the last tenements in America, their windows facing the ocean, brown, tall and square. Elisabeth thought the melancholy housing blocks resembled the thousand-year-old highrise mud-houses in Sana, Yemen. White bulbs flashed above the switchback linking the letters of the name, *Himalaya*. We stayed for an hour on the beach. She rested her head on my lap and closed her eyes in the white cloudy light, her hair spread out in a fan over my knees. I watched her face and the sea. I asked if she still thought of moving back to Copenhagen. She didn't know. Perhaps. We didn't say a great deal that day or the next in the taxi on the way to the airport. She smiled wryly as we stood opposite each other before the check-in barriers. It had been great to meet me. It sounded as if we were never to see each other again, as if nothing special had happened. Then she kissed me briefly and left without looking back. Six months later I stood on another beach with Astrid. It was the day after we arrived at Oporto. We intended to go straight to Lisbon, perhaps with a stop in Coimbra, but first we wanted to see the sea. We hadn't seen it since San Sebastian. We followed the Douro along the increasingly shabby façades with sooty black tiles, rusty balcony railings, lines of sheets and washed-out children's clothes, out to the river mouth where the anglers stood on a sand spit, small and lost in the mist. We drove all the way to Matosinhos and walked across the enormous deserted beach with our backs to the neglected beach cafés and beach cabins and the great oil tanks further away, glittering dully in the misty sunlight. We walked until we could get no further, until we could just stand before the yellowish surf of foam and whirled-up sand, and see as far as we could, out where the sea became one with the fog. I discovered afterwards that Matosinhos and Coney Island lie almost opposite each other, at about forty and forty-one degrees northern latitude. The beach where I sat with Elisabeth's head in my lap trying to imagine what it would be like to leave Astrid, and the beach where I stood with Astrid six months later, after I had taken leave of Elisabeth for the second time. A beach in the old world and a beach in the new, divided by the sea which so many before me had traversed full of hopes, as if the world were not after all one connected place that is merely very large. As if it was a matter of separate worlds.

Astrid was not waiting for me at the airport the first time, in spring, when I came back from New York with the memory of Elisabeth as a blurred, unreal after-image at the base of my fatigue. It was a great relief. I had been afraid she would be standing there holding Rosa's hand with Simon a little in the background, wearing his baseball cap and walkman, restless and impatient because it was rather beneath a sixteen-year-old's dignity to fetch his stepfather from the airport. I had prepared myself so intensively for this reunion in the arrival hall that I had had no time to foresee what else would happen. Would anything happen? As I dozed in the plane my treachery had dawned upon me in all its incalculable dimensions. I couldn't think of it as a mere affair, what had taken place in the East Village during the past three weeks, even though I was now several kilometres above the surface of the sea, alone again, and should have made the air corridor over the Atlantic into an elegant, painless sluice that divided me from my secret and closed again behind me. Of course I knew that an affair like this was something utterly banal when you were an adult who could only smile at your own guileless youth, just as you smile at the old pictures of yourself looking so naïve, with your soft cheeks, dressed in clothes long since dated. I knew very well that it need be nothing more than a harmless diversion without any side effects, that there was no reason at all to make an issue of it or burden Astrid with quite unnecessary pain. But the idea of my own silence was just as painful as the thought of Astrid's reaction if I told her what had gone on in New York. Until three weeks ago I had been the man I had become over the years with Astrid, but I had only been that man because I believed she knew all there was to know about him. I had never wanted to have any secrets from her, on the contrary I had always been afraid of the thought that there might be something I hadn't managed to tell or show her, something she had not seen and seen through. I only dared to believe in her love if I could rely on her loving me despite all she knew about me, despite all my faults and failings. Ten years ago when I kissed her for the first time one winter evening in my kitchen, a strange girl I'd picked up in my taxi and given shelter merely to be kind, and when ten months later she told me she was pregnant, and I replied with my reckless *why not,* I had spontaneously seized the chance to escape my loneliness and become someone in the world, together with someone else, in her eyes and in everything we did together. After Inès left me I had felt as if struck by a curse which made me invisible. It hadn't been in the least like the feeling I had when I lay on the mouldy sofa in the idyllic ruin of my youth among the heaps of broken tiles and watched the birds flying through the roof as I dreamed of being no one. It hadn't been as I had thought in my childish arrogance, and as it said in the poem I had learned by heart: *how dreary to be somebody, how public, like a frog . . .* On the contrary, in the most cruel way, Inès had punished me for my ill-starred passion and transformed me into a hideous toad, slimy and fusty-green with loneliness, and not until Astrid kissed me did I become a person again like everyone else, though not just anyone. For I became precisely that human being she had met so fortuitously and yet liked more than so many others, and I determined on the spot, from one moment to the next, without hesitation and rather irresponsibly, that he was the one I wanted to be, the man she had called forth from invisibility with her gaze. And thus I had closed the door behind me on the innermost room in myself, I thought on board the plane as it grew dark over the Atlantic with unnatural haste. That was how I had turned my back on the room in my overgrown ruin, where I had been myself more than anywhere else because I had the company I needed with the mice and wild cats around me and I did not need somebody else's eyes to hold me fast and prevent me from vanishing. I had escaped invisibility, I thought in my aeroplane seat as I watched the sky turn dark blue above the clouds, but only to disappear from myself and get lost in the visible world's welter of faces and forms and ways of being carried along by the days in the labyrinthine delta of coincidences.

I landed early in the morning. The others had already left when I let myself into the apartment. There was a note from Astrid on the kitchen table, she had laid a tray with coffee and rolls, and Rosa had made a drawing of me, a man in a flowered jacket, standing smiling among skyscrapers only half a head taller than himself. On top of her clumsy rendering of the Empire State Building stood a chimpanzee in spotted bathing trunks. It too was splitting its sides with laughter, and it had what looked like a Barbie doll under its arm, with long wavy hair. I went to bed and slept all day. When I woke up the sun had set. I was roused by Rosa's hand stroking my stubble, and I heard Astrid call her in a whisper. I opened my eyes and saw them for a moment in the doorway of the twilight blue bedroom before they disappeared. I lay still for a little while listening to their distant voices out in the kitchen and the screaming brakes and excited American dialogue in the film Simon was watching in the next room. I felt as if I too was watching a film that had been stopped and now continued again with the same actors, the same plot. I looked at the verdigris-green, illuminated hands of the alarm clock. It was half past twelve in New York, Elisabeth might be working on the picture I had seen her start a couple of days earlier, or perhaps she was walking along First Avenue now with long, quick strides in the sun and wind that made her hair wave like a shining flag. I rose and went into the living room to Simon. He looked at me vaguely, quite lost in the film, then he stood up and embraced me, a little shyly, as if he was really too old for that kind of thing. He asked how it had gone. On the screen behind him a man hung in the air over Manhattan clutching one of the runners beneath a helicopter with a wild look in his eyes, while another man crushed his white knuckles with the heel of his boot. Well, I replied and told him to watch to the end of the film. He smiled apologetically, it was at the very most exciting place, I smiled back and went out to the others. When Rosa heard my steps she came rushing along the corridor and leaped into my arms, nearly knocking me over. I kissed her and carried her into the kitchen where Astrid was peeling potatoes. She stood smiling at us with the potato peeler in her hand until I let Rosa slide down on the floor and embraced her. She had lost some weight, I could feel, she looked beautiful, beautiful and unsuspecting as she stood there recognising me with her eyes, as if she saw all there was to see. As usual when I came back from a journey, I told them what I had experienced and gave them the small presents I had remembered to buy. Later in the evening, when Astrid and I went to bed, it surprised me that she could see nothing, and I made love to her, rough and impatient, as if I could hide behind my violence, as if I wanted to get it over with, in a sudden rage, as if I wanted to punish her for her ignorance, punish her for my own crime. Afterwards she said it was a long time since it had been so good. I kissed her eyelids and she opened her lazy narrow eyes a little and creased her lips into an ironic smile and said she could almost wish I went away more often, so I could come home and make love to her like that.

I lay awake in the dark beside her when at long last we put out the light, for several hours I lay listening to her breathing and the occasional cars driving along by the Lakes. I thought of Simon's bashfulness on the sofa, watching his hair-raising video, of Rosa's happy scream when she reached out her arms to meet me and leaped into my embrace. I thought of Astrid's eyes in the kitchen when she turned towards me and seemed to make my home-coming face regain its outlines in her memory, and I thought of Elisabeth, who was probably sitting eating a tray of sushi she had bought in the Japanese restaurant on Avenue A, while the cat regarded her with its cool, unparticipating eyes. What was it about her that was such a watershed? Was it the earnest timbre of her deep voice? Her profuse wild hair and her hectic, breathless way of making love? Was it the lofty nonchalance of her appearance and the dust that gathered along the walls of her ascetic apartment, self-forgetfully absorbed as she was in her painting? Was it our mutual love for Mark Rothko and Morris Louis, her intuitive, understanding way of anticipating what I was going to say about them and about everything else we discussed because each of us had thought and felt the same thing? Was it this remarkable, finely tuned, undisturbed and noiseless wavelength, where we had found each other without hesitation, because for years we had transmitted on the same frequency without knowing it? Or was she merely an exterior, incidental opportunity that made me open my eyes to what I had ignored for years and forced me to answer the question I had for years allowed to remain unanswered throughout the fleeting, foaming, whirling current? The question Inès had left in me when she kissed me goodbye on the Place de l'Alma a year or two ago and vanished down into the metro, out of sight again. The embarrassing question that had stayed within me after I had answered so maturely and almost didactically, so calm with adult and experienced wisdom. Had I been happy? Or was it merely a conciliatory substitute, this everyday happiness that could stand both daylight and the daily chores, this patient and modest, laid-back bourgeois happiness that could be washed and ironed? Had I gone wrong after all, somewhere on the way through the years? Had I been in too much of a hurry, a little too quick off the mark when I replied to Astrid's unexpected appearance with my flippant, frivolous *why not?* Was my real treachery that ambivalent reply, when Astrid offered me a child and a meaning for my young, pointless and melancholy life? Had I only grabbed at her out of cowardice when she turned up in my self-pitying loneliness, because loneliness had made me cave in? Had she herself been happy, or have I wasted her time? Did I love her, or did it just look like it? Had Inès left an empty room inside me which Astrid was never allowed to enter because I had locked the door and thrown away the key? Had I really believed that I could condemn my own despondency and forget myself in my new life of restless activity, fond duties and humming, quotidian tenderness? Was it there, in my empty interior, that Elisabeth suddenly appeared through a hidden door in the peeling, rotten wallpaper? A door that had been so secret that it was possible to hide its existence even from myself?

The next day I thought Astrid had found me out. When I woke up in the morning and went into the bathroom she was sorting out dirty washing. As I was cleaning my teeth I saw her in the mirror removing a white cat's hair from one of my shirts. Elisabeth's cat had left an astonishing number of hairs in my clothes, which I had carelessly allowed to lie about in her apartment. I rinsed my mouth and told her the Lebanese heart surgeon's cat had kept me company as I wrote. It probably felt as lonely as I was, now its master preferred to stay with his lady friend on Long Island, I said, and it had more or less moved into the guest room with me. While I stood there telling lies with toothpaste foam at the corners of my mouth, it struck me how likely it sounded, as long as I kept the image in my mind's eye of the white cat that lay sunning itself in the window looking out on Orange Street.

Astrid smiled, she didn't think I liked cats, and it was true, I had several times objected when Rosa pestered us to get her a kitten, because I could all too easily see who would end up changing its cat litter and removing its hard, stinking little turds. But this cat had been rather likeable, I said, visualising it strutting around the big old house in Brooklyn Heights or sitting on the window sill watching me write, arrogant and inscrutable. As the days went by it grew easier to manage my economy with the truth. The film continued and I fell into my customary role, after all I did know my lines by heart, I knew precisely when I was in the frame, and what was expected of me. Besides, it had always been one of my characteristics to be slightly preoccupied, even distrait sometimes, which Astrid only thought charming, and at most would tease me about in an affectionate tone. Now I had to ask myself if it was the concentration on my work or an unacknowledged awkwardness towards Astrid, that had been the cause of my growing distraction through the years. I still had my book as a pretext for being absent-minded, and I entrenched myself in my study and wrote a great deal in the weeks that followed. When I was not writing I carried out my domestic duties, and in the evening I was even more attentive and available to the children than I used to be, perhaps in an attempt to compensate for my black conscience. Only when I was alone with Astrid did my fondness become somewhat distanced and conventional, but she was accustomed to that in the periods when I worked intensively, just as she knew the symptoms of a bad conscience when I spoiled the children, anxious lest I should neglect them, absorbed in my self-centred work.

For Astrid my intellectual life had been an inaccessible zone from the outset, and she wouldn't dream of interfering with it, whether out of respect, not wanting to disturb me when I sat at my window overlooking the Lakes bent over my manuscripts, or because my scribblings did not

particularly interest her. I was never offended by her lack
of interest in what I wrote, on the contrary. When I met
her I had in fact felt that she released me from my brooding
solitary nature. Her sure, languid movements, her crooked
smile and her subtle narrow eyes had saved me from myself.
She had drawn me into a sphere of unworried ease, and
even the greyest days had never been ugly or chilling in
their inevitable triviality. With all its necessary repetitions
daily life had rather been transformed into a light, vibrating
mobile of repeated activity, turning gracefully around itself,
set in movement by the warmth between us. I had never
expected her to disturb me in the solitary circles of my
work. It was as if only by keeping outside could she remain
a counterbalance to my abstractions and prevent me from
completely losing sight of the real world. In a subtle way
my intellectual loneliness was the price I had to pay not
to be lonely. Therefore I never thought about her when I
worked, although Elisabeth was constantly on my mind as
I was finishing my book. To think of Elisabeth and write
about the artists of the New York School was the same
thing, not only because she had thought about them in the
same way as I did, but also because for the first time in many
years I had dreamed anew that life and work could merge in
one unbroken movement. For I had indeed discovered it was
possible, in the transient soap bubble in which she and I had
spent the days in the East Village. The thin membrane of the
bubble had broken, but I could not forget its radiance and
iridescence, I could not let go of the idea that it might be
possible to blow up a new and larger bubble that could go
on hovering. Some dreams are so detailed and lifelike that
you go on dreaming them even after you have woken up. I
kept on returning to what she had hinted at once or twice,
that she might think of going home to Copenhagen, and I
indulged more and more frequently in idyllic fantasies of our
living together in another part of town, that she would paint

while I wrote, and get to know Rosa and Simon. It was all very delightful, and Astrid was always conveniently out of sight when I indulged my hopeful hallucinations.

Even before I met Elisabeth, while I was living at the Lebanese heart surgeon's house in Brooklyn Heights, I had found it hard to visualise Astrid clearly. I saw the well-known situations at different times of the day, the same every day, but she remained an indistinct figure, and when I tried to focus on a close-up of her it was always one of those slightly stiff, posed and far too self-conscious portraits that hide more than they reveal. My recollection of her was not that of a clearly defined, fast frozen moment detached from the flashing, unsteady stream of time, for she had been there the whole time, in all the years we had been together. I couldn't catch sight of her because she was everywhere. The recollection of her face couldn't be isolated into firm, unmoving images, it blended together with my diffuse memory of time itself, the continued movement through the years, which made the contours of hours and days flow together in the shining fog of speed, the haste with which everything had happened around us and with ourselves. On the other hand, I could see Elisabeth quite clearly, she merely grew clearer as the weeks passed, after we had parted in the John F. Kennedy airport. She sat with closed eyes and her head leaning back in the sunshine, on the sidewalk in front of a café opposite Tompkins Square, the cigarette between her lips outlined its changing calligraphy of blue smoke in the air, and the transparent shadow of the smoke drew a fine veil over her calm, sunlit face. She stood before her easel in the backlight that made the colour on the canvas glitter like a metal sheet, herself only a grey silhouette with her hair gathered into an untidy turban of loose locks, bare-legged, with stripes of chrome yellow and crimson on her thighs. She sat with legs apart in a sun-ray on the floor in front of the open window, bent over my sheets of manuscript, which she had spread out in front of her while she ate yoghurt, completely absorbed in her reading so she forgot to wipe away the white stripe that emphasised her upper lip and curved upwards at the corners of her mouth like a stiffened, unintended smile. I saw her so clearly in my mind's eye as I sat watching the fresh shining green shoots on the trees along the lakeside under my window. Two weeks later I gave in and called her, early in the afternoon while there was still time before Simon and Rosa came home from school. Her voice was heavy with sleep, it was only half past six in New York. I asked what she was doing. She said the cat was lying on her stomach, and it had its eye on a pigeon sitting outside on the window sill. I said I missed her. She said she missed me too. The words were almost like an impediment between us, they did not connect us, only made it all the harder to reach her. She told me she had a commission to exhibit at a nearby gallery, I talked about my book. It all seemed so dull in contrast to everything I had been thinking after we parted. She asked what it was like to be home. I said it was difficult, that I thought about her a lot. She thought about me too. Was it just something she said? I said I would come to New York, I didn't know exactly when, but I would come. Then we'll meet, she said. There was silence over the telephone, a long, satellite-transmitted silence, faintly hissing, as you imagine the silence in space. I repeated that I missed her, chiefly to fill the hissing emptiness with something, kill the silence that spread out between us all the way across the Atlantic. Soon afterwards we ended the call.

It was not until Astrid left that I began to see her as clearly as I saw Elisabeth then, after I had come home, in calm and clearly defined, easy to grasp images. The images are all I have, and I go on looking at them for fear they too will disappear. But the more clearly I see them, the more incomprehensible they become. Her story is not the same as mine, after all. The pattern of my story hides the story Astrid could have told me if she had not left, and I am only telling my own because she isn't here, but the longer it gets the more she withdraws. And yet I have to tell it if I'm to reach the point where my words die away, the boundary where they have to give up, faced with the distance between Astrid as she appears in my self-centred narrative, and the Astrid who hides behind my pictures of her. Astrid, standing on the balcony on a summer morning looking over the tree tops and the lake with a distant gaze, as if wondering about her life. Astrid, in her coat in the bedroom doorway looking at me silently for a few seconds before she turns and disappears out of sight. Astrid in sunglasses, surrounded by the river's glittering snowstorm of reflections, smiling before the view over Lisbon from one of the ferries to Cacilhas. Her inaccessible eyes and her dazzling smile among the minute houses rising up behind each other on the heights of Bairro Alto and Alfama, brilliant white in the low light of afternoon.

8

We spent the summer by the sea, Astrid, the children and I. While I was in New York she had arranged to rent the house where we had stayed the first summer we were together, when she was expecting Rosa, and where we had holidayed several times. It had originally been a low-ceilinged, thatched fisherman's cottage, enlarged around the turn of the century with an extension on two floors, holding several generations of summer guests at once in its numerous little rooms with faded wallpaper and creaking beds and floors with scrunching sand, furnished through generations, so the place seemed as timeless as the sea outside the windows, below the slope. I did all I could to seem enthusiastic. When I stood among the rose bushes again, on the steps that led down to the beach, and looked out over the empty, uniform sea, time felt longer than it had before, the time that had passed since the night I kept watch after Astrid had been taken away in an ambulance. She had almost lost Rosa, what had become Rosa, the long-legged ten-year-old with brown legs and sun-bleached plaits, who now ran along at the edge of the beach throwing jellyfish at her big brother and screaming shrilly and affectedly when he turned her upside down and threw her into the waves. Here I had sat, on the steps among the fragrant rose bushes, looking out at the dark breakers as I lit one cigarette from the butt of the last one and talked to Astrid as if she could hear me where she was in the hospital. As if it could make any difference, my repeating the same inadequate little words over and over again through my clenched teeth, *hold on, hold on*. And now

I was prepared to let go of it all. I thought of Elisabeth all the time, and I had to make out I had problems with my book on the New York School, explain to Astrid that was why I was so often absent-minded or irritable. In reality the book had been finished for several weeks, I only needed to write a brief concluding chapter and go through the manuscript, but I spun it out and sat for hours bent over the fair copy by my window facing the Lakes and later by the rickety dressing table before the window looking onto the idle and intemperate blue sea, while the others went swimming or lay in the sun. I felt closer to Elisabeth when I was writing of the painters we both loved, just as I had felt closer to her in Copenhagen, perhaps because it was closer to the airport.

After a week by the sea Astrid was brown and lovely, and scented with wind and salt when she lay down beside me. I myself was still as white as a skeleton and smelled of nothing except too many cigarettes and far too much black coffee. I was amazed at her patience and even that irritated me. Elisabeth had come between us, and clearly she had come to stay. It was only by dint of all my concentration that I succeeded in responding to Astrid's caresses at night, and now and then perform a half-hearted and routine shag so as to allay any suspicion. But it was unnecessary, she seemed to think it was my work as usual that distanced me from her, she even tried to comfort and encourage me, which only made me still more morose. When I was not thinking of Elisabeth I thought, for the first time ever, that Astrid had never understood what engaged me. Not only was she ignorant of the fact that I had been unfaithful to her, she had hardly any perception at all of the world where I spent half my life, whereas I had often talked to her about the films she made and showed her how the directors she admired had taken their inspiration from painting in their compositional technique. Suddenly it seemed to me that we had not lived together but beside each other, each in our

own world, with the children as our chief concern. Was I
to stay with her purely for their sake? As I saw it that would
merely make me more resigned until finally I would shut
myself in completely behind my words and my pictures,
because in time it would only be the pattern of repetitions
we had laced ourselves into that could still call me back to
our mutual reality, not Astrid herself and the urge to reach
out to her, the spontaneous tenderness, the recurring desire
that had earlier set the pattern in movement. Would we just
be friends? Could Astrid agree to live with a man who loved
another woman?

There I had to stop my self-justifying defence speech. Did
I really love Elisabeth or had she just become an obsession, a
phantom for my frustrated craving for something different,
another life, a new beginning? I visualised her in the sun
on Tompkins Square, in front of her easel and bent over
my sheets of manuscript, with yoghurt on her top lip,
quite clear but also mysterious. The sight of her struck
me with something resembling pain, but it did not answer
my question, and I knew there was only one way to get
an answer. Once or twice since my return I had dropped
a hint that I might have to go back to New York for a
week or so to undertake supplementary research, and my
alternately melancholy and sullen introversion only started
to diminish when Astrid herself suggested that I should go
again, since I had worked so well over there, where I had
direct access to the pictures of the artists I was writing
about. She really did say that, and I hated myself as I
kissed her, hated myself, because my gratitude could not
be distinguished from the silent, patronising contempt that
oozed out of me behind my smile. But perhaps she was not
as gullible as I fancied, perhaps she had in fact caught
a whiff of what was happening. Perhaps her unexpected
and generous suggestion was just another expression of
the almost aristocratic dignity everyone admired in her,

and which made the more insolent arrivistes in our circle wince when she smiled graciously at their intimidating or bitchy attempts to disconcert her and chisel a crack in her cool façade. Perhaps she had already thought things through and decided she would rather set me free than demean herself by holding on to a man whose love she had already lost. It might even be, I thought in my shadowy room looking out on the dazzling summer days by the sea, that she herself had noticed weariness growing like a distance between us, exhausted as I was by the repetition of everything, by no longer being on the way to some definite place, but further into a future that was no longer so unpredictable as it had once been. Perhaps she was merely waiting with deceptive passivity for me to take the first step. In the state I found myself in, the idea was almost encouraging, and I sucked at it as you suck a sweet until it has melted, dissolved by saliva, leaving only a sticky, sweetish and vaguely shaming feeling in the mouth.

One afternoon while the others were on the beach I called Elisabeth again. I had been on the point of it several times but held back, either because Simon or Rosa had come rushing in or because I'd lost courage at the last moment. It had become all too heavy, all too serious to call her compared with the easy, untroubled way we talked about whatever crossed our minds during the three weeks we spent together. I held my breath when I heard her deep serious voice speaking to me at the other end in its impeccable New York accent, and I was just about to answer her when I realised it was an answering machine I was listening to. She said she was away until the end of August. As I sat with the receiver pressed to my ear and listened to her voice, I saw Astrid come into view among the rose bushes outside, naked and sunburned under her open bathrobe, swinging her wet bathing suit like a child in a cloud of sparkling drops that made the leaves on the bushes flutter as she walked past. She didn't see me as she passed the narrow windows in the low-ceilinged room with bent head, immersed in her own unknown thoughts. The wet sand stuck to her calves and ankles and her beautiful breasts swayed softly in time to her strides, slightly paler than her brown face and legs. Why didn't I go out to her? Why didn't I carry her off to the furthest room of the house in this quiet afternoon hour, while the children roamed on the beach? Why didn't I just forget this hopeless story, why did I sit here clutching the telephone and listening to the message Elisabeth had recorded, most likely several weeks ago, addressed to all and sundry? She hadn't said anything about going away. But perhaps she had only decided at the last moment, after all she was free and independent and could make decisions from day to day. Had she travelled alone or was she with someone? Actually, I knew hardly anything about her or the people she knew. She must surely see others sometimes, and maybe I was not the only man in her life. 'In her life.' The phrase suddenly seemed far too solemn. Wasn't I just a man she had been with for a couple of weeks in the spring? Had it ever been written 'in the cards', as they say, that I should be anything more? I imagined her at this moment sitting on the back seat of a motorcycle driving through the Mojave desert, with her arms round the hips of one of the aspiring young artists in black leather jacket and narrow sunglasses I had seen leaning world-wearily against the bar counters in the East Village. While I sat here at the same time in a thatched holiday cottage, married and bourgeois and filled with longing. I couldn't even see the comedy or complete distortion of being jealous of the woman I had been fucking behind my wife's back.

A few days later I drove into town to meet my editor. Afterwards I went to look at an apartment in the city centre, which had been advertised in one of the Sunday papers. The owner was a journalist with a beer belly and sweat on his upper lip, who was to be stationed in Moscow from the autumn, provisionally for a year, he wanted to let the flat furnished he said as he showed me round. He had exceptionally bad taste, which in a way encouraged me because his smoked glass tables and brandy-coloured leather sofas merely dramatised my revolutionary and brutal determination. If one altered the vulgar furnishings a little Elisabeth and I could have a room each where we could work, hers even had a balcony facing north, and with a bit of goodwill the room could function as a studio. I was amazed at my own self-assured initiative as I questioned the owner about heating costs and the shared facilities of the property. I behaved as if Elisabeth had not only decided to return to Copenhagen, but was also intending to move in with me although I had scant reason for believing any of this. When the journalist showed me the bathroom and proudly pointed out that the gilt armatures matched the brown tiles and mahogany toilet seat, he wiped the sweat from his upper lip and looked at me with a jovially approving glint in his eye, as if he had acquired certain rights now I had seen the way he lived. Was I getting divorced? Or did I just need a discreet little love nest? He really did use that expression. I was speechless, and it struck me as often before that people's heads are probably furnished like their homes. I mumbled something about a working apartment now the children were growing up and needed more space, but he merely grunted contentedly, it was nothing to do with him. It was not only his bathroom that was brown, suddenly I felt brown inside too. He asked for a telephone number but I said I would be away for the rest of the summer. I would call back. *Good luck,* he smiled, sweatily, and his raffish glance, man to man, stuck to my flustered face as he closed the door after me. As I drove northwards I tried to convince myself that the journalist's sticky smile and his brown interior wouldn't need to affect us, and that what had come into being between Elisabeth and me would be the same regardless of where we lived. But what had I actually imagined? What would our new life be like? Would she 'be like a mother' to Rosa, she who was so distrait that she forgot to tie her own shoelaces? Would she and Astrid become 'friends'? Or would she take Astrid's place at the dinner parties with friends? It seemed unthinkable that she would sit in her worn leather jacket and washed-out T-shirt and participate in the worldly table talk in a villa out in the northern suburbs. As I drove along the motorway in the slanting afternoon light that made the cars throw long, deformed shadows on the glittering asphalt, I realised that it was not only Astrid but the whole of my previous life I was about to leave. And perhaps it was not only the thought of Elisabeth that seemed so obsessive, but also the thought of leaving it all. The thought of being no one again and leaving behind me everything I was in the eyes of others, like a snake sloughing its skin. The thought of feeling the empty air in my pores again and breathing in the dizzy sensation that everything was still possible, that my account with the future was not yet made up.

It was Midsummer Eve. I had completely forgotten Astrid had invited guests, they were already sitting with their drinks in front of the house, beside the table among the dog-rose bushes above the sea, the curator, his wife and my mother. He raised his glass in the air when he caught sight of me, with a cheerful, man-about-town gesture, and an enthusiastic roar came from my mother as if it was Santa Claus himself arriving six months late. I turned round as Astrid came out of the house carrying a tray of various tapas and proffering her cheek with an intimate glance, as if she wanted to excuse my own mother's exaggerated and theatrical joy over seeing me again. She smiled, she thought I had run away. I hastened to laugh at her light, ironic tone and sat down with the others. The sun was setting, everyone had left the beach and the shadows began to flow into the hollows in the

sand where millions of heels had trod. I caught sight of
two small silhouettes out in the water, black against the
backdrop of whirling golden reflections below the horizon,
soon afterwards they came up the beach, it was Rosa and
Simon. Had I really thought of leaving them? As if the time
for beginnings were not long ago past, the great shining
openness to everything possible. It was theirs, the openness,
not mine, as they came running towards us across the beach,
their wet bodies glistening in the low light. How would I
ever find the words that could explain why I left them
before time? Before the time when they themselves would
leave us to discover whom they might become. The curator
suggested we had a dip before eating, and I went up to fetch
my bathing trunks. From the window I could look down on
the little group in front of the house. Simon and Rosa stood
with their towels draped like cloaks around their shuddering
bodies explaining something or other with frozen blue lips
and dripping hair, and Astrid massaged their backs while
my mother leaned forward to hear what they said, with
the demonstrative teacher's expression she always put on
when she spoke to the children, as if conversing with two
backward pupils. Astrid looked at me in surprise as I came
down in bathing trunks with a towel slung sportily over my
shoulder. She creased her lips and smiled with her narrow
eyes. Now I must really take care not to catch cold.

The water was actually quite cold. The curator is one of
those who make use of the 'townee's' method when they
brave the first swim of the summer. He cupped water in his
hands and rubbed it into arms and stomach before carefully
easing his skinny body under the surface. I enjoyed the
breathless moment when the water closed around me like
a gigantic ice-cold hand, and I swam quickly out to the
sand-bar to get warm, dazzled by the glittering drops on
my eyelashes. He was puffing with effort when at last he
came up with me. We lay on our backs floating like two

afternoon gentlemen in their chaise-longues in the smoking room. Had I met any interesting people in New York? He had kept his glasses on and they reflected the sun so I couldn't see his eyes. I replied that I had kept to myself most of the time. He smiled his foxy smile. Had I called Elisabeth? I said we had had a coffee together, and started to swim towards the quay of stakes and boulders framing the little bay where the fishermen had once pulled their boats up on shore. I didn't like him calling her by her first name. He swam after me. Charming, didn't I think? I turned towards him, treading water. She was certainly very sweet, I replied, doing my best to sound casual. And he was right, I went on, she was certainly talented. I had already said too much. So had I got to see her pictures? I had the sun at my back, I was no more than a silhouette before the silhouettes of the quay's big stones, but he smiled all the same as if he could see my expression. He knew she would be just my type. What did he mean by that? He smiled again. I needn't worry, it would be just between ourselves, we were friends, after all, weren't we? I swam out, he followed and came up beside me. It was nothing to be ashamed of, a good-looking guy like me, alone in New York, of course it wasn't. Besides, I wasn't the only one to appreciate her talent. He had had the pleasure himself, like so many others, from what he knew she had a liking for men. I started to swim in to the shore. I could see the others in front of the house but only as insubstantial little figures, my mother's wide-brimmed straw hat, Astrid's dark hair as she bent forward to pour into a glass. The curator gave me a chummy punch on the shoulder as we stood drying ourselves on the beach. He was glad I had made myself at home over there. He held up his glasses against the sky and polished them with his towel, blinking at me short-sightedly. Everyone needed to try something different, eh?

The roses resembled coloured Japanese paper flowers in the lavender-blue air when the sun had disappeared behind the calm sea, which reflected the evening sky with a faint, greenish tinge below the horizon. While we were eating, the curator's wife questioned me about my book, and I chatted on about the New York School painters. Everything I said sounded superficial and conventional, but she nodded eagerly as I spoke, simultaneously asking myself if I had got anything out of the past months' work except this handful of tired, complacent clichès. Like Astrid, she had no idea what her husband got up to behind her back. Nor did she know anything of the hidden doors and trapdoors in her apparently harmonious and comfortable life. On the other side of the table my mother was initiating the curator into the most nerve-racking manner in which she had had to confront hidden and painful sides of herself while preparing for her latest role, and he bowed his bald head respectfully as he listened and smiled his slyest and most ingratiating smile almost as if he had in mind to seduce her. His intense gaze made her even more fervent and hand-wringing in her account of how hard it was to be an actor and every evening to bare one's innermost soul to the audience down there in the dark. Astrid went in and out with Simon and Rosa to serve each new course, now and then catching my eye and looking at me affectionately, as if she rejoiced that I had at long last risen to the surface again after the long period when I had been cranky and introspective. I looked sidelong at the curator as I entertained his wife with the stages in Jackson Pollock's development. To this day I don't know if Elisabeth was lying when I asked her if she had slept with him. If he had really been telling the truth when we were out swimming in the sunset, was that perhaps why a year or two later he felt he had a right to place a hand on Astrid's knee when he drove her home after dining with our mutual friends, when I was away? Perhaps he even told her about Elisabeth and me in order to somehow justify the sudden presence of his hand on her knee. In that case Astrid had been clever at concealing her knowledge from me. But on that Midsummer's Eve I was convinced it must be he who lied. And even if there was the least scrap of truth in his chummy confidences, they belonged to a pub or a changing room, not in my memory of Elisabeth and our three weeks in the East Village, floating in our transparent soap bubble outside the world, occupied only with each other and our work. Even if she really had spent a night with the curator, however improbable that seemed, it could not have had the same significance for her as the time she and I had spent together. Or rather, our time together could not have meant so little. Those were my thoughts as I sat chattering mechanically about Jackson Pollock, alternately observing the curator's shining pate and the canine teeth in his foxy smile, his wife's gentle, gullible cow's eyes and my mother's ravaged, dramatic face in which every single movement was distorted into an exaggerated caricature, as if she not only wanted to convince the curator but herself as well that she really thought and felt as she said she thought and felt.

Later on we went to the Midsummer Eve bonfire that had been lit further along the beach. I carried Rosa on my shoulders although she was really too big and heavy, and she grabbed hold of my hair each time I was about to stumble on the loose sand. She told me to hurry, the flames had already taken hold of the witch's clothes, and I heard Astrid and the others laughing behind us when I broke into a run towards the fire with Rosa hooting above my head. There were crowds of people on the beach and I recognised several faces as we passed them. It was almost like taking a walk along Strøget in Copenhagen on a Saturday morning, I thought as I made my way among the figures with dark faces, in white dresses and jackets, which glimmered luminously like the small lines of foam in the blue transparent semi-darkness over the sea and the beach. At a distance the faces were impossible to read, they blended into one with the dark pines of the plantation behind the dunes, so it looked as if the light-coloured dresses and suits were moving of their own volition in and out among each other like lost, anonymous ghosts, chatting and laughing. We move on sand, I thought, and took my place in the group gathered around the bonfire. The flames shot high into the air and the flickering reflection of the fire offset at first glance all the differences in the ring of faces, red-brown like burned clay, like the statues of Chinese warriors I had seen a picture of recently, thousands of life-size clay warriors that had been dug up during the excavation of an emperor's grave, each with his individual features and yet alike, with the same red-brown, uniform complexion. I felt Astrid's hands on my hips and heard my mother laughing loudly at something the curator had told her. Simon was on the other side of the fire talking politely to a grey-haired man who like myself carried a little girl on his shoulders, and a moment later I recognised his father, the film director. Of course he was here too, everyone was here on such a Midsummer Eve, and it really wouldn't have surprised me if I had seen Inès and Elisabeth among the women in their summer dresses, with red-brown cheeks, squeezing up their eyes against the heat from the bonfire. Astrid lifted Rosa down from my shoulders and said she would go back and put her to bed before putting the kettle on for coffee. She probably didn't want to confront the film director, who was having a conversation with the son of his second marriage while his little daughter pulled his hair and his new young wife stood in the background smiling shyly. Would I be standing like that one Midsummer Eve in a few years with a new little child on my shoulders, while Elisabeth shyly looked on as I questioned Rosa on her progress at school, slightly awkward, slightly strange, now we had happened to come across each other?

Next day was overcast. The curator and his wife had

already gone when I woke up. Looking out of the window I saw my mother sitting in front of the house reading aloud to Rosa with clear, dramatic diction, just as she did on the radio, but it really seemed as if she relaxed in the role of grandmother, sitting on the bench among the dog roses with Rosa on her lap and a faded scarf around her dyed hair like a Russian peasant woman. Astrid and Simon went out on the lawn, she asked if Rosa wanted to go shopping with them, and soon I saw the three of them go to the car. My mother remained on the bench with the closed children's book on her lap, gazing at the sea, grey like the sky, grey and bottle green, dappled with darker sections where the sand floor was covered with seaweed. I couldn't recall when I had last seen her sit like that, alone with herself, passive and unmoving, her face resting slackly in its ravaged folds. You could still see how beautiful she had once been, but here before the sea, where she thought no one could see her, she did nothing to divert attention from the baggy weight of her cheeks and the hanging corners of her mouth around the lips that had kissed so many men and allowed the words of so many writers to pass through her mouth. I drank a cup of lukewarm coffee in the kitchen and went out to her. She smiled quietly when she saw me, but didn't say anything. I stood for a while looking down on the empty beach and the tired grey waves breaking in the offshore wind. Then she suggested we should go for a walk. There were no people on the beach. We walked at the water's edge where the sand was damp and firm, past the quay and the burned-out, charred bonfire and further on beside the pine plantation. At first we walked without breaking the silence in the pauses between the dull beating of the little waves. They just about covered the sloping extent of sand and withdrew again at once, the sand reflecting the grey light only for a moment before it sucked in the water and again grew lustreless and gritty. We walked for a long way like this before she finally looked at me.

Time after time over the years I have been surprised that this vain and superficial woman should possess such sharp eyes. I cannot hide anything from her, and I hadn't been able to this time either. Her voice was subdued and completely calm, almost gentle, quite lacking in the usual drama when she asked if I had met someone else. I tried to defend myself, if only for the sake of appearances. What had given her that idea? She smiled but without any sting. I needn't talk about it if I didn't feel like it. I realised I might as well give up. I said I didn't know what to do. She said I was wrong. I knew perfectly well what I should do. That was why I hesitated. What did she mean? She took my hand and pulled me aside a little, just as a wave was about to wash over my shoes. She had hesitated as well, she went on, when she broke up with my father, even if I didn't believe it. She knew quite well I had never forgiven her, and from the start she had seen clearly that she would have to live with that. She had known what she was doing and that was why she had hesitated. Because she knew what she was about, and because she knew she would have to pay the price. It was a pathetic remark, but for once there was nothing at all pathetic about her tone of voice. She asked me to tell her who it was. I held back a bit, mostly because I couldn't decide where to begin. Then I told her how I had met Elisabeth, about the strangely clear and finely tuned wavelength we had immediately found, as if for years we had thought about and experienced the world on the same frequency, without knowing each other. I told her about Elisabeth's pictures and our weeks together in the spartan apartment in the East Village, how when I met her I had discovered that a distance had grown in me over the years, an old gap that had reopened, although I'd thought I had put it behind me long ago. The same old gap I had once more put behind me, together with Elisabeth, for the first time in many years completely present, wholly and fully there in everything I was and held. My mother merely smiled as I was speaking, until I fell silent again, because suddenly the words seemed so inadequate, so imprecise and foolish in their anonymity. She took my arm as we walked across the beach and up the sand dunes, in through the pine plantation, which the wind had shaped into crooked interlacing. When I looked at the wind-blown pine trees I couldn't decide whether to fasten upon their malformation or the stubbornness which kept them growing, despite everything. We could no longer hear the sound of the waves, only the wind's occasional sigh among the grey-green, stiff and sticky needles of the trees.

But what was she like? My mother looked darkly, almost threateningly at me as she asked. I told her about the contrast between Elisabeth's Botticelli hair and her angular face and gawky body, about the contrast between her ascetic lifestyle and her almost hypersensitive sense for the colours and surfaces of things, whether it was a rusty nut she gave me on the street in Soho, or a pumpkin she bought from the Korean greengrocer on Avenue A, merely to keep it on her table to look at and feel with her long, nervously registering fingers. I told her how from one moment to another she could suddenly change between her cool, consistent and merciless faculty for abstract thought and her almost childish, spontaneous and playful whims, as when she woke me up in the small hours because she wanted us to see the sun rise over Brooklyn Bridge. In fact I knew hardly anything about her, I said, but it was not an erotic obsession in the usual banal sense, it was not even so amazing when we lay grappling with each other on her hard futon. If I couldn't forget her it was rather that everything around me, movements, places and things, light and shadows, when I was with her, awoke my old longing just to be, here and now, in the midst of the world. As if I had woken up after sleeping for a long time only to discover that I already was where I had dreamed of being. I could see from my mother's raised eyebrow that even she thought that sounded a touch over the top. That was what it was like, I persisted, what it had been like to wake beside Elisabeth in the morning, as if I had slept for ten years, ever since Inès left me and I grabbed at the first girl who came along, by chance, and rushed to make a life with her, as if it couldn't go fast enough. My mother regarded me for a long time as she lit a cigarette and blew smoke from her nose. I said smoking wasn't allowed in the plantation because of fire danger, and she put her head on one side as she knocked off her ash on the rusty red needles covering the sandy path. Fancy, wasn't it really? Then she stopped. Wasn't Elisabeth too the first girl who happened along, after ten years with a wife and children? I had to admit it. But then, what was the difference? Was it just time that had done it? Time and boredom? She smiled sarcastically. Hadn't Astrid's cheerful nature and lovely face been just as revolutionary as Elisabeth's Botticelli locks and her ability to think in the abstract? I stood for a while looking down at my shoes. Really the two of us were alike, she said, throwing down her cigarette and treading out the stub with exaggerated thoroughness, looking up at me sideways. Would the forest ranger be satisfied? We went on among the twisted pines until the plantation was succeeded by broad-leaved trees.

I might not believe her, but she had actually expected it to happen. I was much too complicated for a woman like Astrid, and she didn't say that to denigrate her, I mustn't think that. She really was a wonderful girl. On the contrary she had feared that I would hurt her one day. Ever since I was a child I had carried a darkness within me, which I concealed from my surroundings and which therefore had only grown denser through the years, impenetrable not only to others but also to myself. It sounded like a speech from one of her television plays I had always switched off as soon as she showed herself on the screen. Formerly she had believed that she had been to blame for my having sought flight in that darkness, where I had hidden for so long that I could no longer catch sight of myself. But in time she had come to the conclusion that she was no more responsible for my closed and secretive nature than she was for the fact that I had inherited her nose and her eyes. I must excuse her, but she could no longer reproach herself for leaving my father. If she understood me now it was only because the decision I hesitated to take was the same decision that she herself had taken then. And I should not rely on this Elisabeth to make it easier to decide. To her it was probably just an affair, what we had had together during my little holiday from the marital grind. She knew me all right, she knew how I always felt everything much more deeply than everyone else. She had not left my father because she was in love with someone else. She had gone her own way because she could not stand dissembling any longer. This so intellectual and spontaneous and ascetic and sensual Elisabeth was merely an occasion, just as her own various affairs had been, and I might just as well realise that now. But she knew it all right, she had the same problem as I did, she went around with the same darkness within her. Of course I didn't believe her, she knew perfectly well I despised her for her mannerisms and prima donna fads, but that was her way of enduring herself. She knew the darkness in which I staggered around like a blind man. She knew the impatient expectation that someone, an unknown totally strange person, would open the door on that darkness, let in the daylight and discover who she really was. But now she had waited for many years, and that person, she had gradually come to realise, that person didn't exist. You had to go out into the light on your own, at least occasionally, when the darkness inside grew too dense and impassable. That was what she had done when she made her escape from my moaning wimp of a father and chose freedom with all its costs. And that was what I was about to do if I could summon enough courage to leave my sweet pretty wife and my sweet children and my cosy, comfortable life, where I was on the point of being suffocated. But it was up to me, and she thought we should stop talking about this business now.

I had never talked to my mother in that way before, and never have since. Even when we were alone together we did not touch on 'that business'. She was right, and so was the Count of Monte Cristo in the chapter I read aloud to Simon and Rosa in the evening: 'There are two strong weapons against every evil – time and silence.' When we arrived back at the house Astrid had prepared lunch, and my mother was overdoing it as usual. The fried herring tasted divine, not just good, and Astrid had never looked as *enchanting* as she did that summer. All things considered there was always something which had *never* been so wonderfully delightful, so shudderingly and ecstatically fantastic, and so her life glided on towards still new, still dizzier heights. We were completely exhausted a few days later when she was obliged to go back to 'her rehearsals' as she always called them, as if the producers and the other actors only breathed to be able to serve as humble and grateful witnesses to the unfolding of her graceful talent. When later I recalled our conversation that summer day on the beach and in the wood, I was amazed both at how much she had perceived and how little she had understood. Her words had hit me, but I couldn't avoid the fact that she was the one who had pronounced them. By insisting we resembled each other, wasn't she only trying to ease her bad conscience by making me her accomplice? Because it would absolve her in my eyes if I repeated her old crime? Otherwise why should it be so urgent for her to get me to leave Astrid and the children? She had boasted of having walked out honestly, not for the sake of some or other man. I reckon she walked out for one or another or a third man's sake, so all in all she was probably right, she

had merely acted in accord with her restless nature. After
she walked out on my father she hadn't spent as much as
a fortnight without having at least one hungry worshipper
whom she could alternately hold off or let in. Not until
age had begun to make itself felt in earnest did she get
to know loneliness, and perhaps it was this new, enforced
loneliness she had tried to transform into something heroic,
retrospectively, when she described herself during our walk
as another Nora, who had left her Helmer out of sheer inner
necessity. Only with the difference that in her case it was
Helmer who was thrown out while Nora stayed on in the
doll's house and turned it into a brothel. If we had ever
again discussed what happened in New York that spring,
she would no doubt have criticised me because I actually did
stay with Astrid. She would have scorned what she would
have seen as my cowardice, but like me she chose to let
time and silence solve my little problem, and with the years
I think she simply forgot what we had spoken of, that we
had ever been for a walk together beside the grey sea among
the contorted pine trees.

The summer passed and with every week I grew better at
concealing my interior unease. Everything was apparently
as usual. Astrid seemed to be convinced it was merely my
'writing crisis' which sometimes tortured me and made me
melancholy. She even asked me when I intended to go to
New York to finish my book, and I replied September would
be a good time, it was too hot in August. I learned to live
with my treachery and neutralise a sneaking contempt for
her, which lured and attracted me at the back of my mind
like a tempting offer of relief from my guilt. The revolting,
secretive contempt of her credulity I made use of to feel
coldness towards her caresses. I fought against it, fought
at least to rediscover a cool, neutral tenderness for her,
for 'everything we had together'. I tried to protect my
tenderness against my guilty desire when I made love to

her, violently, at times almost brutally, as if I could chase away the memory of Elisabeth, if only for half an hour. And gradually I succeeded in splitting my interior into separate worlds and prevented them from coming into contact with each other. Perhaps what they say is true, that you can get used to anything. Perhaps it helped too to think of the hypocritical way my mother had spoken of Astrid's 'cheerful nature' and of how I was far too complicated for a woman like her, and then fifteen minutes later, when we returned to the house, had overwhelmed her with her usual sham and exalted compliments. Her denigrating remarks about Astrid almost resuscitated my loyalty to the woman I had betrayed, and in the following weeks I was especially considerate, sometimes downright affectionate to her, as if she was ill without realising it herself. I rose early in the morning and let her sleep on, I swam and played with the children while she lay in the sun, and when the weather was grey I went cycling with them in the forest. There were times when I discovered that I had completely forgotten to think of Elisabeth, and not until the evening, when quietness descended on me and I sat alone on the steps among the rose bushes looking out over the sea in the eternal twilight of the summer night, did the house become a strange place again, where I felt I didn't belong.

The same feeling lay in wait when I next had an errand in town and opened the door of our apartment. It had been empty for over a month and when I noticed the dusty, enclosed air I thought it was not merely a place we had shut up for the summer. It already resembled a place I had left and would not return to. I dialled Elisabeth's number as I read the headlines of a yellowing newspaper we had left behind on the day we packed the car and drove into the country. This time the answering machine was not on, but a long time passed and I was about to put the receiver down when she answered at last. She sounded out of breath, she had been on her way up when the telephone rang. She was glad to hear my voice, she had been almost afraid of forgetting how it sounded. She had come back from Mexico the previous week, she had travelled around the Yucatán peninsula all alone, it had been horrific. She had been ill in a dirty hotel room with cockroaches as big as armadillos, it came flooding out of her at both ends, and she had lain there wishing I was with her and wondering if she would ever hear from me again. I smiled at the idea of my jealous fantasies about her streaking through the Mojave desert on a motorcycle with another man. She told me it was just as hot and humid in New York as in Mexico, she couldn't bear it anywhere, and it was impossible to get anything done, all she could do was lie without a stitch on gasping beneath the electric fan. I visualised it clearly, her voluminous hair spread out over the sheet, the protruding ribs under her small breasts, her long pale legs, her light grey fearless eyes. She was suddenly so close again, not just a thought, an image, but the person she was, all skin and hair. I said we would soon meet again. Was I coming to New York? She sounded glad but also surprised, she obviously thought by a lucky coincidence some other reason made it possible to meet. I said I couldn't do without her, I had thought a great deal about what had happened. She had thought about it too, she said after a pause, and she really sounded very thoughtful. When was I coming? In September, I said, sometime in September. I didn't say anything about the apartment I had looked at. I wanted to take one thing, one step at a time. Perhaps I was afraid of frightening her, perhaps I already suspected it was a castle in the air, that apartment, a mirage with brown tiles in the bathroom. I couldn't yet know whether Elisabeth was only a cause, a random stranger, who had inadvertently opened the door of my darkness, as my mother put it, so the light had suddenly poured in and dazzled me. I had to see her again to be able to know, I thought, as I mumbled a few tender words of farewell. As if it would be something that could be seen.

One evening in September I landed again at John F. Kennedy airport. I couldn't see Elisabeth anywhere when I walked into the arrival hall, and I wondered anxiously whether she had heard the message I had recorded on her answering machine before boarding the plane. I stood still in the stream of impatiently pushing passengers looking around me in disappointment, when a smiling young woman came towards me. It was the smile I recognised first. She had had her hair cut, her wavy, golden brown hair only reached half way down her neck and she was dressed in a black tailored jacket and a short black skirt and shoes with heels that made her half a head taller than me. I had never seen her in a skirt, as a whole I had never seen her so well-dressed, and as we embraced I was brought to think for a moment of the elegant woman in black I had secretly observed one afternoon in the sculpture garden behind the Museum of Modern Art. Was it for my sake she had dressed like this, to offset the contrast between the Bohemian slattern and her well-dressed bourgeois lover? To show me she could get along in my world, and was prepared to go with me wherever it might be? Or was it someone else who had taught her to make something of her appearance? Was it to make herself attractive to another man's expectant eyes? We stood there in a long unmoving embrace in the midst of the confusion of people and luggage, and I sniffed the unexpected, strange scent of perfume on her neck. In the taxi she laughed at my surprise, and I caressed her naked, delicate neck as she questioned me about my book and told me of the exhibition she had had, and about her journey to Yucatán that suddenly sounded like a long exotic adventure without any stomach problems at all. It was suddenly very real to be sitting in a taxi on the way through Brooklyn talking about this and that, far too real. She was almost frighteningly beautiful to look at, and her new cool elegance made me uneasy, as if it was a first warning that all might not go as I hoped, even though she pressed against me and leaned her head against mine. But to begin with there was something euphoric about our reunion, as if we had cheated the whole world and everything that in the past months had prevented us from being together, and we could hardly wait for the taxi to stop in front of her doorway. We did not let go of each other until far into the night, sweating and breathless. She went into the bathroom, I stayed in bed, exhausted by the flight and our hectic reunion. The cat crept soundlessly around on the bare floors sniffing cautiously at our clothes, that lay jumbled together in contorted heaps. I could hear the water running in the bath, at first with a hard metallic sound, then a soft splashing as it filled up. The rusty taps creaked and then there was silence. I listened to the faraway police sirens, the voices calling in Spanish down in the street, and the cars now and then passing with techno-music beating out through the rolled-down windows. It was a warm night and the windows were open in the house opposite, behind one of them a man was shaving, even though it was past three o' clock, from another a slow tango was playing, and I recognised Astor Piazzolla's passionate *bandonéon*. It was many years since I had heard that recording. When I went into the bathroom Elisabeth lay in the bath with her face covered by a flannel. The greenish water distorted her body slightly, so it seemed flat as photography, and the damp towelling stuck to her nose and eye sockets like a mask. I sat down on the edge of the bath. I said I had thought of what she had talked about a few times. That she had considered moving back to Copenhagen. The tap dripped, and the drips measured out the silence as they struck the water. The little rings made the surface tremble and blot out the image of her unmoving slender body. I said I loved her, she was the one I wanted to be with, and I had decided to leave Astrid, but the drops merely went on measuring the seconds, *plock, plock,* one second at a time as is the case with seconds. Cautiously I took hold of the edge of the flannel under her chin and pulled it until her face came in sight. Her eyelids were closed and she lay unmoving for a long time, before opening them and looking at me with her light grey eyes.

So after all, our hours together, even the most precious, had not had any special consequences. The unexpected understanding, the spontaneous intimacy of each single moment had not been a pact, then, a promise of future moments. They were not to be linked together, they were not a story, or only a story that continuously ended and constantly started again, until one evening it was broken off in the middle of a sentence, just as unexpectedly as when I seized her hand five months earlier as we looked over the Hudson River. Seven years later when I stood pondering Elisabeth's cool, monochrome abstractions at a gallery in Soho, a man of my own age came up and asked if I knew her work. I said I was an old friend, but we had lost contact. He introduced himself as her art dealer and we started to talk. She lived in Vermont now, in a house a long way out in the country, with her husband and their small son. He was a sculptor, very talented. I nodded with interest. The art dealer showed me a photograph hanging on the notice board above his desk in the back room. The picture had been taken in the evening in front of a house of white-painted boards, just after sundown, with a flash. There was a strange contrast between the white flashlight and the sulphur-yellow glow in the narrow section of sky behind the corner of the house. I came to think of Hopper's lonely American houses backed by the evening sky. Their eyes shone red, the black-haired boy in baseball gloves with sun-tanned arms, the dark-skinned man with a black beard standing behind the boy with hands resting on his shoulders, and Elisabeth, standing beside them in an old-fashioned, flowery summer dress, lowering her face so her cheek touched the man's. She still had short hair and looked only slightly older. She smiled as she gazed into the camera with her red pupils. She looked like herself, the smiling woman, and yet it wasn't the one who had lain in her bath one September night seven years before looking at me with expressionless grey eyes. It amazed me that I should have been prepared to turn my life upside-down to be with her, although we didn't really know each other and had only spent a few weeks together in spring. It had needed nothing more, so flimsy had been my ideas of who I was and where I belonged, as weightless as pictures and words.

Of course it hurt, but not as much as I would have believed, when she considerately explained to me that was not quite what she had in mind, not because there was anyone else she would rather be with, but quite simply because she felt good living alone. Moreover, she had decided to stay on in New York. She even dropped a tear for my sake as a little sacrifice to the beautiful story I had made up about us, and I kissed her tear away and pulled myself together. Had the curator been right after all? Was I just another man in the row of men I visualised standing in a long, impatient queue right up to First Avenue? I never found out, it is of no consequence now. The next day I booked into a cheap hotel in Little Italy, but we did go out to dinner once or twice and we talked as we had done from the beginning, about the New York School and everything else we hit upon, on the same wavelength as before. And if I had not weighed down the balance between us with my untimely and drastic plans for the future, I am sure we would have romped around on her futon for another week, observed by her completely indifferent cat, for she was really fond of me, there was a real flow between us when we were together. It was just what it was, nothing else, nothing more. I was not particularly unhappy when we parted, I was paralysed and in a way also relieved. On the day I left we had lunch together in Spring Street where we had first met. Afterwards we stood for a while looking at each other on the corner of West Broadway, before I hailed a taxi. If at that moment she had reconsidered, everything might have been different, but she only patted me affectionately on my shirt front and told me to look after myself. I felt like saying the same, but made do with an adult smile and a kiss on her forehead before getting into the taxi and asking for the airport. Nice lady, but very slim, said the driver in his winning Pakistani accent, as he drove up West Broadway. Yeah, very nice, I replied, turning round on the back seat to get a last glimpse through the back window of her tall slim figure, making its way with long quick strides among the other pedestrians, a moment later impossible to distinguish from the silhouettes of people in motion.

9

Astrid had only stayed a single night in Oporto, then she went on southwards. According to the bank statement she used her Mastercard again at a petrol station outside Aveiro, and later in the day had lunch in Coimbra. The same evening she booked in at the hotel in Lisbon where we stayed for a week, in Graça, with a view over the city and the river, that autumn seven years ago after I came home from New York for the second time as if nothing had happened. Before she left Oporto she may have driven out to Matosinhos, out to the empty beach with the oil tanks and the closed, dilapidated huts with cafés and changing rooms. She may have walked where we walked together in the wind, in the smell of salt and seaweed, out towards the surf that broke on the beach with deafening waves, yellow with whirled-up sand. It might have been misty that day too, so she could not see the horizon, only the dull restless sheen of the waves, that shone like copper further out where the sea and the mist blended together. I made the suggestion as soon as I had got into the car when she fetched me at Kastrup, that we should go to Portugal together, alone together. I don't know why it had to be Portugal, perhaps because we had never been there before. I hit on the idea in the plane as I leafed through the airline magazine and studied the world map with its two half spheres, cut and unfolded like the wings of a butterfly, like separate worlds only connected by the company routes drawn in red lines, that crossed each other, converging from their junctions in the big cities. I had placed my finger on New York, outside Coney Island, and drawn a straight line across the Atlantic between forty and forty-one degrees north, until I hit the coast near Oporto. It had been a stressful year, I said, with my book and all, we needed some time to ourselves. Perhaps we could get my mother to move into the apartment while we were away, and when she was at the theatre in the evening Simon was big enough now to look after Rosa. Astrid smiled in surprise, as she steered through the traffic. Why not?

In the plane, while the sky grew dark over the cloud cover's dazzling, bumpy desert, the paralysis had gradually passed and I wondered at myself. How had it all happened? How had I come to lay my life in the long, slim hands of an almost unknown young woman and leave her to shape it? Had Elisabeth after all been only an opportunity, a pretext? Had I, without knowing it, for years been preparing to leave Astrid? Again I thought of the conversation with my mother as we walked along the beach and among the crooked pine trees. Perhaps she had been right, perhaps I ought to sit down and consider my unanswered questions on a brandy-coloured leather sofa in a rented apartment with brown tiles in the bathroom. But that would not make either Astrid or myself any happier, I told myself. Was it really those brown tiles that made the idea so depressing? The prospect of becoming a gloomy recluse who heated his frozen ready-to-eat meals in another man's microwave oven as he stared forlornly out at the rain? His homeless solitude, drifting in the swirl of empty days? But would we be happier going on together? Once again I recalled the question Inès had asked me a few years earlier when we were in a café on the Place de l'Alma. If I was happy with Astrid. The question had stayed in the background ever since, as time just went by. It had accompanied me as the moon accompanies you when you drive a car at night, never getting its pale, pock-marked face to move an inch in the side window behind the roadside trees rushing past. It was that indiscreet, rigid question about happiness that had made me believe it was time to cut and run from it all. But who had asked the question? Had Elisabeth been anything but a substitute for Inès, now that I was questioning the whole of my adult life? Had she been more than just a delayed revenge for the ancient, musty and malodorous defeat of my youth? Or was it in reality Astrid I had cast in the role of Inès, to have someone to revenge myself on? Was he my true self, the unhappy young man who stood at a window watching Inès disappear among the snowflakes one long ago winter? Had I never been myself again after I betrayed him and took Astrid's face between my hands for the first time? Or was my biggest illusion making him into my original, uncorrupted self? And in that case was I nothing or no more than the sum of the fleeting, distorted shadows that I had cast on the retinas of various women, behind their inscrutable gaze? Was I nothing but this constant metamorphosis? Perhaps it was my fatigue, perhaps it was the turbulence over the Atlantic that made me dizzy and gave me the feeling that all my thoughts were just so many masks that fell, one after another, in tumbling spirals down into the darkness over the Labrador Basin without my ever penetrating behind all the layers of self-delusion and interpretations.

Astrid must have reached Lisbon in the late afternoon. If she had a room with a view she would probably have gone out on the terrace and looked down over the tiles on the staggered roofs between the parapets of the citadel and the river, which is so wide that the opposite side is only a blurred, bluish band when it rains. I imagine her standing for a while with closed eyes and her face lifted in the white light as the rain settles in her hair and pricks her forehead and cheeks and soaks through her blouse with a feeling reminiscent of the light touch of cool fingertips on the shoulders. She may have stood thus and breathed in the scent of dust, dissolved in the dampness. She may have stood like that once more before going in and lying down on the bed fully clothed. I left the door to the terrace open even though it was cool, and eased the shoes from her feet before lying down beside her. We had still not unpacked. I put an arm around her and hid my face in the shadow between us. We were not going any further, it was Lisbon we had made for, the last city in Europe, as she said with an exhausted smile, when at long last the motorway led us in among the suburban tenements of crumbling concrete. She lay on her stomach with closed eyes, I covered her with the bedspread. She stroked my hair with calm slow hands, and the warm air from her nostrils brushed my face with the faint scent of sweat, her perfume. Then we both lay quite still, I with a hand on her back, and I felt her breathing against my palm like a slow movement in the small of her back, beneath the warm piece of skin between her blouse and her tights. I didn't know whether she had fallen asleep. Had she noticed anything in my silence after all? Had a little split opened in her thoughts into which the cold air seeped? The air from an alien world that only on its surface resembled the one where she lived at my side, as we had done for so long. Her world could be inside mine, but there was no room for mine in hers, this difference had arisen, so we no longer knew the same thing. How could I avoid making her less than she needed to be? Ought I not to leave her, now that we lived in separate worlds? Hadn't I already wasted far too much of her time with my melancholy egoism? I could at least have told her what had happened so she could make up her mind whether she would be able to breathe in the other world from which I watched her face, so close to mine, with closed eyes, as if she slept. I could have told her on that October evening in Lisbon, as I lay listening to the rain on the tiles of the terrace, the metal blinds being rolled down in front of the shops, and the scooters pushing their way up the Rua Senhora do Monte. I did not say anything, and that was my greatest betrayal. Not that I had been about to leave her to live with another woman, but that I had come home and driven all the way to Lisbon with her. That I had come slinking back with my secret, suppressed defeat, as if it had been nothing but a little short circuit, a little technical accident. That I lay here at the end of the road and kept silent, as if there was nothing to say. How did it come about that I didn't leave her? Why did I come back so feebly, when my adventure ended up like an abortion, washed out like all the other possibilities one misses or is cheated of on the way through the years? Did I come back for pure convenience? Out of fear of the old, despondent loneliness I still remembered so well? No doubt. But not only for that.

When I lay there in Lisbon that rainy evening and dozed in the half-dark hotel room beside Astrid, exhausted after the long drive, I could not decide whether I had woken from a dream or if I had fallen asleep again after having been awake for a few months. When I met her it had been like waking up from my young dream of Inès. When I met Inès it had been like waking from my dreaming childhood. When I met Elisabeth it felt as if I had been asleep for years. And when I went back to Astrid, I had realised that my dreams of another life had been nothing but dreams set in motion by a pair of light grey eyes that had never seen me as other than the person I was. A married man who reached out to her, perhaps out of boredom, perhaps out of desperation, perhaps because she happened to come by. Perhaps I had spent my whole life in dreaming, perhaps that is how we all spend our lives until the moment comes, early or late, when we awake to pure nothing. Perhaps it cannot be otherwise, perhaps we breathe through our dreams, in separate worlds, as we clasp each other in sleep. That was how I thought of it as I lay beside Astrid one evening in Lisbon seven years ago as the rain eased off and the blue dusk spread around us and I felt her body's warmth against mine in the evening chill.

She had fallen asleep. She wrinkled her brow and mumbled something I could not hear, then her face grew calm again. I couldn't know what she was dreaming. My hand tingled, it was quite numb after resting so long on her back. I pulled it cautiously towards me and rose from the bed. Her face was indistinct, blurred in the dark and hardly recognisable. I went out on the terrace and lit a cigarette and looked down on the street lights and car lights that rose and fell in the darkness. I could no longer see the river, I had to imagine it where the lights tailed off in the impenetrable darkness that spread until the lights began again, faintly twinkling on the other side.

I must have stayed a long time looking at the photo of Elisabeth and her husband and their little son, smiling with red eyes in the flashlight in front of their white-painted wooden house in Vermont. A little too long, I think, for I remember the art dealer cleared his throat and asked if I would like their address. I said no thank you and left the gallery in Wooster Street. I went to the cinema, just to be in a place where there were other people, without having to say or do anything, later I had a meal at a Japanese restaurant, and in the evening I took a taxi back to the hotel in Lexington Avenue. Who knows, perhaps that little glimpse of Elisabeth's life would have made a deeper impression if Astrid had been waiting for me at home in Copenhagen, if I had been able to call her from the hotel room, if I had been able to rely on her answering the phone, because it was the time when she usually came home. Now it was just an amateur photograph of a woman I had once known, almost as strange as the unknown man who had become her husband. Perhaps the truth is as disgracefully banal as that, it is obviously so perishable, the significance you ascribe to a face for a while, feebly attaching it to the features that for a time lend their outline to your tender hopes. The sight of Elisabeth had been as painless as the sight of Inès when I was leaving a cinema with Astrid some years ago and caught sight of her in the throng. But if I had been a little sad at the sight of my old flames, it was not only because they had been transformed into ash but also because they had been extinguished so easily. Nevertheless I had burned myself, and although I couldn't remember the pain I did remember that it had once hurt. Now I burned myself on my images of Astrid. I picked up the receiver and dialled our number, you never know. As I listened to the calling tone I caught sight of myself in the dark television screen, a grey, bent silhouette sitting on the edge of the bed in the anonymous hotel room. I grabbed at the remote control and switched on, just so as not to see the lonely anonymous figure in the curved glass of the screen. I turned down the sound and absent-mindedly watched the cramped news pictures. A river had burst its banks, I couldn't see where it was. Trees, road signs and roofs rose up from the muddy water. Why didn't I just put the receiver down? I visualised the empty apartment, the dark windows onto the Lakes and the façades on the other side, the rows of lit windows. Suppose Astrid had come back after all. A military helicopter hovered in the air, the rotor blades whipped up the water in small waves, and the waves fled in all directions around a rowing boat that had moored up to the top floor of a house from which a covered, mummy-like figure was hoisted up on a stretcher, twisting slowly around itself. Suddenly the receiver was picked up, it was Rosa. I had woken her up, it was six o'clock in the morning at home. I could hear she was glad I called. I asked if she had moved back home, she laughed, she was a bit tired of sweethearts for the moment. Did she have several then? She laughed again. Wouldn't I like to know! I asked if she had heard from Astrid. The reporter stood looking earnestly into the camera as he spoke into his microphone without a sound coming from his lips. She had tried to call Gunilla in Stockholm to hear when I was coming home, but there had been no answer, so they were probably still out in the Skerries. She thought it was dead good that we could think of travelling separately and leaving each other in peace for a bit. The reporter was wearing waders and stood in water up to his waist, moving his lips among the houses in the inundated town. But Simon had called home from Bologna, where he had met a girl he was sold on, so we needn't expect to see anything of him for a while. She said she would fetch me from the airport, and I got out my ticket and read out my flight number and arrival time.

I stayed in front of the television screen's changing incessant stream of people, who spoke or moved among the amputated, jumping snatches of places in the world. It was late and I was tired, but I knew it would be no use going to bed. I came to think of the old idea of time as a river, apparently unchanging and yet never the same. I tried to recall the seven years that had passed since Astrid and I drove to Lisbon and strolled aimlessly beside each other through the narrow streets of Bairro Alto and Alfama, between the scruffy old rattling trams and the sooty, geometric or organic ornamentation of the tiles on the façade. Nothing particular had happened, time had run on with us, the children had grown and we ourselves were slightly older, while Astrid edited her films and I wrote about my painters. I couldn't catch sight of us, the months and the years flowed out into a formless, changing foam, and I only saw us in disconnected shreds of hours and days, that doubled up and turned quickly around themselves like withered leaves on the whirling current before vanishing. When I had thought of Elisabeth and our story, I did so precisely the way you think of an incredible story you have been told, at first with a shake of the head, then with a shrug of the shoulders. As if there is no great difference, as time passes, between what we have experienced ourselves and what we have merely heard or seen on television. Was it really me, or had I just been slightly out of my wits, seized by six months of a passing fit, a last rebellious, ungovernable gesture, before at long last I grew up? When a few months had passed I was relieved that I had shielded Astrid from hearing about my escapade. Why should I hurt her unduly when I myself had got the better of my fantasies of a new and quite different life? Thus I calmed my battered conscience. I could still feel awkward when Astrid responded to my gaze with her narrow eyes. I was ashamed not only of my treachery but also of the thought that I had really believed I could escape from myself and become someone else, different from the man I had become with the years, all the years with her and the children. Who should he have been? If I wasn't in the right place at home with Astrid in the apartment by the Lakes, where then? As the children loosened their grip on us and began to manage by themselves, the days became longer than they had previously been, not so full, and when we met in the evening in the quiet apartment we were almost a bit shy sometimes, as if a little puzzled that time had passed. We fell into a looser, more peaceful rhythm of departure and reunion, now we were suddenly free to immerse ourselves separately in our own pursuits, and on the whole we did as we pleased, because it no longer mattered so much precisely when we came home.

At long last I had stopped asking myself if I was happy, it had become unnecessary, but also futile to ask. After all, you can't be happy the whole time, gasping and salivating in one trembling spasm of happiness from the time you get up until you finally fall asleep with an idiotic smile on your wet lips. I thought of my mother who always tried to make it sound as if she was living on a volcano. Maybe she was, but it was an extinguished volcano, with a barren crater of stiffened lava. Perhaps the question had been wrongly put from the start. If I was happy. Had I reached out to Elisabeth because I thought she would make me happy? More probably I had reached out to her to escape my happiness, in an attack of claustrophobia. Even as a child I had been restless when I heard what, according to the Bible, Paradise looked like. I thought it must get boring in the end with all that lyricism and luxury, and perhaps it was the same insipid taste of eternity that had made me restless and caused me to become rebellious about Elisabeth. The impression that I could see my own future before me with Astrid and the children and later on alone with her when we would no longer have Simon and Rosa as a daily, mutual bond. The defeats and victories of work, the marital boredom and the passing moments of revived marital desire, Sunday outings, dinner parties with friends, profound or superficial conversations about this and that, holiday trips, museum visits, cinema going and everything else you have time for. The whole abundant and yet strangely disappointing catalogue of 'interests and activities' that all the lonely but none the less cheerful and economically independent wretches list in the Sunday papers' lonely hearts advertisements, perhaps in an attempt to seem reliably normal. A perspective of repetitions, as when you are in a Parisian café equipped with mirrors and see the interior repeating itself in an endless corridor of mirrors where you lift the same glass of wine, holding the same cigarette between your fingers, again and again and again, and where you yourself are the same, nauseously the same, vanishing into the perspective. Fortunately that had only been yet another illusion, after all it was never the same day I awoke beside Astrid, even though sometimes it looked like it. Nor were she and I quite the same, year by year, but the change was no longer a question of covering distances, of other worlds, another life, as I gradually came to understand when I had returned to Astrid after my abortive attempt at flight.

The change did not mean we were on the way anywhere,

it played itself out in our bodies and minds. Slowly and
imperceptibly it evolved out of the monotonous spirals of
repetition, so I only occasionally, at intervals of months,
became aware that Rosa's flat, gawky torso had begun to
take on form, or that a faint shadow had started to appear
on Simon's upper lip, that another grey streak had appeared
in Astrid's chestnut brown hair, or that one morning as I
was shaving, the furrows between my nostrils and mouth
suddenly seemed deeper and longer than I remembered them.
We did not feel time as it passed with us, perhaps because
we lived in several times at once. Astrid was still the young
woman who one winter evening had sat on the back seat of
my taxi comforting her little son. I was still the young man
who one summer night had sat among the rose bushes above
the sea repeating my calming mantra, *hold on, hold on*. She
was at one and the same time the woman I had wanted to
leave, and the woman I had gone back to, and I was the man
who had seen her alternately as my salvation and my warder,
as an unexpected, liberating lightness in my life and as a
burden that chained me to the eternally grinding treadmill
of days. When she was on the phone exchanging gossip with
Gunilla in Stockholm I could shake my head and ask myself
how she had ever become the woman in my life. And when
she came into the living room, still with her coat on, and
placed a bunch of white tulips on the window sill, when the
stalks squeaked lightly against each other and she stood there
at the window looking thoughtfully down on the rippling
waters of the lake, I could ask myself how I could ever have
thought of leaving her. When I went into the bedroom and
she lay in bed looking at me, naked, with an unequivocal,
encouraging look, I had sometimes just felt like lying
down with my back to her and falling asleep. And when we
had agreed to meet at a café and I caught sight of her in
the rain on her way across the street, the second before she
saw me, brushing the damp hair from her forehead with a

casual hand movement, I could be overwhelmed by a desire so violent that I had to fold up the newspaper and put it on my lap. It was not the gossip or the tulips, her nakedness and inviting gaze or the hand through her damp hair that alone made the difference, and it was certainly not anything in myself. It was the constant exchange between what happened around me and what stirred within me, between a present that was never the same, when we caught sight of each other afresh, and my restless, changing memories, always announcing themselves in a slightly different light, with a slightly different significance than before.

But how did I get from one thing to another? How had I been able to sit in an aeroplane over the Atlantic on my way west convinced that I would have to leave Astrid to save myself from the detestable perpetuity of repetition, only to get the idea a week later, in an identical plane flying east, that she and I should go to Portugal together? After I lost sight of Elisabeth among the other pedestrians, only a silhouette among the silhouettes in the backlight on West Broadway, my tenderness was still there, the silent, searching tenderness I felt for Astrid when a few weeks later I lay holding her one night in Lisbon, listening to the rain. Tenderness was there, the way her mouth and skin somehow summoned my lips and hands, and there was the old familiarity merely to lie and breathe side by side as it grew dark outside. It was a tenderness that prevailed of its own volition and made its way regardless of what I was just then thinking about her, about us. The palms of my hands knew each hollow of her body, each projection, as if through the years they had formed each other, her body and my hands, her hands and my body. My caresses were more like inscrutable but incontrovertible facts than questions waiting for an answer. It did not matter why we loved, when we made love to each other. I could not know how much or how little she knew, and I no longer knew myself

what to think about all that had happened, and everything
that had moved within me on the way through the years,
my perpetual dizzy wavering between doubts, unanswered
questions and faded hope. Perhaps she had discovered as I
had that the roads and the faces do not mean anything in
themselves, the roads that branch out towards the unknown,
the faces that come to meet you with their alien eyes, where
you might be just anyone. Perhaps she too had been obliged
to admit that to begin with it does not matter which road
you take and who you walk along with because your love
does not mind whom you love providing it is allowed to
run freely along the track you walk, through the eyes you
hold fast with your gaze as you walk. Perhaps she too had
understood that you are not presented with your story, that
you must tell it yourself, and that you do not know the story
before it has been told. That you can never know beforehand
what it means or how much. That the story must be told one
day, one step at a time, whether you tell it in a hesitant or
firm tone, confidently or plagued with doubt. And yet then
she too had wavered, she too had stopped to ask herself if
she had not lost her way, if she had not allowed herself to be
carried away through the chance ramifications of the years
in the arms of the wrong man, torn along by her love's blind
desire to run where she had smoothed the path for it with
her patient steps. And then one morning she had packed a
bag and stood waiting for me to wake up, in the bedroom
doorway, with her coat already on.

Did she notice at some moment that she had shrunk in
my eyes, where she had accommodated herself as if she
belonged there? Did she have to leave me and be alone,
she who had not been on her own for almost twenty-five
years, because she had grown so little in my distant glance
that she was about to vanish out of sight? Or did she feel
that the space my gaze had once opened out around her,
where she had thought she would be able to run as fast

and as long as she wished, had grown too narrow? Did she come to see that I had shaped her too, until she was no more than the one who lived at my side? When did it dawn on her that there was still an unknown woman trying to draw breath through her nose and mouth, a woman I had never set eyes on, behind her well-known features? When did she discover the eyes of that woman in the mirror, through the narrow chinks in her face, where she was accustomed to meet her own familiar glance? Eyes that looked at her in restrained wonderment at how her life had taken shape, as if it had happened while she was asleep. Perhaps she had seen them in the mirrors of hotel rooms on the way, those unknown, wondering eyes. Perhaps they had waited for her in the mirrors of San Sebastian, in Santiago de Compostela, in Oporto and in Lisbon. On the way through those towns she may have looked at me with their wonder, asking herself if he really was the one she had loved, and if she still loved this man. But why had she waited so long? Why didn't she leave me already then, to meet the unknown woman behind the mirrors? Did she doubt whether the other one would be able to draw breath alone, without the protective mask of her well-known face? Had she expected me to tell her what she had already noticed in my silence, until she felt she had waited long enough? Had she expected me to admit that I too was not exactly the person I pretended to be? Or had she already made her decision? Had she stayed for the sake of the children, until they were old enough to cope? I cannot tell what she read in my face, from my glances as we walked up and down the steep alleys of Bairro Alto, slightly uncertain and hesitant, as tourists walk around a strange town because they have nothing really to do. She may have seen and sensed more than I thought. The town always came between us with its trams and sooty tiles, its sparkling river and its smoke from the chestnut sellers' charcoal braziers, the town where I hoped to find her again. We had nothing to hold on to there, so far from the place where we belonged, we had only each other's words, and they ran out so quickly into the strange, greedy silence. We had only each other's bodies in the anonymous hotel room where I lay after our arrival and held her like a shipwrecked mariner as I listened to the rain and saw the light fade and felt the chill air from outside.

Had she been happy? Did I make her happy? I think she was at the start, when I replied to the disturbing news of her pregnancy with my young, reckless *why not?* When with my rash, risky, arrogant *why not?* I took the chance and leaped out into the unknown and to my surprise discovered that I had landed on my feet after circling around in my taxi for months like a solitary astronaut in orbit around the earth. I think I did make her happy in the years that followed, after sitting above the sea one summer night, on the steps among the rose bushes, doggedly adjuring her and our unknown child to *hold on, hold on.* There were a few years, while Rosa was small, when I was completely attentive. Perhaps that is why I remember them so indistinctly. While she was learning to walk, while she was beginning to talk, I was nothing but a happy, tired man who had consigned himself to the hours and the days, adrift in their unthinking maelstrom. I felt in the midst of my life, and I never came any closer to that middle than then, as we were on our way, Astrid and I, from day to day, heedless of where we were going. I think she herself must have thought like that about those years, later, when she felt the cold air of something strange come oozing through an invisible crack in her knowledge of who we were. When I began to be absent-minded, when she began to notice my doubt like an awkward silence, a flicker in my gaze, a sudden clumsiness when I lay down beside her at night.

I must have fallen asleep. It was pitch-dark when I woke up in the hotel room in the Rua Senhora do Monte. The sheet was cold where I had felt her warm side against my palm. I called to her, she wasn't there. I sat for a while on the edge of the bed looking out at Lisbon's glimmering chains of light below the terrace. They could be the lights of any city. I put on my shoes and went down to reception, they told me she had left the hotel half an hour earlier. It was in a quiet residential district with steep narrow streets. I thought I might perhaps find her if I walked around a little. Surely she could not have gone very far. There were only a few people about, two middle-aged women in aprons stood in a doorway talking quietly, a young couple passed on a scooter, the girl leaning her cheek against the young man's back. Suddenly I felt a thin cold stream of water running down my hair and neck. When I looked up I caught sight of an old man on a balcony watering pot plants. He raised his hand in a gesture that was both a greeting and an apology, and said something I did not understand. Some boys were kicking a ball about on the gravel among the peeling plane trees in a small square. The gravel shone with an unreal light in the glare of the orange street lights crisscrossing through the trees' crooked shadows, and the blotched façades resembled theatre décor in the garish light. Behind the closed blinds above the balcony railings I could hear the energetic speakers' voices from television sets and the softer, more scattered voices blending with the sound of clinking china. I sat down on a bench beneath the planes and lit a cigarette, listening to the shouts of the boys and the dull thump of the ball on gravel and the foreign yet homely sounds from the open balcony doors. Of course she had merely gone for a walk like I had, but I still missed her in the same lonely way as when I had travelled alone to a foreign city and left her at home with the children.

I tried to imagine I had left her. That instead of suggesting this trip I had told her what had happened in New York when she fetched me from the airport, as she had so often done before. I imagined saying it in the car or later, in the bedroom, when the children had gone to bed. I don't know how she would have reacted. If she would have broken down, or if she would just have listened and looked at me with the same expression as when she stood looking at me the morning she left. As if she already knew everything. I imagined telling the children. I imagined Rosa weeping and Simon's slightly embarrassed silence. How I would have hesitated a bit, embracing Rosa, before disengaging myself and leaving. I would have rented an apartment, perhaps the one where I had imagined Elisabeth and I would live. I would have furnished a room for Rosa in the room I had envisaged as Elisabeth's studio. I would have fetched her from the apartment beside the Lakes, just as the grizzled film director had once fetched Simon, when he tried for a weekend to be what he had once been. She would have been ready with her little bag and a doll under her arm, and there would have been a moment when she stood between us before she kissed Astrid goodbye to go downstairs with me, a brief moment when Astrid and I would have to look each other in the face. What would we have thought? That Rosa was all that was left? The only proof that we had once loved each other and believed we had arrived at the midst of our life? The place from where everything could be seen and told about? Would I have sat in a rented apartment with brandy-coloured leather sofas and smoke-coloured glass tables reading aloud to Rosa and at the same time thinking she was in fact the result of a mistake, a misjudgement, a rash action? In the seven years that have passed since I sat in the little square in Graça, where the boys ran about playing football, I have sometimes asked myself if I stayed with Astrid only for the children's sake. In that case I should have been relieved when they left home and Astrid packed her bag one morning and handed me over to the silence they had left behind them. But when she left me I myself had begun to believe that the dizziness and doubt had gradually been offset by the weight of time in our changed bodies and by the puzzling gentleness of the unexpected moments when we suddenly caught sight of each other again.

If I had left Astrid I would probably have gone to Lisbon, alone for the first time in ten years, alone in a town where I had never been before. I would have sat looking at the boys kicking the ball over the gravel, their small shouting silhouettes in the orange street lighting, and I would have listened to the scattered sounds from the houses around the square, the sounds from televisions and clinking plates and laughter, of the lives of strangers. It would not have mattered where I was, in which town, it would have made no difference. I don't know how long I sat on the bench among the plane trees, perhaps five minutes, perhaps ten. Behind me I heard the yelling, barking staccato sounds and the deep, distorted, electronic man's voice from a loudspeaker. I turned round. A lad of Simon's age was bending over a flickering video screen behind the bead curtain at the entrance to a small bar. Behind him, by the bar counter, I caught sight of Astrid. She waved. I went to join her. She had been watching me. Where had she been? She shrugged and smiled her crooked smile. Here. I stroked the hair from her forehead and let my hand slide down her cheek and recognised the gesture, the same as when I stood face to face with her in my kitchen long ago, the first time we touched. She too must have recalled my caress, for she smiled again, as she slowly bent her head to one side and leaned her cheek against my hand. I moved my hand to her neck and drew her towards me. I could feel her low voice like a faint, warm puff of air against my throat. What about you? she asked. Where have *you* been? Here, I replied. She looked up at me with a searching glance and smiled again, not so broadly now, as if she had forgotten the smile on her lips whilst thinking over what she saw.

Rosa laughed when I said goodnight, she would go out
for some bread, now I had woken her up anyway, and I
smiled at the thought of all the time there was between us,
she in the apartment beside the Lakes, I in my hotel room
on Lexington Avenue. I leafed idly through the catalogue
of the Edward Hopper exhibition at the Whitney Museum
and paused at the picture of the young woman sitting on
a bed in the sunshine from the window, looking out over
the rooftops with a distant expression, pondering perhaps
at the self-evident thought that the world is what it is,
beneath the boundless sky. That it is nothing else, there
is no more. I lay down on the bed and switched off the
light, observing the dim, colourless outlines of things in
the glimmer of the television screen and the lighted offices
in the building opposite. It helped to lie there in semi-darkness, I could picture Astrid better, the faint after-glow of
isolated moments that faded as I looked at them because
they shone with the light of long vanished days. I thought
of the helicopter pictures of the river inundating houses and
trees, flowing over fields, through forests. I mused that time
is not only a river, but a river that constantly breaks its banks
so you must flee from it as it covers everything behind your
back, flee into the future, empty-handed, dispossessed, as
the river obliterates your footsteps with each stride you
take, each time you pass from one moment into the next.
It is only our own helpless lack of synchronicity, the inertia
of our senses, the illusory power of memory and habit, that
shields us from facing the unknown when we open our eyes
in the morning, washed up on the shore of yet another alien
day. Every morning we tread an unknown path, and we have
only faint and failing memories to tell us who we might be.
Disconnected, frayed memories, that no longer distinguish
between the world we passed en route, and the shadows it
cast in our hollow, clean-swept head as we fled onwards, on
and on. Now and then we overcome our fear of stumbling

and turn round to look back one last time and again one very last time, because we do not understand the strangeness that approaches, and the words we have to name it will still be hopelessly inadequate, and so we flee from the havoc of time, backwards, until we are nothing other than the story there is to tell of all we have lost.

I thought that by writing my story I would come closer to the point when she went away from me, but all my sentences have only been a way of withdrawing myself, while she withdrew herself in the opposite direction. I thought I was writing about Astrid, or about Inès and Elisabeth for that matter, but in fact I was only writing about myself, and when conversely I tried to recall my own thoughts and feelings through the years, I merely interpreted the fleeting and intangible shadows which an Elisabeth, an Astrid and an Inès in turn threw on the vault of my skull's mumbling loneliness. I thought I knew Astrid, but she may have begun to disappear one winter evening in my youth when I rose and walked into my kitchen to the young woman who had stopped in the middle of washing up, with a shining wet plate in her hand as she looked out into the darkness through her indistinct reflection. That unknown woman with narrow eyes and a crooked smile I had taken into my taxi and lodged in my flat because neither of us knew where else I should take her. Perhaps she only became even more unknown, as she turned towards me and I raised my hand and stroked her cheek as an initial sign that I should like to get to know her. Perhaps I got in the way of my own gaze, perhaps my words drowned out the silent breathing, the living silence, that more than any words is the sound of another person. Perhaps she herself came to drown it out when through the days and years that followed she told me details of her story in casual, summary and incomplete fragments, as you do talk about yourself as life goes on with you, so the whole of it is already another story. For her words were addressed to me before they were spoken, already included in the story we were together engaged in telling about each other and ourselves, about those people we were becoming. Just as there are things I never told her, there must be things she never told me, and just as I acquired a secret to keep, there must certainly be people and events that she kept secret from me. When she had released me from my dreams of Inès, long before I dreamed that Elisabeth would release me again, there was a time when I believed she knew everything there was to know about me, more than I was able to know myself. That she could see me as I was, just as I felt I knew her when I woke beside her and whispered her name. But perhaps we were never so blind as when we looked into each other's eyes in order to be recognised. We had a story, and our story ended up containing all previous stories, so that in the end they were only superfluous, backward-looking digressions in the continued narrative of our life together. But there must still be so much else, so much more in a human being than what is told, and what can be told at all. Most of it disappears among the words. It only reveals itself as a hesitation before you speak, a silence when you look down at the floor or out of the window without really knowing what to say. When you have gone for good only the story remains, but when Astrid left she also left emptiness and stillness in me, which I have filled up with words although perhaps I should rather have tried to keep the empty space open by keeping quiet. But I have only my words, and without them I would not be able to hear her silence in the pauses between the words, the cracks and hollow places in my narrative, from which she has withdrawn, just as she came in sight out of nowhere one winter evening, holding a little boy by the hand.

Rosa met me at the airport, as she had promised, when I came home from New York. As we went out of the arrival hall I was about to walk over to the queue of taxis, but she laughed at me and rattled Astrid's car keys. She had passed her driving test while I was away. Now she was really grown-up. She drove hesitantly and uncertainly, and jarred the gearbox each time she changed gear, but I didn't comment. She asked if I minded her borrowing the car for two weeks, I didn't use it a lot, did I? She had arranged to go to Berlin with her boyfriend. Everyone is out travelling these days. Had she found a new boyfriend already? She smiled and shook her head, it was the same one, she had decided to give it a go. I thought of the tonsured installation artist who had sat in my kitchen a week ago looking at me in despair, as I ironed my shirts. But was it all right about the car? Astrid had said OK. I looked at her. Astrid? She smiled as she overtook a bus and swung hard right again so as not to hit the approaching car coming at us with murderous speed. I was still shaken, both because I had looked death in the eye for a second, and on account of her casual reply. Had Astrid called? She smiled patiently as if she thought I must be very tired. Yes, Astrid had called the day before. She thought I had come back. Where had she called from? She didn't know, from Stockholm, she supposed, where else? Had she told Astrid when I would be back? She wrinkled her forehead as if to think about it. No, she hadn't asked, and they had gone on to talk of something else. Had Astrid said when she was coming home? She hesitated for a moment. She had quite forgotten to ask her that. She dropped me at our door, she had to get on at once, the installation artist was waiting. She kissed me on the cheek and I remained standing, anxiously watching as she turned out into the traffic again. You could hear from a long way off when she changed gear. Astrid had called, she would surely call again. Perhaps the last word had not been said.

I picked up the pile of letters from the hall floor and took them into my study. Again and again my eyes ran down the statement of places and times when Astrid had used her Mastercard, a laconic narrative of her movements in names and numbers. She had left this trail behind her, thus leading me back to Lisbon by our old route. There she abandons me, left to my memories. As I sat at my desk before the view of the Lakes, with my coat still on, she has been waking up at the hotel in the Rua Senhora do Monte. Perhaps she sits for a while on the edge of the bed letting her gaze rest on the view, the random slice of town and river. Perhaps she lingers a little longer before getting dressed and walking out of the picture. I imagine her sitting in a ray of sunlight, as she looks out over the roofs of Lisbon and the wide river and its opposite bank, where the invisible car windows catch the sun for a fraction of a second and send its reflections back across the river to her shady room like abrupt and disconnected morse signals. Perhaps she ponders on everything being as it is, as if it could not be otherwise. As if everything was not still undecided. When I remember Astrid in Lisbon seven years ago, I see her walking alone, I cannot see myself. She walks alone, where we walked, with narrow eyes in the clear afternoon sunshine that makes the tramlines glitter in the steep streets in front of her. The sun shone the morning after our arrival, and we walked through Graça, past the market place where the stalls were already being dismantled. We walked without any particular purpose, down towards the blue river, that kept coming into sight between the rooftops when the streets suddenly opened out in sudden falls. I am not present in my few pictures from Lisbon, I only see Astrid, as if I were not there. Sitting in the Rossio, on the pavement in front of a café on the square, where the trams screech close by our table and the sun shines in the thin smoke from the chestnut sellers' braziers as she bends her face and looks down into the coffee cup in front of her, quite lost in thought. Walking in front of me on a path in the botanical garden beneath an arch of trees that filter the sunlight, so both the path and her light-coloured coat are spotted with yellow patches, lifting her face in profile and looking up alertly as a bird's wings flap against the thick foliage of the plane trees. Standing at the rail of the little ferry taking us over to Cacilhas, in sunglasses, smiling her white smile in front of the distant white town. She took only one picture of me, in the ruined church at Largo do Carmo. It had no roof, the sparrows flew around freely between the bare moss-covered walls. I am standing on the grass beneath the Gothic arches outlined like gnawed rib bones against the sky. I am smiling at her, the invisible photographer, but she has taken too long to focus, the smile has stiffened. There is actually no smile left, only a forced, fatuous grimace, as I meet my own gaze, as if I am looking straight through her. As if by looking myself in the eye I open a void into which she has already vanished.